VILLA LOBOS

VILLA LOBOS

MICHAEL ZIMMER

FIVE STAR
A part of Gale, a Cengage Company

GALE
A Cengage Company

Copyright © 2020 by Michael Zimmer
Five Star Publishing, a part of Gale, a Cengage Company

LIBRARY OF CONGRESS CATALOGING-IN-PUBLICATION DATA

Names: Zimmer, Michael, 1955– author.
Title: Villa lobos / Michael Zimmer.
Description: First edition. | Waterville, Maine : Five Star, a part of Gale, a Cengage Company, [2020]
Identifiers: LCCN 2019030887 | ISBN 9781432868406 (hardcover)
Subjects: GSAFD: Western stories.
Classification: LCC PS3576.I467 V55 2020 | DDC 813/.54—dc23
LC record available at https://lccn.loc.gov/2019030887

First Edition. First Printing: March 2020
Find us on Facebook—https://www.facebook.com/FiveStarCengage
Visit our website—http://www.gale.cengage.com/fivestar
Contact Five Star Publishing at FiveStar@cengage.com

Printed in Mexico
Print Number: 01   Print Year: 2020

VILLA LOBOS

CHAPTER ONE

Rio Largo, Texas–June

The sun was barely risen when Ben Hollister and his crew reined up on a low rise east of Rio Largo. Leaning forward, Ben rested both hands atop the flat horn of his saddle as he studied the distant town. The others had crowded up on either side of him, loose-jointed men, weary after their long ride in from San Angelo. For a long moment, no one spoke. They stared at the town with unfathomable expressions, their jaws stubbled, eyes reddened from dust, a lack of sleep, and the unrelenting West Texas sun. Although the early morning breeze felt pleasantly cool, Ben knew it would die soon enough, the temperature rising as their shadows shrank beneath their horses' bellies.

Bobby was first to break the silence, his undisciplined youth like a colt straining against its halter. "Is that it?"

"Christ almighty," Ray Beeler growled in disgust.

Ben glanced down the line of horsemen to where Ray was glaring at Bobby. It didn't matter to Ray, to any of them, really, that Bobby was still learning the ropes. In another thirty minutes they were all going to be putting their lives on the line, and Ben knew no one was comfortable relying on an inexperienced hand. Had it been anyone other than his own kid brother, Ben would have felt the same way.

"Ben?" Bobby said uncertainly, oblivious to the reasons behind Ray's animosity.

"That's it," Ben confirmed.

7

He let his gaze drift over the rest of his crew. They were all good men, steady and dependable. He'd worked with a number of them for several years, and even the newest among them had come on board with solid reputations. Only Bobby was an unknown. Even so, Ben couldn't have turned his back on him. Not with their parents recently deceased, their sisters married to men who already despised the Hollister name. Ben might have wished for a better life for his little brother, something far removed from an outlaw's stormy existence, but destiny seemed to have other plans for the gawky sixteen-year-old. Now Bobby was riding toward his first big job with the Hollister gang, wide-eyed and nervous, but determined not to let his famous brother down.

Ben turned his eyes back to the town they were about to invade. From here, Rio Largo reminded him of chunks of dried mud scattered across the desert floor, its adobe structures blending almost flawlessly into the landscape. Only the Cattleman's Hotel spoiled that image, rising two stories above the rest of the town, its portico like pieces of straw clumped to one side of the squared-off earthen structure.

The town's single street ran north and south, paralleling a stunted river some forgotten wag had named Largo—Spanish for *long*. Having ridden its banks less than a week before, Ben knew the stream ran dry after less than half a mile. But near its source the water bubbled to the surface cool and clean, bountiful enough that the citizens had envisioned Rio Largo as a strong contender for the western terminus of the Texas and Pacific Railroad. Instead, that sought-after prize had gone to Sierra Blanca, a half a day's journey to the south, and although the road between the two communities thrummed with a steady flow of wagon traffic, the longer route north to El Paso was being gradually reclaimed by the desert, leaving the town to hang alone, a withering blossom on a dying vine.

Ben had spent some time in Rio Largo's three saloons while he was there, telling those who would listen that he was thinking about entering a horse in the upcoming races. His declaration had been like a gate opening somewhere upstream, releasing a flood of information and opinions. It turned out there were a lot of people in Rio Largo who still fumed over the loss of the T&P's depot, and the wealth the railroad would have brought with it. That bitterness was a big part of the motive behind what the city's leaders now termed the West Texas Quarter Mile Championships—a horse race pitting the chunkier, heavily muscled cow ponies of the open range over a course where a Thoroughbred's lean shape and longer legs would fail to provide the advantage the animal enjoyed on longer tracks farther east. This was going to be the third year for the event, and in an effort to boost the attraction, the town was sponsoring a boxing contest between a hulking giant from Louisiana named Aloysius le Bâton against any and all comers.

It was going to be a hell of a celebration, the saloon patrons had promised. The city had already contracted with the local stage company to increase its twice-a-week run to every other day, and the hotel was promising to put up a tent behind its stables to accommodate any overflow. The fights would begin at sundown the night before the races and continue until the massive Cajun was either beaten into submission or claimed victory over his challengers. The races would start the next day, with qualifications beginning at noon. Ben had sold his crew on the job by assuring them the town's twin vaults—one at the First Bank of Largo, the other at the Cattleman's Hotel—would be chocked with cash.

"Figure twenty thousand, at least," he'd calculated. "Maybe twice that if we're lucky."

A couple of the men had questioned Rio Largo's isolation, pointing out that they'd been doing all right for themselves by confining their raids to smaller banks and stage lines within a day's fast ride of the Red River, where escape across the border into Indian Territory offered ample sanctuary. But Ben had argued their old haven was no longer assured. Word had been drifting up and down the Red for several months that the Rangers were planning to sweep the outlaws hiding out along the Red River into Texas jails and Texas nooses, and to hell with the legalities.

"Besides," Ben had added, "Rio Largo isn't more than a day's ride from Mexico. We can be across the Rio Grande by nightfall if everyone does their job."

A couple of them had grumbled, but the majority seemed satisfied with Ben's reasoning. Then Bobby showed up, and the gang's mood began to deteriorate. Ben wondered if they would have been as quick to agree if they'd known an inexperienced man—a boy, really—would be riding with them. He had his doubts, especially with some of the brasher members of the crew, like Ray Beeler and the half-breed Delaware they called Little Fish.

Well, it was too late now, Ben reasoned, lifting the reins to his grulla. "Everybody know what to do?" he asked.

"We ain't kids robbin' a candy store," Ray said querulously.

Ben ignored the implication as another dig at Bobby's youth. It was how Ray worked, always poking at open wounds, or scratching scabs off of old ones.

Ray Beeler was a slim man with short dark hair and a snubbed nose that always seemed out of joint about something. His movements were quick and jerky, and his voice could rise to an eerily high pitch when he was angry. Of them all, it was Ray who resented Bobby's addition to the crew most, probably because his own brother had been turned away when he tried to join the year before. Ben had to admit it wasn't fair, but this wasn't Ray's outfit, or his decision. Besides, Ray's brother was already running with a bunch along the middle Brazos; he had options Bobby didn't.

"I reckon we're about as ready as we'll ever be," Ed Dodson said, absently stroking the pointed goatee that hung like Spanish moss from his chin. He sat his horse with a faintly forward cant to his body, narrow shoulders hunched as if to a biting rain. Only a few of the oldest hands—Ben, Mose, and Henry McDaniels—knew of the bullet lodged painfully against Ed's spine, a memento of a running fight with a posse outside of Denison several years earlier.

For Bobby's benefit more than anyone else's, Ben went over the plans a final time. "The bank is two buildings north of the hotel, both of them on the west side of the street. Ed, you and Ray and Bobby take that. Bob, you listen to what these two tell you. They know what they're doing.

"Henry will go after the law." Ben glanced at the older man. "His name's Owen Plunkett, and he'll either be in his office across the street from the bank or having breakfast at the Hub Café next door. If he's not in either place, then stand on the boardwalk outside his office until you spot him. He's a tough old bird, but he's getting on in years, too."

"I'll handle him," Henry vowed.

"If anyone knows how to handle old men, it will be him," Little Fish smirked, thrusting his chin toward Henry.

"You just do your part, Fish, and don't worry about me doing mine," Henry replied.

"I do my part plenty good, and *you* don't worry about that."

"Put a cork in it, you two," Ben said, fixing his gaze on Little Fish. He knew that if any of them took this moment to resist his authority or try to alter their plans, it would be Ray or Fish. Although he wasn't worried about handling either of them, he was glad when Little Fish didn't push it.

Ben turned to Henry, easily the oldest member of the crew,

and as a rule, the least flappable among them. Henry sported a drooping mustache under a lumpy nose, tired blue eyes, and curly gray hair framing a narrow face half-hidden behind a scruff of whiskers. He was wolf-lean and twice as dangerous when riled, which fortunately didn't happen often.

Little Fish, on the other hand, hid his anger like a knife tucked unsheathed inside his boot, so that a man never knew which way it might cut when pulled. He was wiry and reckless, and carried an old Civil War Spencer carbine the way some men did a long-barreled Colt. He was good with it, too. Better than he was with the revolver he carried tucked behind his belt. Little Fish was Delaware on his mother's side and dressed the part—calico shirt trimmed in red velvet, knee-high moccasins, and wool trousers. He claimed his father was a full-blooded American bastard who had been with a raiding party out of Arkansas on the night he raped Fish's mother and left the woman—little more than a child at the time—pregnant and orphaned. He'd left behind the Spencer, too, tossed aside when he spotted a Henry rifle in the dirt next to the body of Fish's dead grandfather. Little Fish said he kept the Spencer because he planned to use it to kill the man who'd sired him, although he admitted he didn't have the faintest idea who that might be; he wasn't even sure where he'd gotten the notion the man was originally from Arkansas.

Ben's grulla shifted under him. He was aware of the others watching, waiting for him to continue, and shifted his attention from Little Fish to Jethro Hill, astride a flaxen-maned sorrel gelding he called Acorn—the only one among them who ever bothered to name his horse.

"You two," Ben said curtly, meaning Jethro and Little Fish. "I want both of you on the street with your rifles handy."

Fish said nothing, and Jethro nodded earnestly. Jethro Hill was another new man, having ridden with them for less than a year. His inexperience showed at times, but he was dependable, and had proved himself so more than once. Like Little Fish, Jethro was a better shot with a rifle than a revolver—most men were unless they practiced—but Jethro was especially good at longer ranges with his .45-75 Winchester.

"Water first, right?" Jethro said, and Ben nodded.

"Water first."

This being new country to them, Ben had decided to bring along a packhorse carrying a pair of pitch-lined ten-gallon water bags. They could abandon the animal if they had to, but if they could keep it with them, that extra water might make all the difference in a hard, fast ride to the Rio Grande. Since they'd already dipped into their supply on the long ride in from San Angelo, Ben wanted Jethro and Little Fish to top off the water bags before the rest of them entered town.

Ben's eyes settled on Mose. "You and I'll take the hotel, old man. Think we can handle it?"

"I can," Mose replied with an amicable grin. "If you have any trouble keeping up, I'll just leave your raggedy butt behind."

"That ought to work," Ben agreed. He looked at his brother. "Any questions?"

Bobby shook his head.

"All right, let's ride, boys. By this time tomorrow we'll be either dead, or stinking rich and deep inside of Mexico."

CHAPTER TWO

Alto Station, Texas–June

Standing stiffly at attention, First Sergeant Andrew Cade thought, *You puffed-up bucket of horse dung.*

He was careful to keep his expression neutral, though, his eyes forward as Lieutenant Colonel Lawrence Hawthorne continued to upbraid his junior officer. Although unable to say anything, Cade was proud of the way the captain was handling himself. Ward Miller had a quiet dignity that men like Hawthorne might sense but would never fully comprehend, much less achieve.

On the other hand, Hawthorne's reputation for castigation was well-known throughout the regiment. It was said he could pinken ears and blister paint from twenty yards away. Cade figured that if there were any new recruits nearby today who had ever doubted the old bastard's ability to rake a man over the coals until he was thoroughly cooked, Hawthorne's dressing-down of Captain Miller would put that skepticism to rest.

For Cade, standing a pace behind and to one side of his commanding officer, there was no surprise at the colonel's fury. And he supposed, all things considered, it was warranted. Cade's discovery that morning of three prostitutes smuggled aboard a troop train bound for Fort Stockton would be a black mark against the company, as well as any officer remotely connected to the incident, for years to come. The best any shoulder board could do under such circumstances was to pass the buck on down the line. With no lieutenant on hand to buffer the thrust of Hawthorne's outrage—First Lieutenant James Tyrell had been sent ahead to ready the premises for the rest of the company—Cade knew where he stood. Only time would tell how much hell Captain Miller would unleash on him before the furor died down.

Keeping his gaze riveted straight ahead, Cade was only peripherally aware of the deep crimson shading the captain's cheeks above his neatly trimmed beard. He didn't know whether the flush of color was from anger or embarrassment, but he guessed he'd know soon. Colonel Hawthorne was winding down like a watch spring losing its tension, the blaze in his eyes dimming to smoldering coals. At last the colonel issued his dismissal, returning the captain's salute with sloppy disregard and a final order to "See to it, immediately!"—spat out like pieces of hard gristle.

Pivoting smartly, Captain Miller marched away, his stride over the rumpled terrain as smooth as if on parade back at Fort Bliss. Cade quickly fell in behind and slightly to Miller's left. It wasn't until they'd covered probably fifty yards that he risked a backward glance. Hawthorne was still standing in the shade of the canvas fly of his large tent, like a chunk of deeply rooted red oak left where it was because it was too damn tough to hack through with an axe. Judging from his stance, he was still ranting, too, this time at an orderly who stood rigidly at attention to one side of the shelter.

Cade turned away, his lips drawn tight in a grimace of distaste. He and the captain were making their way swiftly down the length of the stalled train, the morning sun throwing their shadows far in advance. Their differences in appearance were especially obvious in silhouette. Where Miller was tall and slim, Cade was both shorter and stouter. Not fat—there wasn't an ounce of excess weight to be found on his five-foot-eight-inch frame—but compact and strong, chest and shoulders broad, his legs slightly bowed from nearly a lifetime in the saddle. Not apparent in the contours of his silhouette were the sandy shade of his hair and mustache, the crow's-feet framing his eyes, or the stubborn set of his jaw.

El Paso, where the company had boarded for its journey eastward, lay some fifty miles to the northwest, their destination half again that far eastward, to Fort Stockton, where they were to be stationed until the garrison's permanent closure in the next couple of years.

It had been a provision of the government in granting the railroad its license that the Southern Pacific and its subsidiaries provide free transportation for the army in times of conflict, but the reality was that there had always been large discrepancies between what Eastern railroad officials considered conflict and the military view of a situation. Less than six hours out of El Paso, the string of cars had been side-railed at Alto Station to await the passage of a westbound train carrying railroad officials headed for California. Hawthorne and his officers had been impatiently twiddling their thumbs ever since.

Cade didn't think there was any doubt the delay was part of what was burning the colonel's britches that morning, but he also knew the match that had set it aflame waited ahead. Narrowing his eyes beneath the upcurled brim of his campaign hat, Cade studied the three women gathered under a loose guard at the rear of the train. Even from here, their attire was eye-catching. Skimpy at best, yet vividly ablaze in shades of purple, yellow, red, and green—like brilliantly colored canaries framed against the tawny landscape.

The women had been smuggled onto an equipment car shortly before the train's departure from El Paso by troopers from Miller's company. Their presence had come to light barely an hour ago, but the news had moved swiftly up the chain of command to where Hawthorne had been forcing down a breakfast of cool porridge and weak coffee; better provisions awaited them at Fort Stockton, which they should have reached last evening, and Cade wondered if that hadn't fed into the colonel's sour disposition that morning. He was a portly man with a fondness for rich foods, good wine, and cushioned chairs, and had studiously avoided any form of bivouacking since attaining the rank of major.

Although Miller's stride never faltered, a drawn-out exhalation of breath confirmed his readiness to speak. Cade lengthened his stride to come up to the captain's side.

"I should have caught this, Sergeant."

"I think we both should have," Cade allowed.

"Well, it's done, and Hawthorne will probably nail it to my record with a spike, but there's nothing that can be done about it."

Cade figured the captain was right. A more forgiving commander might have chewed Miller's ass ragged, but then let it drop. Hawthorne wasn't like that. He would store the information in a file in his head to be used against Miller as the need arose; having it permanently attached to the captain's records would strengthen his grip on the officer. It was a raw deal for Miller, but it was also the military, and odds were there would come a time when Hawthorne wanted something only Miller could supply—an endorsement or an alibi—and the captain would be hard-pressed not to provide it if he wanted to keep his own career viable. In Cade's opinion, it was a sad reality that damn few men rose through the ranks on merit alone.

"What do you want done with the women, sir?"

"I want them out of camp, immediately," Miller replied. "Pick six good men, Sergeant, and take Corporal Poe with you. You'll have to use an ambulance for the women. Take along enough supplies to last you three days. You should make it in two, but

17

there's no point in taking any chances. I want Poe and one other man on the wagon and a four-mule hitch, the rest of you to be mounted. Your orders are to escort these women to El Paso and deposit them in front of the Cosmopolitan Saloon. After that, return the ambulance and stock to the stables at Fort Bliss and await further instructions."

"What will those instructions be, Captain?"

"If I have anything to say about it, you will proceed from there to Fort Stockton to rejoin the company. It remains to be seen whether your return will be by rail, or overland with the livestock and ambulance."

"Yes, sir."

Miller came to an abrupt halt. Cade did likewise. Staring into the captain's eyes, he saw the anger that still burned there.

"I want this thoroughly understood, Sergeant. No man in your squad is to have carnal relations with any of these prostitutes. That is under threat of severe punishment."

"Yes, sir."

"I mean severe, as in I'll shoot any son of a bitch who disobeys that order."

"Yes, sir, I'll make sure the men understand."

"They'd better, by God. Now go ahead and get ready. I want you on your way in thirty minutes."

"Yes, sir."

Cade spun away as Miller turned a pensive gaze north across the dry desert. The sun was barely two hours into the sky, and the heat was already clamping down. A thermometer set in the shade under one of the equipment cars yesterday had registered ninety-six degrees by midafternoon. It had been quite a bit hotter in the sun, and summer barely begun.

Corporal Frank Poe was idling near the morning mess when Cade arrived. He came over to where the sergeant had stopped next to a flatcar carrying a trio of military conveyances.

"What's the word from the top?" Poe asked.

"No one's smiling."

"No, I guess not. What does Hawthorne want done with these doves?" He gestured to where the women were sitting in a colorful cluster on the far side of the breakfast fire.

"We're taking them back to El Paso."

"Train, wagon, or do we make 'em walk?"

"We'll take an ambulance." He slapped the iron-shod wheel of the refurbished Rucker towering above him on the flatcar. "This one. Morgan, Elkins, Riley, Talbot, Schultz, and Hendricks will provide escort. You're coming, too."

"Me?"

"Captain's orders."

Poe's lips twitched to suppress his grin. Cade knew it pleased him that Miller had personally chosen him to accompany the squad. Poe was a good soldier and a natural leader. It wouldn't be long before he was wearing sergeant's stripes. Cade was glad to have him along.

"What do you want done?" Poe asked.

"Get this ambulance on the ground. I want a four-mule hitch with you and Riley on the box, everyone else mounted." He stepped away from the flatcar. "Let's get to it, Frank. We're pulling out in thirty minutes."

Poe nodded and strode off to find some men to unload the ambulance. Taking a deep breath, Cade walked over to where the Cosmopolitan's whores were warily eyeing his approach. He recognized only one of them, a Mexican named Lucia. Although he'd never gone to her crib, he had talked to her at the bar a time or two and enjoyed her company. He could tell by her expression that she remembered him as well.

Halting in front of the women, he briefly considered unleashing the same kind of hell against them that he'd used earlier on the troopers who had smuggled them onto the train, then decided against it. Although he doubted his choice of words would have offended anyone, it was his mother's upbringing that stayed the fire on his tongue.

"Ladies—" he began, then stopped as laughter rippled from the throat of a redhead wearing a stained purple gown.

"I think you got the wrong idea about us, Sergeant," she said.

Cade sighed, already regretting his decision to follow the dim advice of his ma.

"Just shut up and listen," he said irritably. "Every one of you knew better than to crawl onto this train." He quickly threw up a hand when the redhead's mouth popped open to protest. "Don't say it, because I'm not interested." After a pause and another deep breath, he went on. "It is Colonel Hawthorne's orders that you be returned El Paso. You may take my word for it that there are those who favored leaving you here to fend for yourselves."

"But you ain't gonna do that, are you?" the redhead said, crossing her arms over her chest in almost Custeresque bravado.

"You test my patience and you might damn well find out," Cade returned stonily. He shook his head. "I'm not going to deal with each of you individually. Pick a leader, then have her come see me. Meanwhile, get ready to move out. We're leaving in twenty minutes."

"If you're looking for someone to blame, then I'm probably the one you want," Lucia said, rising from the cask of molasses where she had been sitting. She was short and full-figured, with dark eyes, hair the color of coal, and a complexion that did nothing to hide her Spanish ancestry; yet for all that, her words carried barely a hint of Mexico, and her tone seemed refined.

"You're behind this?" he asked.

"I'm the one who talked these women into coming with me, yes."

"You're Lucia?"

20

"Lucia Mendoza, and you're Sergeant Cade."

He nodded. "Who put you up to this, Miss Mendoza?"

"There's no call to stand on formality, Sergeant. My name is Lucia, and you already know all there is to know about who put us up to this. A couple of your troopers came to me with a proposition. I took them up on it."

"Names would make it easier on you, once we get back to El Paso. I know the men we have in chains now weren't the only ones involved."

"Names would make it easier for you, not for me or us." She tipped her head to the side to include the other women.

"Then tell me who first approached you with this plan."

Lucia laughed shortly. "There wasn't much planning involved, beyond the greedy needs of your men, Sergeant. If there had been, if your soldiers had thought to bring along what we needed, like food and a couple of buckets for our business, you'd never have found us."

Eyeing the stubborn cast of her face, Cade decided there wasn't going to be time to sort it out today. The half hour Miller had given him was already whittled down to twenty minutes, and there was still a lot to be done.

"All right," he relented. "I've got a few more things to say, and I'll make it brief. It's going to take us two days to reach El Paso going cross-country like we will. During that time, you will obey orders like any other soldier in my company. If you don't, you'll get the same punishment they would. Your money-making days are over for this trip, ladies. Keep your knees together and your skirts down until you're released from my command. Is that understood?"

The rusty-haired woman snorted, glanced at the others, then leaned to one side and spat into the dirt, her sputum tinged brown. A tobacco chewer, Cade noted.

21

"Hell, Sergeant, after last night I could use a few days off," she said.

Cade ignored the remark. He studied the third woman, auburn-haired and of slight build, her shoulders sloped as if carrying burdens unseen by others. "What's your name?" he asked.

"Hattie Wilkes."

He paused a moment to absorb that and what her subdued posture told him, then turned back to the redhead. "And yours?"

"Fanny," she said, leaning forward and smacking her butt. "Fanny, get it?"

"What's your full name?"

"Fanny O'Shea, sweetheart. What's your name?" She snorted again—a habit of hers, Cade decided—and grinned, the dark discoloration of her teeth confirming her tobacco habit. Bone-thin and hatchet-faced, her bare shoulders looked nearly white against the deep purple of her gown.

"You already know my name," he said curtly, then pointed to where Frank Poe was supervising the unloading of the Rucker ambulance from the flatcar by six burly soldiers. "That's Corporal Poe. He'll be second in command. You will obey him the same as you do me."

"What about them others?" Fanny O'Shea asked. "They got names?"

"Their names are no concern of yours," Cade replied. "The three of you will deal directly with either Corporal Poe or myself, and no one else."

Fanny snorted, and Cade swore under his breath. "All right, ladies, collect your gear and get ready. We're pulling out in fifteen minutes."

He walked over to check on the progress of the men as they set the ambulance on the ground with loud grunts and muttered curses. Morgan, Elkins, Riley, and Talbot were already bringing in the horses and mules from where they had been turned loose that morning to graze as Schultz and Hendricks sorted through sacks and crates from a boxcar for supplies. Cade spotted a couple of men loafing nearby and ordered them to fetch four twelve-gallon water kegs, and to make sure they were completely filled before securing them inside the ambulance, under the bunk that would serve as a seat.

As soon as Poe's men had the ambulance rolled safely away from the flatcar, Elkins and Riley began backing the mules into their traces, while the others saw to saddling the horses. The men worked with a disciplined efficiency that swelled Cade's chest with pride. They were just about finished when Captain Miller showed up. He nodded approvingly as Cade came over.

"Well done, Andy."

"Thank you, sir."

"Arms and ammunition?"

"Fifty rounds for the Colts, twice that many for the Springfields."

"You shouldn't need them," Miller said.

"No, sir, we shouldn't."

Neither stated the obvious. The Comanches, Mescaleros, and Lipans were mostly confined to reservations, but West Texas still crawled with renegades and badmen from both sides of the border. Cade didn't anticipate trouble—they would be eight strong and well-armed—but they wouldn't lower their guard until they'd safely reached El Paso, either.

"Have the women any other clothing, Sergeant?"

"I haven't asked them."

"Do," Miller said. "If this is all they have, requisition something more appropriate from the quartermaster." He held up a hand, his taut smile standing in pointed contrast to the seriousness of his demeanor. "I don't expect our QM to have lady's dresses in stock, but he should have something more suitable than what they're currently wearing. I imagine they'll need the smallest sizes available, and I want them in full attire—shoes to caps, union suits to coats or jackets."

"Yes, sir."

"Have your men been fed?"

"Not yet. We were sidelined with our discovery of the stowaways this morning, but I'll see that they have something to eat before we pull out."

Miller glanced behind him. Cade followed suit. Hawthorne, like a tyrant, was standing in front of his tent nearly a hundred yards away, his fists clearly balled on his hips as he glared in their direction.

Exhaling heavily, Miller said, "Have the men take their breakfasts with them, Sergeant. They can eat in the saddle. The women, too." After a pause, he added, "Do what you feel is necessary after you're out of Hawthorne's sight, but until then, let's try to appease the man."

"Yes, sir," Cade acknowledged.

Miller looked at him with a rueful smile. "Good luck, Sergeant," he said, and thrust out a hand.

Grasping it firmly, in surprise, Cade said, "Thank you, sir."

Miller walked away, and after a pause, Cade took off in search of a kettle big enough to hold breakfast for the ten men and women he would be escorting to El Paso. Although he wouldn't have admitted it to anyone, he was relieved that the captain didn't appear to hold this fiasco against him personally. It made him all the more determined to see the mission completed without incident.

Eight men and a trio of doves, Cade mused to himself. What could possibly go wrong?

CHAPTER THREE

Rio Largo was ready to celebrate. Even at this early hour of the morning, excitement hung in the air like the coppery aftertaste of a recently passed electrical storm. The town had strung a banner across its single thoroughfare with the word *WELCOME* in old English script. In smaller, more easily read type beneath that was *3rd Annual West Texas Quarter Mile Championships.*

Bunting, new enough that the desert sun had yet to dull its radiant colors, dotted both sides of the street, and vendors were already setting up booths and blankets to hawk wares of roasted ear corn, sugar cones, cinnamon-laced fried pastries, fireworks, and tortillas filled with spicy meats.

Ben Hollister kept his horse to a walk as he made his way down Rio Largo's broad main street. Mose rode by his side. Neither spoke, nor needed to, and there was no outward sign of the anxiety that squirmed through their guts like snakes tumbling from their dens in the warm spring sunshine.

Ben was aware of the others strung out lazily behind him, like cowhands wandering in off the range. It was the image he wanted, that of men who had ridden a great distance to join in the celebration, and he thought they were pulling it off in fair fashion.

Jethro Hill and Little Fish were already in place, having ridden into town with the packhorse thirty minutes earlier to fill the water bags at the steel tanks below the springs at the north end of town. Jethro had remained close to the tanks afterward,

25

while Little Fish returned to the community's southern terminus with the packhorse, taking up an unobtrusive position where he could keep an eye on the street, as Jethro was doing from the north. Ben didn't acknowledge Little Fish's presence as he led his men into town, but he did note from the corner of his eye the small nod the mixed-blood Delaware gave him, indicating that, so far, all was in order.

Henry McDaniels had ridden in alone shortly after Jethro and Little Fish. Ben spotted his horse hitched to the railing in front of the sheriff's office, and wondered if he'd tracked down Rio Largo's solitary lawman yet. Listening to the gossip inside Jim Hannagan's Second Chance Saloon when he came through town the preceding week, Ben had been impressed with what he'd learned of the old lawdog. Owen Plunkett might be in his sixties now, but he'd been a heller with both rifle and pistol when he was younger, and was still as tough as knotted oak.

They came to the hotel first, and Ben and Mose peeled off and swung down to tie up out front. Ray and the others rode on past. Ben deliberately kept his gaze turned away from them, not wanting to attract any more attention than necessary. The fact that they were strangers in town shouldn't be a problem— the boxing matches and horse racing had brought in plenty of those—but he didn't want anyone noticing their measured approach to the town's two largest businesses.

Ben and Mose climbed the hotel steps together. Although both men were wearing black, knee-length frock coats, Mose's was puffed out in the middle like he was sporting a good-sized belly. Had anyone been paying attention, they might have noticed that Mose's slim face and skinny legs belied a hefty man's build, but it was early yet, and no one paid them any mind as they entered the lobby.

The Cattleman's wasn't fancy and never had been, but the floors were polished and the chairs and settees scattered around the room were clean, the fabric suffering only a minimum of wear. The counter was on their left, and after a quick glance to determine the rest of the lobby was empty, Ben headed in that direction. The clerk on duty was a young man with slicked-down hair and bushy sideburns that added a false breadth to his hollow cheeks. A smirk tugged at the corners of his mouth as Ben and Mose ambled over.

"If you're looking for a room, you're three days too late," he chimed before they'd come to a complete stop.

Ben put a hand out to touch his friend's arm, but it didn't do any good.

"We're not looking for a room," Mose replied quietly. "We're looking for the combination to the hotel's safe."

The clerk's expression widened to a simper. "If you gentlemen think for one minute—" Then he shut up, his smile vanishing as he stared cross-eyed down the muzzle of Mose's revolver, resting intimidatingly on the tip of his nose.

Henry McDaniels exited the sheriff's office and gently pulled the door closed behind him. The jail had been unoccupied, but Ben had warned him it might be. Next door was the Hub Café, and that's where he headed. There was a single, multipaned window next to the door, its glass powdered so heavily with dust from the street that he couldn't see anything inside. Not wanting to draw undue attention to himself, he didn't try too hard.

He paused inside to get his bearings. The café was larger than it appeared from the street, narrow but deep. A couple of dozen customers were scattered across the room; a pair of harried-looking women in matching aprons bustled among the tables to serve them. One of them noticed Henry's entrance and said, "Grab a seat anywhere, mister, and we'll be right with you."

Henry smiled and politely touched the brim of his hat.

"Thank you, ma'am." He'd already spotted a stout-built individual sitting at a table hugging the wall several rows back from the front door. In the restaurant's dim light, the man's star seemed to beckon.

Keeping his stride casual, Henry made his way to the lawman's table. Although careful not to make eye contact, he noticed Plunkett's eyes following him closely. It wasn't until the last minute, barely a table-width away, that Henry allowed himself to meet the sheriff's gaze. Affecting a friendly smile, he said, "Owen?"

Caught off-guard, the lawman leaned back in his chair. Henry crossed the distance between them.

"Owen Plunkett, right?"

"I don't know you, stranger."

Henry pulled out a chair and sat down. As his waist disappeared below the level of the table, he slid a short-barreled .41 caliber revolver from inside his vest and pointed it at the sheriff's midsection, although he was careful to keep it shielded from the rest of the room. He was still smiling as he cocked the weapon. Only Plunkett seemed to hear the polished steel ratcheting into place. His eyes narrowed dangerously, but he didn't move.

"I reckon you know me, huh?"

"Only by reputation," Henry said.

"If you're looking to build yours as a gunman, you're lacking ambition."

"Oh, I'm satisfied with my current reputation."

"Might it be one I'm familiar with?"

"It ain't likely," Henry allowed, then nodded toward the lawman's plate—fried eggs, scrambled sausage, thin-sliced potatoes garnished with onions, and a biscuit on the side, slathered with butter and jam and already half-consumed. "I'll tell you what we're gonna do, Sheriff. We're gonna sit here calm as can be, a couple of old acquaintances catching up on the past, and as soon as one of those pretty gals comes over, I'm gonna order a cup of coffee. In the meantime, you're gonna finish that breakfast like you've got all the time in the world."

"Mister, you've bit off a mouthful. You figure you've got the teeth to chew it down to size?"

"I figure I do." Henry nodded toward the blue enamel of the lawman's plate. "Go on, Sheriff, take a bite before your eggs get cold."

Ray Beeler was first through the front door of Rio Largo's only bank. Ben Hollister hadn't put him in charge, hadn't put anyone in charge, which was why Ray decided to assume the role himself. It pleased him that neither Ed Dodson, who was older and more experienced, nor Bobby Hollister protested the move. Not that Ray would have given a rat's hind end what Ben's little brother thought. As far as Ray was concerned, bringing the kid along on a job like this was plain lunacy. There wasn't much he could say about it, though, since it was Ben who'd put the outfit together all those years ago, who had kept it more or less successful and intact over the years, too. But the kid's presence did irritate the hell out of him. His ignorance was a danger to them all.

The First Bank of Largo was a squatty little adobe building with a worn wooden floor and bars over the windows. Ray figured the whole place could have been dismantled with axes in a couple of hours. All except for the safe, which sat wrapped inside an iron-strapped cage similar to some of the jail cells Ray had found himself lodged in over the years. The cell door was open, though, and that was a plus, even if the safe itself was closed.

A chest-high counter ran across the rear of the room, where a pair of tellers were handling the early morning transactions. A chubby man with curly gray hair sat at a desk in the right rear corner of the room, his back to the lobby as if hoping that might discourage interruption. A plaque on his desk read: *Manager.* Short lines of waiting customers were queued before each window, but no one was acting impatient or chagrinned; the festive mood of the town seemed contagious.

After assessing the room with a glance, Ray nodded to Ed, who leaned close to whisper instructions into the kid's ear. Drawing his revolver, Bobby moved over in front of the door, while Ed sidled to one side where he could keep an eye on the twin lines of customers. Sliding his Colt from its holster, Ray walked up behind the heavyset man at the desk and tapped one broad shoulder with the gun's barrel. The man swung around with an annoyed scowl that instantly dissolved when he spotted the .45's muzzle hovering not quite six inches from his nose.

Behind Ray, Ed Dodson loudly stated, "Sorry for the interruption, folks, but this is a holdup. Ever'one of you raise your hands and do as you're told, else I'll have'ta put a bullet through your briskets."

There were several startled exclamations and one vehement curse, but with a trio of revolvers leveled down, no one resisted. Ray pushed the .45's front sight under the bank manager's chin to tickle his wattle.

"On your feet, fat man, and over to the safe."

The bank manager had to use the arms of his chair to rise. On creaking legs, he made his way to the open cell and walked inside. Ray followed as far as the door, then stopped where he could keep an eye on both the room and the safe's steel door. As the bank manager pressed his fingers lightly to the dial, Ray said, "If there's a gun in there, make damn sure you don't get anywhere near it."

The banker hesitated, then swallowed audibly. "There is a revolver on the top shelf, although I can assure you I have no intention of reaching for it."

"Then I'll want you to back off as soon as the door's unlocked. I don't even want you to open it. Understand?"

"Yes," he immediately replied, and his hand trembled as he began turning the dial.

Ray glanced into the lobby, but no one was looking his way. They all had their eyes on Ed Dodson and Bobby Hollister, and not one of them had lowered his arms. Ray smiled. It appeared that Ben's well-laid plans were going to work out just fine, after all.

"How long are we going to continue this charade?" Owen Plunkett asked, swallowing the last of his eggs.

Henry McDaniels tipped his head toward the lawman's plate. "You got a couple bites of potatoes left. Let's finish those and see where we stand."

"I don't *have* the combination," the hotel clerk pleaded pitifully, and considering the number of gashes Mose had already carved into the kid's cheeks with the barrel of his revolver—the front sight in particular made an effective cutting tool—Ben finally believed him.

"Hold on," he said quietly, interrupting Mose as he was about to deliver yet another downward stroke to the clerk's face.

Mose scowled fiercely but lowered his weapon.

"All right, then who does have it?" Ben asked.

"The day manager."

"Where?" Mose snapped, and the clerk flinched. Ben hadn't seen a hint of a smirk from the kid since hauling him out from behind the counter and hustling him into the hotel's small office, under the second-floor stairs.

"In his room, I believe. He lives here."

"Which room?"

31

"Ground floor, other side of the stairs."

"Keep an eye on him," Ben said, holstering his Smith and Wesson. "I'll go see."

Mose poked the clerk's stomach with his gun. "You'd better not be lying to us, sonny. It's gonna make me mad if you are."

The clerk shook his head. "No, sir, I'm not lying, I swear it."

"I'm swearing it, too," Mose assured him, and Ben smiled as he exited the tiny office.

Spotting a heavy walnut door in the wall next to the stairs, Ben strode to it and tried the knob. It was unlocked, and he shoved it open and stepped inside. A slim man in shirtsleeves—a vest and jacket hung off the back of the chair where he sat at a small table reading a newspaper—looked up as Ben closed the door behind him.

"I beg your pardon," the man said.

"You the day manager?"

"I am the manager, day or night. My name is Rogers. I suppose it was young Leonard who assigned me the title of day manager?"

"It was the kid behind the counter."

"Leonard," the manager confirmed in a disgruntled tone. "He has ambitions beyond his abilities."

"I'm not really interested in Leonard's ambitions," Ben replied and slid the Smith and Wesson from its holster. "On your feet, friend. I need your assistance in the other room."

Rogers studied the revolver thoughtfully, then sighed and stood. "Robbery, I suppose?" He reached for his vest.

"You suppose right, and you won't be needing that vest."

"I would feel undressed in public without it."

"Now, why does that make me suspicious?"

"I wouldn't have the foggiest notion what sparks your suspicions, sir."

"I'll tell you what, you step away from that vest and let me have a look at it, and if I don't find a hideout gun in one of the pockets, I'll let you put it on. But if I do, I'll put a bullet through your foot. How does that sound?"

Rogers hesitated only a moment, then said, "Very well," and headed for the door, leaving his vest and jacket hanging from the back of the chair.

The lobby was still empty, for which Ben was grateful. Inside the cramped office he elbowed the door closed, and Rogers jerked to a halt.

"Good heavens!" he exclaimed when he spied the clerk's battered face. He turned to Ben. "What is the meaning of this, sir?"

"We want that safe opened," Ben replied coolly. "If you don't want to look like your friend there, you'll quit your cackling and get to it."

Rogers's lips parted, then slapped shut. He crossed the room to the safe and knelt in front of it. Mose shoved the clerk against the back wall and told him to stay out of the way, then he and Ben moved closer to where Rogers was carefully rolling the dial. It was so quiet in the room, Ben would have sworn he could hear the tumblers falling into line; he was certain he heard the lock's final, crisp snick as the cam rolled free. Rogers reached for the latch, but Mose smacked the back of his hand with the barrel of his revolver. Rogers yelped and jerked it away.

"Don't get so itchy," Mose chided him, then reached over the manager's shoulder and turned the latch. He grinned when the door swung open.

Ben was smiling, too. He started to speak, then shut up as another series of clicks reached his ears. For a moment he thought the sound came from the safe. Then the pattern registered in his mind and he turned just as the clerk pulled the trigger on a little over-and-under derringer.

The sound was deafening in the tiny room, and Rogers

squawked and fell back as if shot. But it was Mose who took the bullet, the lead slug entering near his right shoulder blade, then driving down through his chest to exit below his breastbone. He slumped forward into the safe and the door banged closed.

Ben spun and fired, and Leonard was flung into the wall by the force of the bullet. His feet seemed to kick out from under him as if yanked, then he folded in a heap against the baseboard. Ben turned the Smith and Wesson on Rogers, but the hotel manager already had both hands as high into the air as he could get them, blubbering about not wanting to die. Looking at Mose, Ben saw the shock of awareness that blazed from his old partner's eyes. He was sagged against the front of the safe while blood flowed out from between the fingers he had pressed over his abdomen. Cursing, Ben dragged him out of the way, then grabbed Rogers by the shoulder and pushed him toward the safe.

"Open it, and be quick," he yelled, the Smith's muzzle quivering from the rage pounding through his veins.

"Damnation, Ben, the little jackass shot me," Mose breathed wetly, the words barely audible through the ringing in Ben's ears.

"I know he did. How bad is it?"

Mose tried to answer but coughed instead, spraying the front of his frock coat with a pink mist. He wiped his lips, then stared at the bloody froth staining his fingers. "I'd guess it's pretty bad," he said, then coughed again and closed his eyes.

Hearing the telltale rattle from Mose's lungs, Ben knew his old partner's time was short. He leveled the Smith on the back of Rogers's head. "Get it open now, you sonofabitch!"

"Yes, sir, it . . . it's open." Rogers pulled the steel door back, then scuttled out of the way. His eyes were wide, his face like risen dough. "Please, mister, I didn't know Leonard had a—"

"Shut up," Ben snapped. He stooped to unbutton Mose's

frock coat. Inside, mimicking a potbelly, were a pair of heavy canvas money sacks, with flaps on top that buckled closed. Ben tossed one of them to Rogers and told him to get busy. Then he walked over to where Leonard lay curled against the wall. Staring at the body, he wished he could kill him a second time, only slower, with more pain.

Clearing his throat, Rogers said, "Here it is," and Ben turned to find him holding up a single, limp sack.

"What the hell, is that it?"

"Yes, sir, nearly fifteen hundred dollars."

"Where's the rest of it?"

"I beg your pardon?"

"The rest of the money, damnit. With all the men in town looking to bet on the fights and races, there has to be more money than this."

"I'm sure there is, but most men wouldn't keep it here."

"Why not?"

"Because . . ." He hesitated, then gulped. "Because they'd be afraid someone would steal it, sir."

After a stunned pause, Ben snatched the bag from the manager's fist. "I'm walking out of here. I want you to stay put until somebody comes looking for you."

"Yes, sir."

Ben walked over to where Mose was propped against the wall. His chest rose and fell shallowly, and his eyes had taken on a glaze Ben knew well. Kneeling, he placed a gentle hand on the dying man's shoulder.

"Mose, can you hear me? Mose!"

Mose's head came around, his eyes struggling to focus. "You get it?" he asked, the words more gurgled than spoken.

"We got it," Ben said, and Mose's lips peeled back in a macabre grin; twin ribbons of blood dribbled from each corner of his mouth, collecting in the stubble on his chin.

"You'd best get outta here, pard."

"I aim to. I just wanted to say goodbye before I left."

"It was a good ride," Mose burbled. "How many years . . . it been?"

"Twelve, I'd guess. I'm not sure anymore."

"Yeah, twelve feels . . . 'bout right." He looked at Ben and smiled a final time. Then the light went out in his eyes and his head tipped to the side.

Ben staggered to his feet, a low, agonizing sound welling up past the constriction of his throat. Watching him, Rogers moaned and dropped to his knees, his lips moving swiftly in prayer. But it wasn't the hotel manager Ben turned to. It was Leonard. Raising his pistol, Ben fired once, then again and again, until the Smith was empty and his ears ached from the repeated blasts inside the confined space. Rogers fell forward and covered his head with his arms, as Leonard's torn body seemed to deflate before Ben's eyes, flowing out from the wall as if turned to liquid.

Hands trembling, Ben released the catch in front of the Smith and Wesson's hammer, and the barrel and cylinder tipped forward, ejecting the empties. He walked to the door and threw it open. A thick, gray cloud of gun smoke spilled out before him. He followed it into the lobby as he slipped fresh cartridges into the Smith's chambers. A man stood on the landing to the upper floor with an old cap and ball Dragoon revolver held gingerly in one hand. He stared at Ben, then took a step backward. Ben slapped the Smith and Wesson closed with the palm of his hand and raised it toward the man on the landing, who abruptly dropped the Dragoon and scrambled back up the stairs to disappear around the corner. Sucking in a deep breath, Ben turned for a final look at Mose. Then he strode through the front door to the street.

CHAPTER FOUR

Cocking his head to one side, Ray listened as the sound of gunshots rolled down the street. Glancing apprehensively across the room, he said, "What's goin' on out there, kid?"

Bobby stepped over to the door and peeked outside. After a few seconds, he shook his head. "Nothing, there's nothing happening out there."

"What are the people on the street doin'?"

"They're looking at the hotel."

Ray swore and ducked into the cage where the bank manager was filling a pair of gray canvas bags with cash, carefully arranging the bills and coins for optimum balance. Ray poked him in the back with the revolver's muzzle, causing the manager to glance peevishly over his shoulder.

"Do you want this job done right?" he asked, "Or would you prefer—"

Ray thumbed the Colt's hammer to full cock. "I want it done now, fat man."

The manager's gaze dropped to the gun pointed at his chest, then he nodded and began shoving the money roughly into the bags. Ray eased back to where he could see the customers still standing in line. No one had moved, not even to lower their arms. If this had been his job to orchestrate, Ray would have ordered every damn one of them to empty their pockets of cash and valuables. But Ben had been specific about that.

"Let's not get everyone riled," he'd said when outlining his plan to relieve Rio Largo of a good share of its finances.

"The law is gonna be after us no matter what we do," Jethro had pointed out.

"The law in Rio Largo is one old man. Let's not give him a reason to raise an army of outsiders to come after us."

The others had immediately agreed. Even Ray had grudgingly nodded his consent. But that had been a week ago, back in San Angelo. Standing here today, staring at all these bank patrons waiting to be fleeced, he was experiencing a change of heart. Then another series of shots rattled down the street, and he knew they were running out of time.

"Ed," he barked. "Check those gents' pockets and see what they're carryin'."

Dodson shot him an uncertain look. "That wasn't the plan."

"I'm changin' the plan, and I'll take any spurring Ben wants to dish out about it."

Ed hesitated only a moment, then shrugged and moved toward the line of customers nearest him. "Keep your hands up and your mouth shut," he instructed his first victim as he reached inside the lapels of a gray suit coat to search for a wallet.

The bank manager grunted as he lifted the two heavy canvas sacks. With a bag in each hand, he shuffled over to where Ray waited outside the cage.

"That's good, fat man. Now put 'em down here beside me, then get back inside the cage. You tellers, too."

"People are starting to get real excited out there," Bobby said from the front door. His voice sounded taut, almost jittery.

"Keep a tight rein, boy. We'll be out of here in two shakes."

Ed was making quick work of relieving the waiting customers of their valuables. It took only a couple of minutes to make his way down both lines. He tossed what weapons he found toward a front corner of the bank, shoving wallets, watches, and any interesting-looking trinket into his pockets. By the time he finished, Ray had moved over to stand next to Bobby at the door.

Out on the street, men were gathering across from the hotel. A couple of them had already drawn their revolvers, but no one was paying any attention to the bank. Ray figured that wouldn't last. Sooner or later, someone was going to figure out what was going on.

"All right," he said tersely, shoving both money sacks into Bobby's hands. "Let's go say howdy to the townsfolk."

For a time, Jethro Hill believed it was all going to go as smoothly as Ben had predicted. He and Little Fish had ridden into town before the others and filled their water bags at the steel tank below the springs. McDaniels had been only a few minutes behind them, and even as Jethro and Fish were returning the bags to their panniers, Henry was dismounting in front of the jail.

Jethro watched the older man's confident stride as he left his mount tethered to the rail out front, looking for all the world like a scruffy gentleman on a morning stroll. Even when he reappeared a few seconds later and made his way down the boardwalk to the Hub Café, he'd done so without any hint of anxiety. McDaniels entered the little restaurant, and when he didn't soon reappear, Jethro knew he'd located the town's sheriff—*deputy* sheriff was the official designation, working for the county sheriff's office out of El Paso. Ben had predicted Plunkett might be there, eating a late breakfast as the town prepared for the upcoming festivities.

With the water bags secured, Jethro and Little Fish remounted their horses. Little Fish took charge of the packhorse, leading it back down the street to the opposite end of the town; Jethro guided his sorrel over next to a badly eroded adobe pen, empty now but still smelling of hogs. Little Fish was barely in place when Ben rode into town from the south. Mose was at his side. Ray, Ed, and Ben's little brother, Bobby, whom they'd picked up in San Angelo barely a week before, brought up the rear in loose formation. Only Bobby acknowledged Little Fish's presence, giving the half-breed a quick, low wave. It made Jethro wince to see it. That was exactly the kind of ineptness Ray had been complaining about ever since the younger Hollister showed up.

Well, it was too late to do anything about it now. The stone had been kicked loose the minute Henry entered the Hub; it was rolling now, picking up speed, and nothing was going to stop it. Not with Ben and Mose already inside the Cattleman's, and Ray and Ed and Bobby swinging down at the bank. It was worrisome, though. Although things seemed to be going just fine, Jethro knew hell generally broke loose without warning, and that it paid to be ready. That was why he'd shucked his Winchester as soon as Little Fish took off with the packhorse, and why he sat his own mount, Acorn—the sorrel's light red coat and flaxen mane reminded him of the acorns that grew in the orchard behind his parents' house back in Missouri—with his rifle butted firmly to his thigh, a round chambered and his thumb on the hammer. Still, when the echo of the first shot reached him, he felt more sadness than concern.

"I knew we'd bit off more'n we could chew," he told Acorn as he heeled the horse away from the deserted hog pen. He let the Winchester fall forward over the crook of his left arm where it would be quicker to shoulder when the shooting started in earnest. Then, hauling up in the middle of the street, he waited to see what developed.

Owen Plunkett was glaring hard. Henry returned the visual examination calmly, without blinking. He was aware of others around the restaurant looking their way, no doubt wondering what the lawman intended to do about the increasing sounds of gunplay coming from the street.

Henry was wondering about that himself. During the planning stages of their raid on Rio Largo, they'd recognized the possibility that something might go wrong. No matter how carefully Ben had crafted this scheme of robbing two businesses at the same time, then getting out of town without gunplay, there were always contingencies that couldn't be foreseen—missteps made or just plain flukes of bad luck. Like the company of Texas Rangers that unexpectedly showed up in Santa Clarita as they were holding up the local express office. They'd lost two good men making their escape, but those kinds of things happened no matter how carefully a man plotted. Now it seemed like it was happening again, and Henry needed to decide how he wanted to handle it.

"Are we going to sit here all day?" Plunkett asked impatiently.

"No, we ain't," Henry replied, coming to a decision. "We're gonna get up and walk outside like we're goin' to see what all the fuss is about, and if anyone says anything, you'll tell 'em it's just some drovers blowing off steam."

"They won't buy that."

"You'd better damn well make 'em buy it," Henry threatened. "I ain't takin' my pistol's front sight off your belly until I'm convinced we're in agreement."

"Sheriff?" someone said tentatively.

"Just a minute, Don."

Neither man looked his way. Henry made a quick, upward motion with his chin. "Let's go see what all the ruckus is about, Owen," he said, raising his voice so that those sitting nearby could hear.

"Why sure, *stranger*," Plunkett said, leaning heavily on the last word.

41

"You try that again, lawdog," Henry said quietly, "and I'll pull the trigger and take my chances in the ruckus you're gonna cause with a hole punched through your gut."

Plunkett nodded, and Henry did likewise. He could tell the sheriff believed him, and that was three-quarters of the battle right there.

They stood together, and Henry let his short-barreled revolver hang along his thigh, half hidden beneath the hem of a ratty sack coat. Plunkett's revolver was still holstered, but Henry knew he couldn't take it away without revealing his hold over the lawman, and he didn't want to do that if he didn't have to.

"Sheriff, is everything all right?" the man Plunkett had called Don asked. He looked confused by the lawman's unhurried response to the escalating gunfire outside.

"I said, not now, *Don.*"

"But . . . I'm Dave."

"Son of a bitch," Henry growled, then whipped his revolver out and brought it down hard on top of Plunkett's head. The lawman dropped to his knees and the color drained from his face. He swayed there a moment, then toppled forward like a felled tree. Pointing his revolver at Dave, Henry said, "You so much as twitch, mister, and I'll blow a hole between your damned eyes."

A woman at one of the tables next to the front window screamed, and a man at the counter demanded to know what Henry thought he was doing. Lifting the revolver above his head, Henry fired a round into the ceiling, and pandemonium erupted throughout the café. Men and women scattered, tipping over chairs and crashing into tables. Dinnerware slid to the floor in sprays of color—the blue of shattered china mingling with yellow egg yolk, pieces of browned meat, tan biscuits, and pale milk gravy.

Shoving panicked customers out of his way, Henry beat a

hasty retreat to the front door. On the street he saw Ben Hollister loosening the reins to his mount in front of the hotel. At the bank, Ed and Bobby were already in their saddles. Jethro Hill was jogging his sorrel toward them on a tight rein. People had already gathered on the boardwalks, but so far only a couple of them had pulled their weapons; they stood uncertainly, still not sure what was happening.

Henry ran to where his mount was hitched in front of the jail and jerked the reins loose, but when he tried to get a foot in the stirrup, the horse spooked from all the chaos and began sidestepping away from him.

"Whoa, you jugheaded son of a bitch," he cried as the horse dragged him into the middle of the street.

Men were pouring out of the Hub, most of them with their guns drawn. Henry fired once into the wall above their heads, driving them back inside. No one was returning fire yet, but they soon would. It was only a matter of time—seconds, not minutes—before Rio Largo's main street would start humming with lead, and Henry figured if he wasn't in the saddle when it began, he was going to be a damn hard target to miss.

Mose wasn't anywhere to be seen, and Jethro knew instinctively that Ben's old partner wouldn't be riding out of town with them. Alive or dead, poor ol' Mose was staying behind.

Two doors up from the hotel, Ed and Bob were struggling to hold their mounts steady as Ray stood in front of the bank's open door and fired inside with his revolver. The canvas sacks Ed and Bob had brought into town with them looked like a couple of stuffed geese hanging from their saddles.

Although Acorn kept fighting the bit, Jethro managed to keep him under control. When he spotted a couple of men peering around the corner from the alley next to the Hub, he swung the horse sideways in the street and started firing methodically at

43

the building, keeping the duo in the alley and those inside the café pinned down until Henry managed to jam a foot in the stirrup and swing his free leg over the cantle. The horse didn't wait for him to find his seat. It took off in an explosion of dust, head thrown high in a panic, nostrils flaring. But by then Henry was firmly planted and he let the animal have its head, riding low to make himself as small as possible.

Ben Hollister was already making tracks south to where Little Fish had brought his mount out of the shadows of a rambling stable. The half-breed was firing his Spencer steadily, peppering the fronts of the businesses that lined both sides of the street. Jethro was doing the same from the north, his Winchester's heavy bullets like fists slamming into the buildings. Ben was riding at a slow lope, firing behind him with his revolver while gripping the reins to Mose's horse in the same hand that held his own reins.

Ray Beeler was the last of them to fork his saddle. Jethro held Acorn back until Ray was mounted. Then, with everyone racing south amid a hail of returning gunfire, Jethro gave the sorrel its head. It took only seconds to fly past the center of town, where armed men were crowding the doorways and alley mouths to get a shot at the fleeing outlaws.

Jethro kept shooting until his rifle was empty, then returned the Winchester to its scabbard and drew his Colt. He held his fire, though. The worst of the shooting was already tapering off as they moved out of range, and he began to breathe easier as the cluster of businesses near the center of town gave way to scattered residential structures. They were just about clear of the place when a blast like a small cannon—or a large-bored shotgun—erupted from the window of a small, flat-roofed adobe house next to the road.

Up ahead, Ed Dodson's revolver was snapped from his hand, and Bobby Hollister was flung forward over his saddle horn. In that same instant, Jethro felt a tearing burn in his thigh, and cried out in pain and surprise. For a moment the world seemed to blur into a gray fog. He was aware of the fluid motion of his horse and could clearly hear the roar of the wind as it rushed past his ears, but his sight dissolved into a watery blur and his senses briefly disconnected from his body, as if the two existed side-by-side rather than as a single entity. Then his vision returned and he grabbed his saddle horn with both hands. His revolver was lost, his hat as well, and when he looked to his side, he saw Henry McDaniels leaning close to slip the reins from his weakening grasp.

"Hang on!" Henry cried, and Jethro nodded that he would, just before the world faded out once more.

CHAPTER FIVE

Sierra del Capulín Mountains
Chihuahua, Mexico—June

Lounging in the shade of a brush ramada, leaning back on one elbow with his ankles crossed, José Yanez tried hard to maintain an air of disinterest in the nearly naked individual sitting across the trade blanket from him. From a distance, José might have looked half-asleep. Inside, his gut was taut, his every nerve tingling. Geronimo was not a man to insult, and José knew his affected indifference could easily blow up in his face if the war leader took his feigned insolence personally. But José had come here to trade, and trading with the Apaches never came without risk.

Geronimo, wearing only a loincloth, knee-high moccasins with upcurled rawhide toes, and a faded blue-and-white bandana on his head, sat cross-legged with his elbows resting on his knees, staring intently at the seven stubby carbines lined up before him. To one side sat a pair of wooden crates, the lids popped off both of them to reveal stacks of pasteboard boxes, each one containing twenty rounds of .45-70 cartridges for the single-shot Remingtons. The carbines were José's ace in the hole, the miniscule leverage he was gambling on to keep Geronimo's infamous rage toward Mexicans in check, and his own life moving forward.

The craggy-faced Apache raised his head to peer into José's eyes, as if to gauge the sincerity of this overture within their depths. Gathered in front of a wickiup several yards away, nearly a dozen warriors stirred in anticipation of a decision. In the early morning light just peeking over the rim of the canyon wall at José's back, they reminded him of wolves salivating before a fattened calf. Without closer scrutiny, which he thought might not be prudent at the moment, he couldn't tell what the war-weary Apaches were hungering for. Was it the carbines he had brought into their camp? Or was it José himself, he and his men being well-armed but hugely outnumbered?

Sensing Geronimo's impatience, as well as his reluctance to open negotiations by speaking first, José pulled his legs under him and sat up.

"Has Goyaałé decided?" he asked, using Geronimo's birth name—He Who Yawns—in what he hoped would be viewed as a gesture of respect for the war leader's prominence.

"There are more?" Geronimo asked in his poor Spanish, thrusting his chin toward the carbines.

"Many more," José assured him, then leaned forward to tap one of the ammunition crates with a blunt finger. "And plenty of cartridges to kill the white-eyes above the border."

Geronimo made a dismissing motion with his hand. José knew he considered the indistinct line separating the territories of Arizona and New Mexico from the states of Chihuahua and Sonora as just more foolishness from two races of people he had never understood. A border to Geronimo—to any Indian, José thought—was a river or a mountain range, and certainly nothing a true warrior couldn't cross with impunity. That the blue-clad soldiers from the north and the gray-attired troops below the line refused to pursue the Apaches beyond these intangible barriers both puzzled and appeased the war leader. It was a stupidity that served the Apaches well.

"When?" Geronimo asked, moving a finger to indicate the carbines.

"Two moons," José replied without hesitation.

Geronimo studied him silently for a long minute, his distrust unmistakable. José returned the Apache's scrutiny guilelessly. He had already explained how the big ships brought American goods to Mexico, and how he had established a connection with a warehouseman in Matamoros who promised to slip a crate of carbines—packed seven to a box—and at least two crates of ammunition out of every second or third cargo ship that docked at his battered wharf. He just wasn't sure the Apache believed his lies.

"Two moons," Geronimo repeated, his gaze returning to the weapons and ammunition his warriors so desperately needed. Then, his expression never changing, he made a motion toward the carbines and ammunition crates. Immediately several braves stepped forward to confiscate the munitions and whisk them from sight. When they were gone, Geronimo said, "I like this deal you bring me, Yanez, and in two moons when you return with more rifles and cartridges, I will pay you for the guns you brought me today."

José had stiffened when the Apaches vanished with his merchandise. Now his nostrils flared in anger. Sensing he was on dangerous ground but unwilling to back down, he said, "I will need payment today, Goyaałé, in order to purchase more rifles from the man who works on the big ships."

"The man who works on these ships is of no concern to me." Geronimo rose and stepped clear of the ramada. The morning sunlight striking his face at an angle deepened the shadows under his prominent cheekbones, and heightened the enmity in his eyes. "In two moons, Yanez."

José scrambled to his feet. Geronimo watched stoically, without any hint of fear, as José took a step toward him. One of José's hands started to reach for the slim-bladed *belduque* sheathed at his waist, then slowly fell away.

"You wish to challenge me, Mexican?"

"I wish for payment, Goyaałé. It is only fair."

Geronimo's voice softened, yet there was no mistaking the threat it carried. "You know of Kas-Ki-Yeh?"

José's throat went dry at the mention of the town outside of which Geronimo's family—his wife, children, and mother—had been slaughtered by Mexican troops, while Geronimo and others from his tribe had been in town bartering with traders and shopkeepers. It was said by men whose opinion José trusted that it was after Kas-Ki-Yeh, or Janos, as the Mexicans called the town, that Geronimo's heart had turned dark with a need for revenge that the blood of a thousand innocents had yet to cleanse. The last thing José wanted at that moment, with him and his men surrounded by warriors, was for Geronimo to dwell too long on what had happened at Kas-Ki-Yeh.

"We will go," he said. "And in two moons, if the ships are not delayed, we will return with more rifles and ammunition, and trinkets for your women to pin to their dresses or put in their hair."

"Our women do not want your cheap brass and glass beads, Yanez. Bring us guns and bullets. With those, we will take what we want."

Then Geronimo walked away, leaving José standing rigidly with his fists clenched, pulse throbbing at his temples, until a horse nickered from behind him. Turning, he saw his men waiting anxiously in the shade of cottonwoods across a small stream fifty yards away. Snapping his quirt sharply against his leather leggings, José went to join them. As he waded the shallow waters he saw that their horses were already saddled, packs lashed securely to their mules.

Despite Geronimo's double cross with the Remingtons, they had done a fair business with the other merchandise they had brought with them to *Apacheria*. Cloth, needles and thread, small kettles and iron utensils, flint-and-steel fire starters, ground corn, beans, and tobacco had been bartered for items of gold and silver—crucifixes and other religious artifacts taken in raids across Northern Mexico and the Southwestern United States made up the bulk of the Apaches' trade—plus paper money from both sides of the border and clothing taken from the dead, boots and hats, gloves and coats. Too much to carry for a people constantly on the run.

José's Second Lieutenant, Francisco Castile, waited next to the creek, holding the reins to his own gray as well as José's buckskin. The thunder on José's face told him the deal had gone sour before his companion exited the water.

"He would not trade?" Castile asked in Spanish.

"You did not see?"

"Not from here, no."

"He took the Remingtons, but said he would not pay for them until we returned with more arms and ammunition."

Scowling, Castile said, "Did he not understand that these were all the rifles we have?"

José shrugged. "I told him there would be more."

"More? Why?"

"Because I wanted him to believe we would come back." He jerked the buckskin's reins from Castile's hands. "How do you think that cutthroat would respond if he thought we could not bring him more weapons, eh? I will tell you. He would cut our throats from ear to ear, then take our weapons and our horses." José shook his head in disgust. "No, we gambled that we could deal with the Apaches as we once dealt with the Comanches, that we could hold back our best and make a better deal, but we were wrong."

"I'd like to cut that bloody son of a whore's throat," Castile said quietly, glancing across the creek to where several dozen wickiups were scattered across the canyon floor.

"There would be a bounty to collect, and don't think I didn't consider it." José paused, and a grim smile stretched across his face. "They would have paid us handsomely, from both sides of the border, and given us medals to hang on our chests."

"I don't need a medal," Castile replied. "But Geronimo's head, that I would display with pride. I would put it on the horn of my saddle and take him with me everywhere."

"It is a good thought," José agreed. "But in truth, neither of us would live long enough to put it anywhere." He gathered his reins above the buckskin's neck, then stepped into the hard leather of his saddle. "Come on, let's leave this place before Geronimo changes his mind."

Castile gave him a sullen look, followed by a wry smile. Then he, too, swung into his saddle. The others—Antonio Carrillo, Pedro Suarez, and Javier Diaz—were already mounted. With their pack mules in tow, José led them away from the Apache camp. His scalp crawled all the way out of the canyon, and his back continued to itch in anticipation of a bullet or arrow for miles as they crossed the rolling hills east of the Sierra del Capulíns. It was early afternoon when he finally led his men into a side canyon and began to feel like he could lower his guard. After a few miles they came to another shallow stream, and in the towering cottonwoods flanking it awaited a rough-hewn community of *jacales* and brush shelters covered with uncured hides or ratty blankets, none of which would have shed much rain were the summer monsoons to appear.

Juan Carlos Cordova, First Lieutenant in José Yanez's *Cazadores de los Médanos*—his Hunters of the Dunes—was first to climb to his feet. He came to the edge of the trees to greet the traders as they rode in out of the sun. José smiled and stepped down to embrace the man in a bear hug.

"Mi teniente," he cried. *"Mi amigo."*

"Mi capitán," Juan Carlos replied, then reached up to sweep

José's sombrero from his head. "And your scalp is intact." He laughed. "You have earned me much silver, my friend. There are those here who thought that rascal Geronimo would take your hair as well as the guns."

"Tell me who doubted my ability to deal with that devil, and I will have them drawn and quartered."

But Juan Carlos only laughed again. "Let's wait to pronounce sentence until I've been paid." His gaze moved on to the others, dismounting and leading the mules into the center of the camp to begin unpacking. "You were successful?"

"Only in that we escaped with our lives," José replied dourly. "Geronimo kept the carbines. We were only able to trade our smaller goods for some gold and silver and a few small banknotes."

Juan Carlos cocked a brow. "Is that not why you approached the Apaches?"

"I approached the Apaches to set up a trade for rifles and ammunition, as we once did with the Comanches. Not for baubles for their women."

"Rifles?"

"He promised Geronimo even more guns," Francisco said from where he was loosening the cinch on his gray.

"More?" Juan Carlos looked puzzled. "Where would we find more arms?"

"We would have found them . . . somewhere. Maybe from your cousin in Matamoros."

"That was a one-time transaction, *Capitán*, a crime of convenience. It is not as easy to steal from a ship's cargo as some might think."

José's smile disappeared. "You would tell me what I already know, Juan Carlos?"

"No, never!" the lieutenant replied, and raised his hands as if in supplication.

José nodded, satisfied the man understood his place.

After a pause, Juan Carlos said, "Then we will not become traders?"

"Not as long as I am *capitán*. No, we tried in good faith, but the Apaches are not like the Comanches. There is too much hatred between our people and theirs." His smile returned. "We are *soldados*, my friend. You need to remember that the next time your cousin wants to sell us guns."

Although aware of the glances exchanged between his two lieutenants, José chose to ignore them.

After a pause, Juan Carlos said, "I will remember, and in truth, it is good to hear that we are still soldiers."

"Eh, why is that?"

"Yesterday, Luis returned with news that a band of Apaches is camped half a day's ride south of here. They are making their way north, probably to join Geronimo, but they are in no hurry."

"How many?"

"Seven warriors, some children, and three women. Fourteen scalps in all, plus weapons and horses."

José growled low in his throat, the sound like that of a dog about to attack. "Then maybe our long journey will not be as unsuccessful as I had feared."

One of the men came up to take José's horse, leading it away to be unsaddled, then watered at the creek before being turned loose on hobbles to graze on the rich grass growing along the stream. José nodded his approval, pleased with the mien of respect on the *soldado*'s face, and that he appeared proud to be part of a company of men brave enough to enter the camp of their enemies, and to ride out again unscathed. José's gaze moved on, roaming the camp and the rough men who occupied it. He wondered what Geronimo would have said had he been aware of the thirty-plus men under José Yanez's command. Would he have been as free in displaying his scorn as he examined the Remingtons placed before him? Would he have been so quick to take the weapons with only a promise to pay later?

Perhaps, José admitted to himself. That Apache was an arrogant bastard, guided by hatred and utterly lacking in fear. And the numbers still favored the war leader's position. But José couldn't help but think the outcome might have been different had he gone into Geronimo's camp with all of his men, as a war leader himself, rather than a humble trader. It had been his mistake, his miscalculation, and his focus shifted briefly, thoughtfully, to Juan Carlos, whose cousin had offered them the guns. But no, despite Juan Carlos's petitions, the decision to trade had been his, and there was nothing he could do about it now. But maybe there was something that could be done to salvage this latest venture—over five weeks lost to tracking down that wily Apache bastard—and only a few pieces of gold and silver and some worn, bloodstained clothing to show for it. Barely enough to recover the costs of the munitions they had lost.

The thought of the seven warriors who unknowingly awaited their fate to the south brought a hard smile to José's lips.

"We ride tomorrow," he announced suddenly, loudly, so that they might all hear. "I am tired of wandering this land like vagabonds. It is time we returned home."

"To San Fidel?" Francisco asked, his expression hopeful.

"No, to Villa Lobos."

It was the name the citizens surrounding San Fidel had begun calling the town not long after José Yanez and his Hunters had taken up residence there.

Villa Lobos.

House of Wolves.

Chapter Six

They made good time that first day. Better than Cade had anticipated. He'd put Trooper Riley on the Rucker ambulance to handle the lines of the four-mule hitch, with Corporal Frank Poe on the seat beside him, carrying a single-shot Springfield across his lap. Cade and the others rode horseback, with two on rear guard and the rest up front. In such open country, he'd seen no need for flankers.

The women—Lucia, Hattie, and Fanny—rode inside out of the sun, on a bunk folded down from the sideboard. They'd rolled the canvas walls up about a foot on each side to allow air to circulate, although it hadn't helped much. Lucia and Hattie endured both the sweltering cauldron and the Rucker's lurching tempo in dogged silence, but Fanny had set up a steady string of oaths and complaints within ten minutes of leaving the stalled train, and hadn't stopped until midafternoon when weariness and a raw throat finally overcame her other discomforts.

Poe confessed to Cade that evening that her incessant carping had nearly set his ears to bleeding. He meant for the comment to be taken lightly, but Cade didn't see the humor in it. He was still smarting over the reprimand Colonel Hawthorne had given Captain Miller that morning, and by extension, himself. He considered the women's presence on the train to be his failing, and knew it would be a long time before he was able to laugh about any part of it.

They'd followed a rough lane paralleling the Southern Pacific tracks for several hours that morning—the remnants of a wagon road the tracklaying crews had used during the line's construction—but abandoned the trace in favor of an arm of the old Butterfield mail route that once ran between Sierra Blanca and El Paso. Although competition from the railroad had rendered stagecoach traffic obsolete along that section of the trail, the road was still in decent shape, and Cade was counting on it to cut at least half a day's travel off their return.

They made camp that evening inside a clump of stubby mesquite—the first trees they'd come to all day—surrounded by creosote bush and low, rolling hills. The presence of the mesquite, as well as the halfway decent graze they found within the spiny grove, indicated water somewhere beneath the surface, although there was no sign of it aboveground. Not even a hint of dampness to the soil.

The lack of moisture wasn't a concern. Cade had ordered enough water brought along in kegs to keep the stock satisfied at least as far as the river road south of El Paso. They could refill their barrels there if they had to.

He set Morgan and Riley to organizing the camp, Elkins, Schultz, and Hendricks to tending the stock, watering them first, then currying their sweaty hides as the animals fed on molasses-sweetened oats fed from nose bags. When the horses and mules were finished eating, they were hobbled and turned loose to graze or roll. Elkins and Hendricks kept watch to make sure they didn't wander off.

Hattie and Lucia fixed the evening meal—side pork and beans, along with a couple of pans of corn bread salvaged from the breakfast mess that morning, and a small pot of coffee. It was standard fare for a march and no one complained; surprisingly, not even Fanny, although her expression as she chewed on the beans spoke freely of her discontent.

When the light started to fade, Cade ordered the stock

brought in. They tied the horses and two of the mules to a rope stretched high between the trunks of a pair of sturdy mesquite trees at the edge of the clearing. The other two mules, still green-broke and rebellious, were led deeper into the trees and hitched to individual limbs, where they weren't as likely to get into a kicking fray with the other stock. Cade ordered a single guard put out on three-hour shifts to patrol the camp's perimeter, and to keep a small fire burning.

The men were unrolling their blankets when Cade and Poe walked over to where the women idled near the rear of the ambulance. As he already had several times that day, Cade reminded himself not to smile when he saw the women in their cavalry attire—trousers and blouses, kepis for their heads, thick-soled brogans on their feet. Yet even from thirty feet away and at the dim edge of the campfire's light, he thought there would be no mistaking their sex. Lucia stood out in particular, and he wondered who had chosen her blouse; he also briefly wondered if he wouldn't have picked a size or two larger if he'd been there when the uniforms were issued. It kind of surprised him to re-alize he wasn't sure he would have.

Lucia looked up expectantly as they approached. Hattie glanced their way as well, then averted her eyes. Fanny snorted and shook her head.

"I knew that sergeant'd be first to crumble," she said contemptuously as the two men came near. "Officers always are." Then she leaned to one side and spat a gob of tobacco into the shadows behind the wagon.

Ignoring the remark, as well as the trail of brown spittle Fanny wiped from her chin with the back of her hand, Cade spoke directly to Lucia. "We have blankets for all of you. You're welcome to either bed down out here or in the ambulance."

"I been sitting on that damn board you call a bench all day," Fanny retorted, swiping the back of her hand across her trouser leg. "I'll sleep on the ground. It'll be softer."

"Just be careful some rattlesnake doesn't crawl into the blankets with you," Poe said in his teasing way.

"If that snake's got two dollars, he'll be welcome, and probably a hell of a lot more fun than any of you soldier boys."

"That's enough, Corporal," Cade said mildly.

"You, too, Fanny." Lucia looked at Cade. "She's right, though. I'd just as soon stretch out on the ground as spend any more time in that torture chamber you call an ambulance."

"It's your choice," Cade said, then turned to Poe. "Corporal, see that these women have what they need to be as comfortable as possible for the night."

"Will do, Sergeant."

Cade returned his gaze to Lucia, who met it with a frankness he found oddly disquieting. A scowl worried his brows, until Fanny snorted and said, "I believe that soldier boy likes you, Loosh."

"Hush," Lucia said irritably, and moved her eyes away from Cade's.

Lightly touching the upcurled brim of his campaign hat, Cade said, "Goodnight, ladies," and walked away. Fanny laughed, Lucia repeated her appeal for her to shut up, and Poe said something Cade didn't catch. Then he was out of earshot, and glad for it. He walked past the fire to check on the picket line, where he found a trooper brushing down one of the mules.

"Riley?"

"Hello, Sergeant."

"What are you doing out here? I thought these animals were already taken care of for the night."

"Aye, they have been, but old Hank here likes the extra attention, and I'm prone to stay on the good side of any beasty that likes to kick."

"And when did old Hank ever take a swipe at you?"

Riley's teeth flashed in a good-natured grin. "Why, he never has, Sergeant, and that's why I keep brushin' on him and Molly here." He tipped his head to the other mule on the highline, both of them wheelers.

"Do you take care of your own mount this well?"

"Aye, that I do, and I miss the old plug. I wish I could've brought him with me."

Cade smiled. "Keep up the good work, Riley, and one of these days you'll be wearing corporal's stripes."

"Now, that'd be something to write home about. Me old ma told me I didn't have what it'd take to be a soldier. Said I was too bullheaded, she did, so I made up me mind right then and there to prove her wrong. I reckon an extra set of stripes on me sleeves'd set her straight, don't ye?"

Cade laughed, his first of the day. "I'm not so sure about that, Riley."

The private's brush slowed. "Not so sure? Why's that?"

"I think maybe your mother knew what she was talking about when she challenged you the way she did. She might be proud if you became a corporal, but I doubt that she'd be surprised."

"Challenged, ye say? How'd the old girl challenge me?"

"Think about it," Cade said, turning his back on the puzzled trooper and returning to the fire. The coffee pot was still there, though empty and already scrubbed clean.

"I didn't put it away because I wasn't sure we wouldn't have a pot or two in the morning," Hendricks said.

"I appreciate the forethought, but doubt the outcome," Cade replied, sinking to the ground a few feet away from the fire. It would be chilly by morning, but it wasn't cold enough to hug a blaze just yet.

"Tired, Sergeant?" Morgan asked absently from where he lay atop his bedroll a dozen feet away.

"Just taking advantage of some slack time, Trooper."

"Me, too," Morgan replied sleepily. He was still fully dressed, save for his boots, which sat upright beside him. His socks, gray when new, looked almost black in the light of the gently dancing flames.

Cade dug a pipe and a cloth sack of Genuine Durham from his kit and carefully filled his meerschaum's chipped, soft-red bowl. Bats flitted overhead, and off in the distance a coyote yipped, then even farther away a wolf howled as if to intimidate the lesser creature.

With his pipe lit to satisfaction, Cade leaned back against his saddle. He puffed contentedly, staring into the flames as the day's tensions flowed from his body. He was tired—as much from the assignment as from a day in the saddle—and intended to slide into his blankets as soon as he finished his pipe. He was just about there when Poe returned from getting the women settled.

"Trouble?" Cade asked.

"Not if you don't count the redhead's constant yapping."

"I don't." He stretched, stifled a yawn, then leaned forward to knock the dottle from his bowl. "I'm about ready to turn in, Frank. Can you do a final check on the picket before turning in?"

"Will do," Poe replied, hiding his own reactive yawn behind a sun-browned hand.

Cade was returning his pipe to its case when he heard a commotion from where the horses were highlined. He glanced curiously at Poe, then the two of them started to their feet together. They were stopped by a voice from the darkness behind them.

"Don't get up, Sergeant!"

Cade hesitated only a moment, then rose all the way, although careful to keep his hand away from his holstered Colt. His men remained seated. Even Poe sank back to the ground at the command of the unseen intruder. But they were all fully awake and keenly alert. Before Cade could turn to face the man to his rear, another stepped into the light in front of him, carrying a revolver he had leveled on the troopers gathered around the fire. Within seconds other men were moving into the firelight, each of them carrying a fully cocked firearm.

"Who are you?" Cade demanded.

"That's nothing you need to know," said the voice from behind him, and Cade turned to find a weary-looking man in a black frock coat standing at the edge of the light, a cocked Smith and Wesson revolver locked tightly in his fist.

"You're in charge?" Cade said.

"As much as anyone, I guess."

"Let me tell you up front, mister, we're not carrying payroll or extra arms, but this is still a military affair, and you're interfering with army business. Are you sure you want to do that?"

"Sergeant, I don't give a damn what your business is out here. All I need from you right now is for you and your boys to keep your mouths shut and do what you're told."

There was more movement from beyond the firelight. Then an older man with a drooping mustache came in from where the cavalry horses and the two wheel mules were highlined. Riley marched in front of him, a mix of anger and embarrassment swirling in his dark Irish eyes. A second man in a calico shirt and knee-high moccasins, his raven-black hair hanging below his collar in back, arrived from another direction with Schultz being prodded along in front of the muzzle of a stubby Spencer carbine; the disarmed trooper glanced apologetically at Cade and shrugged. Before Cade could speak, a high-pitched whoop sailed out from behind the ambulance, followed by an equally elevated laugh. At first Cade thought it was one of the women. Then he recognized it as a man's cackle, as sharp as splintered glass. Seconds later a slim man with close-cropped hair came

61

around the rear of the ambulance herding the women loosely before him.

"Damnation, Ben, look what I found," he crowed.

The man with the oversized mustache who had brought Riley into the light exclaimed, "It's wimmin!"

"It sure as hell is. Three of 'em," the short-haired man answered. "I don't know if these damn Yankees have found a new way to recruit soldiers, or if they're just so hard up for fighters they'll take anyone, but I sure as hell approve." He poked Fanny in the back with his pistol and gave her a final shove toward the fire. "They was just standing over there lookin' lost," he added, a tinge of wonder in his voice.

The man in the calico shirt and moccasins, a mixed-blood, laughed mirthlessly. "Ray can sniff out a female like my old beagle used to sniff out rabbits."

"You're just jealous of my abilities, Fish," Ray chortled.

The man Ray had called Ben—the one in charge—moved closer to the fire. "That's enough," he snapped. "I want everyone over here by the fire, now. You women, too." He looked at Cade. "I can see your mind working, Sergeant, but don't be so stupid as to think you'd stand a chance in hell of pulling off whatever you have bubbling around in that brain of yours."

"What I'm thinking is that you and your men are stepping hip-deep into a peck of trouble," Cade said.

"You keep on ruminating in that direction. It just might keep you and your boys above ground and breathing." He glanced at the man with the mustache. "Grab their guns, Henry, and toss them over there by the wagon."

While Henry did that, Ray and Fish crowded close to the women. Fish reached out to touch one of Lucia's breasts, and she angrily slapped his hand away. Laughing, Fish said, "I like the scrappy ones."

"You two stay away from them gals," Ben ordered, then called into the shadows beyond the firelight. "Ed, bring Bobby in here."

"And Jethro," Ray added, his gaze darting to Ben, settling on him with a brazenness Cade was quick to note.

"You just keep an eye on these soldiers and make sure none of them decide to try to earn a medal for bravery tonight," Ben said, before turning away.

It took Henry only a couple of minutes to gather the squad's Springfield carbines and Colt revolvers and dump them in a pile under the Rucker's tailgate. As he did, a middle-aged man with a narrow goatee walked into camp leading a pair of horses. A wounded man was slumped in the saddle of the first animal. Behind them came a third man—young, his face etched in pain—riding a red-dust sorrel and leading a small remuda of saddled stock by their reins. All three were bloodied. The man on the sorrel had a rag tied around his thigh and the one with the goatee had a bandana circling one hand. But it was the fellow slouched over his saddle horn—tied to it, Cade realized—who looked the worse of the lot.

"You got any bandages in that ambulance, Sergeant?" Ben asked.

"Some," Cade replied. "Poe, go get the medical kit."

"You stay where you are, Poe," Ben said sharply. He looked at Cade. "You're not giving the orders tonight, Sergeant, so you tell me where it is and I'll have Henry fetch it."

"It's behind the seat, a small satchel."

Ben glanced at the older man with the drooping mustache, but Henry was already moving in that direction, the man with the goatee tying his horses to the Rucker's rear wheel.

Cade studied the intruders. After twenty years in the military and nearly a dozen wearing sergeant's stripes, he'd already pegged several of them. Ben was their leader, smart but tired. Ray and Fish would be the troublemakers. Henry was one of the solid hands, a man Ben would depend on to watch his flank. He wasn't sure yet where the others fit in, but doubted it would be long before everyone settled into their places, like cogs on a wheel.

"You boys sit down," Ben told Riley and Schultz, but they both looked to Cade first, remaining where they were until he nodded for them to do as instructed. Ben smiled at their defiance but didn't remark on it. To the women, he said, "You ladies make yourselves comfortable, too. We're going to be here a spell." He glanced at Cade and his eyes narrowed speculatively. "Am I going to have any trouble from you, Sergeant?"

"It's possible."

Ben seemed to consider that for a few seconds, then shrugged and holstered his weapon. "Ray, you and Fish keep an eye on these boys." He started toward the ambulance, where Henry was crawling out of the back with a medic's kit in a leather satchel. Then he stopped and turned. "And keep your hands off those women."

"By damn, there's a limit to how much bossin' I'm gonna put up with, Hollister," Ray said threateningly.

"We've got men who need tending to, Beeler. Until they're taken care of, you'll keep your pants buttoned and your eyes on these soldiers, or you'll by damn answer to me."

Ray Beeler's jaw rotated jerkily, like he had a quid of old tobacco stuck in his cheek, but after a few seconds he nodded grudgingly. "All right, but I ain't leavin' here 'til I've spent a little time with one of these gals, I'll tell you that right now."

Ben Hollister continued on to the ambulance without reply, and Cade struggled with a memory. Hollister, the Hollister gang. He'd heard of them. Bank and train robbers from around North Central Texas. He'd heard of Ray Beeler, too, a gunman of some note in that same area. If that was who they were, they were a long way from their old stomping grounds, although

Cade supposed even outlaws had to move on eventually. Especially those whose reputations grew too large to find safe places to hole up. He studied the others—the mixed-blood called Fish and the older man with the walrus-sized mustache called Henry. He'd never heard of either of them, but that didn't mean anything. Some men liked to keep up on that kind of thing, but Cade never had. He'd been kept occupied enough with all the Comanche and Apache troubles along the border.

The wounded man tied to his saddle didn't make any sound as he was cut free, then laid facedown on one of the bedrolls Poe had furnished the women, but the man on the sorrel did when he dismounted—a sharp grunt followed by a shallow curse as he clung to his saddle and waited for the pain in his leg to dissipate. Twisting partway around, Ben said, "You got a lantern or a lamp in that wagon, Sergeant?"

"There's a little bull's-eye in the side toolbox."

Henry pushed stiffly to his feet and disappeared around the far side of the Rucker. Cade heard the lid on the wooden box bolted to the wagon's sideboard creak open, then slap shut with a bang. Henry came back carrying a small tin candle lantern, mostly enclosed save for an adjustable aperture in the body. He opened the curved door and struck a match to light the candle inside, then closed it and fiddled with the adjustment until he had a bright narrow beam he could focus directly on the wounded man's injuries.

Cade walked over, ignoring Ray Beeler's command to stay where he was.

"I wouldn't push Ray too far, Sergeant," Hollister said quietly. "He's a good Southern boy, and not overly fond of Yankees."

"How bad is he hurt?" Cade asked, leaning in for a closer look at the youth stretched out facedown on a blanket.

"Bad enough," said the man with the goatee.

Taking a guess, Cade said, "You're Ed?"

The guy's head jerked up. "Ed Dodson. How'd you know?"

"Your boss, when he told you to bring Bobby in. And this is Bobby?" He nodded to the young man, little more than a kid, laid out beneath them.

"Bobby Hollister," Dodson replied.

"You talk too much, Ed," Ben said without looking up. He and Henry had tugged the boy's shirt up past his shoulder blades, revealing a badly bruised area surrounding two tiny puncture wounds in his lower back, just to the left of the spine. Had they been smaller, Cade might have guessed he'd been snakebit.

"What happened?"

Dodson's lips parted as if to reply, but Ben pegged the older man with a look that immediately shut him up.

"You don't have to worry about me knowing what you did," Cade said. "If you're Ben Hollister, then I figure you and your boys had your hands into someone else's till. I'm asking about this guy." He indicated the young man. "Is he your brother, or your son?"

"My brother," Ben replied gruffly.

"He's been shot," Ed Dodson added.

"Gutshot," Cade clarified, watching Ben for his reaction, knowing he'd have a better idea of their own situation by it.

Rocking back on his heels, Hollister rubbed a hand helplessly over his lips. Without looking up, he said, "Can you help him, Sergeant?"

"I can't do a damned thing for him, Hollister. You know that. He needs a doctor."

"Yes, he does, but unless you've got one handy, I'm going to have to make do somehow."

"Sorry."

Ben didn't speak. He didn't even move for nearly half a minute. Then he slowly stood, and his hand came up to cover the grips of his Smith and Wesson.

"I can help," said a voice from the fire, and the two turned as one, both of them scowling.

"Who said that?" Ben demanded.

"I did," and the woman called Hattie Wilkes, who had barely spoken since Cade discovered her crouched inside an equipment car early that morning, rose and took a hesitant step forward.

"The hell!" exclaimed Ray Beeler.

"What do you know about doctoring?" Ben asked skeptically.

"I wasn't always . . ." She hesitated, and her gaze dropped.

"I'll be damned," Ben said softly. "Whores." He looked at Cade. "You're escorting a wagonload of whores."

"We're taking them to El Paso," Cade confirmed.

"From where?"

"We were on our way to Fort Stockton when they were discovered. We're returning them."

"Troop train?"

Cade nodded. He was staring at Hattie, wondering if this was some kind of gambit on her part, or if she really knew what she was talking about.

"Sum'bitch, Ben, maybe we oughta find us an all-purpose gal like this to tote along." Grinning, Ray reached out to grab Hattie's butt. She jumped and spun and took a swing at him, but he dodged the blow easily, laughing at her indignation.

"What's the matter, honey? You ain't gonna claim no one's ever grabbed—"

"That's enough, Ray." Ben was studying the girl thoughtfully. "You're not a doctor."

"No, but my father was, at Chickamauga."

"You a Southern girl?" Ray asked in surprise.

"We lived in Chattanooga, downstream from the battle. The army didn't have enough surgeons, so when they started bringing their wounded into town, my father was forced to help."

"They?" Ray echoed. "Who's they, girl? Which army?"

"Does it matter?" she asked.

"It does to me, by God. I had kin at Chickamauga."

"A lot of people had kin there," Ben said. "And it doesn't matter to me whose side her daddy doctored for. What I want to know is how she thinks she can help tonight." After a pause, he added, "How old are you, anyway? Chickamauga must have been twenty years ago."

"I was twelve," Hattie replied with a defiant thrust to her chin, something Cade hadn't seen in her before. He noticed Lucia and Fanny were listening attentively, and wondered if this was the first they were hearing of her past as well.

"We were overwhelmed with wounded," Hattie continued. "My mother began assisting my father immediately, but even before the battle was over, they brought me in. I just helped with the simple chores at first, but the longer it went on and the more soldiers they brought to us, the more involved I became."

"But you don't have any real experience treating these kinds of wounds, do you? And what you might've seen was twenty years ago?" Ben started to turn away, but Hattie's words stopped him.

"I'd wager I have more experience than you do, and maybe more than anyone else here."

Ben was silent a moment, as if considering both her reply and his options. When he looked at Henry, the old-timer shrugged. "I don't reckon it can hurt. Sure as hell, none of us know what to do."

Ben glanced at Cade, who shook his head.

"I don't have any experience with this kind of a wound, either."

"All right," Ben said, and motioned Hattie forward. "Come over here and take a look, but I'll warn you, if you try anything suspicious, I'll bust a cap on you as quick as I would any man."

Hattie didn't move. She was staring at Hollister, and Cade could tell her mind was working swiftly, seeking some kind of an advantage. After a minute, she said, "I want to make a deal."

"The only deal I'll make is to let you live."

"That's not good enough."

"It's all you're going to get," Ben said, his voice rising.

"Let her talk," Cade interjected quietly.

Ben gave him a disgruntled look, then shrugged. "All right, what kind of deal?"

Hattie tipped her head toward Ray Beeler and Fish. "You keep these men, all of your men, away from me and my friends, and I'll do everything I can to help your brother."

"The hell," Ray growled, but Ben nodded with barely a pause. "All right. What else?"

"You'll let us go. Not now, and not me, but Lucia and Fanny. They haven't done anything to you."

"Okay. Anything else?"

Hattie shook her head. "That's all. I just don't want my friends hurt. Or these men," she added, waving a hand toward the troopers gathered around the fire.

"You've got yourself a deal," Ben said. He looked at Ray. "You heard her, Beeler. You, too, Fish. All of you, stay away from these women, or you'll have to deal with me, and I'm not in a forgiving mood right now."

"Well, I ain't in a deal-makin' mood," Ray replied coolly. "You ain't speakin' for me, Hollister. Not no more."

"Yes, I am," Ben replied. "And I will be until we reach Mexico."

Henry spoke up from where he was still kneeling next to the younger Hollister. "Hell, we're almost there, Ray. Let's not throw it all away because you can't keep your britches buttoned."

Michael Zimmer

Fish moved over to Beeler and leaned in close to whisper in his ear. Whatever he said brought a frosty smile to Beeler's face. "All right, we'll wait until we get to Mexico before settlin' up." Then his gaze shifted to Hattie. "Before we settle up on everything."

CHAPTER SEVEN

José Yanez and his scout, Luis Huerta, had reconnoitered the Apache camp after dark last night, and found that it was as Juan Carlos had told them the day before, following José's return from Geronimo's camp in the Sierra del Capulíns.

Seven warriors, some children, and three women. Fourteen scalps in all, plus their weapons and horses.

Satisfied the numbers were correct, the odds well in their favor, José and Luis had slid back off the hill to return to where the rest of the Hunters waited several miles to the north. Now, with dawn's light spreading over the dry hills, they were back, surrounding the camp on three sides in anticipation of the Apaches' emergence from their brush lean-tos and wickiups. José had kept the slim-shouldered Luis with him, trusting the younger man's keener eyesight and greater experience with Apaches, although he knew when the battle was joined, it would be his own skill as a leader—as *El Capitán*—that would carry the day.

José liked that title: Captain. It was much better than the simple leader, or boss, that the men had called him early on. Before he brought organization to these ragged misfits of deserting soldiers, bandits, and revolutionaries. He'd considered other appellatives, such as chief and commander, but *captain* implied rank and a certain prestige, and José had desired both as more and more men descended on San Fidel to join him.

Luis had been one of those recent recruits, but already adept in the ways of the hunter, *el cazador*. Captured by Lipans as a boy, he had lived with the tribe for nearly ten years before making his escape. Eventually he had arrived in San Fidel to join José's small company. Thirty-six men in the field now, and another dozen guarding the garrison at Villa Lobos. Although Luis was still half-wild and occasionally unpredictable, his hatred of Apaches was always dependable. That was why José trusted him now, confident the young man would do everything in his power to assure victory.

As they crept closer to the scattered wickiups, José caught a whiff of the peculiar odor of tiswin, a kind of beer made from fermented corn that was popular with some of the tribes. Luis had informed him last night the Apache women were brewing fresh batches of the stuff, which they would present to Geronimo in a gesture of friendship.

"They want to join his band to share in the plunder Goyaałé takes from the Mexicans and *Norteamericanos* they kill," Luis whispered to José as the two men awaited the coming battle. "These are not Chiricahuas," he added. "They are Mimbreños."

José nodded absently, straining to pick out details from the camp in the weak light. It didn't make any difference to him who they were. He had fought Mimbreños before, and knew they would be as fierce as Geronimo's Chiricahuas when the fighting started. In the end, all that mattered were the scalps he and his men would take, and the horses and gear they captured.

And the women.

José had no use for Apache women himself, but that was only because he had accepted the Lord as his Savior, and knew it was unholy to rape a woman he was not wed to. Although others of his company held no such compunction, José had resolved to remain pure in his heart until he returned to San Fidel, where his current wife maintained the house he had confiscated from a wool trader on the central plaza. Only then would he satisfy the animal-like cravings of his sex in a union that would not offend the Church. What happened to the women captured during the periodic raids made by him and his men were between them and the Lord, and José wanted no part of that discussion.

The Mimbreño camp sat on a narrow flat that jutted from the side of the hill like a swollen eyebrow. There was a trio of enclosed shelters at the nearest end—wickiups the *Indios* used when they were going to be in one location for more than a few days—and a couple of small lean-tos covered with deer and javelina hides. The leather-lined tiswin pits where the liquor was fermenting had been dug between the two dissimilar shelters like a trench between the upper and lower castes of larger cities. José wondered if that meant anything here, at least in regard to their impending attack. As far as any differences between individual Mimbreños, he knew that by the time his men were finished, there would be no such distinctions; the dead would all be as one, an idiot's scalp worth no less than a chief's.

José had split his men into three equal forces before their final approach on the site. He had personally taken command of the hill east of the Mimbreño camp, where he would have an unobstructed view of the *Indios* as they left their shelters to greet the new day. His two lieutenants—Juan Carlos Cordova and Francisco Castile—had taken positions with their companies to the south and north of the slumbering Apaches. Only the western side remained unguarded, a steep slope rising nearly a hundred meters above the slender bench. Anyone attempting escape in that direction would be in full view of José's men, gunned down long before they reached the top.

Luis's slight nudge brought José's head up with a snap. Across the narrow canyon a figure had stepped out of a wickiup. José squinted, but the light was still too poor to make out whether it was a man or a woman.

Luis cleared up the mystery.

"The woman."

"What woman?"

"The one the men talk of."

"Ah, *sí*, her." He was silent as he considered the young woman with the long, coal-black hair hanging to her waist. Luis had described her to Juan Carlos in detail, and Juan Carlos had passed the description on to the men in an attempt to fuel their passion for the fight. José felt a moment's sympathy for the young *mujer's* plight. He thought that if she were lucky, a bullet would take her in the first volley, allowing her to avoid the indignities that surely awaited her if captured. For a brief moment he contemplated killing her himself, then chided himself for such selfishness. His men had been without female companionship for nearly six weeks now. They deserved the spoils of a good fight. And what did he care of a Mimbreño woman, José asked himself as he recalled those within his own family who had died under an Apache knife or lance?

He became aware of Luis watching him, perhaps having spotted his furrowed brow.

"We are ready, are we not?" Luis asked.

"*Sí*, we are ready," José agreed as other Mimbreños began to take shape in the predawn light. He could make out all of the women now—two old crones kindling a fire, the young squaw with the long hair checking on one of the tiswin pits. A couple of children hovered near the older women as if in anticipation of the fire's warmth, while several of the men walked out to check on the horses.

Three men elected to remain behind and were talking among themselves. One of them lifted an arm to scratch lazily under his arm. No one seemed the least suspicious that they were being observed. José did a quick count of the Apaches, and smiled when he was finished.

"They are all there?"

"*Sí*, all except for the two youngest," José replied, meaning a toddler and an infant that one of the older women cared for. Grandchildren, perhaps. When he'd asked, Luis had seemed as confident the young woman was not the mother as he was that the mother was not among them. Luis did not know why she was absent, and José didn't care.

He had removed his sombrero before wiggling up the last few meters of the ridge overlooking the camp. Brushing a strand of lank, dark hair from his forehead, he leaned forward and raised his hand. A metallic murmuring ran outward from his position as the men to either side readied their weapons for firing. José waited only a moment, then brought his hand down sharply. In an instant, a roar filled the narrow valley. Smoke rolled forward from three sides in a dirty froth; lead whined and a horse screamed. On the small flat across the canyon, Mimbreño warriors twisted and jerked as marionettes in unskilled hands.

The remaining Apaches scattered, and José cursed his men's poor aim. Although nearly half of the Mimbreños were down—a couple of them writhing on the ground—neither of the youngsters and only one of the older squaws were felled in that first volley. Worse, two of the horses had been shot, one of them continuing to scream in a way that made the flesh across the back of José's neck ripple.

Two of the warriors were still on their feet, both armed and returning fire with lever-action rifles as they backed toward the wickiup where the younger children slept. The long-haired squaw and the remaining older one had already darted inside. They reappeared seconds later with the infant and toddler in their arms. The other children were already fleeing toward the horses. The women and one of the warriors ran after them. The older woman mounted first. She set the toddler in front of her, then accepted the infant from the younger one. Seconds later, a bullet from a Hunter's rifle swept her from the horse's back, tossing her toward the camp like windblown trash. The warrior with them fell next, twisting first one way, then the other as half a dozen bullets tore through his body. The warrior who had stayed close to the wickiups collapsed next, then the eldest child, a boy probably no more than nine or ten.

Carrying the infant and toddler in her arms and yelling for the remaining child to come with her, the young woman began scrambling up the steep hill behind the wickiups. Even as José lowered his rifle, men from Francisco's command were abandoning their positions and racing through the scrub to intercept her. Seeing them, the men to either side of José rose and started plunging down the rocky defile, yelling and whooping as if the battle had already been won.

José sighed as he watched his Hunters clamber over the craggy terrain. He sometimes wished he had more disciplined troops. Men who obeyed without question, who were guided by pride in their company and respect for their leaders.

At his side, Luis was slowly rising. Although he'd already reloaded and his expression was eager, he wasn't taking part in the chase. Picking up his sombrero and clamping it on his head, José stood next to him to watch as the final scenes were played out across the canyon. It was Francisco's men who caught up with the young woman first. They swarmed around her, forcing her to the ground until all but her screams remained. The children were tossed aside as inconsequential, although they would be brought back to the camp after the men were finished with the squaw. Their value would be in markets farther south, where wealthy *hidalgos* would purchase them for household help.

Juan Carlos's men were still fifty meters away when Francisco's detachment overwhelmed the woman. In resignation, they turned their attention to the camp and began plundering it for spoils.

"Selfishness," José muttered in disgust.

"They are no worse than you or I," Luis replied.

"Eh, how can you say such a thing? Look at them. Like wolves on the carcass of a calf. And it will be worse when they start dipping up the tiswin, even though it is not yet finished fermenting. They will drink until they are drunk, and drunk, they will become worse than animals. They will be like demons. Worse than demons."

"We brought them here," Luis reminded him quietly. He was looking at José, his dark eyes solemn. "For our own purposes, we brought them here to do what we were not strong enough to do on our own."

José scowled but refused to answer.

"Think about it," Luis continued. "You will see the truth in my words."

"I would rather cut my ears from my head than listen to such words."

Smiling thinly, Luis said, "Let me know when you are ready, and I will loan you my knife."

With his back propped to the Rucker's rear wheel, Ben Hollister stared solemnly into the gray distance. His coat was buttoned all the way up against the dawn chill, the unholstered Smith and Wesson a solid weight in his lap, easy to reach if needed. He sat quietly, without motion, and although his body ached and his eyes felt as if they had become trapped within a bed of sand, it wasn't his own discomfort he dwelled on.

He had to force himself not to look at Bobby, not to hover over him like some damn vulture waiting to see what happened next. Even so, he was acutely aware of the boy's presence just a few feet away. As far as Ben knew, his little brother hadn't so much as twitched since they'd laid him on a bedroll behind the ambulance. If not for the shallow rise and fall of his chest, it would have been easy to imagine him dead, and the thought made Ben's throat constrict until his breath whistled softly with each exhalation.

Bobby's continuing unconsciousness was baffling; it didn't fit the nature of his injuries. There was no doubt the twin puncture wounds in his back were serious, but they weren't the kind of injuries that normally rendered a man comatose. And especially not for this long. There had to be something else going on, but Ben didn't have any idea what it might be.

He glanced at Hattie Wilkes, sitting on a crate at Bobby's side, and wondered if he'd made the right decision putting his faith in her. She hadn't said much last night after examining the bruised flesh in the light of the bull's-eye lantern. The heavy buckshot—Henry had estimated them at .32 caliber each, based on what he'd pried from the cantle of Bobby's saddle—was lodged somewhere deep in the boy's guts, but Hattie hadn't been able to locate them with the gentle probing of a finger, and she'd refused to cut into him without knowing where the shot had come to rest.

"I could easily do more damage than good," she'd said.

"Then what are we going to do?"

Her reply sent a shiver coursing down his spine.

"Do you believe in prayer, Mr. Hollister?"

"No, Miss Wilkes, I don't."

"Then maybe you should wish for luck."

"I don't believe in that, either."

They'd stared at each other in strained silence, until Hattie finally turned away, dropping to her knees at Bobby's side and drawing a blanket over him. Ben had withdrawn to the Rucker's rear wheel, where he'd sat mutely ever since, a brooding despair gnawing at him. Now, as a new day crept slowly over the desert landscape, he knew he had some tough decisions to make. And he was equally certain that no matter what choices he settled on, there would be trouble. Either from his own people, or Cade's.

Ben's gaze drifted to where the sergeant sat close to the fire, still awake, still alert. It was more than his own crew seemed capable of. Although Little Fish was still on his feet, standing idly to one side keeping an eye on the soldiers, the majority of his men were scattered around the clearing, sprawled in exhaustive slumber.

Ben could forgive Jethro Hill for his negligence. He had a hole through his thigh from the same charge of buckshot that caught Bobby, but the others seemed determined to try his patience. It was as if they sensed that this would be their last job together as the Hollister gang, even though Ben hadn't told anyone yet that he'd decided to quit the trade. Not even Bobby.

He regarded Ray Beeler for a moment, curled on his side across the fire from Cade. Ray still had his revolver close, cradled to his chest like a child's toy, but his steady snores told Ben he would be next to useless if the sergeant's men attempted to retake the camp. They likely would have already tried, if not for Little Fish's vigilance.

With a surge of impatience, Ben pushed to his feet and stalked over to where Ray was laying with a single blanket draped over his hips and legs. Giving his frustration free rein, Ben drove his toe into the man's back hard enough to elicit a grunt made up of equal parts pain and surprise. Then he stepped back as Ray staggered to his feet. He spun around with a curse, wild-eyed and crazy mad until he spotted Ben. Then he straightened warily, but didn't holster his revolver.

"What the hell'd you do that for?"

Ben spoke harshly. "Get the others on their feet."

"Why?"

"Because I told you to."

Ray glanced slowly around as if searching for a cause to Ben's anger. Spotting Bobby, he nodded and holstered his Colt. "All right," he said, but made no move to comply.

"What's goin' on?" another voice asked, and Ben saw Jethro struggling to sit up. The young man looked around as if not quite sure where he was or how he'd gotten there, but when Ben asked how he felt, he replied that he was fine.

"Just a little stiff," he added, although Ben thought the pinched look to his face belied the assertion.

"Can you ride?"

"Sure, whenever you're ready."

"Get your boots on. We'll be pulling out soon." He walked back to where Bobby lay unmoving, aware of Cade's eyes following him. Hattie watched his approach with an expression of concern.

"Mr. Hollister, your brother is in no shape to travel. He needs rest, and time to heal."

"I'm afraid time isn't something we have a lot of, Miss Wilkes."

"Hell," Ray said, "time is something we ain't got any of."

Ben turned. Although the gunman hadn't moved from where Ben had left him, the others were awake and climbing stiffly to their feet. Henry and Ed—both older men—looked worn out. Ben could appreciate their fatigue. Yesterday had been a long day, and it had come on the end of an even longer journey from San Angelo. They were all tired, but they couldn't stop now.

"Go throw our saddles on those Yankee horses," Ben said to Ray. "You." He pointed at Lucia. "Get some breakfast started. Henry, bring the mules in and get them harnessed."

"No," Cade said, rising abruptly.

"Sergeant," Ben warned, "I'm tired, and I'm out of patience. We're taking your horses and your firearms." He jerked a thumb over his shoulder, toward the Rucker. "And we're taking the ambulance. What we're leaving you is your lives, but you need to understand that's an offer, not a guarantee."

"The ambulance?" Ray echoed. "The hell!"

"Go saddle the horses," Ben repeated.

"You know well as me that Largo lawman has a posse on our tails right now, and Mexico is still a good thirty miles away," Ray argued.

"Then you'd better get busy."

"It sounds to me like you're in enough trouble with the law," Cade remarked. "Are you sure you also want to tangle with the United States Army?"

"I'm sure," Ben said. "Now shut up and sit down."

"I can't let you do this, Hollister."

"Fish," Ben said. "Sit him down, and if he gives you any trouble, use your rifle butt."

"Be easier I just shoot him," Little Fish replied.

Ben knew the half-breed could do it without compunction, too, but he didn't want any blood spilled if it could be helped. "Just sit him down, and keep your finger off the trigger unless someone makes a play. No point letting that sheriff know where we are, if he's close by."

Little Fish nodded. To Cade, he said, "You put your ass on the ground damn quick, soldier, or I will settle this another way." Keeping the Spencer pointed at Cade's chest, he used his left hand to lightly pat the grips of a Bowie sheathed on his hip.

Ben sighed but let it go. Glancing at Dodson, he said, "Ed, give Ray a hand saddling those horses. We'll ride the army's bays today, but we'll take ours along, too." He turned to Bobby. Hattie was sitting beside him with one hand resting gently on his shoulder. "What do you think, sister? Can we move him?"

She didn't look up. "Not if you don't want to kill him."

Something lurched inside of Ben's chest, like a noose yanked

81

hard and tight around his heart. But they didn't have a choice, and he said as much to the woman.

"Then leave him here," she urged. "Sergeant Cade can look after him."

"We can't leave him. There's a deputy sheriff following us. If he shows up, he'll put his cuffs on Bobby and there won't be anything Cade can do to stop him. It'd be a civil matter, not a military one."

"Then let the sheriff have him. He can see that your brother is taken care of. They might put him in jail, but at least he'll be alive."

"I know that sheriff's reputation, Miss Wilkes. He wouldn't let a wounded man slow him down. He'll follow us all the way to Mexico if he has to, and pack Bobby along with him. Across the saddle if that's what it takes." He glanced at his brother . . . so damn young. "That would kill him for sure."

"Yes, it would," Hattie agreed.

She finally looked up, and Ben was surprised that there was no fear in her face. The others—the Mexican called Lucia and red-headed Fanny—were intimidated whenever he spoke to them. He wondered what it was that made Hattie different. Was it truly a lack of fright? Or did she simply no longer care?

Shaking his head to dislodge the question, Ben said, "We'll have to take him with us in the ambulance, and I'm afraid you'll have to come, too."

"I expected no different."

After a pause, he added, "And the others."

Hattie's eyes widened. "That wasn't part of our agreement, Mr. Hollister. You don't need Lucia and Fanny. I've already said I'd come with you."

"They'll be my insurance that you keep your word, Miss Wilkes. And I'll keep mine. My men won't bother any of you so long as you keep my brother alive."

"You can't expect me to perform miracles, Mr. Hollister. Your brother's odds of survival would have been flimsy enough if he'd received immediate medical attention. After being in the saddle for Lord knows how long yesterday, then putting him in that ambulance today, you are almost certain to seal his fate."

"I don't have any say over what fate does with him, but I do have a say over what happens to you and your friends, and I've already given you my word on that. We're going, ma'am, and your friends are coming along, at least as far as the border. I'll let them go after we reach Mexico."

"That isn't fair, Mr. Hollister," she said quietly.

"I know it isn't, but that's the way it is."

Hattie's lips thinned in angry frustration, but she didn't have much of a choice, either. Not if she cared about what happened to her friends.

Turning, Ben walked over to where Cade was still standing next to the fire. He drew his Smith and Wesson when he got close.

"You were told to sit down, Sergeant."

"I don't see any sign of rank on your sleeves."

Ben thumbed the revolver's hammer to full cock. "This is my rank, Cade. Now, sit down."

Chuckling, Little Fish said, "That is General Smith and Wesson, soldier. Yesterday, the general put a man in front of a firing squad because he did not do what he was told."

Cade's gaze moved uncertainly from Fish to Ben.

"Let me clarify what Little Fish is saying," Ben offered. "Yesterday, a clerk in the Cattleman's Hotel in Rio Largo didn't do what he was told. I had to kill him. I didn't want to, and I don't want to kill anyone today, but once I've made up my mind, I don't do a lot of debating. So get this through your head. We're taking your wagon, your horses, and your guns. We're also going to take most of your food and water. It's not something I particularly want to do, but we need the ambulance, and we'll take the rest to keep you from following us."

"Oh, we're going to follow you," Cade assured him. "To hell and back, if that's what it takes."

"I don't think so. You might follow us to the Rio Grande, but by the time you get there on foot, we'll be deep into Mexico, out of reach."

"Your brother won't make it that far, Hollister."

"You don't know that, Sergeant. No one does. But either way, we're taking your stuff, and there's nothing you can do to stop us that won't get you and your men killed. Is that understood?"

After a long moment of silence, Cade nodded grudgingly. "All right, take them. But understand this, Hollister. We're going to follow you. Every step of the way."

CHAPTER EIGHT

Ben couldn't stop a crooked grin from tracking across his face as he studied the fiery little sergeant. He had to admit he liked the man. He had no doubt Cade would put a bullet through his head as fast as any man there if he got the chance. But he still liked him. Cade reminded him of himself, when he was younger and still believed in causes.

Cade's men had observed the conversation between them in silence. Now the corporal made a move as if to stand up, until Little Fish bobbed the Spencer's muzzle toward him. Frowning, Poe settled back down.

"What are you saying, Andy?"

"I'm saying our hands are tied," Cade replied in grating tones. "I've got a gun on me and there are others on you, but mostly, there are guns being held here by men who wouldn't hesitate to kill any of the women in our charge if they thought it would get them what they wanted."

Cade paused and looked directly at Ray Beeler, who mugged a grin back at the glowering sergeant. Cade was right, though. Ben knew Ray wouldn't think twice about gunning down anyone who got in his way, man or woman.

"So we're just going to stand back and let these pirates take our horses and guns?" Poe asked.

"That's what we're going to do. And we're going to trust"—here Cade fixed his eyes on Ben—"that Hollister keeps his word about not letting any harm come to the women. Isn't that right, Hollister?"

"You just worry about taking care of your own men, Sergeant. You're going to have a rough enough time of it out here on foot to worry about what we're up to." He glanced to where Ed Dodson was saddling the cavalry mounts, using their own tack instead of the military's rigs. "Ray, I thought I told you to saddle those horses."

"I was, 'til that sawed-off Yankee started struttin' around like a damned banty."

"Go help Ed," Ben said, and after a charged pause, Ray did as he was told.

Ben sensed a warning in the gunman's anomalous silence, a showdown looming between them. He knew that once they were within Mexico's embrace, he'd have to be ready for whatever came his way, because Ray wasn't the kind of man who believed in fair fights.

Over by the wagon, Henry McDaniels stood back from where he'd just buckled the last tug to the off-side wheeler. Henry ran his gaze critically over the harness, then nodded as if satisfied he'd gotten it right. Leaving the wheelers in place, he went out to fetch the two lead mules the troopers had tied off separately. Ben had asked the private called Riley about that last night, and the private explained the leaders had been kept away from the rest of the stock because they were still green broke and difficult to manage.

"Young and rambunctious," was Riley's description of the pair, "and more'n a little onery from the rough treatment they got from a freighter bound for Chihuahua City, before the quartermaster at Fort Bliss bought 'em. Give 'em a few weeks in harness and some gentle handling, though, and they'll be sweet as peppermint candy, you'll see."

Ben had no reason to doubt the gangling Irishman, and the

mules seemed docile enough, so he watched absently, without concern, as Henry loosened their lead ropes and started toward the ambulance with the animals in tow. But they'd barely made it halfway across the clearing when one of the mules bared its teeth and pinned its long ears to its neck. Ben thought to call a warning, but he was too slow. Clamping its jaws over Henry's forearm, the mule chomped down hard enough to send blood spurting in several different directions.

The color seemed to drain instantly from Henry's face, and his mouth opened wide as if to scream, but the only sound that came out was a shrill hiss that probably couldn't have been heard more than a few yards away. Then the mule reared with Henry's arm still in its teeth and shook its head like a dog killing a rabbit. This time when Henry opened his mouth, the whole camp heard him.

"Hey!" Jethro Hill bellowed, gimping toward the mule on his injured leg. Ed started that way, too. The mule dropped to its feet, and with a final toss of its head, released its grip on Henry's arm. With a pitiful moan, the older man slumped to the ground.

Ben started instinctively in that direction. Then some sixth sense warned him and he whirled and fired in a single smooth motion. His bullet slammed into the dirt at Cade's feet, bringing the sergeant to a tottering halt on his way to the ambulance, where the soldiers' weapons had been dumped the night before. Corporal Poe and a couple of the troopers—Riley and Talbot—were also halfway to their feet, but Ben's shot froze them where they stood.

"That's far enough, Cade," Ben hollered, rocking the Smith and Wesson's hammer all the way back. "You, too, Poe. The three of you sit down, and don't twitch a muscle."

Poe and Riley obeyed with undeniable reluctance. Only Talbot continued to rise, coming to his full height as he glared at Ben.

"Sit down, Private," Cade ordered.

"I reckon not, Sergeant." Talbot's voice quivered with suppressed fury, and Cade's voice sharpened.

"I told you to sit down."

Talbot hesitated, then tore his eyes away from Ben and began to slowly lower himself to the ground. But he wasn't fast enough to suit Little Fish, who took a swift step forward and drove his fist into the trooper's back. Talbot stiffened and his body arched as if he were seeking a better view of the sky. Ben cursed, knowing before anyone else what had happened. When Little Fish stepped back, Talbot collapsed, and the others, the soldiers, saw Fish's Bowie clenched firmly in the half-breed's fist, its blade shining with blood.

"This way, gents," Ben said loudly, drawing the troopers' attention away from the fallen man. He let his revolver's muzzle sweep the stunned prisoners. "Anyone tries anything, he gets a bullet in his gut," he warned. Then, noticing the outrage on Cade's face, he moved the Smith over to cover him. "Don't even think about it, Sergeant. It'll only get more men killed."

"There was no call for that," Cade said, staring at Little Fish.

"He was told to sit down," Little Fish replied indifferently.

"He was doing it."

Laughing from where he was standing next to one of the army's bays, Ray said, "Not fast enough, huh, Fish?"

Ben swore again, and for a moment he wondered if he shouldn't just go ahead and shoot Ray now and be done with it. He figured he'd have to sooner or later, and at least this way he wouldn't have to worry about Beeler gunning him down from ambush. But something stayed his hand, and the moment passed. Ben knew that Ray thought the soldier's death was funny, and that he would likely be making small jokes and barely concealed barbs about it for the rest of the day, most of them aimed at Little Fish.

Glancing at the half-breed, Ben saw no hint of a smile on his face. Fish's carbine was pointed at Cade's heart, held tightly in his right hand, while his left continued to hold the bloodstained Bowie half-raised, as if ready to fire or charge in an instant. Talbot's death had meant as much to him as crushing a beetle under his heel.

"Sit down, Cade," Ben ordered.

"No, I don't believe I will."

"You better sit down, soldier-man, before I slice a damn big hole out of your belly," Little Fish said.

Cade's jaw seemed to mutate into a rigid shelf above his neck, but he didn't move.

"Goddamnit, sit down," Ben flared.

"Is this the kind of control you have over your men, Hollister?"

"It was you who started this when you made a play for a gun."

"Then shoot me, not one of my men."

"It ain't your decision who we shoot, Yankee, or who we cut," Ray said in that reedy tone Ben had learned to dread.

"I'm not going to tell you again," Ben said softly, and this time the sergeant did as he was told, although without taking his eyes off of Little Fish.

You damn fool, Ben thought of Cade. Then he released the Smith and Wesson's latch to expel the empty cartridge, before replacing it with a live round. He snapped the cylinder back in place and walked over to where Henry McDaniels was sitting on the ground, his legs splayed before him. Sweat was pouring from the older man's brows and his eyes were glazed. Jethro had used his Barlow to slice the sleeve of Henry's shirt from cuff to collar. Ben winced when he saw the wound. The flesh had been torn nearly to the bone where the mule's huge teeth had mauled him, creating kaleidoscopic swirls of blue, black, and red. Blood flowing from the shredded meat was pooling on the hard ground under his elbow.

Ben glanced over his shoulder to where Hattie Wilkes was still sitting with Bobby. He motioned her over. "Bring that medical bag with you," he called.

His head swiveled as he searched for the mule that had mangled Henry's arm, but the animal was nowhere to be seen.

"They both skedaddled back into the mesquite," Ed said.

"Did you see which way they went?"

"Straight into the middle, far as I could tell. I was mostly trying to help Henry."

Ben stared into the trees, but didn't see either animal. Finally he shrugged and returned the Smith to its holster, accepting that he'd have to let the mule live unless he wanted to waste time looking for it.

"Ed, go put the soldiers' rifles and pistols in the wagon, and make sure they aren't easy to reach. We're taking them with us."

Ed nodded and took off, passing Hattie on her way to where Henry was sitting, his color growing more pallid by the second. Jethro tried to hitch himself out of her way, but when he took his hand from the older man's shoulder, Henry's eyes rolled up and he tipped over backward, unconscious.

"Damnit," Jethro cried.

"It's okay," Hattie assured him. "He'll be easier to care for this way."

Jethro stood and limped over to join Ben, his own color kind of pasty in the strengthening light.

"It looks pretty bad, don't it?"

"It does," Ben agreed.

"Knew a man got his arm tore up like that in an auger at my daddy's mill. They sent for a doc, but he just whacked 'er off."

"There's a reason they call them sawbones," Ben replied flatly. "Let's let the woman have a look at it."

90

"She did a good job on my leg last night. It's still sore as a broke preacher, but I watched her working on it, and I'd say she knows what she's doing."

"She'd damn well better."

"Shoot, he'll be okay, Ben. Miss Wilkes'll see to that."

Then he hobbled off to look for the missing mules.

Ben stayed where he was, staring at the curve of Hattie's slim back under its Union blue tunic, but in his mind he was seeing Henry as he had been—as they'd all been, once upon a time—recalling the years they'd ridden together. It was Henry who had taken young Ben under his wing shortly after the war's end, teaching the youngster what he knew of the outlaw trade after having ridden with bushwhackers during those bloody years across Kansas and Missouri. It could have been Henry's crew, had he wanted it, but the older man had made it known from the beginning that he didn't.

"I'd druther have chiggers up my ass," he'd insisted, and had seemed satisfied to watch Ben take over the reins.

Henry hadn't protested when Ben brought Mose, then Ed Dodson, into the fold, and those had been some good years, too. Before Ray Beeler and Little Fish fell in with them. Before Jethro Hill showed up as well, although Ben had no regrets about Jethro. Then Bobby joined them in San Angelo, deepening a wedge between Ben and some of the others that had been growing wider for some time now.

By the time Ed got the firearms stowed away and returned to help Ray finish saddling the army mounts, Jethro was limping back into camp, shaking his head negatively.

"I couldn't catch 'em," he told Ben. "I found 'em back in the brush, but every time I got close, they'd take off like they was goosed."

"You want me to run 'em down?" Ed volunteered.

Ben shook his head. They already had two mules in harness.

91

With the sun pulled nearly free of the horizon, they needed to start rolling.

"Drag that extra harness out of the way, then climb up and grab the lines," he told Ed. "Cade, have a couple of your troopers help lift my brother into the ambulance." He looked at Lucia. "Is that food ready?"

"Yes."

"Pack it up and stow it inside, then stay there. I'll want you to help Miss Wilkes with the wounded. You, too, Red," he told Fanny. Walking over to where Hattie was still bent above Henry's arm, he said, "How's it coming, sister?"

"It's bad," was her terse reply. "A lot of muscle was torn away from the bone."

"Is it bandaged?"

She looked up. "No, of course not. I'm still cleaning the deeper incisions, then he'll need stitches to close it completely."

"Is it still bleeding?"

"Some, yes."

"Then get it bandaged. You'll have to finish it on the trail."

"While we're moving? I'm afraid that would be impossible."

"You've got no choice," Ben said kindly. "None of us do. We're pulling out, now."

"Do you not care about your men, Mr. Hollister?"

Refusing to rise to the bait, he said, "Not with a posse hounding us, Miss Wilkes, and that is surely what's happening. Now, please, get a bandage on his arm, and if you can't finish it on the move, you'll have to finish it tonight. Cade, I told you to pick some men to help get my brother inside."

"Riley, Morgan, get the kid into the wagon. Be easy, he's hurt bad. And bring back a shovel." He looked at Ben. "I'm going over to check on Talbot."

"No need for that," Little Fish said with a taut grin. "He plenty dead, that one."

"I'm gonna check on him anyway," Cade replied.

"Let him check his man, Fish," Ben said. Then a moan brought his attention back to where Hattie and Jethro were helping Henry to sit up.

"Come on, old-timer," Jethro said gently. "We're going to Mexico."

"Damnation," Henry wheezed, his weathered flesh the color of cold ash above the scruff of his beard. He wouldn't have made it to his feet without Jethro and Hattie each slipping a shoulder under his arms, let alone across the camp to the Rucker.

Leaving Little Fish to guard the troopers, Ben followed them to the ambulance. Cade's men, Riley and Morgan, already had Bobby inside. Staring at his little brother's comatose form, Ben felt the muscles pull tight across his chest. Why the hell didn't the kid wake up?

Mounted on one of the army's bays, Ray led a horse over for Little Fish. Cade's men were all standing now, gathered in a knot behind Corporal Poe. All except for the sergeant, who knelt at Talbot's side with one hand on the dead man's shoulder as if to offer him belated comfort. Ben stepped into the saddle—his own—cinched to a well-put-together mount Ed had left tethered to the Rucker's rear wheel. With Henry settled inside, Jethro took the reins to another bay, then rode over to loosen the halter rope on the sorrel he called Acorn.

"Christ sakes, kid, leave that animal behind," Ray exclaimed. "It's played out after yesterday."

"He's coming with me," Jethro replied, soft-spoken but firm. That was something Ben had always admired about the younger man. If Jethro thought he was right, he wouldn't be deterred.

"They're all coming with us," Ben said, before Beeler could work up a reply. "Loosen those halters, Ray. I'm putting you and Little Fish in charge of the spare stock. We'll switch back to

93

our own horses tomorrow, after we cross the Rio Grande." He glanced at Cade. "You'll find your guns and horses there, if you follow us that far."

"We'll be right behind you," Cade promised, and Ben smiled.

"I've no doubt you will. Just don't get too close, or I might have Fish do some long-range shooting with that Spencer of his. Those blue uniforms of yours would make mighty fine targets in this kind of country." He looked at Ed. "Let's roll," he said, and Dodson released the Rucker's brake and hupped the two harness mules into motion.

After freeing the weary mounts they'd ridden hard the day before, Ray swung in behind them with a string of oaths that could have reddened the cheeks of a teamster or brought a preacher to his knees. Ben and Little Fish waited until the others had cleared the camp, before reining after them.

CHAPTER NINE

Owen Plunkett was feeling out of sorts that morning, and not just because of the hearty cuff that son of a bitch with the ragged mustache had given him yesterday. Still, he knew it could have been worse. The blow could have been delivered with a lot more force. Or it could have come down on top of the head, instead of striking him at an angle above the ear, knocking him senseless for a while but not causing any permanent damage to skull or brain. It still hurt, though, and the fact that he had to wear his hat—*not* wearing one wasn't an option in that country—at what he considered an uncharacteristically jaunty angle peeved him all the more. He was a lawman, damnit, not some damn fop from Philadelphia.

The posse was a burr in his britches, too. Eleven of them, the majority of which he estimated would cut their pins and run the minute Ben Hollister and his crew of cutthroats decided to stop and fight.

And what the hell else would they do? he thought irritably.

Holding his tall roan back, Owen waited in exasperation as a few stragglers clumsily scaled the sides of their mounts to find their seats. He knew a lot of them were already worn out. It showed in their bobbing heads and slack expressions, in cheeks as red as ripe cherries from windburn, and lips badly chapped but not yet cracked. It didn't surprise him. Most of the posse were businessmen who had lost a good chunk of their savings when the bank was robbed. They wanted their money back, but would have been satisfied to find it dropped somewhere along the trail so they could turn around and go home, and never mind the two men killed in yesterday's raid.

A few of them were drovers, in town for the festivities but eager to throw in for the adventure of chasing outlaws. In Owen's experience, drovers were a steady enough lot when sober, but most of them were still so wet behind the ears it was a wonder they didn't drown in their sleep. Of them all, only Bill Rowland, Simon Butler, and old Pete Maddox had any real experience running down fugitives. Pete had been a Texas Ranger back in the '60s, and Bill and Simon were former deputies; those three were the ones Owen would trust when the time came to fight.

Had he been thinking clearer yesterday, he would have winnowed his posse down to a more efficient force before leaving town. He'd have given the townsfolk the boot right off, and made sure the drovers knew what was expected of them. But he'd still been woolly-headed from the blow the old man in the Hub had dropped on his head, and had simply put out a call for anyone with a good gun and a fast horse to saddle up and meet him in front of the jail. He'd hoped quick pursuit would put them within range before nightfall, but Hollister's men were riding good stock, and by the time darkness forced them to stop, Owen feared they might have actually lost some ground, rather than gaining any.

As he saddled his horse that morning, Owen had given some serious consideration to sending a number of men back to Rio Largo. He suspected the majority of those he picked would have welcomed the dismissal. But he couldn't forget—couldn't forgive—what Hollister's men had done to his town. It wasn't just the money they'd taken or the men they'd killed—Leonard Collins at the Cattleman's Hotel and an innocent bystander from Sierra Blanca named Jim Potts, a horse trader by profession who had come to town to watch the races, and had been struck by a stray bullet during the gang's wild departure—but what the outlaws had destroyed within the community itself, the damage they had done to the town's *spirit.*

Having seen it happen before, Owen knew it would be a long time before the citizens of Rio Largo fully recovered from the raid. They would be jumpy and depressed, and a lot of them would consider themselves, and the town, lacking in the face of adversity. Hollister's men needed to pay for that, and it was Owen's opinion that the gang's capture and return would go a long way toward reassuring the town that good would prevail, and that while evil might occasionally rear its head, the people of Rio Largo were up to the task of defeating it.

No, he'd decided as he lowered the mare's stirrup, it was important that they continue on as a group, and not give up after a single day's effort. He could revisit the idea of sending the weaker men back tonight if the chase lasted that long, and it was beginning to look like it might. Tracking had been difficult. West Texas hadn't received any rain since March, and Lord knew that had been skimpy enough. The ground was hammered down tight and hard, reluctant to give up its information.

They were barely two miles out of camp that second day when Owen relinquished his lead position to Pete Maddox, who had more experience following a trail than any of them. But Pete was in his late fifties now, and his vision wasn't what it used to be. He kept having to dismount to examine the ground, to distinguish between the passage of horses and common dents and scratches in the desert hardpan.

Owen's roan kept rattling her bit as the posse crept forward, thrusting her chin against the restraint of her reins. She was a spirited animal, and eager to be off. Owen shared her impatience. He kept scanning the horizon in hope of spotting some telltale sign of the gang's passage, but the land before them continued empty, a flat terrain blanketed in creosote bush, pilled with ocotillo and towering yucca.

Off in the distance, barely ruffling the skyline, stood a low range of mountains called the Sandbars. Instinct told Owen that was the gang's objective. The mountains, and then the Rio Grande on the other side, and finally Mexico and safety—assuming the outlaws reached it in time. Owen was determined not to let that happen. Sooner or later they would find some clue to confirm the gang's destination—the pass they would use to cross the mountains, or which direction they'd take if they decided to go around. When that happened, Owen was determined to pull his posse away from the dim trail, to gamble that they could beat Hollister and his men to the river before the gang could cross into the haven that was Mexico.

Cade was on the move even before Ben and Little Fish were out of pistol range.

"Schultz!"

The stocky German snapped to attention. "*Ja,* Sergeant?"

"You came in here last night without your carbine or revolver."

"*Ja,* the half-breed . . . I did not hear him, Sergeant. It was like out of the darkness he come, but no sound—"

Cade cut him off with a quick, downward slash of his hand. "What happened to your firearms?"

"Into the trees the 'breed he threw them."

"Go get 'em, and be quick about it. What about the rest of you? Any more weapons?"

"I snagged a pistol," Morgan said, pulling his shirttail out to allow a service revolver to drop into his hand. "Got it out of the toolbox when I fetched the shovel, but it was the only one I could grab without drawing too much attention to what I was doing."

"Good man," Cade said, pleased. "Anyone else?"

"Aye, the pistol I was wearin' when the old feller snuck up behind me last night," Riley said. "Pulled it outta me holster, he did, and tossed it over the horses."

"Go find it."

Riley nodded and took off.

"Frank, take two men and round up those mules the old man let get away."

"Will do, Sergeant. Elkins, Hendricks, let's go!"

"What about me, Sergeant?" Morgan asked.

Cade glanced at Talbot's crumpled form. "Find that shovel and start digging," he said stonily.

It took a while to get the grave deep enough. The sunbaked earth was like concrete, and had to be chipped away rather than tossed aside. Even with the sun barely risen and a cool breeze out of the west, Morgan was soon sweating heavily. When Schultz and Riley got back, Cade had them help. He took on the task of readying the body for burial. He emptied the dead man's pockets first, removed his belt and holster, then wrapped the corpse in a blanket that he tied closed with pieces of rope cut from the highline. By the time Poe, Elkins, and Hendricks returned with the runaway mules, they had the grave down about four feet, and Cade called it good.

They buried Talbot with little ceremony other than the few remembered words Cade spoke over the grave after it was filled in and tamped down. Afterward, he distributed their few remaining weapons. He kept Schultz's Springfield for himself, using the rear strap from a saddle boot to fashion a sling for it, and let Morgan keep the revolver he'd filched from the ambulance, but he had Riley turn his revolver over to Corporal Poe. Riley started to protest, but shut up when he saw the look on Cade's face. Schultz kept the remaining revolver.

They saddled the mules next, filling their kits with cartridges and food but leaving behind jackets, blankets, and any personal item that wouldn't aid them in their pursuit. The water kegs were still in the ambulance, but they had canteens that they fastened to the McClellan saddles. When they were ready, Cade stood back to eye the provisions and weigh their odds. Two mules for seven men, a trio of revolvers, and a single-shot Springfield carbine. They had plenty of ammunition, but not much food and an extremely limited supply of water for what he had in mind. On the plus side, they were all good men, every one of them hungry for revenge, and Cade knew that would mean a lot before it was all over. He just wasn't sure it was going to be enough to catch up to Hollister and his men in time.

Gathering the troopers close, Cade outlined his plan. "I want to try something I've heard about but never seen done. It might not work, but we've nothing to lose in trying. Poe, you and Elkins are the two lightest men. I want you both in the saddle. The rest of us will grab onto the cantle straps and hang on tight. Take a loop around your hand if you have to. Corporal Poe and Elkins will move out at a trot, and the rest of us will jog alongside. If this works, the mules should do most of the work, and have us moving along twice as fast as we could manage walking. We shouldn't be as winded, either."

"A Comanche trick," Morgan said.

"So I've heard," Cade agreed. "All right, let's get ready." He waited until Poe and Elkins were mounted and the others had taken positions to either side of the mules. The jack—Lester, who had taken a chunk out of Henry McDaniels's forearm—laid his ears back threateningly when Morgan and Riley moved close.

"Careful of those front hooves," Poe cautioned from his seat.

"Aye, the back ones, too," Riley said worriedly. " 'Tis a menace from either end, this one."

"He'll either be minding his manners by the time we catch

up with Hollister, or you and me'll be beat raw and likely dead," Morgan spoke across the saddle.

"Just watch his hooves and teeth," Cade said, coming alongside the jack and taking the nearside blanket strap in a firm grip. He gave the men a final glance. All six were watching him expectantly, clinging like ticks to the sides of their mule. "All right, give him some heel," Cade told Poe. "Let's see if we can make this work."

Poe led out, reining his mule away from the camp at a walk for the first few yards, then tapping the jack's ribs with the sides of his stirrup. Although Lester was a harness mule, he seemed to understand the saddle, and, once they were moving, to not mind the men hanging off his sides. Finding his stride, Cade was soon trotting along at a pace several times faster than he would have believed possible. It was hard to keep an eye on the others, though. The best he could do was squeeze a few quick peeks over his shoulder, and then all he saw was a lot of bobbing and sweating faces. Even so, they were able to maintain that gait for nearly four miles before Cade gasped out a command to halt.

Poe hauled in on the reins, and Cade, Riley, and Morgan immediately released their holds on the saddle's straps. Riley and Morgan staggered to either side and collapsed atop the flinty soil, while Cade walked off until he was well clear of Lester's hooves and teeth before bending over and placing his hands on his knees. His pulse was thundering in his ears and perspiration dripped from the end of his nose to form nickel-sized puddles in the dirt under his face, but he was pleased with the distance they'd covered in such a short a time, proud of the men who had made it work.

Elkins reined up nearby, and Schultz and Hendricks did the same as Morgan and Riley. Poe and Elkins dismounted and loosened the cinches on their saddles, even though the mules

101

didn't seem particularly winded. Leading his mule over, Poe said, "Are you all right, Andy?"

Cade nodded but didn't reply. He was still puffing heavily, and not entirely sure he wasn't going to end up sprawled on the ground like the others.

"Ol' Lester here did pretty good," Poe commented.

"Noticed," Cade huffed.

"He might make a better saddle mule than harness stock."

"Yeah." Cade said no more, and after a moment's pause, Poe took Lester away.

They rested for fifteen minutes, then returned to their places. "You'll have to keep an eye on the trail," Cade told Poe, taking a hold on the pommel strap.

"It hasn't been hard to follow so far." He nodded toward the twin lines pressed into the hard earth by the ambulance's narrow iron rims. "It'd be a lot harder, a lot slower, too, if we didn't have those wheel tracks marking the way."

Cade nodded agreement. Hollister's men were still well ahead of them, but he knew the Rucker would slow them down considerably once they reached the arroyo-scarred mountain range rising before them.

They jogged and ran for another four miles, then slowed to walk a half mile more before Cade called a second halt. This time he flopped in the dirt beside the others, his heart hammering, legs threatening to knot up in cramps.

"Sergeant," Hendricks wheezed. "I ain't sure—"

"And I'm not interested," Cade interrupted. He wiped sweat from his brows, then struggled to his feet, afraid that if he remained seated too long his stiffness would worsen. "Walk it off, Hendricks. Elkins, grab a couple of canteens. I think we've earned a drink."

"No sight of them yet," Poe offered. "I haven't even seen any dust." He was standing next to Lester, having removed the saddle to allow air to reach the mule's back. Both animals were beginning to sweat now, the hair around the cinch rings growing dark with moisture as the sun rose higher.

"It took longer to get on their trail than I figured it would," Cade admitted. "Can't be helped. We'll catch up sooner or later."

Poe nodded—skeptically, Cade thought—and led his mule away.

He walked over to where the others had gathered around Elkins to stake a claim on one of the canteens. "Make it a short one," he instructed the men.

"Don't know that I can, Sergeant," Hendricks replied. He'd already taken one long pull and was lifting the canteen for another when Cade wrenched it away from him.

"This has to last us to the Rio Grande, Hendricks, and we'll be watering the mules out of it before the day's over. Take it easy now, or you'll do without later on when it gets hot."

"Jaysus," Riley breathed. " 'Tis already near hot enough to bake a man's toes through his boots."

"You know what it's like out here," Cade said.

"Aye, from horseback, not runnin' alongside the swelterin' beasty."

"Think what the beasty's feeling," Morgan said with a dusty grin.

Cade walked over to Elkins's mount, another jack they called Roman, and ran a hand over the animal's flanks. To Poe, he said, "We'll water them the next time we stop."

Poe nodded, and he and Elkins tightened their cinches as the men took their places.

"Join the cavalry, me mother said," Riley mumbled. " 'Tis better'n walkin' in the infantry."

A couple of the men laughed, and Cade said, "Let's march, Corporal."

CHAPTER TEN

They rode fast after leaving the scene of the slaughter—naked and mutilated bodies missing scalps, fingers, and ears; plundered wickiups, discarded clothing, and their own stinking vomit after becoming sick on the sour-tasting tiswin, not yet fully fermented.

The majority of his command rode with churning stomachs and reeling senses after half the morning spent in debauchery. José Yanez led them, but there was no pride in his bearing. His men, his Hunters of the Dunes, disgusted him. Or most of them did. A few—the scout, Luis Huerta, and his best *soldados*, men like Antonio Carrillo, Pedro Suarez, and Javier Diaz—were dependable, and not easily distracted by spoils.

And to a lesser extent, so were his lieutenants, although both of them had to tread cautiously within their own companies, else risk being voted out of the position. Such were the hazards of a volunteer army. José knew he could face similar consequences if enough men became disillusioned with his leadership.

They rode steadily through what remained of the morning, keeping their horses to a swift, ground-eating trot for much of that time. José was taking them southeast toward the settlements along the Rio Grande, where he felt they might be, if not safer, then at least partially shielded by more tempting targets for any pursuing Apaches. And José knew that if the ravaged camp of Mimbreños was discovered soon enough, the Apaches would come after them. Only time would tell if Geronimo himself took up the pursuit, abandoning his planned raid into the United States in order to seek revenge against the Hunters.

The sun was near its zenith when a shout from the rear of the splintered column moved up its ranks. Without slowing, José glanced over his shoulder to where Francisco had pulled away from his men. He was gesturing toward a low range of hills on their left, and José's eyes narrowed when he spotted the Indians. He eased back on the buckskin's reins, bringing his mount to a walk. He counted seven heavily armed warriors sitting their ponies less than two hundred yards away, their tawny desert mounts coalescing almost flawlessly into the landscape.

Francisco spurred his gray horse forward, reining in alongside José without taking his eyes off the half-naked *Indios.*

"What do you think, *Capitán*? Are they Apaches?"

"*Sí,* but are they *our* Apaches?"

"Who else?"

"Another band? Maybe even Lipans or Mescaleros?"

"Either would be as bad as Geronimo's Chiricahuas."

José was not sure he agreed with that, although he suspected the differences would be minimal. Arguing that one tribe of Apache was worse than another would be like debating the damage inflicted by a diamondback rattlesnake's strike versus that from a Mojave green. Of one thing he was certain. Whoever these men were, they would be exceptionally more deadly if they knew of the destruction his men had inflicted upon the small party of tiswin-making Mimbreños that morning.

José regarded his lieutenant briefly. It had been Francisco's command that had captured the young woman and children, and it was they who held them prisoners now.

"Go back and have your men cover the captives with blankets," José ordered. He raised a hand above his shoulder, bringing the column to an uneasy halt. Twisting around in his saddle, he motioned Juan Carlos forward. So far the Apaches hadn't moved. Not even their horses' heads seemed to swivel in the searing heat, and for a brief, hallucinatory moment, José wondered if they were real or just figments of their collective imagination.

The iron-shod tapping of hooves on the stony ground brought his head around. Juan Carlos Cordova was riding forward at an easy lope. He reined in at José's side, his expression filled with dread.

"*El Diablo* has found us," he remarked tautly.

"So it appears."

"And your plans, *Capitán*?"

"To see what these dogs want," José replied, nodding toward the distant horsemen. He still counted seven, but feared there might be more hiding beyond the summit or among the rocks and brush just below it, on this side of the ridge. "Take your men and ride toward them. How they react will reveal their plans."

Juan Carlos seemed troubled by the command. "It is a trap, don't you think? Why else would they expose themselves to us in this manner?"

"That is what I want you to find out, *mi teniente*. Is this a trap, or only a passing party of hunters? If the latter, we might consider adding to our collection of scalps, eh?"

He twisted around in his saddle to observe the ragged column of rough-hewn *soldados*. They were all staring east, as if transfixed by the silent, unmoving presence of the seven *Indios*. Like mice under the paralyzing gaze of a snake, and as that image solidified in José's mind, a chill shot down his spine. He swung his head wildly in the opposite direction and spotted instantly what they had all missed with their attention focused on the mounted warriors—a score or more of Apaches moving swiftly afoot over the rugged terrain. Even as his eyes fell upon them, the first shots rang out, a rippling volley that dropped several men from their saddles and sent panic tearing through the rest of them.

José's throat seemed to close as he drove his spurs into the buckskin's ribs. The horse squealed shrilly in pain and fright, then reared briefly before springing forward. José let the animal have its head as he clawed for one of a pair of revolvers holstered at his waist. No command to flee was given, either by him or his lieutenants. Nor was one needed. The Hunters were already in flight, riding low over their mounts' withers, yelling and cursing as the sound of gunfire raked their flanks from both sides and iron-tipped arrows arched through the sky like birds of prey.

The Apaches' attack proved quick but deadly. When José threw another desperate glance over his shoulder, he saw numerous horses running after them with empty saddles, stirrups flapping like broken wings. With a furious bellow, he began firing at the clouds of gun smoke that dotted the landscape like tattered gray blossoms sprouting from the desert floor. The seven decoys had kicked their ponies into motion, their ranks swelled by other warriors pouring over the top of the ridge to join them.

Without any kind of organized retreat, it was every man for himself, and those to the rear of the column—Juan Carlos's company—were soon shredded by the Apaches' fire. José heard their screams for help even above the thunder of the guns and the pounding of nearly two hundred hooves, but there was nothing he could do. Not without leading the rest of his men back into a decimating field of fire. All that was left was to empty his revolvers—one at a time—at the swarming Indians and continue his own escape.

The Rucker was slowing them down, no doubt about that. No surprise, either. After several brief halts throughout the day, Ben called for a longer rest around midafternoon, ordering Ed to loosen the harness on the mules and give them water.

"But don't—"

"I know," Ed interrupted with a dismissive wave of his hand. "Don't over water 'em."

Ben nodded and stepped down from his saddle. They were well inside a low range of hills now. On the far side lay Mexico, still a good distance away. Ben sent Ray Beeler back to check on pursuit, then told Little Fish to let the loose stock spread out to graze. Jethro sat his mount close to the wagon, his head bent over his chest in slumber, his injured leg hanging free of its stirrup to ease the pressure on his wound. He was sweating heavily and looked feverish—worse now than he had that morning.

Ben let him sleep. After tying his mount to one of the Rucker's wheels, he stepped around to the rear and peered inside. The women stared back guardedly, but Ben's gaze went straight to Bobby.

"He hasn't come around yet," Hattie Wilkes replied to his unspoken question.

Ben ordered the other women to get out and find some shade, then crawled inside and settled down next to Hattie. "Is there any change in the way he's breathing?"

"No, it's still fast and too shallow. He needs rest, but he isn't getting it. How much farther is it?"

"It'll be a while," he replied dourly. "I'm not familiar with the area, but according to a map I picked up in San Angelo, we're probably still six or eight hours shy of the Rio Grande."

"Six or eight hours?" Her gaze searched his face. "That's too long."

Ben knew it, but didn't have a reply. Placing his hand gently on his brother's shoulder, he said, "Bobby?"

There was no reply. He knew there wouldn't be, but he had to do something. Pressing down until his fingers indented the pale, febrile flesh, he tried again.

"Bobby, can you hear me?" His voice roughened and grew louder. "Damnit, Bobby, wake up."

"He can't hear you, Mr. Hollister."

"You don't know that. Goddamnit, you don't . . ." He swayed back with a loud exhalation. "Whoa, I'm sorry."

"For what?"

"For cursing and nearly losing my temper."

"I'd say anger is an appropriate response, and cursing oftentimes accompanies it."

He gave her a thoughtful look. "No offense, sister, but you don't speak like any whore I've ever met."

"To be just as frank, sir, you don't speak like someone I would think capable of robbing banks."

"Yeah, well . . ." His words trailed off. Behind them, on the other bunk, Henry groaned softly, and Ben shifted around to examine the older man's injury.

"He's hurting," Hattie said quietly.

"What can you do for him?"

"For the pain? Very little, although if we remained here long enough I could cleanse his wounds and stitch the torn flesh closed."

"We won't be here that long. What can you do for him now?"

"There's salve in the medical kit, but I'd want to disinfect the arm first."

"Disinfect? What's that?"

"It kills the small bacteria that can poison the blood."

Ben stared back suspiciously, uncertain how to respond.

"I don't pretend to understand the science behind it, Mr. Hollister, and I don't know how much good it actually does, but I don't believe disinfecting a wound would harm it, either. And many people, medical professionals, do believe it helps."

"How do you do it?"

"Pure alcohol is the preferred method, but whiskey would

work. Do you have any among your men?"

Ben laughed softly. So did Ed Dodson, returning from where he'd left the mules hobbled on the sparse grass along the trail.

"Do you think we could scrape up a bottle or two of whiskey?" Ben asked him.

"I reckon we could scrape up three or four without too much effort," Ed replied, then turned to where Little Fish had the spare saddle horses loosely gathered on a small bench above the ambulance. Ben watched through the Rucker's rear entrance as Ed eased into the cavvy. Ed acted oblivious to Little Fish's stoic gaze as he dug a bottle from the pommel bag on his saddle and brought it back to the woman.

"What about you, Mr. Dodson?" Hattie asked, tipping her head toward the crudely wrapped bandage around his hand, still damp with blood.

"Aw, this ain't so bad, Miss. See to the youngsters, first."

She nodded. "All right, but don't neglect it. Even a small cut can become infected if it isn't tended closely."

"Yes, ma'am," Ed replied, and Hattie turned to Bobby, pulling the cork from the whiskey bottle with a professional ease.

Ben watched silently as she lifted the boy's shirt and pulled the loose bandages aside to reveal his wounds. The flesh around the small punctures looked tighter and brighter than they had that morning—and was there a smell emanating from them, as well? He wasn't sure, and didn't know if he wanted to. With a strained curse, he abruptly exited the ambulance, dropping to the ground and moving away on unsteady legs.

Spotting Lucia and Fanny sitting in the shade of a boulder to his right, he moved left instead, staring back the way they'd come that morning without really seeing anything. His jaw was set rigidly and there was an unfamiliar tightness in his chest as he struggled to suppress the image of Bobby lying immobile inside the ambulance. It took some time before he was able to shake the feeling of helplessness that wanted to grab him and pull him under. It took even longer to focus on the land before him. Not that there was much to see. They'd climbed some in altitude since leaving the flats, but with the hills thrust up on either side, his view was limited; the sinuous wash they'd followed into the hills disappeared around the shoulder of a low bluff not even a quarter of a mile away.

Ben had no doubt that they were being hunted. What worried him was that he didn't know how close their pursuers might be. Cade and his men weren't a concern, but there had to be a posse out there somewhere, and that was a problem he couldn't ignore. Not with the slower pace the ambulance was forcing them into.

The trouble, Ben reflected, was that he didn't know what kind of a posse was trailing them, how it was organized or who was in charge. If it was just a bunch of riled-up townspeople, the odds were good that pursuit would be disorganized and inefficient. But if Plunkett was in charge—assuming Henry hadn't killed or crippled him when he'd clubbed him over the head with a gun butt—it would be a different story. A posse like that, put together by a skilled lawman, would likely be smaller and quicker, made up of capable men with enough supplies and good horseflesh to get the job done.

With another whispered curse, Ben turned his back on the winding course of the dry wash and returned to the Rucker's side. Squatting in the vehicle's meager shade, he quietly rolled and lit a cigarette. He inhaled deeply, his first smoke in nearly thirty-six hours. It felt good rolling into his lungs, soothing his jangled nerves, easing his doubts. After a couple of minutes, Jethro stirred and seemed to come awake. He sniffed and looked around until he spotted Ben in the wagon's shadow.

"Where we at?" he croaked.

"West of where we were this morning."

Jethro blinked several times as if trying to make sense of Ben's cryptic reply. Then he shrugged and stiffly dismounted. Even weakened by his wound and sizzling with fever, he took time to loosen his horse's cinch.

"Where's Acorn?" he asked, meaning the sorrel he'd brought with him from San Angelo.

"You dropped his reins a few miles back. I tied them to his bridle and shooed him in with the rest of the horses."

Jethro thought about that for a minute, then grunted his thanks. He held his hand out and Ben gave him what was left of his cigarette.

"Why don't you have Miss Wilkes look at your leg?"

"She took care of it last night."

"Wouldn't hurt to have her check it. You look like you have a fever."

"Maybe I do. My brain feels kind'a foggy, even with my eyes open."

"You could ride inside with the others."

"Naw, I'll be fine. I just need some rest." Then he sat down and put his back to the ambulance's front wheel and let his head tip forward until his hat brim nearly touched his chest.

"Christ," Ben whispered as he gently slid the cigarette from the younger man's fingers.

They'd taken a beating this time, no doubt about that. Mose dead and two men badly wounded, then Henry laid low by a malicious mule. Ed's hand was still seeping blood, too, and that couldn't be good. They'd be in a tight spot if that Rio Largo posse caught up.

Finishing the cigarette, Ben dropped it and ground it out under his heel. When he looked up he saw Ray coming around the shoulder of the low bluff, and walked out to meet him. The look on Beeler's face confirmed his fears.

"They're followin', all right."

"How close?"

"Couple of miles."

Ben's tired eyes widened. "A couple of miles!"

"They caught them mules we left behind. Now they're hanging off the sides like lumpy packs."

Ben hesitated. "What do you mean, hanging off the sides?"

"Cade and his soldiers, damnit! They're hanging onto their saddles and runnin' alongside them army mules the old man let get away this morning. Who the hell'd you think I was talkin' about?"

Ben didn't tell him that he'd been more worried about the Rio Largo posse than he was Cade and his troopers.

Chuckling self-righteously, Ray said, "I knew we should've gone after them mules."

"Yeah, I seem to recall you telling me how you wanted to hang back long enough to find them," Ben replied dryly. "Maybe long enough for Plunkett's posse to show up and give you a hand, huh?"

The grin abandoned Ray's face. "The hell with you, Hollister," he said, then jerked his mount around to ride off.

"Tell Fish to bring the horses in," Ben called after him.

"Tell him yourself," Ray fired back.

"Jackass," Ben muttered after Ray's retreating form, then walked out far enough to catch Little Fish's eye and wave him in. Returning to the Rucker's rear entrance, he peered inside. Hattie had removed the bloody bandage from Henry's arm and was gently bathing the torn flesh. Henry was still unconscious, but he was groaning faintly and moving his head back and forth as if trying to find his way out of the darkness.

"How is he?" Ben asked.

"Worse than he was this morning." She gave him an annoyed flash of her eyes—dark brown, he observed, though flecked with slivers of gold. He chided himself for noticing.

113

"You didn't expect him to improve by jostling him around in this wagon all day, did you, Mr. Hollister?"

"Please don't push me, ma'am."

"He is seriously injured, but I expect him to live if infection doesn't set in. I will do all that I can to see that it doesn't."

"Thank you, but right now you'd better get ready to move. We'll be pulling out in a couple of minutes."

Hattie nodded curtly and returned to her ministrations. The clop of hooves drew Ben's head out of the ambulance. Little Fish had brought the horses in. Chivying them out of his way, he rode over to the wagon.

"Cade's men are getting close," Ben told him. "I want you to ride back and see where they are. If they're still following, lay into them with that carbine of yours."

"Kill them?"

"They were warned," Ben replied coldly.

Little Fish's expression was stoic, his eyes like dusty black stones, without emotion. "What about the money?"

"We'll split the money in Mexico, like we've already discussed."

"Be hard to split fair if I get shot by one of them soldiers."

Weighing his response carefully, Ben said, "Are you afraid?"

Little Fish's brows shot up, and Ben was satisfied that the half-breed's pride had been pricked.

"That's what I thought," Ben said. "Right now, it's only you, me, and Ray that's not carrying lead in our hides or bleeding into rags, and Ray and I are going to have our hands full getting this outfit into Mexico."

Ed had come around to eavesdrop. Always the practical one, he said, "You're the best tracker in the bunch, Fish. You'll find us without no trouble, and you've got that rifle that bites worse than it barks."

After a pause, Fish lifted the Spencer as if seeing it for the first time and admiring its beauty. "Shoots pretty good, this gun," he allowed, then smiled. "Okay, I will go. I am not afraid." With a short, sharp bark, like a fox on the hunt, he wheeled his mount and galloped back the way they'd come.

Noticing their preparations, Lucia and Fanny came over without being summoned and climbed inside. Ben woke Jethro and waited until he'd hauled himself weakly into the saddle before going to help Ed hitch their single span of mules to the wagon. Ray circled the spare stock and got them moving. With the mules in place, Ben stepped into his saddle and rode around back for a final glance at Bobby. He was aware of Hattie watching him expectantly, but he no longer had the words and quickly reined away before she saw the fear in his eyes.

Chapter Eleven

Owen Plunkett leaned forward to rest both hands on top of the narrow horn of his stock saddle. Although aware of the impatient murmurings from behind him, he kept his attention focused on the small clearing in the middle of the stand of mesquite the locals called *Bosque Solo*—the Lonely Woods.

In that flat desert south and west of Rio Largo, the patch of stubby chaparral was a well-known landmark. Old-timers claimed if you sunk a well deep enough you'd find water, but so far no one had been ambitious enough to take up the challenge. In Owen's opinion, the lack of decent graze surrounding the tiny grove would have made the effort pointless anyway. Other than serving as an out-of-the-way camping spot because of its firewood, there was little nearby to attract even a sheepherder.

What was keeping Owen's attention riveted on the clearing today was the ashes of a recent fire, along with everything else littering the hardpan around the still-warm pit. There had been at least one small wagon—Owen could see that even from where he sat his restive mare—and probably a dozen or more horses hitched nearby, judging by the droppings. A pile of McClellan saddles and other gear heaped in a pile close to the fire hinted of a military presence, and a story yet to be deciphered. Pete Maddox was working on that now. He'd left his horse in the care of others as he slowly paced the clearing, eyes cast to the ground as he attempted to sort out the tangled spoor.

Tom Holden, owner of Largo Saddlery, and Cyril Rogers,

manager of the Cattleman's Hotel, were doing most of the grumbling. Owen reasoned that with an outstanding mortgage on the saddle shop, the loss of Holden's savings was going to be a major setback to the saddler, not to mention a blow to the town if he went out of business. It wouldn't have made much sense for Holden to want to turn back unless you considered the man's physique. Tom was five-foot-four and probably weighed two hundred and fifty pounds, and his face revealed his misery. Even his horse was showing signs of distress.

Owen suspected the loss was less personal for Cy Rogers, who had trusted neither the hotel safe nor the bank with his wages. Cy was there only because his business associates— especially those who had favored the hotel's safe over the bank's—expected it. That and because Hollister had killed his night clerk, and the townspeople would feel Cy owed his young employee at least a token effort of pursuit.

Tom and Cy weren't the only ones mumbling their desires to return to Rio Largo, but they were the loudest. Owen was expecting Cy to be the first among them to voice a protest, but he couldn't say he was overly surprised when it was Tom Holden who finally nudged his horse forward.

"I think we're done, Sheriff, and we need to accept it."

Owen sighed before glancing over his shoulder at the saddler. "I'd think you, as much as anyone, would want to keep going, Tom."

"Hell, I'd like to, you know that, but I can't. The inside of my legs are just about rubbed raw now."

"I reckon you can go on back if you want," Owen replied indifferently, turning away from the saddler, "but the rest of us are going on. At least as far as the Rio Grande, and I won't guarantee we'll turn around then."

Cy Rogers's head jerked up. "What do you mean, we won't turn back at the Rio Grande?"

"What I mean is, I ain't going back, not yet." Owen shifted partway around in his saddle to eye the weary posse. Raising his voice, he added, "Why don't you boys just go on back to your wives and mothers. You're just slowin' me down with your complaining."

"That's not fair, Sheriff," Tom Holden protested.

"I ain't trying to be fair. I'm trying to do my job, and I ain't gonna let others hold me from it."

"Look around you, Owen," Rogers cried, sweeping a hand toward the abandoned camp. "Are you telling me Hollister didn't join up with the rest of his gang here?"

"We don't know what happened here, Cy, but I'm not seeing anything to make me believe they picked up reinforcements."

"For all we know there could be fifty of them, raiding nearby towns while Hollister's bunch tore hell out of Rio Largo."

"Like I said," Owen repeated with strained patience. "We don't know what happened here, and until I—"

"Maybe we do," Pete Maddox called from the far side of the clearing, where the tracks of the wagon had pulled out to the west.

"Maybe we do what?" Cy demanded.

"Know what happened," Pete replied, returning to where Owen and the others waited. "Looks to me like Hollister's bunch jumped an army patrol and stole their horses and wagon."

"Jumped a bunch of soldiers?" Cy echoed skeptically. "I'd have to say I have my doubts about that, Mr. Maddox."

"You can doubt what you want," Pete said, stopping next to Owen's roan and putting a hand on the mare's shoulder. "That's the way I read it. Looks like the soldiers hung onto a couple of mules, judging from their tracks, and are following as best they can."

"How many men?"

"The soldiers? Half a dozen, at most."

"Why the wagon?" Holden asked.

"Looks like Hollister has some wounded."

"We figured they did," Owen said, then thrust his chin toward the clearing. "What else?"

"It's hard to peg," Pete admitted. "The ground ain't giving up much detail, but there's four saddles stacked next to a fire they had going last night, and a fresh-dug grave over yonder."

Owen glanced briefly at the mound of recently turned earth. It was one of the first things he'd noticed when they halted at the clearing's edge.

"Any idea who's inside?" he asked.

"Nope."

"But they're still heading for the border?"

"Uh-huh. Just a hunch, but I'd say they'll cross the Rio Grande near San Ignacio."

Owen nodded thoughtfully. Although it seemed a likely option, he didn't want to count on it yet. From what he knew of the Hollister gang, they had been operating out of the Red River country, near Indian Territory, for a number of years. If so, they were a long way from home, and probably didn't know the shortcuts the way men like he and Pete Maddox did. That could prove to be to the posse's advantage, but only when they were certain they knew which way the outlaws were headed.

"All right, boys," he said, gathering his reins. "Let's keep moving."

"What about those of us who don't think it's worth going on?" Cy challenged.

Owen paused only a moment before heaving around in his saddle to lay a withering scowl on the hotel manager, then the posse as a whole. "I told you you can go on home. I sure as hell ain't gonna stop you."

Turning his back on the posse, Owen gave the roan its head. Pete stepped aside to allow him to pass, then took the reins to

119

his own mount and pulled himself into the saddle. He fell in beside Simon Butler. Bill Rowland brought up the rear. Owen didn't waste any time mulling over what the rest of the posse might decide. As far as he was concerned, he had the best of the party right here with Maddox, Butler, and Rowland. Truth was, he was almost disappointed when he heard the clatter of hooves and looked back to see the rest of them loping to catch up—Cy Rogers and Tom Holden among them.

They did well, but by midafternoon Cade had to accept that their pursuit of the Hollister gang was winding down. Gasping a hoarse command to stop, he let go of the McClellan's strap and staggered away from the sweating mule. The others did likewise, scattering like so many lost chicks before collapsing to the ground.

They'd stopped in the middle of a dry wash just inside a line of hills that rose before them in a series of jagged summits, like the worn teeth of some ancient predator. The Rucker's tracks lay plain before them in the sandy draw, leading toward a gap in the hills no more than a couple of miles away. Cade knew they'd find the Rio Grande on the other side of the low mountain range, but didn't have any idea how far that might be. A mile . . . maybe ten; he suspected somewhere in between.

Dismounting, Poe stripped the saddle from Lester's back, then tore some clumps of grass from the edge of the wash to rub the animal down. Elkins was doing the same for Roman. Cade slumped back against a boulder, then immediately jerked forward, away from where the stone's absorbed heat threatened to burn him through his shirt. He cursed without enthusiasm and scooted into the scanty shade of a creosote bush. When he took off his hat and ran his fingers through his hair, it felt as if someone had dumped a bucket of warm water over his head. Off to the east, waves of heat shimmied above the rugged terrain they'd recently crossed, and the sky appeared pale and featureless, not a cloud in sight. Other than the heat, nothing stirred. Not even the wind, and Cade closed his eyes against the fiery view. He figured they'd covered close to twenty miles so far, and he was pleased with that, but didn't want to think about the distance they had yet to cover.

After a while Poe came over leading his mule. The animal's head was lowered, and a thick rope of drool hung from its lower lip. "Sergeant," Poe said quietly.

"Yeah?"

"These mules are about played out." He sounded almost apologetic about bringing it up.

"I know."

Poe hesitated, then cleared his throat. "I'm thinking if we don't slow down, we might end up killing one or both of these animals."

Cade looked up to meet Poe's eyes. "Do you have a problem with that, Corporal?"

"It's not something I want to do, but if that's your order, we will."

Relenting, Cade said, "Let's hope we don't have to." He sat up and looked around, taking in the details of their immediate surroundings for the first time since staggering away from the mule's shoulder. The heat reflecting off the hills was palpable, like standing too close to a hot stove, and graze was scarce. "How much water do we have left?" he asked.

"Enough for one more swallow for each man, then maybe half a hat for each of the mules. We could likely make it to the Rio Grande on that if we walked and took our time, but it'd be better if we waited until after the sun goes down."

Cade shook his head. Waiting wasn't an option he intended to consider.

"Then you still think we can catch up?"

121

"One way or another. That ambulance has to be slowing them down. If not on the flats, then surely up above." He nodded toward the low pass before them. "I don't know that we've gained anything yet, but I don't think we've lost much ground, either. That'll be to our advantage when we get deeper into these hills."

Poe didn't reply, but Cade could tell he was considering their odds, weighing the pluses and minuses. His thoughts were running along similar veins. Although determined to catch up, he was worried about what kind of shape they'd be in when they did. Looking at his men now, worn damn near to nubbins from their long, mule-aided run across the hot Texas desert, he doubted if they'd present much of a challenge to Hollister's men even if they could get between the gang and Mexico in time.

Bringing his gaze back to Poe, he said quietly, "Ready?"

"As we'll ever be, I suppose."

Rising stiffly, Cade said, "Elkins, grab a couple of canteens for the men. One swallow apiece, no more."

"Just one?" Hendricks said.

"You heard the sergeant," Poe said, dropping Lester's reins and walking over to free a canteen from where he'd left it on his saddle. "Hendricks, loan me your hat. I want to water these mules."

"With my hat?"

"Damnit, have you gotten hard of hearing today?"

"I just don't want mule slobber in my hat, Corporal."

"I don't have to use it if you don't want me to."

"Ye can use mine," Riley volunteered. "I reckon a waterlogged hat'd feel mighty good about now, even if there is a bit of mule snot in it."

Hendricks scrambled to his feet. "No, we can use mine."

"I figured you'd change your mind when you thought about

it," Poe said wryly. He unplugged the canteen and Hendricks took off his pale campaign hat with its yellow braid and deep sweat stains climbing all the way to the crown. He was just holding it out, gripping it on either side by its wide brim, when a shot cracked from the hills above them. Hendricks grunted and took a step backward, and the hat slipped from his fingers.

"Take cover," Cade yelled, but the men were already running. All save Hendricks, who stood with his hands still half-raised, staring at the spreading red stain on the front of his shirt.

Cade wiggled under the limbs of the creosote bush where he'd sought shade earlier—poor shelter from a bullet, but hopefully enough to shield him from the gunman's view—and brought the carbine from his shoulder. A second shot struck the mule called Lester in the middle of the forehead, and he dropped as if his legs had been yanked out from under him. Spotting a wispy puff of gun smoke rising from a veed notch between a couple of boulders nearly two hundred yards away, Cade sent a round whistling into its center. The whine of his bullet off stone came back to taunt him as a miss, but he hoped he'd let their ambusher know they weren't without some ability to fight back.

Lunging to his feet, Poe ran into the wash and grabbed Hendricks around the waist, taking him down in a dusty roll that placed them both within the shelter of the arroyo's low bank. On Cade's right, Schultz was returning fire with his revolver. Cade knew the range was too great for much accuracy from the Colt—so did Schultz—but he was hoping the steady flow of lead would keep whoever was shooting at them occupied for a few seconds. Meanwhile, he fingered a fresh cartridge from his belt, expelled the spent brass from the Springfield's chamber, and replaced it with a live round. He slapped the trapdoor closed, cocked the carbine's stiff side hammer, snugged the weapon to his shoulder, and brought the sights back onto the jumble of rocks from where their bushwhacker had last fired. But he didn't pull the trigger. He wanted a solid target, and was counting on spotting one as soon as Schultz was done.

With his Colt emptied, Schultz rolled onto his back and began ejecting the spent rounds. Cade firmed his grip on the Springfield, both eyes open as he scanned the fractured boulders above them. Nothing moved, and after several minutes his finger began to relax on the trigger. As cluttered as the slope was, he knew whoever had shot at them could have easily crawled away. Could even now be fleeing, while he and his men huddled under their skimpy cover.

"Anyone see anything?" Morgan called.

"Just smoke, and not much of that left," Elkins replied.

"What about Hendricks?"

"Frank?" Cade inquired without taking his eyes off the distant rocks.

"He's alive," Poe replied, but Cade didn't like the tautness of the corporal's words.

"Morgan, work around to your right," Cade called just loud enough for the trooper to hear him. "Keep your head down and take your time, but I want someone up there flanking that position. Schultz, are you ready?"

"*Ja*, Sergeant, my pistol, it is reloaded."

"Move up on the left, but be careful, damnit."

"*Ja*, hokay."

"Frank?"

"I'm here."

"Come on up where you can keep an eye on those rocks. If whoever is up there starts shooting again, I want you to lay into him with everything you've got."

"I'm not likely to hit anything from here."

"Just put some lead up there, give Morgan and Schultz all

the cover you can."

"What about Hendricks?"

"Damnit, Frank, get up here and do your job before someone else gets hit."

Poe said something Cade couldn't make out—possibly to Hendricks—then darted forward through the scrub. Cade watched close but didn't spot any movement from above. After a moment to ready themselves, Morgan and Schultz started working their way through the brush and scattered boulders. Cade remained where he was, sweat stinging his eyes, the sun burning his shoulders where the fabric of his shirt was drawn tight. The Springfield's walnut stock seemed to grow warmer the longer he kept it tucked to his cheek, but he didn't look away, and only blinked to keep the worst of the sweat from reaching his eyes.

It took Morgan and Schultz nearly twenty minutes of cautious climbing to reach the spot where the gunman had opened fire. Cade waited tensely as the two men ducked from sight. A moment later, Schultz appeared on a flat-topped boulder to the left of the shallow notch and waved his hat above his head.

"There is here no one, Sergeant, but we found—"

The shot came from another hundred yards beyond where the ambusher had originally fired, and Schultz jerked violently, half turned, then tumbled from his stone platform. Cade fired immediately but knew he'd missed. Morgan also opened fire, while Poe darted from cover and began clambering up the steep slope toward the bushwhacker's newest position. Cade swore and quickly reloaded, but no more shots came their way, and by the time Morgan and Poe reached the spot from where the gunman had fired, he'd vanished a second time.

Cade watched grimly as Poe and Morgan continued their upward climb after the killer. Within minutes, both of them had disappeared from view. Cade waited a bit longer, then stood and walked over to where Hendricks lay on his back against the wash's low bank. His eyes were closed, his complexion pale, but he was still breathing. Cade knelt by his side and waved flies off the trooper's bloody shirt.

"How are you doing, Hendricks?"

His eyes popped open, wide and startled. "Sergeant?" he gasped.

"Yeah, I'm here. How are you?"

"Maybe you ought to be the one tellin' me," Hendricks replied in a voice made raspy from heat and dehydration.

Cade set his carbine aside. Poe had already cut the shirt away from where the bullet had entered Hendricks's torso just below the rib cage. Cade eased the fabric up to have a look.

"Pretty bad, huh?"

Cade gently laid the material back over the wound. "Yeah, I suppose it is. How's the pain?"

"I'd have expected it to be worse than this," Hendricks confessed. "My legs hurt more from where they were cramping when we first got here than my side does."

"That's good," Cade said, patting the man's shoulder.

"Christ, is it that bad?" Hendricks whispered, staring at Cade's hand. He looked suddenly fearful, as if the sergeant's tenderness brought home the seriousness of his wound.

"Just rest," Cade told him.

Elkins scurried over in a stooped jog, although Cade felt certain the gunman had moved on. There would have been more shooting by now if he hadn't.

"What can I do, Sergeant?"

"Stay with him," Cade instructed. "Riley?"

"Over here," Riley called, poking his head above Roman's shoulders. When the shooting started, the unarmed trooper had grabbed the mule's halter and hustled him into the relative safety of a cluster of boulders several yards away.

"Are you all right?"

"Aye, me and the beasty both, though I'm thinkin' I'm a mite more scared than he is."

"Bring a canteen over here and help Elkins."

Riley nodded and led the mule back into the wash. After tying him to a creosote bush growing along the arroyo's edge, he found a canteen and took it to Elkins. Cade grabbed another canteen and the Springfield and started up the steep grade to look for Schultz. He found him without much effort, crumpled at the base of the boulder he'd been shot from. The ambusher's bullet had taken him squarely in the back, shattering his spine and tearing through his heart before exiting his chest.

Swallowing back the bitter taste of anger, Cade walked over to where he had a clear view of the upper wash. Pulling his hat brim low over his eyes to shield them from the sun, he stared toward the shoulder of the hill where Poe and Morgan had disappeared probably half an hour earlier. He was starting to worry, but there wasn't much he could do about it, and there was nothing he could do for Schultz.

Slinging the canteen's strap over his shoulder but keeping the Springfield handy, Cade skidded back down to where Elkins and Riley were watching over Hendricks. Elkins had taken off his shirt and draped it over a creosote bush for shade, but there was precious little relief in its shadow. Although still alive, Hendricks's breathing was fast and shallow, and his flesh looked like polished marble. He didn't reply when Cade spoke his name, although his eyes darted under closed lids.

It was another twenty minutes before they spotted someone coming toward them from above, taking his time tramping through the scrub. From here, he was little more than a dark smudge against the lowering sun. It wasn't until he reached the cluster of boulders where Schultz lay that Cade recognized him as Morgan. He watched as the trooper sidetracked to check on

Schultz, then ducked behind the rocks where their ambusher had fired the first time. When he reappeared a couple of minutes later, he came on down the rest of the way without making any effort at concealment.

"Where's Poe?" Cade demanded as soon as Morgan joined them.

"He went on alone," the trooper replied, accepting a canteen from Elkins and drinking deeply. Cade didn't reprimand him for the extra water. Patting his cracked lips delicately with the back of his hand, Morgan said. "Corporal sent me back to report. I told him he should come with me, but he was set on following the man's trail."

"Just one man?"

"Yeah." After a pause, he added, "Schultz is dead."

"We know," Elkins replied. "The sergeant already checked."

Morgan nodded and looked past Elkins to where Hendricks still lay close to the arroyo's bank. "What about him?"

"Dying, I'd say," Elkins replied, though quietly so that he wouldn't be overheard.

"Bastard," Morgan said softly, meaning their bushwhacker. Then he turned to Cade. "We found these, right before Schultz was hit," he said, dropping a pair of empty copper cartridges into Cade's hand.

Cade studied the casings solemnly. Spencer rounds—from two hundred yards away and downhill.

"That half-breed, the one who knifed Talbot, he carried a Spencer," Morgan said.

"Yeah, I remember."

"I figure he killed Schultz, too."

"It's possible."

Morgan's brows rose questioningly; Elkins and Riley also looked surprised.

"I'd say there's little doubt about it, Sergeant."

Cade looked up. "Did you see him?" His gaze moved from Morgan to Elkins, then on to Riley. "Did anyone see him?"

"No, but who else could it have been?" Morgan countered. "Spencers aren't all that popular out here anymore, not with men like that."

"It could have been anyone," Cade returned bluntly.

But Morgan wouldn't be swayed. "I don't think so," he replied stubbornly.

Cade sighed and bounced the empty cases in his palm a couple of times. "I don't, either," he admitted. "But I'm not going to count anything as fact until I'm convinced it is."

He waited until Morgan grudgingly nodded. He was angry, Cade knew. They all were. It was natural, considering what they'd been through, the humiliation they'd been forced to swallow from Hollister and his crew. It would have been different, he told himself, if not for the women and his concern for their safety.

Deciding not to push it any further, Cade jerked his head toward Hendricks. "Go say your goodbyes, Morgan."

Morgan hesitated, then nodded and stepped around Cade, his expression wooden. Cade raised his eyes to the winding arroyo. He wished Poe hadn't gone on alone, especially if it was the half-breed who had ambushed them. Poe was a good man, but Cade wasn't sure he'd be a match against a cold-blooded killer like Fish. Tossing the empty copper into the scrub bordering the wash, he wondered if any of them would be.

CHAPTER TWELVE

Although the sun had set, the sky was still light when Ben Hollister pulled his horse to a stop on the east bank of the Rio Grande. Ed Dodson whoaed his mules a few yards downstream, and the two men quietly studied the fast-flowing river. After a couple of minutes, the whore called Lucia Mendoza poked her head out of the front of the ambulance to look around, then crawled into the driver's box with Ed.

"I know this place."

Ben gave her a speculative glance and wondered if she was telling the truth. Suspicion had become a constant companion the last few years, and although he was as weary of that as he was the outlaw life he led, he wasn't ready to abandon it yet.

"Is it always this high?" Ed asked the woman.

Lucia was still standing, looking almost wistfully across the river at Mexico. A strong breeze flowing south with the current had caught her dark hair and was blowing it back off the shoulders of her military blouse. The soft evening light accentuated her subtle beauty, as the clothing did the curves of her body. Under different circumstances, Ben thought he would have been deeply attracted to her, but something had changed in the last day or so.

Lucia stared quietly at the river for several minutes, then shook her head. "No, it isn't," she replied to Ed's question. "There must have been a heavy rain somewhere upstream. Either that or the melt is just now getting here."

"Melt?"

"Snowmelt." She looked at him. "From the mountains."

"Lord Almighty, woman, where's there a mountain 'round here high enough to pack snow?"

"In Colorado."

"Colorado?" Ed stared at the rushing waters, as if contemplating melting snow that had come all this way for the sole purpose of blocking his entry into Mexico. Finally he leaned over the wheel and spat into the sandy soil. "That's a damned long trip for a snowball," he grumbled.

"Normally you could cross here without getting your feet wet," Lucia said to Ben.

"How long do you figure before it goes down?"

"There's no way to know. It could go down tonight, or it might not budge for a week."

As she spoke, two more heads appeared from the ambulance's interior—Hattie's and Fanny's. Ben glanced at Hattie, and his gut gave an unfamiliar lurch. If not for Fanny O'Shea, he feared he might have said something stupid, and for once he was glad for the brash redhead's presence.

"Where we at?" Fanny demanded.

"Not far from the village where I was born," Lucia replied.

Straining forward, Fanny peered first upstream, then down. "I don't see no village."

"It's upriver from here."

"How far?" Ben asked, pulling his eyes off of Hattie to follow Lucia's gaze.

"Three or four miles, if I remember right."

"Is there a bridge there?"

Lucia smiled at something she must have considered humorous. "No, there is no bridge."

"How's the crossing there?" Ed asked. "Better'n this un?"

"No better, maybe worse."

Ben studied the river's twin banks. They were low on both sides, but the current was swift, keeping the reeds along the shore swaying wildly. Without actually riding into the stream to measure its depth against his horse's shoulder, he estimated it at four or five feet toward the middle. In still waters, that wouldn't have been intimidating, but running fast like this was, it could easily tip a wagon, or even pull its team under and drown it.

He stepped down from his saddle and pulled his bridle from the grulla's head.

"Unhook your mules, Ed, and let them drink," he said.

Downstream, Ray Beeler had already driven the loose stock to the river's edge, where the horses immediately dipped their heads to water. Crawling out the rear of the ambulance, Hattie filled a collapsible canvas bucket at the shore and returned to the wagon without taking time to slake her own thirst. When his horse had its fill, Ben led it back to the Rucker and tied it to a rear wheel. Then he walked past the loose stock to where Jethro's horse was also drinking. Jethro sat his saddle listlessly, staring into the purling water. Ben placed a hand on the younger man's knee and gave it a gentle shake.

"Climb down, *amigo.*"

Jethro didn't respond for a moment. Then he roused himself and looked at Ben. "Are we there?"

"Just about." He nodded to the far bank.

"Is that Mexico?"

"That's it. Are you ready to cross?"

"Sure." He started to lift his reins, but Ben caught them instead and slid them from his fingers.

"Why don't you get down and have a drink first, then rest a minute. We'll all cross soon enough."

"I ain't sure if I got down, I could get back up, Ben."

"That's all right. We'll get you in your saddle."

132

Jethro looked around until he spotted the loose stock, his sorrel among them. "I think I'd like to ride Acorn into Mexico."

"Sure, but right now get down and take a drink, then sit in the shade until we're ready to move."

Jethro nodded and dragged his right foot from its stirrup. Ben had to hang onto him while he dismounted to keep him from crumbling to the ground. He guided him to the riverbank and eased him down on his knees, then helped him lean forward to drink. When he was done, Ben made sure he was far enough back from the water that he wouldn't fall in and drown. He returned to the ambulance, arriving just as Hattie appeared at the rear entrance.

"Oh, Mr. Hollister!" she said, startled.

"Ma'am," he replied, then tipped his head toward the vehicle's interior. "How are your patients doing?"

"I believe Mr. McDaniels is coming around. His fever has broken and he seems to be resting."

"And Bobby?"

"I don't think his fever is as high as it was earlier. Or perhaps it's because the sun has gone down and there's a breeze, but his forehead doesn't feel as warm as it did this morning."

"Then that's good news?"

"Yes," she said, and an unexpected smile briefly lit her face. "I hope so, at any rate." She held a hand out. "Help me down, please."

"Yes, ma'am," Ben replied, and felt an odd moment of confliction as she placed her hand in his. "I . . . I just want to . . ." He looked up helplessly.

"You're welcome," she said quietly, and Ben nodded and helped her to the ground.

"You gonna help me out now, fancy britches?" a brassy voice piped up.

He glanced past Hattie to where Fanny O'Shea was leaning

out the back of the wagon. She was grinning broadly, her tobacco-stained teeth like twin rows of rotting fenceposts between heat-cracked lips.

"Or is it only Hattie you're hankerin' for?" she added snidely.

"Miss Wilkes is earning her keep by attending to the wounded," Ben replied. "When you do something productive, I'll help you out as well."

Fanny cackled loudly. "Come by my bed tonight, Hollister, and I'll show you how I earn my keep."

Glancing at Hattie, Ben felt strangely gratified by her expression of restrained embarrassment. He tipped his hat to her, turned his back on Fanny's outstretched hand, and walked around to the front of the ambulance. Fanny hooted and called him a couple of obscene names, but she was laughing about it. Or maybe she was laughing at him and his foolish behavior, one as deserved as the other, he feared.

Ray had dismounted and led his horse over to where Ed was hanging onto the lead ropes of the two army mules. Ed was watching the mules drink. Ray stared along their backtrail toward the low mountain range they'd crossed that afternoon.

"Where do you figure Fish got to?" he asked Ben.

"I don't know."

"He should've caught up by now, unless he got tangled up in a trap."

"Little Fish ain't a man to do what you'd expect," Ed said. "It wouldn't surprise me one bit if we found him waitin' for us across the river."

"We crossing over tonight, Ben?" Ray asked.

"Yes."

"That Mex woman said the river might go down by morning," Ed reminded him.

"Or it might not go down until next week. I'd rather cross now, in case it rises even higher overnight."

Ed shrugged as if he didn't care, but Ray seemed to approve of the decision. "Quicker we get into Mexico, the quicker we can split the money and go our own ways."

That brought Ed's head up. "You splittin' off on us, Ray?"

"We're all splitting up," Ray replied, grinning. "Ain't that right, Ben?"

Ed frowned. "Ben?"

"He's right," Ben confirmed. "Bobby's going to need a lot of rest, even after he's on his feet again."

"Hell, we could all use some rest," Ed said. He sounded puzzled by the direction the conversation had taken, not yet grasping all its implications.

Ben kept his mouth shut and reminded himself that Dodson was a good man in most respects, consistent in his reliability. But he was also slow of hand and thought, and Ben found it annoying that he was only now starting to understand what some of the others—Ray and Little Fish, and even Henry, before he'd been laid low by a contrary mule—had already realized and accepted.

"You ain't trackin' this straight, ol' hoss," Ray told Ed. "It ain't rest Ben is wanting, it's to be shed of us."

"That true, Ben?"

"Not altogether, but I suppose it's close enough. I've got Bobby to think about now, and I don't want him following the same trails I did."

"Your little brother is damn well old enough to find his own trails," Ray pointed out.

"Maybe, but it's not going to happen that way."

There had been an unexpected tautness in Ray's words, and Ben half turned to keep an eye on him. He wondered if this was where the gunman intended to make his play. He seemed to be considering it. Then he grinned suddenly, looked at Ed, and winked.

135

"You can come with me if you want to," Ray said. "Let the Hollister boys figure out for themselves what life is like for men with prices on their heads and no one to watch their backs."

"I'd just as soon stay with Ben, if he'll have me," Ed replied.

"I don't know where I'll end up," Ben said. "All I know for sure is that I'm giving up on outlawing."

"Hell, that'd suit me," Ed said, smiling as if a conclusion had been reached and agreed upon. Ben didn't see any reason to dissuade him. There would be time enough later on to decide which direction they all wanted to take.

"All right," he said, turning away from the river. "Let's get those mules back in their traces. Ray, you and I will run the loose stock across the river, then come back and help float the ambulance over." His gaze fell on Jethro, sitting close beside the stream with his mount's reins held loosely in one hand. The horse was pulling up clumps of grass, and Ben figured it wouldn't be long before it slipped free and wandered off to seek better graze. From his expression, Ben wasn't sure Jethro was even aware of the animal's presence.

"We ought to just shoot him," Ray muttered.

"No, we'll put him in the ambulance with the others. Come on, daylight's fizzling and we still have a lot to do."

They got the horses across without trouble, although they had to swim them for about ten feet just past mid-channel. The wagon proved a little more difficult, but with Ben and Ray on the upstream side with ropes running from their saddle horns to brackets on the inside of the bed, they kept the vehicle upright and the wounded men dry; the women got a little wet when the river swirled inside, several inches deep across the floor, but it was nothing to cause harm. Ben and Hattie had already put Jethro inside to sit on the bunk next to Henry McDaniels. Henry was also sitting up, his arm bandaged and in a sling. He was conscious now, and insisted he'd feel all right in another day or two.

"It's gonna take more than a mule's nip to keep me down," he said, but Ben wondered if he wasn't trying to convince himself as much as anyone else.

Jethro kept asking about Acorn and struggling to leave the ambulance until Ben finally tied the sorrel to the tailgate with Jethro's saddle on the horse's back. He'd had to assure the younger man he could ride again just as soon as they reached the far shore, but by the time they got across, Jethro seemed to have lost his desire to ride. It was apparently enough just to have the horse in sight, and Henry voiced no complaint when Jethro stretched out on his bunk and fell asleep.

Coiling their lariats afterward, Ray said, "Where to now?"

"North." Ben glanced at Lucia, sitting beside Ed on the wagon's seat. "We're going to find that town Miss Mendoza mentioned and see if they have a doctor."

"They won't," Lucia said.

"Maybe they got one after you moved away."

She looked at him like he'd said something too ridiculous to acknowledge, then shrugged and smiled dismissively.

"Move out," Ben said quietly, and Ed hupped his team into motion.

Swinging wide behind the extra stock, Ben and Ray hazed them after the wagon, following a rough, two-track road that ran parallel to the river. The light was already fading when they left the crossing. It was full dark by the time they reached the town. Ben swore and trotted his horse up beside the ambulance. Ed had already stopped the rig at the head of the street and was leaning forward to squint at the dilapidated buildings. From behind, Ray's laughter floated eerily over the abandoned town.

"You could have told me it was deserted," Ben charged.

"I thought maybe someone came here with that doctor you

mentioned. You know, after I moved away."

"*This* is the town you was talkin' about?" Ed blurted. "Damnation, gal, there ain't but a handful of houses to the whole shebang."

"It never was a prosperous place."

"Is there a store?"

"Or a cantina?" Ray added from where he sat his mount near the rear of the ambulance.

"There was a store once, with a cantina inside along one wall," Lucia said. She pointed to a sprawling adobe edifice, its roof partially caved in. "That was it."

"What happened here?" Ben asked.

"Apaches. They attacked the town and killed most of the men, then kidnapped a lot of the women and younger children and took them into the Sierra Madres, farther west."

"Why didn't they take you?"

"Who said they didn't?"

"You escaped?"

"I was . . . sold . . . to a rancher in Sonora named Hardy, an old man who wanted a young wife. I was fifteen when he purchased me. I was seventeen when he died."

"Is he the one who taught you English?"

"Yes." Her voice turned bitter. "Samuel Hardy was a stickler for proper pronunciation and sentence structure. He said he wouldn't tolerate ignorance, and that I had to learn to read and write, in English, or he'd make me sleep in the shed with the pigs."

"He sounds like a bastard," Ed declared.

"He was, although he never beat me like the Apaches did."

"What happened after he died?"

"I went to El Paso and became a whore."

Ben started to glance toward the dark opening of the ambulance, but stopped himself in time. It made him wonder, though, how two fairly well-educated women came to share such a similar story. He didn't know anything about Fanny O'Shea, but from listening to her heavy Eastern accent, her coarse humor and frequent flatulence, he wouldn't be surprised by whatever path had brought her to prostitution. But he couldn't understand why Lucia and Hattie hadn't found something better for themselves. Then a voice whispered from deep within: *Why didn't you?*

It was as much an accusation as a question, and he shook his head to drive it away.

"Anybody living here now?" he asked, and wondered if anyone detected the ragged edge of his words.

"Ghosts, I suppose."

"Ghosts?" Ed gave her a wary look. "Real ha'nts, you mean? You've seen 'em?"

"No," Lucia replied, smiling. "It was just an observation."

"Well, don't you go observin' too much," he warned, then leaned past her to speak to Ben. "Let's make camp out here tonight, and go in tomorrow."

"No, let's go see if anyone's around. Maybe we can buy some decent food."

"Or whiskey," Ray added.

"I don't know, Ben," Ed said plaintively, staring down the vacant street. "What if there is ha'nts?"

"If there are, Ray'll shoot them for you," Ben said, tapping heels to his mount's sides.

There wasn't much to see. A wide street with less than two dozen buildings in varying stages of disrepair. Many still showed the stain of the fires the Indians had set after overwhelming the town, like shadows of the dead imprinted on the pale adobe walls. Yet there were signs of recent activity, too. A hard-packed trail following one side of the street, a lingering scent of woodsmoke, and the unmistakable odor of manure—horse, mule, or burro.

Although most of the shutters hung open or had been torn off completely, those in a house near the far end of the street had been firmly closed, as was its heavy door. Halting in front of the small adobe structure, Ben slipped the Smith and Wesson from its holster and rested it on his thigh. Ed stopped the mules some distance away, and Ray allowed the cavvy to ramble as he rode forward. Ben called to Lucia, "Can you still speak Spanish?"

"Of course."

"Then tell whoever is inside to come out with their hands empty. Tell them we won't hurt them, that we only want to buy some food and maybe some medicine if they have any to spare."

Lucia spoke too rapidly for Ben to follow, but he did catch a few words, including *medicina* and *comida*. They waited but no one replied, and the silence hanging over the battle-scarred village seemed to grow vaguely ominous.

"Ben," Ed called, and his gray goatee seemed to tremble under his chin. "Let's get the hell outta here. We can come back tomorrow and poke around."

"Hell's bells, Dodson," Ray said scornfully. "I always figured you for a tough son of a bitch. Now here you are actin' like a scared kid."

"I ain't scar't of anything I can see or touch, but ha'nts is something I don't want no part of."

"Shut up, you two," Ben said mildly. He was leaning forward in his saddle, trying to listen, but there was too much ambient noise—his horse's breathing, the small creaks of saddle leather, the faint squeaks of bats overhead; even the wind seemed to want to muffle the town's message.

"Whoever is here is probably frightened and hiding," Lucia said. "Leave them alone. They won't have medicine, and look around you. Do you see any crops?"

"They've gotta eat something," Ray said.

"Rats and mice," Lucia replied. "Rabbits. Maybe fish caught from the river. But there won't be anything decent to eat, and very little that is poor." She was looking at Ben. "Please, you're wasting your time here. You must know that."

Ben glanced at Ed, then Ray. Before he could make up his mind, Henry poked his head out the front of the ambulance to cast his lot with the others.

"Let's get outta here, Ben. We're too damn close to the Rio Grande. You know that skimpy river won't stop Plunkett if he thinks we're nearby."

Ben eased back in his saddle, looking at Lucia. "All right, then where do we go from here?"

She seemed surprised by the question. "You're asking me?"

"I am, and if you don't answer, I'll kick that door open and kill every son of a bitch I find inside."

Lucia hesitated as if trying to decide how serious he was. Then she shrugged and pointed over her shoulder. "There are small villages all along the Rio Grande, but none that will have what you want. The nearest town that might is southwest of here."

"They'll have a doctor?"

"Possibly. I've never been there myself."

"How far?"

"My father could walk it in five days. With the wagon, you should make it in three." After a pause, she added, "I said *you* should be able to make it there in three."

At first Ben didn't know what she meant. Then it came to him. When she saw that it had, she went on.

"You promised you'd let us go after we crossed the Rio Grande."

"I'm afraid we'll need you to ride along with us for a few more days," he replied.

"Then you are a liar, as well as a thief?"

Chuckling, Ray said, "He's a lot worse than that, sweetheart."

"Shut up, Ray."

"Aw, hell, Ben, they already know what kind of men we are. No sense sugarcoatin' it."

Ben pulled his horse around to face the wagon. "I told you to shut up."

Ray laughed and waited, and then his expression gradually hardened. "One of these days, Ben, you're gonna push me an inch too far."

"Anytime you're ready, Beeler."

"No, not tonight, and not here." Then he laughed again, to show he wasn't frightened, and reined away to gather the stock.

Ben took a deep breath before returning the Smith and Wesson to its holster. He looked at Lucia. "All right, what's the name of this place?"

"Here? This is San Ignacio."

"No, the place your daddy used to walk to in five days."

"That town was once called San Fidel, but now it's called something else."

"What's that?"

"Villa Lobos."

CHAPTER THIRTEEN

They came together at a place called *Rocas Quebradas*—the Broken Rocks. It was a favored camping place for the Hunters, especially when they were returning from a long raid or trading expedition. Not that there was much difference between the two.

José Yanez rode at the head of the six men who had stuck with him after the Apaches' attack on their column that afternoon. The rest of his command had scattered like flushed quail. Not in cowardice, but to escape. It was a trick they'd learned from the Apaches, to break up into smaller and smaller bands until pursuit became futile, then to meet again at some predetermined site. In this part of the country, that was *Rocas Quebradas*.

Nightfall caught them many miles short of the Rocks. They could have stopped until moonrise—the giant orb was nearly full and would have provided them plenty of light—but José opted instead to give the buckskin its head, allowing the horse to set both pace and direction. By the time the moon finally crested the horizon, the stone slabs with their numerous tanks and monoliths lay within sight, less than thirty minutes ahead.

Quite a few men had already straggled in by the time José and his six arrived, but there were no fires to greet them, and even less warmth in the bleak stares fixed on him and his men. José hadn't expected a campfire, not in Apache country, but the sullen looks from the men were worrisome. They would bear watching, he decided, and any show of dissent would have to be crushed quickly.

José guided his buckskin to the middle of the small basin and dismounted. There was no forage for the stock. Despite the abundance of water in the numerous tanks, the soil here was too hard, the water too contained, and what little grass did grow was quickly consumed by wildlife. It didn't matter. It was the water they needed. Tepid, at best, if there had been no recent rains, occasionally gelatinous, but always available if a man was desperate enough.

José handed his reins to one of the men who had ridden in with him, confident the buckskin would be cared for, then strode almost casually to the center of the basin. The moon was high enough now to shine its light into the jumbled boulders; in its glow the animosity of his men was like a low hum, though more felt than heard. Loudly, his voice bouncing back off the rocks, he said, "Where is Juan Carlos or Francisco Castile?"

One of the men sitting by himself looked up. "Maybe they are where you left them, eh?"

José tipped his head thoughtfully to one side. The speaker was leaning back against a *carreta*-sized boulder several rods away, his round face darkly stubbled, his *botas* stained with old blood.

"What is your name, *amigo*?"

"You know my name, José."

"Ah, but you don't seem to know mine. It is not José, not to you, hombre. To you, I am *El Capitán*."

The man rose and tipped his sombrero back on his head. José recognized him as one of Juan Carlos's men, whose unit had been hardest hit in the Apache attack that afternoon.

"Do you know me now, *El Capitán*?"

"Yes, I know you. You are Benito Reyes."

"*Sí*, Benito Reyes. Brother to Sebastián, uncle to Esteban."

"Also under Juan Carlos's command."

"No longer, *mi capitán.* I saw them both for the last time this afternoon, as the *Indio diablos* tore at them with their knives. They were like dogs, those savages, ripping into the flesh of a weakened calf."

"Then your brother and nephew died bravely," José said. "Will you dishonor their deaths now with your insolence?"

Benito took a half-step away from the boulder where he had been sitting. He was a large man, as had been his brother and nephew, his hands blunt and square; they seemed to swallow the grips of his revolver as he closed his fingers around the badly scarred walnut. José was aware of others watching from the shadows, waiting to see what Benito would do, and how he would respond.

Waiting, he knew, to see who would lead them away from *Rocas Quebradas* when the sun came up the next morning.

"There is no dishonor in demanding an able leader," Benito said, raising his voice so that everyone would hear.

"We have fought the Apaches before," José reminded him. "And we have lost friends and family, as well."

Benito made a sound of harsh dismissal in his throat. "What we walked into today was not a fight, José. It was a slaughter." He flung his free hand, the one not attached to his holstered revolver, around the basin, an arena surrounded by house-sized boulders, slanting stone pillars, and the flat, staring eyes of the Hunters, José's *Cazadores de los Médanos.*

"Look, *Capitán!* Where is your command?"

"The others will be here before dawn."

"*Ba!* You spin lies like a spider spins its web. We are all that remain."

José sensed movement behind him, a stirring in the shadows close to the rocks that he dared not turn to face, or even acknowledge. He wondered where the six who had followed him into the *Rocas* had gone. Did they have his back? Or were they also waiting to see who won this violent tribunal between José Yanez and Benito Reyes?

But José would not be drawn into a battle against such uncertain odds. "Before dawn," he repeated, his voice ringing among the boulders. "Then we will see who lies."

Silence, charged with tension, greeted his declaration. Then Benito eased back and allowed his hand to fall away from his revolver.

"At dawn," he agreed. "Then we will make our decision and ask ourselves if José Yanez will continue to lead the *Cazadores* of Villa Lobos."

Dusk brought relief from the unrelenting heat, along with a cooling breeze that flowed up over the crown of the Sandbar Mountains east of the Rio Grande to nose among the weary troopers like a curious hound. Cade turned his face to it and closed his eyes.

"This'll do," he announced, taking a deep breath that, for the first time in hours, didn't feel like it was searing his lungs.

Muttering quiet consent, the men broke apart to see to their responsibilities. Elkins stripped the McClellan from Roman's back and led him out of the way, Morgan flipped the saddle blanket upside down to dry, and Riley dug through their packs for hardtack and jerky. The men gathered close as Riley passed out the slim rations, then settled down around the saddle like it was a campfire—something close and familiar, Cade assumed, taking a seat between Morgan and Riley.

At first a solemn hush enveloped the decimated squad as they mulled the losses they'd incurred that day. Talbot's death seemed a month past now, but they'd buried him only that morning, laying him to rest among the mesquites where they'd spent the previous night. They buried Schultz at the base of the hill where the ambush had taken place, covering him with stones because they hadn't brought along their shovel. Hendricks had been interred next to him, barely an hour later.

Corporal Poe's whereabouts were still unknown. Cade had been half-afraid they'd find him somewhere along the arroyo leading to the low pass over the Sandbars, but there had been no sign of him along the way. Now, waiting for better light to continue their trek, the men began to speak of Poe in tentative voices.

"I still say it was Hollister's redskin that bushwhacked us," Morgan said gruffly.

"Likely was," Elkins agreed.

"And he probably got Frank, too."

Riley's head jerked up. "Naw, ye don't know that, Morg. Not for certain sure, ye don't."

"The corporal would've been back by now if he was alive," Morgan insisted.

"You don't know that, either," Elkins said. "Poe's stubborn. He won't quit a trail until he's followed it to the end."

"Aye, the corporal's still trackin' the bogger, is my thinkin'," Riley said, although with a trace of uncertainty in his voice.

"Not after dark."

"Well, hell, Morg, of course not after dark, but ye don't think he can just whisk 'imself up here aside us with a witch's spell, do ye?"

"Damnit, we should've seen some sign of him before now."

"He'll show up when he's done what he needs to do," Cade said mildly.

Riley seemed to perk up at that. "Ye believe so, Sergeant? That Poe's still kickin' at the traces?"

"I do. If it was Little Fish who jumped us this afternoon, then he did so from ambush, and he killed Talbot standing behind him with a knife while Talbot was unarmed. But Poe is armed, and he knows Fish is out there somewhere stalking him. Stalking all of us. That changes the odds, as far as I'm concerned."

"Little Fish is an Indian, though," Morgan said.

"Half," Riley responded.

"Half or whole, being Indian doesn't make him invulnerable," Cade said.

"Damnit, the bastard's already killed three of us," Morgan said, striking his knee with the side of his fist. "And something else no one's mentioned. That first shot that got Hendricks came from at least two hundred yards away. Two hundred yards with a Spencer, and a carbine, at that."

Cade nodded somberly. He'd carried a Spencer for a few years in Kansas, immediately following the War Between the States, and although he'd liked the weapon just fine, he was also aware of the carbine's limited range. Anyone who could hit a target with one at two hundred yards had to be considered a good shot, and a dangerous adversary.

Deciding it was time to drop the subjects of Poe's whereabouts and the identity of their ambusher, Cade stood and brushed cracker crumbs from the front of his shirt and trousers. The moon was already peeking over the rim of the earth, like a pale chip of freshly exposed bone; its light flowed across the pass, illuminating the Rucker's tracks as twin shadows scratched into the tan earth.

"Time to go, men," he announced. "Before Hollister gets any farther away than he already is."

There was no grumbling as they rose and prepared to move out, and Cade nodded appreciatively. Their self-censorship underscored their determination to catch up with those who had abused and humiliated them that day. After Elkins saddled the mule, they shared the last of the water from the canteens, giving most of a hatful to Roman and splitting the rest among themselves. Then they started out, stiff-kneed and sore-backed, all of them limping to some degree but none of them riding. Cade had given up their Comanche-style pursuit after losing Lester.

Midnight came, then moseyed on without them, and the air that had turned pleasantly cool at supper now began to draw a chill through their sweat-dampened clothing—from hats to feet, and especially along their spines. Had Hendricks still been with them, Cade was certain he would have been complaining. And Cade would have had to bite back his irritation with the man. Still, he missed the constant bellyaching, along with the easy ribbing of the others in response. That was something else they'd lost to the Hollister gang.

The trail going down was easier than the one they'd followed up, crossing hard ground rather than following a sandy wash. It wasn't as steep, either. Cade kept looking out over the land toward Mexico for a light to mark the outlaws' campfire or a cloud of dust made pale by the moon that might indicate the gang wasn't too far ahead. Even the dark course of the Rio Grande would have been a welcome, if disappointing, sight, if for no other reason, affording them a goal. Instead, he saw only more of what they'd left behind yesterday, a dry land pocked with clumps of greasewood, scarred with crooked lines he recognized as arroyos.

They halted again at moonset and curled up to doze as best they could with their throats dust-coated, their lips cracked and beginning to bleed. Hunger nagged like a small child tugging at his mama's skirt, but it was thirst that tortured them with a more primitive fury. Lying on his side with the others while Elkins stood first watch, Cade felt around on the ground for small, smooth pebbles that he popped in his mouth like peanuts. The little stones activated his salivary glands, and that helped for a few minutes, but it never lasted, and he was soon scratching for more pebbles.

Dawn came slowly, spilling down over the western slopes of the Sandbars after first spreading out across the flats below. Morgan was on watch by then, but Cade was already awake. As tired as he was, he didn't think he'd dozed for more than a few minutes at a time, a dream-broken slumber filled with twitching muscles and a pounding at the back of his skull he knew was from too much sun and not enough moisture. He sat up and tried to spit to clear his throat, but couldn't raise enough saliva. In a voice like tumbling gravel he called the others to their feet. Once again, no one complained, but the look of exhaustion on their faces was disturbing, and it occurred to him that if they didn't reach the Rio Grande soon, they might not reach it at all.

They started out as they'd finished the night before, with Cade leading and Morgan and Riley following. Elkins brought up the rear with Roman trudging faithfully at his back. The morning started pleasantly cool, but that didn't last. By midday the sun was hammering down as if to spite them. Cade's vision swam and his feet stumbled over stones and dips in the trail he wouldn't have noticed yesterday. He kept glancing over his shoulder to make sure no one fell behind, and his concern grew as the hours passed and the men became more slack-jointed. He didn't think any of them knew quite what to make of the water flowing across their path. Not at first. Cade stopped and blinked, and Morgan bumped into his back. He mumbled an apology, then added a raspy, "Hey."

"Yeah," Cade replied in a voice equally frayed. Then he was shoved rudely aside by Roman as the mule trotted past them to the river's edge.

Flopping to their bellies upstream from where Roman stood hock-deep in the cooling water, the men drank deeply, sucking in more than they should have. Elkins crawled away after a bit and vomited into the sandy soil, but then came back for more.

It was Cade who finally pushed to his feet and reached for the mule's lead rope. Roman gave a fluttery bray and shook his head in protest, but Cade held firm and the mule gave up and allowed himself to be led out of the stream.

"Come on," Cade barked to the others. "You've had enough." He was watching Elkins, but thought the man would be okay with a little rest. "Morgan!" he snapped. "Get out of there!"

"Damn, Sergeant—"

"On your feet, and that's an order. You, too, Riley."

"Aye," Riley exhaled, but rolled onto his back instead to let the calmer water close to shore lap against his shoulder and the side of his face.

Observing him, Morgan did the same, and Cade found no fault in their refusal to stand. He tied Roman to a piece of driftwood, then sat down on the log and toed off his boots and socks before wading into the river up to his knees. Elkins crawled in after him, then allowed the current to float him around until he was sitting chest-deep in the current.

For a long time then, no one spoke. Occasionally Cade would fill his hat with water and pour it slowly over his head, but mostly he just stood there while his body cooled and the throbbing in his head subsided. When he judged enough time had passed, he waded out and led Roman back to drink some more. He used his hat to pour water over the animal's neck and withers, and the mule closed his eyes and brayed comically, the sound of his pleasure echoing like a rusty trumpet for miles in every direction.

They rested there for a couple of hours, stripping naked one by one to bathe and wash out their uniforms as the others stood guard. Cade was the last one in, and he felt the same reluctance he'd seen on the faces of the others when he finally climbed out and walked over to where he'd left his clothes to dry over a bush. When they were all dressed, he ordered Riley to bring out the last of their hardtack and jerky. Although water was plentiful for now, he knew they'd soon need more food. He'd spotted a couple of antelope east of the Sandbars, but had seen only a roadrunner and lizards on their trek that morning. He had some decisions to make, and absently reached for his pipe and tobacco before remembering he'd left that luxury back at the mesquites with the rest of their gear and tack.

Walking away from the others, Cade chewed thoughtfully on his last piece of jerky as he contemplated the Rucker's tracks, dipping down into the river, then coming out on the far shore, solid and deep. He regretted not catching up before Hollister, his men, and their hostages made it into Mexico. By law, he and his troopers were forbidden to continue their pursuit onto foreign soil. From this point on, the theft of government property and the kidnapping of the women would—should— legally be in the hands of the two nations' diplomats. But Cade knew what that would mean. Whatever fates awaited Lucia, Hattie, and Fanny would long since have been concluded before news of their abduction reached the state department. By the time Mexican officials were contacted, the women would be lost forever.

Cade had looked briefly for the horses and weapons Hollister had promised to leave behind when they reached the Rio Grande, but he didn't find them. Nor had he expected to. Making his decision, Cade swallowed the last of his jerky and walked back to where the others waited. "I'm not exactly sure where we are, but I'm guessing we're pretty close to Camp Rice," he declared.

"Rice?" Morgan looked up.

"You know it?"

"I've heard of it."

"We've all heard of it," Elkins said. "Not much to the place, is what they say."

"It's a small post, but it's a lot closer than Fort Bliss or any town that I'm aware of. I figure if you start now, you ought to be there by sundown." Cade nodded south. "I *think* it's in that direction. If I'm wrong and you don't reach it by noon tomorrow, turn around and try upstream."

"You're not coming with us?" Morgan asked.

"No, I'm not. Riley, give me your revolver. I'll take the mule, and I'm going to keep the Springfield, too."

"Ye goin' after 'em, are ye?"

"I am."

"You're going to invade Mexico on your own?" Morgan asked.

"I'll leave my stripes on this side of the river, and I'll ask that one of you keep them safe for me until I get back."

Morgan and Elkins exchanged glances. Riley spat into the dirt.

"You could come with us," Elkins suggested.

"If I thought I could requisition a fresh horse and supplies from Camp Rice and continue on into Mexico, I would, but the commander there wouldn't approve it, and I'd be forced to stay on this side of the river if I received a direct order not to go after the women."

"Meanin' that without a direct order forbiddin' it, ye figure ye can go?"

"That's about the size of it."

"Seems to me ye be splittin' that hair mighty fine, Sergeant."

"That I am, Riley, so hand over your revolver and belt. I'll take the extra cartridges the rest of you have, too."

No one moved to comply. To Morgan, Elkins said, "What'd you think?"

"I think I'll go with him."

"No, you won't," Cade replied. "This could well be a court-martial offense, and I won't allow anyone else to risk it."

"What if we come along, anyway?" Elkins asked.

153

"You're not. I'm ordering all three of you to go to Camp Rice, and that's not something I intend to discuss further."

"Are ye gonna have authority over us poor troopers once ye've crossed the Grande?" Riley queried.

"As long as I'm wearing these stripes, I'm still in charge."

"Aye, but ye said yeself ye'd be leavin' those stripes behind."

"I also said this is something we're not going to discuss. You men head for Rice. When you get there, tell the post commander I went into Mexico as a civilian, and that I'll report back as soon as I return to the U.S. If they want to prefer charges, they can do so then."

"I think you're missing the point, Sergeant," Elkins replied quietly. "If you go into Mexico as a civilian, you won't be wearing your stripes."

Cade could feel his temper building. "I'm wearing them now, Trooper, and I'm giving you an order that I expect to be obeyed."

"Aye, and we expected to be in El Paso by now," Riley said.

"Looks like we're going with you," Morgan added. "Whether you want us along or not."

Gritting his teeth, Cade took a threatening step toward Morgan, but the soldier held his ground, as all good soldiers did. It was Cade who stopped, his eyes moving from Morgan to Elkins, then to Riley, before coming back to Morgan, and for the first time in years he felt at a loss for words.

"He means it, Sergeant," Elkins said. "We all do."

"Ye can whale away on us all ye want, but it won't change our minds."

"You're a bunch of damned fools," Cade said. "If you do this, every one of you will end up in a stockade. Assuming the Federales don't find us and put us in front of a firing squad first."

"We're going after the son of bitch who killed Talbot and

Schultz and Hendricks, and probably Poe by now," Morgan growled.

"We're going to bring those women back, too," Elkins said. "Our orders were to deliver them to El Paso, and that's what I intend to do."

Cade looked at Riley, an unspoken question in the arch of his brows.

"Aye, they speak for me, Sergeant. We'll be goin' with ye, all the way."

"Fools," Cade grumbled, but he felt a deep sense of pride. And relief, as the odds of rescuing the women rose to something that made it seem almost possible.

"All right," he said. "If I haven't taught you jugheads any better by now, I doubt if I can before we cross into Mexico. I want anything you're carrying that can identify you as a soldier of the United States left behind. Empty your pockets, and Elkins, check the packs on the saddle. Morgan, cut the canvas off any canteen that has a U.S. stamp on it."

"It's a McClellan saddle, Sergeant, and Roman is carrying a U.S. brand on his hip."

"Just do the best you can," Cade replied, peeling his damp shirt off over his head. He used a small hunting knife carried in a sheath on his belt to start slicing through the thread holding his First Sergeant stripes to his sleeve.

"Sergeant," Morgan said quietly, and Cade looked to where the trooper had his chin jutted toward their backtrail. "Looks like we've got company."

"Spread out," Cade ordered, dropping his shirt and picking up the Springfield.

"I don't know who they are, but it's not Hollister's bunch," Elkins said, shading his eyes with the palm of his hand.

Cade made a rough count and came up with twelve men, one of the horses carrying double. The leader was a large man riding a tall roan. The rest looked like a hodgepodge of drovers, drifters, and townspeople. For a minute, Cade thought a couple of them might be injured or wounded, but as they drew closer he realized they were just worn out. It was Elkins who identified the man riding the saddle skirt of a seal brown.

"I'll be damned," he said. "Look what the wind blew in, boys."

Riley whooped and Morgan gave a cheer, but Cade quickly shuttered their elation. He'd spotted Poe, too, but he wasn't ready to celebrate without knowing the full story. As they came nearer, Cade noticed a badge pinned to the leader's shirt, and figured the odds were good that they were chasing the same quarry. The lawman raised a hand while his posse was still some twenty yards away, bringing his column to a halt.

"You'd be Cade?" the lawman called.

"Andrew Cade, First Sergeant. It looks like you picked up one of my strays."

The lawman chuckled. "Found him back in the hills, thirsty and lame. He's yours, if you want him."

"I do," Cade said, and Poe slipped from the seal brown's back and hobbled over to stand next to him.

"We're chasing the Hollister gang," the lawman said. "Your corporal here tells me you're doing the same."

"We are. Or were, until they slipped into Mexico without us."

"You gonna let that stop you, Sergeant?"

Cade's gaze narrowed as he considered the lawman's reply. Then he motioned toward the river. "Why don't you boys come on in and have a drink? We might need to discuss our options."

156

CHAPTER FOURTEEN

The road leading away from San Ignacio was hard and flat, and they were finally making good time. The land around them looked anemic in the pale moonlight, as flat as the bottom of a skillet. Riding in advance, Ben kept an eye out for a place to stop for a few hours, but the desert hugged the road tightly on either side, thick with greasewood and sprawling patches of cactus, an unrelenting sameness to the country that could make a man think he wasn't moving at all.

Eventually the road began to climb, a gentle grade toward a low mesa at least a dozen miles southwest of San Ignacio, but it wasn't until they reached the top that the flora began to open up. Spotting a gap in the vegetation on their right, Ben motioned the wagon off the road.

"This is far enough," he announced, although if the stock hadn't been so worn down by the day's unrelenting pace, he might have had them push on into the night to take advantage of the cooler temperatures.

Ed guided the mules off the road and to a stop as Ray hazed the cavvy past the ambulance toward what skimpy graze was available. Riding back to the wagon, he dropped tiredly from his saddle.

"God almighty, how far did we come today?"

"Halfway across Texas, by my reckonin'," Ed replied, setting the Rucker's brake and climbing down stiffly from the wagon's leaf-sprung seat. "My hind end feels like raw meat on a pumpkin."

Ben dismounted nearby, the muscles in his long legs protesting as they stretched into new positions. "Fifty miles," he said in a dry voice. "Maybe sixty."

"And a big chunk of it uphill, crossin' them mountains," Ed declared.

Henry was still sitting on the wagon's seat where he'd kept Ed company that afternoon. Raising his head to Ben, he said, "Another day like this and we'll kill these mules."

"Some of the horses, too," Ed furthered. "Not ours, but those Yankee nags look about played out."

"Yankee horses would," Ray said.

"We won't push this hard tomorrow," Ben told them. "We're deep enough into Mexico now that Plunkett's posse won't follow, and Cade's soldiers can't. Not without causing a ruckus with Mexico."

"This ain't much of a place to stop," Ed remarked. "Not enough grass here to feed a june bug, let alone a bunch of hungry four-legged critters."

"We'll move on first thing in the morning," Ben assured him.

"How about we divvy that money now?" Ray said, turning away from where he'd just stripped the saddle from his horse and dropped it on the ground next to the ambulance.

"Not until Little Fish catches up."

"Fish might not catch up."

"If he doesn't by the time we reach Villa Lobos, we'll split the money there."

Ray's voice rose a couple of notches. "I ain't sure I want to ride along that far, Ben."

"Villa Lobos'll be all right with me," Ed said quickly, before Ben could reply.

"That'll work for me, too," Henry said. "If things were different, I'd probably side with Ray, but I ain't myself tonight; Jethro and Bobby are still in bad shape, and Fish ain't caught up yet. Let's give it a few more days."

"That's bullshit," Ray said darkly.

"I know, but let's do it anyway," Henry said.

Ray hadn't taken his eyes off of Ben, but now he smiled and relaxed. "Maybe so," he agreed in a mocking tone. "I still aim to have a little fun with one of these whores, and that chestnut-haired gal from Chattanooga has caught my fancy."

"No," Ben said mildly, shifting around to face Ray. "You'll stay away from her. From all of them."

"We'll see, Ben. We'll sure as hell see." Ray jerked the halter from his mount's head and shooed the animal toward the rest of the herd.

They made a cold camp that night, eating jerky and dried apples washed down with canteen water. Later on, Ben and Hattie returned to the ambulance with the bull's-eye lantern to check on the patients. Ben's gut tightened in dread as he crawled in after the woman, but Bobby was still breathing. It was that same quick, shallow rise and fall of his chest that scared the hell out of him, but it was better than no movement at all.

Jethro was lying on the bunk across from him and seemed only partially conscious. He was muttering something unintelligible, his good leg moving slowly up and down the bed. Perspiration had darkened his shirt and the blanket under him, and his hair was soaked.

Ben spared him only a glance, then turned the light on his brother. "How's he been?" he asked Hattie.

"Better, I think. His fever has lessened."

"Has he said anything?"

"No, I'm afraid not."

Ben inhaled deeply, his lips pressed tight. "Is . . . is there anything you need?"

"I don't need anything, but these men," she motioned to Bobby and Jethro, "could use a clean bed that isn't continually jarring their wounds open. A warm meal and a doctor wouldn't hurt, either."

Returning her straightforward gaze, Ben was surprised by his lack of anger at the accusation in her words. He knew she blamed him for their situation, and especially his refusal to seek medical assistance in the states. But she wasn't asking for anything for herself, only for the injured. It was an attitude he hadn't seen much of since the war, and he both admired it and regretted not having sought it out sooner in life.

"You overheard what your friend said in San Ignacio?"

"That help is still three days away? Yes, I heard."

"We'll do the best we can between here and there," Ben said, as he moved to the rear of the ambulance and dropped to the ground.

Ray, Henry, and Ed had settled down close to the wagon. Ed was smoking a pipe, the smell of tobacco oddly comforting. It was something familiar, Ben thought, like the aroma of meat roasting over a fire, or the scent of an approaching storm on a hot summer day. It reminded him vaguely of home, before the war.

The army horses they had ridden that day had been turned loose to graze, while the mounts used in the Rio Largo raid were brought close and fed a bait of oats from the Rucker's side box. Ed had already removed their nose bags and double-checked their halters and lead ropes. Then he and Ray bridled and saddled the horses in case they needed to make a middle-of-the-night escape. It was a holdover from the Civil War, or the War of Northern Aggression as they preferred to call it, and a habit Ben had insisted they continue in the years since, sleeping with their horses close and their guns handy.

Ben looked around until he spotted Lucia and Fanny in their

blankets on the far side of the road, already settled in for the night. Near the Rucker's rear wheel, Ray chuckled crudely.

"I invited both of them to share my bedroll, but they wasn't interested."

"I don't blame 'em," Ed said emphatically.

"That's because you're too damn old to remember what it's like to bed a woman," Ray countered.

"It wouldn't be much fun around here, anyway," Henry added tiredly. "I've already plucked a couple of fishhooks outta my ass."

"Fishhooks?"

"Cactus. I keep forgettin' most of you boys ain't Texas-bred."

"That's all right," Ray said, his attention still focused on Lucia and Fanny. "Waiting is just gonna make it all that much sweeter." He raised his voice, even though Ben knew the women could hear him just fine. "Ain't that right, darlin's?"

"You should've took you a bath at that river," Fanny retorted. "I might'a considered crawling into your blankets tonight if you had."

Ray laughed and folded his hands behind his head.

Picking up his bedroll, Ben carried it to the opposite side of the ambulance and found a spot close to the road that looked free of cactus and sharp rocks. He took off his boots and gun belt and lay down on top of his blankets. It was a clear night, the moon riding high and nearly full amid a spray of stars, and the breeze was comfortably cool after a brutal day of blazing sunlight.

Considering the last several nights of wakefulness, Ben should have dropped off immediately, but sleep eluded. He couldn't get Bobby off his mind. It had been a mistake to allow him on the Rio Largo raid. He should have called it quits as soon as his little brother showed up in San Angelo. Bobby was a gawkish kid with no experience save stocking shelves in his family's

161

store, burned to the ground along with several other businesses when a fire broke out in a livery several buildings down from the Hollister Emporium.

Fate had cast Bobby to the wild winds; their brothers-in-law had sent him to San Angelo, claiming they couldn't afford to be associated with the Hollister name. It had been a fluke the two brothers had met there on the banks of the Concho River, one lost and alone, the other embittered and looking for an excuse to leave his old ways behind. It could have been a perfect opportunity . . . but the Rio Largo job had already been set into motion, and Ben couldn't back out. Not at the last minute, and not on men like Mose and Henry and Ed, whom he'd ridden with for years.

The wagon springs creaked and Ben glanced around to see Hattie Wilkes crawling out of the back of the ambulance. The sight of her brought an unfamiliar ache to his chest, a sense of further loss he didn't fully understand. He watched as she started around the side of the wagon where the others were in their bedrolls, then paused before turning back. She came in his direction, and he cleared his throat to announce his presence, not wanting to alarm her. She stopped with a flinch, then came on.

"Mr. Hollister?"

Ben sat up. "Yes, ma'am?"

"I wasn't sure it was you."

"It is. I came out here to get away from the others."

"Do you wish to be alone?"

"No, ma'am, but I do like to keep my distance from Beeler as much as possible."

"I can't fault you for that." She came closer, as tentative as a deer. "Your brother seems to be sleeping."

"That's good news?" It was a question.

"Yes, I think it is. Sleep rather than unconsciousness." She

162

smiled. "If there's a difference."

"Seems like there should be."

"Mr. Hill's leg has taken an infection. I do fear for him."

"Did you try whiskey on the wound?"

"I did, but unfortunately not soon enough. If it continues to fester, I may have to lance the area to release the purulence."

Ben didn't have a reply for that, and after a while, Hattie shifted uncomfortably.

"I suppose I'd better go," she said. "I just wanted a bit of fresh air."

"You're welcome to sit a spell." He pulled the top blanket from his bedroll and handed it to her. She paused before accepting it, then folded it into a square and placed it on the ground several feet away before sitting down on top of it.

Ben tried to think of something to say, something that might atone for what he and his men had put her through, but nothing came to mind. He decided there was no justification for what they'd done, and the realization shamed him. Yet he didn't want her to go away. He liked that she had accepted his offer to sit, that she hadn't turned away from him as she had from the others.

He had thought about her often that day. Noticing the way she looked in her Yankee fatigues, with her auburn hair wind-tangled under her kepi, her expression haggard from the strain, seemed inappropriate under the circumstances. But there was something about her that drew him in. The depth of her brown eyes, the calm acceptance of her situation. And the way she'd volunteered herself in an effort to prevent the abduction of her friends. He'd known her barely twenty-four hours and could easily have believed she despised him for her predicament. Yet he sensed neither animosity nor concern in her nearness to him. He wondered if he would have felt this way if not for Bobby, and his own determination to give up outlawing. Was

Michael Zimmer

she merely a piece of an unrealistic dream, a desire for something he'd feared lost forever?

She had been looking away. Now she turned, and he noticed her smile in the moonlight. "Are you always so pensive, Mr. Hollister?"

"Why don't you call me Ben?" he replied, and her posture stiffened. "I'm sorry."

"No, it's all right." She stood and picked up the blanket and handed it to him, leaning slightly forward as if to not get too close.

"I meant what I said," he told her, accepting the blanket and dropping it to the ground at his side.

"About what?"

"About no harm coming to you or your friends."

She smiled again, an expression of sadness. "Is that really your decision to make?"

"If not mine, then whose?"

"Whoever stands up to you first, I suppose. Mr. Beeler, or the Indian, if he returns."

"They're still my men," Ben replied gruffly. He wanted to stand, to face her and make her believe he was man enough to back up his promise, but he sensed that if he so much as started to rise, she would flee back to the ambulance.

"Good night, Mr. Hollister," she said, and he swallowed hard against the melancholy that rose in his throat.

"Good night, Miss Wilkes."

Ben lay back to stare at the stars. It was a long time before he drifted into a restless slumber.

Ray's shrill cursing brought him scrambling from his blankets. Rising with gun in hand, Ben looked around wildly, but there was nothing to see other than desert, taking shape around them as the light of the new day grew stronger.

164

"What is it?" he demanded.

"It's that goddamned Mexican whore, is what it is," Ray yelled. "She's gone."

Ben turned a slow circle without spotting her. Over by a clump of greasewood where she and Fanny had slept he saw only red hair and a single lump under a blanket. But none of the horses were missing. "Maybe she needed some privacy," he suggested.

"Like hell," Ray growled. "She skittered."

"On foot?"

"Hell, she's Mex, Ben. She can probably outrun a mustang."

Ed threw back his blanket and stood up to scan the area, but Lucia was nowhere to be seen. He turned a questioning eye to Ben, who had lowered his revolver. "Where'd she go?"

"I couldn't say," he replied, although he no longer believed she'd gone into the scrub to relieve herself. He thought Ray was probably right that she'd taken off in the night, and tried to decide if it mattered.

"Good riddance," he said, and stooped to pick up his gun belt.

"Good riddance?" Ray echoed. "What the hell does that mean?"

"It means we don't need her," Ben said, returning the Smith and Wesson to its holster before strapping it around his waist.

"Is that it? That's all you got to say?"

Ben sat back down on his bedroll and straightened his socks before pulling on his boots. He didn't reply, even though Ray stood there glaring at him.

"Christ in a bucket," Ray finally exploded, stalking toward where the horses were tied. "If no one else is gonna take care of this, I'll do it myself."

"Leave her be," Ben called, and Ray spun around.

"Not this time, Hollister. This time you ain't givin' the orders."

Rising to his feet, Ben squared around to face him, his hand resting on the Smith's grips. "Yeah, I am," he returned quietly.

The others were awake now, Henry sitting with his back to the spokes of the Rucker's front wheel, Fanny bare-chested and cross-legged in her bed, the blankets heaped around her waist. Movement at the back of the ambulance and a darkness against the vehicle's shadowy interior announced Hattie's presence as well.

Ray stood as if turned to stone, save for his right hand, which trembled above his own revolver. Ben could see the rage burning in the gunman's eyes. He thought he should have been worried, possibly even afraid, considering Beeler's reputation, but he felt only weariness, a desire for it to be over.

"Ben," Henry said softly.

Neither Ben nor Ray looked around, but they both waited for the older man to continue.

"Ray's right this time, Ben," Henry said. He struggled to his feet, his injured arm shining wetly where it had started oozing blood again during the night. "If that gal goes back to Texas, she ain't likely to be a threat. But she's from these parts, and that means she might know where there are Federales stationed. If she takes a notion to go there and tell them what happened, letting her go could end up biting us in our asses."

Ray snorted. "I ain't worried about any damn Federales, old man."

"And I ain't worryin' about what worries you," Henry countered. "But I am fearful of what that Mexican gal might do." He was looking at Ben as he spoke. "Go get her, hoss. I'll keep a tight rein on this jackleg." He nodded toward Ray. "He won't bother the women, and if he tries it, I'll bust a cap on his butt."

"God almighty," Ray erupted. "What the hell's happened to this bunch? We used to be all of a same mind."

"Most of us still are," Henry replied calmly. "Now pull in your horns and let's get rolling. We're still too close to the Rio Grande to suit me."

Cautiously, Ben straightened and allowed his hand to fall away from the Smith and Wesson's grips. "What do you say, Ray? It's your call."

"All right," Ray breathed, and the fire died from his eyes. "Just make sure you bring her back."

"I'll bring her back," Ben said. "And while I'm gone, Henry's in charge. You savvy that?"

"Yeah, I savvy it. Now you savvy this. As soon as we reach Villa Lobos, I'm collectin' my share of the money, then I'm cuttin' my pin with this sorry outfit."

"What you do after we reach Villa Lobos will be your business," Ben agreed. "Until then, you do what Henry tells you to do. And stay away from the women."

Ray tensed as if to push it further, but Ben turned away and began rolling his blankets. When Ed went to fetch the mules, Henry walked to the rear of the ambulance and told Hattie to get down.

"You, too, girl," he called to Fanny. "Get some breakfast ready. Ray, fork your horse and bring in the loose stock."

"What the hell do we want with those army horses? They're still used up from yesterday."

"You just go get 'em. We'll decide what to do with them down the road." He looked at Ben. "You need anything, youngster?"

"A bite of food before I ride out."

"Get your horse ready," Henry told him. "I'll get you some grub to take with you."

Ben tightened the grulla's cinch, strapped his bedroll behind the cantle, and checked that his Winchester was firmly booted. Hattie came over as he was slipping the headstall over the gelding's ears and handed him a cotton sack.

"There are some biscuits and beef in there," she said. "I didn't know how long you'd be gone."

Ben hefted the sack experimentally. "This'll be enough. I should be back by tonight."

She hesitated, then looked out to where Ray Beeler was riding toward the horses they'd taken off of Sergeant Cade's men the day before. "Will he listen to Mr. McDaniels?" she asked.

"He'd damn well better."

"Is that supposed to reassure me . . . Ben?"

This time, he did flinch. Then he smiled and reached out to lightly touch her cheek with the back of his fingers. She shuddered slightly but didn't pull away. "He'll stay away," Ben said. "Henry's tough enough to handle him, and Ed will back him up if he has to. How's Bobby?"

"The same. He needs rest, and shelter from the heat. Yesterday was brutal for him and Mr. Hill both."

"There's nothing I can do, Hattie. They'll both have to hang on until we reach Villa Lobos."

"I know," she said, stepping back. "Be careful, Ben."

"I will," he promised, and climbed into his saddle. "I'll be back before you know it."

"I'll be watching for you," she replied, and when she smiled, it nearly took his breath away.

He reined his horse around and rode off at a swift trot, and had to fight the urge to look back.

CHAPTER FIFTEEN

Francisco Castile had to be dead. There was no other explanation. Had he not been killed—or worse, captured—José was certain he would have rejoined them by now.

Juan Carlos Cordova had survived, even though his company had been nearly annihilated in the Apache's ambush. Only five of his command had lived through the assault, and three of them were seriously wounded. Juan Carlos had come through yesterday's running battle only because he had been summoned to the front of the column by José minutes before the *Indios* launched their attack.

In a quick count that morning, as the light of a new day crept through *el Rocas Quebradas,* José had counted twenty-one men. Twenty-one, out of thirty-six. He held no illusions about what had become of those who had been captured. By now they were all dead; the lucky ones had been killed instantly.

Only Luis Huerta and his scouts remained unaccounted for. They had been sent back early yesterday to search for pursuit from Geronimo. It remained to be seen whether they would return today, or if they had also fallen to the Apaches.

José and Juan Carlos sat together, smoking corn husk *cigarillos* and talking quietly. Juan Carlos knew of the challenge one of his own had issued to José last night, but the subject had not come up in their conversation that morning. Watching his lieutenant's face, bewhiskered and streaked with spent powder, scarred over the years by knuckle and knife, José wondered

169

what Juan Carlo's reaction would be if Benito Reyes bested José that morning. Would he smile and take command of *el Caza-dores de los Médanos*—José's Hunters of the Dunes? Or would he order Benito executed and insist on an election to democrati-cally choose their next leader? Not that it would come to that. José had no intention of losing to a hulking brute like Reyes. But it would have been interesting to know how his old comrade felt.

"We will wait until midmorning," José finally stated, coming to a decision on a matter he and Juan Carlos had debated for some minutes—whether to pull out immediately, in case the Apaches were still following them, or wait awhile longer in case others were still making their way to the Rocks.

Juan Carlos was not pleased with the decision. He had seemed moody and distant all morning. But he didn't argue. Rising, he said, "I will have what food is left prepared for breakfast."

José nodded and stood. There would not be much. Juan Carlos's men had been in charge of the pack mules when the shooting started. Nearly a half-dozen animals carrying plun-dered items, merchandise traded from Geronimo, and the sup-plies his men needed for their return to Villa Lobos had been lost. Without the mules they had no skillets, no coffee or flour or extra tobacco; only what the men carried on their saddles or in their pockets.

The long-haired Mimbreño squaw and two children had also been lost, abducted by their attackers, although José did not mourn them as much as he did the supplies. He had found that hostages were always difficult to keep alive until they could be sold, especially the females. It was the missing food and other items that presented him with a dilemma.

With his thoughts thus occupied, José watched absently as Juan Carlos made his way across the small basin where the Hunters were gathered. But when he saw his lieutenant and the hulking Reyes exchange a glance and a nod, his head snapped up. Had that been merely an acknowledgment of one another? Or was it a signal between the two?

José studied Benito through narrowed lids. He was standing alone near the same boulder from which he had issued his challenge last night. José thought he looked nervous but determined, and he turned his gaze to where Juan Carlos had come to a stop near the remnants of his command. There was no concern in Juan Carlos's expression, just a flat expectancy, and a chill wormed its way up José's spine. Grimly, he dropped his right hand to the revolver on that hip and started across the tiny basin.

"You are still here, Benito," he called while still some distance away.

"Where would I go?"

"Maybe into the rocks to find a hole to crawl into."

"I am not a coward, José."

"Then you have not reconsidered since you so foolishly opened your mouth last night? I am saddened, Benito, but you must learn that I am your *capitán,* not your friend. I will be addressed as such."

Taking a deep breath, Benito pushed away from the stone's sloping shoulder. "A *capitán,* a true leader, would not have led his men into such a trap as you did yesterday. My brother is dead, José, and so is his son, my nephew. Yet here you stand, alive and untouched, demanding the same respect I would offer willingly to any skilled commander."

José was aware of the others watching and waiting, a hunger in their eyes born of grief. They wanted revenge for yesterday's losses, and far too many of them would not care who suffered the consequences . . . just as long as someone did.

It was to be expected, and José's lips curled back in an ugly grin. "I am growing weary of this conversation, cur. Last night

171

you made it clear to me, to all of us, that we would decide this morning who would lead my Hunters. I am here now to answer that question."

Benito's eyes darted past José to where the others had paused in their morning routines. One of those men, José knew, was Juan Carlos Cordova, and he felt a deep regret for the lieutenant's betrayal. A silence settled over the Rocks. After a moment, Benito raised a hand to wipe it across his shirt front, as if to dry the sweat gathered on his palm.

José's smile widened at this tiny act of submission. "Now, Benito," he said, and palmed the revolver from his right-side holster.

Benito also reached for his weapon, but doubt slowed his reaction. The muzzle had barely cleared leather when José's first slug drove deep into his torso, just below his sternum. Benito grunted loudly and his pistol seemed to spin from his fingers as if yanked by some unseen force. He leaned forward and his hand came up to press against the spreading red blossom on his shirt.

Benito's eyes expressed his disbelief, and José nodded in satisfaction. He had seen that look before, and knew its outcome. He turned a slow circle, but no one stepped forward to pick up the challenge. José's gaze settled on Juan Carlos, but the *teniente* made no move, spoke no word, and after a long moment José sought out one of the few men he still trusted.

"Antonio."

Antonio Carrillo took a step forward. "*Sí, mi capitán?*"

"This man," he motioned toward Reyes, "will no longer need his weapons. Take them and distribute them to whoever has use for another gun. His horse and whatever else he has we will take with us to Villa Lobos to distribute among the needy."

"He has a wife, *mi capitán.*"

José shrugged. "She is of no concern. Perhaps in the future

172

she will choose her husbands with more care."

"She did not choose Benito," Javier Diaz spoke up. "Benito took her, after shooting her first husband."

"Ah, yes, I had forgotten." He nodded. "Then it is fitting that she receive what little this dog has to offer. Antonio, you will see that my wishes are carried out."

"*Sí,*" Antonio responded without hesitation, already striding purposefully toward where Benito still stood next to the boulder where he had spent the night, his head lowered as he stared dully at the blood seeping through his fingers.

"But not his guns," José amended loudly. "Or his horse. Whatever you find in his saddlebags belongs to his woman, but his weapons and that pretty palomino will remain with the Hunters."

He turned to Juan Carlos, standing silently among what was left of his command. Juan Carlos returned the look without expression, just a hard flatness in his eyes, a taut compression to his lips. José wondered if there was any gratitude for his captain's survival beneath the lieutenant's scarred mien. Or was it only disappointment?

Owen Plunkett pulled his mare's head from the stream and led her back to dry ground. He could feel Cade's gaze following him, and knew the sergeant wanted to talk. Owen didn't. The truth was, he didn't give a damn how the army had gotten sucked into Ben Hollister's web, but he had no intention of allowing Cade's problems to interfere with his pursuit of the gang. Then he sighed in annoyance, because what a man wanted and what he sometimes had to do to honor his responsibilities and keep his self-respect were two vastly different arenas.

Dropping his mare's reins to the ground, Owen walked over to where the stubby Yankee sergeant was still pulling threads from the chevrons on his shirt.

"You reckon we need to talk, Cade?"

"Probably wouldn't hurt," the sergeant agreed, lowering his shirt.

"The name's Owen Plunkett. I'm the law in Rio Largo, and a deputy sheriff for El Paso County, although my office is in Largo and I serve as the city marshal there when it's needed. Most folks call me sheriff." He paused. "You've heard of Rio Largo, haven't you?"

"Some. There was supposed to be a big horse race there, if I remember right."

"Quarter-mile championships," Owen confirmed. "Should've gone off a couple of days ago."

"But you were robbed, instead."

"You know about that?"

"I know a man named Hollister and his boys rode into my camp night before last and stole my horses, guns, and some . . . guests we were escorting back to El Paso."

Owen allowed a smile to slope across his lips. He enjoyed the slight reddening of the sergeant's face, and figured it must be galling for him to admit his patrol had been waylaid by the Hollister bunch. Then Cade went on, and Owen's smile vanished.

"I hear they treed you and your town, as well."

"They got the drop on us, that's true, but they didn't steal our horses and guns."

"We'll get 'em," Cade said.

"You intend to keep runnin' after them like a bunch of yapping pups? Yeah, your corporal told me about that little Comanche trick, trotting alongside your mules. I admire your pluck, Sergeant, but it ain't a pace you can keep up." He glanced at the patrol's solitary mule, drying in the sun after its cooling trip into the Rio Grande's waters. "Your mule's fagged to rawhide, Cade, and in case you ain't noticed," he jerked a thumb

over his shoulder, toward the river, "that's Mexico over there."
His gaze dropped to the shirt in the sergeant's hands. "But I
guess you ain't gonna let that stop you, huh?"

"No, I'm not. What about you, Plunkett? Your jurisdiction
ends at the river, same as mine."

"Let's just say I got a personal investment in bringing
Hollister back."

"So do I."

"Then you're going after him?"

"I am," Cade confirmed. "You?"

Owen nodded. "Just as soon as I whittle some of the deadfall
from my posse."

"We could go together," Cade suggested. "Especially if you're
sending some of your men back. We need horses and guns, and
you can supply them."

"No, I can't," Owen returned flatly. "These men will need
their horses to get home. If we were back in Largo, I could loan
you some of the county's rifles and shotguns, and maybe talk
one of the local merchants into supplying the rest, but I won't
order these men to give up their arms out here. There are
bandits, outlaws, and renegades roaming all up and down this
river. You know that as well as I do."

Cade took a deep breath, then nodded crisply, and Owen
knew the conversation had reached its conclusion.

"I wish you luck, Sergeant, but if I was to offer advice, it
would be that you and your men hike back to the nearest army
post and let the commander there know what happened."

"I'll wish you luck, as well," Cade said, then returned to
removing the stripes from his shirt.

Owen walked over to where his posse was scattered along the
river's shore. They watched his approach curiously, anxious to
hear what he had in mind. Owen knew the majority of them
wanted to go back to Rio Largo, probably as much as he wanted

them to. He suspected the drovers had also given up on the thought of attaining any kind of glory by trailing the Hollister gang into submission. They were a young and reckless lot, but they had jobs to get back to, too. That left Bill Rowland, Simon Butler, and old Pete Maddox, men he'd trust with his life, and knew he might well have to after they crossed the Rio Grande.

Owen's gaze settled on Cy Rogers and Tom Holden, pegging them as spokesmen for the townspeople. "You boys go on home. You drovers, too. I appreciate all of you volunteerin', but I don't need you no more. Bill and Simon and Pete and me'll go it alone from here."

Surprised registered on Cy Rogers's face. "You mean you intend to follow Hollister into Mexico?"

"That's what I mean."

"You'll have no authority over there," Tom Holden said.

Owen lightly tapped the side of his holster. "I'll have enough," he said, and Pete Maddox chuckled and looked at Tom to see what he had to say about that.

But Holden, Rogers, and the others—even the drovers—seemed content with Owen's decision.

"Good luck," Tom said, before hauling his flabby bulk into the saddle and kicking his mount away from the river.

Cy and the others followed silently. Cy looked angry, as if anticipating what the town might think when he returned empty-handed while the posse's oldest members continued on. A couple of the cowhands also looked subdued, like they were embarrassed to be quitting in the middle of the job, but Owen felt no ill will toward the drovers. This had never been their fight. The townsmen were a different story, but Owen wasn't sure yet what he felt toward them. He'd need to ponder it when he got back.

Gathering his mare's reins, Owen stepped into the saddle and rode over to where his remaining posse waited. Forcing a grin, he said, "You old-timers reckon you're up to treeing the Hollister gang?"

All three laughed, and Pete added, "Let's get 'em roped, Owen. My woman had a pot of beans started before we left. I'd like to get home in time to help her eat what's left."

Frank Poe came over just as Cade finished removing the second chevron from his shirt. The fabric where the stripes had been was a deep blue, revealing how much the desert sun had faded the shirt in just the three weeks since he'd purchased it new at Fort Bliss.

Cade dropped the chevron atop the sloping driftwood and pulled the shirt on over his head. Down by the river the posse was breaking apart, the bulk of it turning toward the rugged hills they'd just crossed, on their way home. Only the sheriff and a trio of older men lingered, and Cade's eye told him they were all experienced manhunters, despite their advanced years. He nodded his approval. He'd heard of Owen Plunkett. Back in the day they said he'd been as tough as they came, afraid of no one. He still looked like he could handle himself. Cade figured he was wise to cut himself loose from the others.

"We could take those horses," Poe said quietly, inclining his head toward the retreating townsmen and drovers. "I don't suppose they'd put up much of a fight."

"Probably not, but I figure we'll be in enough trouble when we get back without adding theft to our woes."

"Having decent horses and good guns might help us get back."

Cade glanced at him with an amused glint in his eye. "You sure some of Hollister ain't rubbed off on you, Frank?"

"I want that son of a bitch and his bunch of cutthroats to pay for what they did, and I especially want to see that little half-breed bastard dangling from a hangman's noose."

177

Cade's smile faded. "We're not going after them for revenge. We're going after them to fetch those women back to El Paso. Whatever happens after that is just gravy on biscuits, as far as I'm concerned."

"We'll have to catch them first."

"We're not stealing anyone's horses or guns to do it, so put a cork in that wish and call it good."

After a long hesitation, Poe nodded and started to walk away, but Cade summoned him back.

"What happened out there?"

"With the 'breed?"

"Yeah."

Poe shrugged. "I went after him."

"Without permission."

"I was on my own. I did what I felt was best."

"Since you haven't said anything, I figure he got away."

"Yeah, he got away. We played cat and mouse all over those hills. He was trying to lure me into a trap, but I wouldn't fall for it. Finally it got dark and I guess he took off. I tried easing up on where I'd last seen him and waited for dawn, but he wasn't around when it got light."

"Damnit, Frank, he was armed with a carbine, and all you had was a revolver. It's a wonder you weren't shot."

"He tried, but he isn't as slick as he thinks he is."

"That doesn't change anything," Cade said, frustrated by the risks his corporal had taken. "You'd better start using your head, or you're liable to lose it somewhere out there to a Spencer's bullet."

Poe was glaring now, and his voice rose until the rest of the troopers and even some of Plunkett's dismissed posse members took notice. "We're going to lose them if we don't find some horses and guns, and you're letting everything we need just ride away."

Cade's gaze narrowed, and Poe shook his head and looked away.

"Why don't you go down to the river and cool off," Cade said quietly. "We'll cross in a few minutes."

Glancing at Cade's chevrons, sitting atop the driftwood, he said, "Do you want me to take my stripes off, too?"

"Have Elkins do it while you're soaking."

Poe nodded and moved off. Cade watched Owen Plunkett and his three remaining posse men enter the Rio Grande. He took note of where the bottom seemed to drop out from under their horses, making them swim for several yards before they found solid footing again, surging out the far side of the river streaming water. On shore they stopped long enough to pull on their boots, which they'd tied around their necks, along with cartridge belts and firearms. Then they mounted and rode away, heading straight west into the desert as if the lawman already knew where he'd find Ben Hollister and his gang.

Chapter Sixteen

José Yanez waited until midday, rather than midmorning, before reluctantly ordering his Hunters away from *el Rocas Quebradas*. As they filed out of the small central basin where they had regrouped, he wasted but a single, contemptuous glance on Benito Reyes. Benito was still breathing, but the effort to draw air into his slowly collapsing lungs was growing more difficult as the day wore on. If the bullet high in his gut didn't soon kill him, the hammering rays of the early summer sun would.

Benito sat naked and sweating in full view of the departing column, his guns and clothing stripped from his massive frame at José's orders. He stirred briefly as the sound of passing hooves penetrated the haze of his suffering. Raising his head, he fixed José with a murderous stare, but José only grinned before flashing the dying man an obscene gesture. Then he jabbed the buckskin's ribs with the rowels of his spurs and loped up to where his scouts—Luis Huerta and his three had returned shortly after dawn, surprising them all—rode in advance of the battered company.

"What do you think, *amigo*?" José asked the younger man. "Have the Apaches returned to their wickiups, or do they still follow us?"

After a pause, Luis said, "I did not mention this earlier because there were other ears nearby, but we found the site of yesterday's fight, and what was left of *Teniente* Cordova's men."

José's expression turned wary. "And what did you find?"

"What you would expect of Apache prisoners, although I believe the Blessed Virgin must have been watching over them. *El Indios* were in a hurry, and spent only moments at their torture."

"And what caused this great hurry that pulled the Apaches away from their pleasure?"

"Nothing that I could identify." He looked at José. "You need to remember, *mi capitán*, that you control a large command of experienced fighters. Perhaps it was your return that the Apaches feared."

Luis's assessment brought a scowl to José's face. He hadn't considered a counterattack, and the thought of what they might have seized—scalps, horses, weapons—soured his mood.

"What of the woman and children?" he asked.

"The long-haired woman and the children were freed by the Apaches. Even now they are fleeing north to join Geronimo."

That news brought a relieved smile to José's face. "Good, then the danger has passed."

Luis shrugged, and José chuckled.

"You are right, my friend. For us, danger is never far away. But it is still good that we are no longer followed, and that these Apaches will take word of our victory to the thief, Geronimo."

"Is that something to wish for?" Luis asked doubtfully.

"What, are you afraid of that coward?" José laughed, his mood soaring. "Ride ahead with your scouts, Luis, and use your hawk's eyes to watch for fresh prey. We may yet return home as heroes."

Thinking he would locate the runaway without much effort, Ben Hollister kept his horse to an easy lope as he backtracked toward San Ignacio. It wasn't until he'd dropped down off the mesa into the bleakness of the valley floor that he began to doubt that assumption. After several more miles, he pulled up and stepped down to examine the roadbed. Their tracks from the day before—horses and wagon—were easily discernible in the thin layer of dust covering the hardpan, but Lucia Mendoza's footprints were nowhere to be seen.

Lifting his gaze to a horizon furred over with endless scrub, Ben uttered a hollow curse. He should have known better. Lucia was smart. She wouldn't have counted on darkness alone to elude her captors. She'd utilize her own cunning to exploit the scant desert cover. And, too late, he reminded himself that she had grown up in this country and probably knew it intimately. Ben should have taken all that into consideration before leaving their camp atop the mesa. He should have sorted out her trail there, then stuck to it like a hound to the scent.

She could be anywhere out there. A dozen miles away by now. Or close enough to chuck a rock at his head. There was no way of knowing, and suddenly, Ben decided he didn't care. Lucia had been right when she accused him of being a liar as well as a thief. He'd promised to let them go once they reached Mexico, then hadn't thought twice about recanting that pledge. Well, the hell with her, he thought. And with an unexpected smile, Ben gathered his reins and stepped into the saddle, reining back toward the mesa where Hattie Wilkes waited, watching over Bobby.

By midafternoon the sun was hammering at them like clubs in the hands of a maniac. Cade walked up front with the Springfield held ready in both hands, unsure of what to expect on this side of the border, where Federales and rurales were the authorities and he and his men were intruders.

Elkins followed leading Roman, the mule's saddle empty save for the canteens they'd filled at the Rio Grande. Poe, Morgan, and Riley brought up the rear. They were making their way north, following the Rucker's tracks along a rutted trail running parallel to the river.

Cade found Hollister's line of travel baffling. He'd anticipated the outlaw plunging straight into the state of Chihuahua once they crossed the river, putting as much distance as possible between himself and his pursuers. Even assuming that neither Plunkett's posse nor Cade and his men would cross into Mexico, this vaguely northward course seemed inconsistent with what he knew of the outlaw's character. It was keeping his men too close to the border, too vulnerable to U.S. patrols making a lightning raid into Mexico to snatch the outlaws back into the states.

It wasn't something a smart man would do, and for all of Hollister's flaws, Cade knew stupidity wasn't one of them. There had to be a reason Ben was taking his men along this route, and the likeliest of them was his little brother. Nothing else made sense. There had to be a town somewhere up ahead, and a physician to look after the wounded. If that was Hollister's plan, the gang would have to hole up there, at least for a while. And with any luck, that was where Cade and his troopers would catch up.

But there was another piece of the puzzle that nagged at him. Why had Plunkett and his men taken off across the desert when the ambulance's tracks clearly led north along the Rio Grande? It seemed obvious to Cade that the old lawman knew this country intimately. Certainly better than Cade or Hollister did. Plunkett had a plan, which meant there was another destination somewhere to the southwest, and a reason Hollister would have to take his men in that direction.

Once again, Cade's thoughts returned to the wounded men, and Bobby in particular. That had to be it. Wherever the Rucker's tracks were bound for now, Plunkett knew they wouldn't find any medical help there, and that eventually the outlaws would have to turn inland, away from the river. And somewhere along that line, Plunkett intended to cut them off.

Cade briefly considered altering his own direction, but just as quickly dismissed the idea. He had no real assurance that Plunkett had a plan to intercept the Hollister gang, and no idea what he and his men might face if they tried marching into the heart of the vast Chihuahuan desert. He was pretty sure of what they wouldn't find, though, and glanced over his shoulder at the canteens hanging from Roman's saddle. No, they were better off sticking to the Rucker's trail. It might be slower, but he thought it was wiser. And it was possible that wherever Hollister was striking for now might have horses, guns, and ammunition that they could purchase.

"Sergeant!"

Cade stopped and turned. "What is it?"

"Over there," Morgan replied.

Sighting along the path of the trooper's extended arm, Cade spotted a lone figure struggling through the brush toward them.

"Where?" Riley asked, squinting.

"About a mile out," Elkins said. "Where that chaparral comes to a point."

"Aye, I see 'im now," Riley murmured.

"Good eye, Morgan," Cade said.

"He looks about done in, don't he?" Riley observed, then leaned forward as if those few extra inches might make a difference. "Damn me, boys, if I don't think yon bogger's a soldier of our own makin'."

"A soldier?" Cade narrowed his eyes in the blinding light. "Are you sure?"

"I believe so, Sergeant."

"Looks like it to me, too," Poe said.

"Wait here." Cade slipped the reins from Elkins's hand and stepped into the saddle. "Keep a sharp watch," he warned. "He could be a Federale."

"Or a deserter," Poe added.

184

Cade reined toward the distant figure. He wasn't expecting a trap, from either Federales or deserters, but he was a cautious man. It was how he'd made sergeant, and why he was still alive today.

He kept the mule to a walk as he wound through creosote, rambling patches of cactus, and stunted mesquite. The Springfield was butted to his thigh, his thumb curved firmly over the hammer, index finger on the trigger. Within half a mile he recognized the deep blue of a Union uniform, but it wasn't until he was within a few hundred yards that he realized who was wearing it. With a startled curse, he drove his heels into Roman's sides, and the mule took off at a shuffling trot—the best Cade could get out of the animal after yesterday's long trek across the desert.

The figure stopped and started to turn away as if to flee, then came back around to stare silently. Then she waved, and Cade breathed, *"Lucia!"*

The mule slowed of its own accord as they drew near, and Cade reined up and swung to the ground. Loosening a canteen from the McClellan's saddle, he rushed forward as the woman's knees buckled and she dropped to the ground.

"Lucia," Cade said, dropping down beside her and yanking the cork from the canteen's mouth.

"Andrew," she said in a husky voice, like a deep exhalation. "I thought for a minute you were Hollister . . . or an Apache."

"Drink," he ordered, and raised the canteen to her cracked lips. After several long swallows, he took it away. "How long have you been out here?"

"I slipped away last night, but I've been running all day."

"Where are the others?"

She made a vague motion behind her, toward a low mesa far to the southwest.

"There," she whispered, then reached for the canteen. He allowed her three more deep swigs, then lifted it from her grasp.

"More," she demanded.

"In a bit." He tugged the bandanna from around his neck and poured water over it, then used it to brush her forehead. Soaking it again, he ran the cloth around the back of her neck, then down the front of her chest where she'd loosened the buttons on her tunic.

"How do you soldiers stand a uniform in this weather?"

"We get used to it."

She made a sound that he took for laughter. "No wonder the Apaches are running circles around the army. If Geronimo dressed like this, he'd collapse before a soldier's bullet ever reached him."

"I'll bring that up to the colonel the next time I see him," Cade promised, and they both laughed. He poured more water over her face and upper chest, straight from the canteen.

"Maybe I'm not going to die, after all," she murmured.

"Did you think you were?"

"I was starting to think I might." Then her brows furrowed. "What are you doing in Mexico?"

"My orders were to escort you and the other women to El Paso. I'm following orders."

Smiling, Lucia said, "You are full of shit, Andrew Cade, but I am so very glad to see you."

"I'm glad to see you," he replied, then blinked at the unanticipated words.

Lucia chuckled. "It doesn't hurt, Sergeant."

"What doesn't hurt?"

"Letting in a few feelings."

Cade glanced over his shoulder to where his men were patiently waiting. He cleared his throat, and she laughed again. He brought his gaze back to hers with a conceding smile.

"Can you ride?" he asked.

"I can do anything you need me to do," she said, staring straight into his eyes, and this time he didn't look away.

Cade helped her stand, then steadied her as they walked to Roman's side. Lucia had to try twice to get her foot in the stirrup. Then she looked at Cade and said, "You're going to have to put your hand under my butt and give me a boost. Do you think you can handle that, Sergeant?"

"I can handle whatever you need me to," he replied, and felt immediately foolish.

Hanging onto the pommel with her left hand and the cantle with her right, she said, "Push, Sergeant," and he shoved up with his palm on her buttocks. Mounted, she looked down with a teasing grin. "That wasn't so bad, was it?"

"No, it wasn't," he agreed. "In fact, I could probably get used to it real quick."

Her smile fading, Lucia said, "So could I, soldier boy." Then she pulled the mule around and started for the road.

Cade watched a moment, admiring the way the trousers fit her thighs and accentuated her calves, and especially the way she swayed so lithely in the saddle, then wondered what he was thinking. He was a soldier, and she . . .

Shaking the thought from his head, he propped the Springfield over his shoulder like a clunky fishing pole and followed Lucia back to where his men were gathered on the wagon track. Riley cheered as soon as he saw who it was, and Morgan and Elkins had big grins plastered across their faces. Even Poe looked mildly pleased.

As Cade walked up, Riley said, " 'Tis amazin' what a stout wind can blow in, ain't it, Sergeant?"

"It is, for a fact," Cade agreed, then took hold of the mule's near-side rein near the bit. "You said the others were behind you?"

"Yes, up there." She pointed southwest, toward the mesa

187

Cade had noticed earlier.

"How far?"

"From here, maybe twelve miles. But they won't be there now."

"Jaysus," Riley breathed. "Ye been hikin all that way? 'Tis a wonder ye ain't still out there, croakin' ye last."

"I walked farther than that," she said. "I went straight east, into the desert, before circling back to the north. I knew Hollister would follow me as soon as it was light enough, and I didn't want my trail to lead straight back to San Ignacio."

"What's San Ignacio?" Cade queried.

She indicated the rutted path they had been following ever since crossing the Rio Grande. "The town where I grew up isn't far ahead. Another hour, at most."

"Can we get some horses there?" Poe asked.

"No," she replied without hesitation, then looked at Cade. "The town was nearly destroyed in an Apache raid many years ago. There are still a few people living there, and I think I know who they are, but I don't think they will have any horses to spare, if they have any at all."

"What about guns?"

"There might be a few, mostly muskets and old pistols. We were a poor people, and bandits have kept us that way."

"You said you know them?"

"I think so. A woman named Anna Gonzales and her son, who is . . . damaged, after nearly drowning in the river. There may be others."

"If there aren't any horses in the village, what about nearby ranches?" Poe continued stubbornly.

"At one time there was a small ranchero a half day's ride west of the village, and a mining camp north of that, but I don't know if either are still there."

"The woman, Anna, would she know?" Cade asked.

"Yes. If it was her smoke I smelled last night, she would know."

"Then let's go find out," Cade said resolutely, letting go of the mule's rein.

It was a long hour's hike into the battered shell that had once been San Ignacio. By the time they arrived, their feet were dragging, scooping up clouds of dust and dispersing it to either side like the wake from the bow of a ship. Their view of the town did nothing to lift their sagging spirits. Most of the buildings had been abandoned for years, their adobe walls crumbling above the windows where the flames set by Apache marauders had weakened the outer layer. Cade estimated that at one time there might have been a hundred or more residents living here. Now he would have guessed it deserted, but Lucia disagreed.

"They are here," she assured him, her head swiveling as if sensing out the hidden locations of the citizens. Standing in her stirrups, she shouted in Spanish, her words echoing between the empty buildings. Cade followed it roughly, his command of the language tenuous at best, picked up from Mexican packers, Apache scouts, and frontier cantinas. After a pause, she repeated it in English. "I am Lucia Mendoza, the daughter of Edwardo and Rosa Mendoza. These men are not here to steal or destroy. We wish only to purchase a few supplies. We have money." She glanced quickly at Cade, who nodded affirmation. "Coins that can be used here or in Texas."

She dismounted and handed the reins to Elkins.

"Wait for me," she said, and started down the street.

Cade watched her disappear around a curve in the gently winding street, then motioned to his men.

"Let's find some shade," he said, and led them to the side of what must have once been a cantina, the faded images of liquor—mugs of beer and bottles of mescal—remaining above the entrance for those who couldn't read. Riley went inside but was back within minutes, his disappointment obvious.

"Not even a drop of the devil's brew."

"What's the matter, Riley?" Morgan asked. "Isn't it already hot enough without pouring whiskey down your throat?"

" 'Tis a warm day, to be sure, but a swallow or two of beer'd help me forget the heat."

"I could've used a beer, too," Elkins said dolefully.

"Why don't you two unsaddle that mule and rub him down if you're needing something to occupy your time?" Cade said.

Riley groaned, but it was his only protest as he walked over to help Elkins with the mule.

Poe and Morgan made themselves as comfortable as they could with their backs to the cantina's front wall. Cade paced impatiently. He kept eyeing the buildings within sight. Although the raid had happened years before, its essence lingered—the wailing of women and children, the screams of dying men—as if absorbed into the bullet-pocked adobe walls.

It was a long time before Lucia returned. The shadow of the cantina had stretched most of the way across the street before Cade spotted her striding swiftly toward them.

"Damn me, boys, but she's lookin' like a woman again," Riley commented as he struggled to his feet.

Lucia was dressed in the simple garb of a Mexican woman from a poor village. She wore a brown skirt tied off at the waist, a loose-fitting top with sleeves that came down only as far as her elbows, and a shallow neckline. The flat-soled leather *zapatos* on her feet looked more like moccasins than shoes. There was a belt at her waist, a sheath carrying a slim, long-bladed knife, and a smaller pouch opposite it that Cade figured held the necessities of a desert-bred woman—flint and steel, a little charred cloth to start a fire, maybe a needle and some thread. A *rebozo* in subtle reds and yellows against a black background was draped over her shoulders; later, when the temperature dropped with the sun, she could pull it up over her head like a scarf and wrap the ends around her neck and over her shoulders for warmth.

Her gaze was fixed almost challengingly on Cade as she approached, but he had no idea what could have sparked her defiance. He liked the dress, though, and wondered if he should tell her so. Not now, but later, when they had a moment alone.

"What did you find out?" he asked as she stalked into the cantina's shade.

"It is not as I was beginning to fear," she replied. "There are more people here than I thought there would be."

"What about horses and guns?" That was from Poe.

"A few horses, maybe some guns, too, if you can pay for them. But they won't take vouchers or script, only gold and silver."

Cade considered their options and knew they were few. He'd left the troop train with a single double eagle in his pocket, along with the authority to write a voucher in case they needed something between Alto Station and Fort Bliss. He figured twenty dollars would go a long way in a village like this, where the people were poor, but he knew horses and guns would come at a steep price.

"Frank," he said, turning to Poe. "How much cash are you carrying? The rest of you, too. I'll need it all." He dug the double eagle from his pocket, then took off his hat and dropped the coin inside before passing it on to Poe. When it was all tallied, they had thirty-one dollars and a few pennies. He looked at Lucia and gave her the count. "Will that be enough?"

She smiled. "Yes. For what is available, that will be enough. Follow me."

She led them to the far side of town, then down an alley to a small pen and lean-to shed in back. A dozen or more men and twice that many women and children were waiting there for them.

"These are the people of San Ignacio," Lucia said. "The woman with the red *rebozo* is Anna Gonzales, my mother's sister. The man with the large mustache is Hector Martinez. The village has no official leader, but the people look to Hector when guidance is needed. These people, my people, have survived here by leaving the main street as the Apaches left it. They have built their homes in the brush, where they won't be easily discovered."

Scowling, Cade said, "I doubt if that'd fool an Apache."

"I know that, and they know it as well. But they also believe it sends a message, and so far the Apaches and bandits have left them alone. That is all they want, to be left alone to live their lives. To raise their children and their crops, and to pray to the Blessed Virgin for rain." She looked at him, her eyes sad. "There is never enough of anything in San Ignacio, but rain is what they desire most."

Cade nodded and thought it sounded like a pretty good life. Not a soldier's life, but an honorable one.

"Where are the horses and guns?"

"Where is your money, Sergeant?"

Cade handed her his hat and she took it to Martinez. They spoke quietly for several minutes, and from time to time the old man would look their way, but his weathered face remained impassive. Finally, Lucia motioned him over.

"They have two horses and two mules. One of your soldiers will have to ride double."

"No, that'll work. We'll have five with Roman."

"Your mule is tired, Andrew, and I am light. I will ride Roman."

"I can't allow that."

"Either I go with you, or there will be no trade. Hector and I have already discussed this."

"Hector isn't giving the orders here," Cade said firmly.

"Then, Sergeant," Lucia replied with feigned sweetness and a brittle smile, "you may go to hell and see how many horses the devil will sell to you and your men."

"We're not going out there on a lark, Miss Mendoza," Cade replied.

"*Miss* Mendoza?" she mocked him. "Let me tell you something, Sergeant, I know exactly where we are going. I've lived here, and I know this land. But more importantly, I know where Hollister is going. Do you?"

Cade hesitated. He'd thought earlier he had a pretty good idea, considering the direction Plunkett and his men had taken after crossing the Rio Grande, but the truth was he had no inkling where the Rio Largo lawman might be headed. Or Hollister, for that matter.

"I am capable, Andrew," Lucia said quietly. "And I promise you, I will be more of a help than a hindrance."

Speaking from the other side of the small pen, Morgan said, "She speaks Spanish, too, Sergeant."

Cade swung around to peg Morgan with a warning glare. "I don't need your help here, Trooper."

Morgan shrugged and Riley patted him on the back, raising a small cloud of dust that puffed up above his shoulders.

Cade turned back to Lucia. The others, he noticed, and Hector in particular, were watching the exchange between them silently, although not without judgment. Cade wondered if any of them spoke English. As much as it aggravated him to admit it, he figured it couldn't hurt to have someone along who knew the language and the culture.

"It looks like you have me over a barrel, Miss Mendoza," he allowed stiffly.

"Then I will come with you?"

"If that's what I have to do to outfit my men, but we'll also need saddles and ammunition, food and blankets."

She looked momentarily concerned. "Don't be too hard to deal with, Andrew. These people are poor. They will trade honestly, but they have little to spare, and won't barter their future for a few coins."

"I'm not looking to cheat anyone. I just want to get you, Hattie, and Fanny O'Shea back to the States."

"As do I."

"Then we agree?"

"Yes, we agree." Then her smile returned. "On one final condition."

Cade felt the tension flow out of his shoulders. "That I call you Lucia?"

"No," she replied, appearing startled by his assumption. "That I also get a gun, and that when the shooting starts, I will be there to put a bullet through Ray Beeler's heart."

CHAPTER SEVENTEEN

Ben took his time returning to where they'd spent the night. He was worried about Bobby and looked forward to seeing Hattie again, but he was also happy to be on his own for a while. Ed's sour disposition and Ray's cockiness that was like a thorn between his toes, even Henry's woeful expressions, had become a drain on his soul. He liked them—or at least he liked Ed and Henry—but it was nice to enjoy the countryside in solitude, despite its heat and desolation. This wasn't farmland, and it probably wouldn't provide much graze for ranching, but there was a certain beauty in its harshness, a prickliness he understood. It was a land that would never be truly conquered. You either lived with it or it killed you, and he liked that.

He wondered what Hattie thought of the land. Not here, but somewhere with better grass and good water, a place to settle down and make a home. Not that it mattered. He was fooling himself to think there could ever be anything between them. Still, the thought of starting over, of building something fresh and clean for himself and Bobby—it spoke to something he sensed had been missing in his life.

He studied the thin line of vegetation marking the course of the Rio Grande, nearly lost in the haze of distance. In between lay rocky ground and scrub, rattlesnakes and scorpions. He wondered if Lucia Mendoza had made good her escape. A part of him hoped she had. Her value as a hostage—if she'd ever had any to begin with—had been deflated by their arrival in Mexico.

Her absence was one less concern he'd have to deal with once they reached Villa Lobos.

He was looking forward to that. A few more days and then, whether Little Fish had caught up by then or not, they'd split the money and go their separate ways.

Riding along loose and easy, Ben began to whisper the lyrics to a song they'd sung early in the war, before the Yankees' pounding began to take its toll.

We are a band of brothers, and native to the soil,
Fighting for the property, we gained by honest toil;
And when our rights were threatened, the cry rose
      near and far,
Hurrah! for the Bonnie Blue Flag that bears a single
      star.

Then far ahead and to the north he spotted a vulture circling on an updraft, and his throat went suddenly dry, and the song wilted in his throat.

José watched the last of the floating vultures—specks recognized only by the pattern of their flight—begin its long glide toward *el Rocas Quebradas,* half a day's ride behind them. Envisioning the birds' meal brought a grim smile of satisfaction to his lips. He wondered if Benito Reyes was dead yet, or if the sorry scavengers had begun their feast on a live carcass.

At his side, Juan Carlos said, "He is dead now."

"It doesn't matter. I hope he is alive, so that he can feel their beaks tearing at his flesh."

José was aware of his lieutenant's puzzled surveillance. He knew the man didn't understand the animosity that burned in his gut. Nor did Juan Carlos recognize the simmering distrust that now existed between them. The memory of the look that had passed between Benito and Juan Carlos that morning, as well as the expression on his lieutenant's face after José shot Reyes, haunted him. Juan Carlos had clearly been disheartened by the outcome. He'd wanted Benito to win and José to lose—to die among those lonely boulders so that he, Juan Carlos, could assume command of the Hunters.

When he thought about it, José decided it made sense that the two men had conspired. And who, he asked himself, would Juan Carlos have selected as his lieutenant?

"The traitor," José breathed, and cut a sideways glance at Juan Carlos. Friends? Perhaps once, but no longer, and maybe never.

"Riders," Juan Carlos spoke quietly, thrusting his chin to the east, where a sliver of dust cut into the late afternoon sky. "More than one, I think."

"Luis," José replied.

"Perhaps."

José fixed his once-trusted comrade with an acrimonious stare. "It is Luis."

For a strained moment, Juan Carlos didn't reply. Then he nodded and said, "Yes, it must be Luis returning."

"Never doubt me, my friend," José replied, his voice low but hard.

"I would not," Juan Carlos agreed.

"Good, because loyalty cannot be questioned. Do you understand?"

"Sí, mi capitán."

The horsemen beneath the approaching dust were beginning to take shape now. "It is Luis," José said with even more certainty than before. "He has found us some new prey."

The road running southwest from San Ignacio was in better condition than Owen Plunkett would have expected, considering the lack of cart tracks in the road, and the manure that marked the route looked to be months old, picked clean by scavenger bugs and dried nearly to dust by the early summer sun. Only the thin wheel prints of the army ambulance and those of the horses Hollister and his men had stolen from Cade and his boys betrayed recent traffic, and Pete seemed convinced they were less than twelve hours old. They weren't catching up, not yet, but Owen expected they would.

It had been nearly ten years since Owen had traveled this country. He'd been trailing a trio of horse thieves who, like Hollister, had thought they could evade the law by crossing the Rio Grande into Mexico. Owen and his men had found the tail twisters in a cantina in San Fidel, and put an end to their thieving right there, without the bother of a trial. He was hoping they'd catch up with Hollister's men before reaching the town, but even if they didn't, he felt confident they would find them in San Fidel. Or Villa Lobos, as Pete Maddox had informed him the community was now called.

Owen had puzzled over the new information. "Why'd they change it?"

"Couldn't tell you," Pete had replied. "It was a Meskin goatherder told me, and I asked him that same question, but he just said he wouldn't go there no more. Said it was a bad place."

Owen had nodded at that. He'd learned on his first visit that San Fidel was a rowdy town, but he doubted it was anything he and his men couldn't get a rope around. Even with its new name. Smiling crookedly, he'd said, "They're gonna get a new appreciation of bad after Hollister's bunch hits town, but it won't last."

The others had laughed, and Owen had let the matter drop, but the changed name continued to nag at him. In border Spanish, Villa Lobos loosely translated as Village of Wolves or House of Wolves. It was a title that didn't correspond with what he recalled of the place. It had been wild, sure, but not bad enough to scare a goatherder into never wanting to return. Something had happened, and a little tingle of warning climbed Owen's spine.

He tapped his heels to the roan's sides, urging the mare into a jog, and the others quickly followed suit. He didn't tell them why, but he suddenly wanted to catch up with the Hollister bunch *before* they reached San Fidel . . . or Villa Lobos.

Ray Beeler swung his horse around and rode back to where Ed Dodson had brought the mules to a halt at the edge of an arroyo cutting diagonally across the road.

"What's the matter, grandpa?" Ray demanded.

"Mind your manners, sonny," Henry McDaniels fired back.

The two old-timers were sharing the ambulance's seat, while Jethro Hill drifted in and out of consciousness in back, stretched out on the fold-down cot McDaniels had occupied yesterday.

McDaniels still looked peaked, his cheeks lightly flushed and his shoulders drooping like he'd spent the day hauling a hundredweight of oats on his back, but he was improving steadily, and had regained much of his querulous disposition. Bobby was still riding inside, his heart ticking as of their last stop at noon, although Ray wouldn't have given odds on the kid lasting until nightfall.

It was a damn sickly outfit he was crossing dangerous country with, and for not the first time he toyed with the idea of cutting his pin and riding on into Villa Lobos alone. Ben would raise holy hell if he did, but Ray about had his fill of the mighty Ben Hollister.

There had been a time when he considered Hollister one of the best highwaymen in the Southwest. Someone to ride the river with from dawn to dusk. But lately—and especially since his runt of a kid brother had showed up in San Angelo looking as lost as a half-drowned kitten—Ray had been having some serious doubts about Hollister's abilities. Or at least his judgment. Like quitting that rich territory up along the Red River to come way the hell down here into a country that looked like it could chew a man up and spit him down a hole without half trying.

Ray eyed the loose horses as they wandered up. They were following without being herded now, like cattle on a drive. Or sheep, and he grimaced at the image and spat as if to rid himself of a bad taste. What the hell was he doing down here? This was no land for a man with ambition, and Ray figured he had that by the shovelful. He needed to head on back to their old haunts along the Red and put together his own crew. Not the kind of men Ben seemed content to settle for—kids like Bobby and Jethro, or old farts like Mose and Dodson and McDaniels. He'd seek out competent gunmen like Little Fish and his own brother, whom Hollister had given the boot when he tried to join the outfit. That memory still gnawed at Ray, and it had only gotten worse after Bobby was allowed in. Welcomed into the bunch, by God, as if he had something to offer other than the humor Ray and Little Fish found in watching him try to figure out life on the owlhoot.

Yeah, he had plans—but not yet. First, he needed his share of the money they'd taken from Rio Largo. Then he had a personal score to settle with Hollister. After that, if Ben didn't bring back the Mexican whore who'd run off last night, Ray intended to have a little fun with Hattie Wilkes.

He looked at Dodson, leaning forward over the footboard to study the arroyo, and his temper flared. "Goddamnit, what's the matter, old man?"

"Ain't nothing the matter. I just don't want to tip my wagon."

"You've crossed a dozen of these gulches today, and Lord knows how many yesterday, when we didn't even have a road to follow."

"That's all right. I took my time with those, too. That's why I still got all four wheels on the ground, and not pointed at the clouds."

Movement at the back of the ambulance caught Ray's attention. The redhead, Fanny O'Shea, had climbed down. Now she came up front to study the situation.

"What the hell do you want?" Ray demanded.

"I wanna know when we're gonna get to that town Loosh told you boys about."

"Now, you'd have to ask *Loosh* about that, wouldn't you?" Ray sneered.

Fanny looked at him with a cocky grin, knuckles planted firmly on her hips. Ray could tell she'd lost a lot of her fear over the last couple of days. Probably because she realized they weren't going to kill her. And really, Ray thought, what else did a whore have to fear?

"What are you so grumpy about, cowboy?" Fanny asked.

"Nothing you'd want to hear," Ray replied.

"You ought to get back in the wagon, miss," Ed said. "I'm gonna tackle this on an angle."

"And you can't do that if I'm not inside with all them sick boys?" She was still looking at Ray, still grinning boldly. "I swear it stinks to high heaven back there. That Hollister kid messed himself again. Hattie cleaned him up, but there ain't much she can do about the smell."

Ray's mood began to change. "Maybe you ought to ride ahead with me," he suggested.

"Maybe I ought to."

"Ed told you to get your ass back inside," McDaniels said, scowling at Ray.

"And I'm telling her she can ride up ahead with me," Ray countered. He glanced at Fanny, then nodded toward Jethro's sorrel, standing among the loose stock behind the ambulance. Although still saddled, Henry had removed the gelding's bridle that morning and strapped it behind the cantle. "You know how to tighten a cinch and slip a bit?" he asked.

"Sure do."

"Then do it, but be quick. Ol' Ed here is itchin' to cross this arroyo . . . at an angle."

When Fanny took off, Ray smirked at Henry. The old codger didn't look away and he didn't like it, but there wasn't much he could do about it. Ben had made it clear that morning that Henry would be in charge until he got back, but everyone understood the person actually in charge was the man with the quickest pistol—as long as he was willing to use it. And Ray didn't think anyone there doubted his willingness to shoot if crossed.

Fanny caught the sorrel without effort—the damned horse was almost like a pet—and led it away from the cavvy. Ray watched her struggle with the knot holding the bridle in place as Ed hupped his team into the arroyo and out the other side, the vehicle's tall box swaying wildly from side to side but rolling on through. Ed kept the wagon moving, and it wasn't long before a couple of the loose horses started after it. Soon they were all moving out lazily. Only Acorn remained standing, trained well enough to know what was expected of him.

Looking his way, Fanny said, "He's too tall, I can't see the knots holding the bridle."

"Maybe the problem is you're too short."

She stuck her tongue out at him but kept plucking at the saddle strings. Ray watched and grinned, but eventually he grew impatient with the delay and hollered, "Come on, Red, you ain't crippled."

"These knots is too tight!"

"Aw, the hell with this," Ray said, pulling his mount around. When he did, Acorn took a step to follow.

"Hey, wait," Fanny called in alarm.

202

Ray twisted around in the saddle to rest one hand on his bedroll. "You got thirty seconds to get that hoss bridled and your hind end in the seat. After that, I'm moving on, and that sorrel can come with me."

"I'm trying, damnit!"

Ray had to smile at the hint of desperation in her voice. He'd thought for a while she might be faking it just to get his goat. Now he knew her struggle was real. Not that it changed his intentions any.

"Better try a little harder," he said. "You're running outta time."

That was when the first knot came free. She flashed him a triumphant smile, then hurried around to the other side to loosen the second knot. Ray didn't own a watch—what few he'd taken in robberies he always sold or tossed—but he was willing to bet she had the horse bridled in under a minute. It took only a few more seconds to tighten the cinch, then shimmy up into the seat.

"The stirrups are too long," she complained.

"Still sounds like you're too short to me," he replied, giving his horse its head. Fanny kicked the sorrel up alongside, flashing him a tobacco-stained grin.

"What's gonna happen to us when we get to Villa Lobos?"

"I couldn't say. I'm gettin' my share of the money, then I'm gonna spend a little time with your friend up there." He nodded toward the ambulance, a couple of hundred yards ahead of them by now, and just disappearing over a low rise. "Then I'm headin' back to Texas."

"What about me?"

"Red, I don't give a good goddamn what happens to you."

Fanny's smile vanished, and damned if her eyes didn't mist up, too.

"Then the hell with you, Ray Beeler. I was thinkin' real hard

203

about letting you come into my blankets tonight, but you can sleep with a cactus for all I care."

"Lady," Ray replied coolly. "If I ever decide to crawl into your blankets, I sure as hell ain't gonna ask for your by-your-leave."

"If you think you're—"

"Shut up!" He jerked his horse to a stop, his expression turning to stone as the sound of gunfire drifted toward them on the hot desert wind.

The hoot owl's call rang across the land, and the hairs along Ben's arms stirred uncomfortably as his hand darted for the Smith and Wesson. Laughter bubbled from a nearby draw as the revolver cleared leather.

"Is a good thing I'm not a savage redskin," a voice called. "I would have your scalp on my belt before you know I was near."

Ben swore, then eased the Smith and Wesson back in its cradle. "You're lucky I didn't blow your damned head off."

A horse snorted as it was put up over the arroyo's rim. Little Fish appeared astride one of Cade's army mounts. He had his Spencer balanced across his saddlebows, but that wouldn't have slowed him down if it came to a shooting match.

"If you had not put your pistol back, I would have shot you first," he replied, and Ben figured the odds were fair that he might have.

"Where the hell have you been?"

"Riding around, looking at the country."

"Thinking of settling down out here, are you?"

"Thinking one of us should do a little scouting, and not believing we are free just because we crossed a little mud puddle." He pulled up a few yards away without returning the Spencer to its scabbard. "They didn't stop at the river."

"Who didn't stop?"

"None of them. The sheriff, them army boys. They all follow us."

Ben frowned. "You're sure?"

"Sure, I'm sure. They follow the river north the last I saw them army boys, but still walking. Plunkett is closer."

Ben reined his horse partway around to scan the country, but it appeared empty in every direction. "Where's the lawman?"

"Up ahead of us, not behind. They cut cross-country after leaving the Rio Grande."

"Did you follow them?"

"For a ways I did. Then I go back to check those army boys. I can't be everywhere."

Ben turned his gaze forward, following the Rucker's tracks in the road as far as the crown of the next hill.

As if reading his thoughts, Little Fish said, "They crossed south of here."

"How long ago?"

"The width of a man's hand, held to the sun."

"About an hour?"

Little Fish shrugged.

"Take a gander at these tracks and tell me how far ahead the ambulance is."

"The width of a man's hand."

"About an hour?"

Another shrug.

"You figure they'll cut one another's trail down the road?"

"I figure that is what Plunkett has in mind," Little Fish replied soberly. "I figure he has been this way before, and he knows where this road takes us. No telling where he will set his trap, though. Maybe he will get around in front, or maybe he will come up from behind."

"Maybe he'll wait until dark?"

205

"Maybe, but I wouldn't. Too easy for a man to get away in the dark."

"How many men does he have riding with him?"

"This side of the river, three."

"Three!" Ben laughed and eased back in his saddle. "Hell, that won't be much trouble."

"Old men, too."

"Even better."

"Maybe. Or maybe there is a reason Plunkett sends all the young bucks back to Rio Largo."

"Yeah," Ben said thoughtfully. "Maybe there is." He glanced up the road. He'd been taking his time ever since turning back from his pursuit of Lucia. Now he felt a sudden impatience to catch up, a sense that hell was about to descend on the Rucker, and on Bobby and Hattie.

"Let's ride," he said tersely, and the two of them heeled their mounts into a gallop.

They were making their way southwest at an easy jog. Pete Maddox was up front where he could keep an eye on the Rucker's tracks. Owen was close behind, then Bill Rowland and Simon Butler, trailing by about twenty yards.

Spotting the single horseman waiting for them in the middle of the road half a mile ahead, Owen eased his roan mare up alongside Pete's bay. Uneasiness flowed through his gut like a fistful of worms.

"Meskin," Pete pronounced without slowing.

"Looks like," Owen agreed, his eyes moving swiftly from side to side, seeing nothing to cause alarm. But something had him worried, and it was a feeling he took seriously. "Let's walk a ways," he said, and brought his horse out of her trot.

"You thinkin' this might be trouble?" Pete asked.

"Feels that way."

After a pause, Pete said, "It sure as shootin' does. How do you want to play it?"

"I reckon we'll just ride on up and introduce ourselves."

Pete nodded and moved his hand back to his Colt. "That suits," he growled.

The rider had his back to the lowering sun, making it difficult to pick out any details other than his silhouette—the broad brim of his sombrero, the wide horn of his Mexican saddle with its sweeping tapaderos cinched to a sturdy buckskin, a short-waisted jacket above twin revolvers jutting out from both sides of the man's hips like handles on a jug.

It was those twin pistols that Owen kept coming back to. They weren't the kind of firearms a common vaquero would carry, and by the time they were within fifty yards of the buckskin's rider, Owen felt certain they were in for a fight.

Raising his hand in a friendly gesture, the horseman shouted in a kind of sing-song voice, *"Hola, mi amigos!"*

Owen brought his roan to a halt. *"Hola,"* he called in return, then waved the man forward.

The man refused, then called out again, still in Spanish. Owen replied in kind, while Pete translated for Bill and Simon.

"Come on in, friends," the Mexican said. "We will have some coffee and talk. Maybe you are looking for some cattle to buy, no?"

"We are looking for some men who might have passed this way."

"Men?" The Mexican shook his head. "I have seen no men. Only yourselves." After a pause, he added uncertainly, "How many men?"

"Twenty," Owen replied. "They are my deputies."

"Deputies! You are in Chihuahua, my friend. You have no authority here."

"Then we will leave, as soon as we finish our business."

207

Michael Zimmer

"That sounds wise," the Mexican said. "Tell me, who is your business with?"

"The citizens of San Fidel. There are some bad men heading toward their village, and I want to warn them."

The Mexican laughed with what sounded like genuine humor. "I think that you are too late by several years to warn the people of San Fidel. That village no longer exists. Today it is called Villa Lobos, and it is already ruled by bad men."

Taking a deep breath, Owen called, "Are you one of those bad men, my friend?"

"Yes, I think probably I am." Then he flicked his quirt in a small gesture that immediately brought a dozen horsemen piling out of a ravine to the north.

Simon Butler uttered a dry curse, and Owen felt his blood surge. The Mexican on the buckskin was still laughing when Owen gave to command to "Give 'em hell, boys," and palmed his Colt.

All four of them got off shots before any of the Mexicans could return fire, but it did little good. Owen saw his first bullet strike a horseman in the thigh. Another was spilled from his saddle by a shot from either Bill or Simon. Pete fired at the man on the buckskin but missed. He fired a second time, then the back of his head exploded in a bloody mist. Owen got off three more rounds as he yanked his horse around and drove his spurs into the mare's ribs, but the air around him was humming with lead, and at least two of the bullets struck him—one in his side, a glancing blow that carved a deep path through his flesh, the other smashing the wrist of his left hand—before his mount caught its stride.

Bill was clinging limply to his saddle, his horse plunging sideways against the reins. Simon was already racing back toward Texas, but he hadn't covered twenty yards before a pair of men darted from the brush on foot to cut him off. One of

208

them carried a shotgun, and its charge swept Simon from his saddle like a scythe through wheat. The other raised a rifle, and Owen swore in frustration that he should die like this, cut down in the middle of a Mexican desert with no one to know what had become of him, to see that he was given a proper burial, and for the men of Rio Largo to drink a toast in his honor later that night at Jim Hannagan's Second Chance Saloon.

CHAPTER EIGHTEEN

Luis Huerta walked over to where José was staring down at the old man with the star pinned to his shirt. The *Norteamericano* was still alive, but he wouldn't be for long. José just had to determine how he wanted the man to die.

"Three killed," Luis reported solemnly.

"Three," José repeated softly. "Three of our own."

"And three of theirs." Luis put a hand on his revolver. "Shall I kill this one now?"

"No, not yet." José eyed the *Tejano's* wounds, the one in his side and another in his wrist, then a third high and to the side, breaking his collar bone. Squatting, he slapped the old man's face. "Hey, hombre, can you hear me?"

The lawman's eyes flickered open. "I hear you," he replied in heavily accented Spanish.

"You killed three of my men."

"If I could have, I would have killed every one of you sons of bitches."

José looked at Luis and laughed. "A tough one, eh?"

"So he thinks," Luis replied. "But he will die, no different than the others."

José stood with a sigh. "Yes, he will die, but maybe not like the others." He studied the men who had ridden with him— Luis and his scouts and what remained of Juan Carlos Cordova's command. But not Juan Carlos. José had ordered him to stay behind with the rest of the Hunters, those wounded in the

Apache ambush and Francisco Castile's command.

Had stealth not been a factor, José would have brought them all with him, but here the desert was more open, difficult to conceal a large group. Besides, there had been only four of them, well-armed but old. José should have known they wouldn't be easy to take, though. Old men didn't live into their gray-haired years in this country if they were not tough and hard to kill. And none of these men had been easy to kill. Especially their leader.

"I hope," José said quietly, so that only Luis heard him, "that when I am old and wrinkled like this one, that I will still have the heart of the wolf."

"The others died as men should," Luis agreed. "It remains to be seen if this one will."

"Let us find out now," José said, drawing one of his Colts. He cocked the weapon, then leaned forward to point it at the old man's head. "Do you have any last words you wish to say, old man?"

"Yes, you can kiss my hairy old—"

José fired, the Colt recoiling in his hand, the body beneath it jumping simultaneously. The old man's eyes widened briefly, then partially closed as his body stilled.

"See," José said softly, letting the revolver hang at his side. "He died as well as any man I have ever known."

"What of the others?" Luis asked. "Those with the wagon and the extra horses?"

José didn't respond. He ejected the spent cartridge from his revolver and silently replaced it with a live round, never taking his eyes off the still-angry face of the dead lawman. He was having a hard time putting away his feelings for the old one.

Luis stood quietly to one side, patiently awaiting his captain's command. José appreciated that. Turning away from the old man, José walked over to the lawman's horse. He took a moment to admire the roan's clean lines, then accepted the reins from one of his men and stepped into the saddle. The others were already mounted and ready, the dead *Tejano* deputies stripped of clothing and boots, their weapons affixed to the saddles of their horses. Only the old man's body remained untouched, and Luis gestured to one of his scouts.

"Get his guns and boots and anything else of value, but have respect. He was a true warrior."

The man singled out dropped instantly from his saddle and moved to comply, and José nodded his approval. It was good that Luis Huerta commanded such obedience from his men. He was a man to nurture, José thought, and maybe, when the time came to remove Juan Carlos—as José knew it eventually would—Luis might be the one to take his old lieutenant's place. But not yet. Luis was still too young, his hatred for the Apaches, for all *Indios*, too consuming to make a competent leader.

José motioned for his men to move out. Luis, mounted, rode up beside him.

"Do we go after the wagon now?"

José chuckled. "You are too impatient, my friend. No, not yet. They have likely heard our gunfire and will be wary. We will return to pick up the rest of my Hunters, then we will wait until the *Norteamericanos* stop for the night before we approach them."

"And if they do not stop?"

"Then we will plan accordingly, but do not worry, Luis. They will stop. By sunset, they will be huddled inside their wagon like rabbits under the hawk."

Ben eased back from the crest of the low ridge where he and Little Fish had witnessed Owen Plunkett's final minutes. Ben felt chilled inside, like someone had jammed an icicle down his throat. The lawman's death didn't bother him—it served the old bastard right for being where he had no legal authority to be—but the callousness of the slim bandit chief had caught Ben unprepared. It didn't take him long to realize why. Looking at Little Fish, he said, "They know about the ambulance."

The half-breed nodded. "Probably."

"They'll go after it."

Little Fish gave him a puzzled look, as if wondering what he was leading up to.

"Bobby's in there," Ben said. He didn't add that Hattie was also with the ambulance.

"It don't look good for them people with the wagon," Little Fish admitted.

"Let's go," Ben said, starting back to where he and Fish had left their horses. He stopped when Little Fish started talking.

"I am wondering where is the money we took from Rio Largo?"

"It's in the wagon. You saw Henry put it there."

"I saw him put the bags in the toolbox with the soldier guns, but when I look in there last night, it was not there."

Ben turned around fully. "You were there last night?"

"Sure, I was there."

"Why didn't you stay, or let someone know you were okay?"

"It didn't seem to me like you was too worried about where I was."

Ben was aware of Little Fish studying him, head cocked puzzledly to one side. Ben had seen that look before and recognized it as a trait of Fish's, growing up in a red man's world, trying to make his way through the white man's.

"I think maybe we better talk this out, you and me," Little Fish said, moving the Spencer just enough to let Ben know the seriousness of his position.

"All right, yeah, we've been wondering where you were. But we also knew you could take care of yourself."

"Either that, or I was dead?"

"That's about the way we figured it," Ben said, and Little Fish grunted and allowed the Spencer's muzzle to drop.

"Do you know where the ambulance is now?" Ben asked.

"Not exact where, but maybe pretty close."

"Can you get us there before those bandits find it?"

"Depends on the bandits."

Little Fish moved back to the crest of the low ridge and raised his head behind the same creosote bush they'd used to shield themselves earlier. Ben followed, peering through the spindly limbs and small yellow blossoms to where the four dead lawmen lay scattered across the road. Little Fish pointed with his chin to where the bandits were even then riding away, quartering off the road to the northwest.

"They are going to find the rest of their men," he stated.

"How do you know that?"

"I just know. There are more men somewhere, otherwise they would have followed the wagon right away."

"Then we have some time?"

"Not very much, I don't think." He was quiet a moment, thinking. Then he pushed back off the ridge to face Ben. "I think maybe I don't want that Rio Largo money no more."

"You're giving up your share?" Ben asked incredulously.

"Not all of it." Little Fish brought his Spencer back up, swinging it around to cover Ben. "I think what I will do is trade my share of the maybe money for what you have in your pockets now."

"That's a bad play, Fish. I don't have two bucks in my pockets, and less than fifty in my saddlebags. Your share of the Rio Largo money ought to top three thousand, at least."

"I think maybe I'd rather have the sure money than what is in that wagon, because I don't think that wagon is going to be around much longer."

Ben's eyes narrowed. "You said you checked the wagon last night and the money wasn't there?"

"Not in the side box, but it was dark. Or maybe you moved it, or someone moved it." His expression changed subtly. "Or maybe someone slipped it out of the wagon and hid it. Maybe that is what happened. I think I will go back and see if I can find it along the trail."

"If you're the one who took it, Fish, you won't live to spend it. If I don't come after you, Ray and Henry and the others will."

"I am not afraid of them, but I did not take the money. Maybe it is still in the wagon. I don't know, but what I think is this. If the money is there, them Mexicans are going to be the ones who keep it, and anyone who tries to stop them is going to be dead pretty damn quick. That is what I think."

"All right," Ben conceded. He dug several coins from his vest pocket and handed them to Little Fish. "The rest is in my saddlebags."

"Let's go get it," Little Fish said. "But first, you give me your pistol, okay. That way you don't get tempted to shoot me."

Ben eased the Smith and Wesson from its holster and handed it over. "Satisfied?"

"Sure, I'm satisfied." He nodded toward Ben's mount. "Now the rest of it."

They walked back through the scrub to where they'd left their mounts tied to the sturdy trunks of a couple of creosote bushes. Ben's grulla lifted its head at their approach, and he spoke quietly and patted the gelding's shoulder before moving to the saddlebags. Ben carried his cash in a little pouch tucked in the front corner of the near-side bag. After several years riding together, Little Fish knew that. What he didn't know, what none of them knew, was that Ben also kept a .32 caliber Colt pocket revolver next to his poke. In twenty years of riding the owlhoot, he'd never had to use it, but it was always there, always fully loaded with its grips up, easy to grab.

Reaching into the saddlebag with both hands, Ben moved aside the extra clothing he also carried there. He pulled the money pouch out first, using his right hand, and Little Fish took a step closer. Fish didn't see the .32 in Ben's left hand. Nor did Ben notice the Spencer's hard walnut stock until just before the heel of its steel butt plate slammed down on top of his head.

The world seemed to explode before Ben's eyes in a blinding white flash. He sensed himself falling, but managed to thrust the .32 up and pull the trigger. Behind the roaring in his skull he heard Little Fish cry out, and he pulled the trigger twice more before the white swallowed him whole.

The sun was setting by the time their trading was finished. The village had little to offer that would be of value to fighting men, and what they did have was old and of poor quality. Even then, Cade had to dicker hard to get what they needed.

As San Ignacio's citizens trudged slowly back into the brush, Cade began distributing the merchandise. He'd managed to purchase three horses—Indian ponies, judging from their small size and colorful markings—of reasonable soundness, and a pair of mules that looked like they would be more at home pulling a *carreta*. Saddles and tack had been an added expense. Cade bought two Mexican rigs, a beat-up Dragoon that had probably come to Chihuahua during the Mexican War in '46, and a Texas stock saddle with cracked, peeling leather. That still left them a saddle short; someone would have to use a blanket held in place with a surcingle unless they could locate something better before moving out.

The blankets they got for their bedrolls were locally woven and of good quality, as was the food—venison, frijoles in a chipped clay pot, and parched corn in leather sacks—all of it spiced in one way or another with chili.

The villagers bartered hardest for their firearms. Cade understood their reluctance. They were giving up protection for a little coin to jingle in their pockets, although Hector Martinez had let him know most of them hoped to purchase better guns with the money they got for these older weapons.

The troopers had their own limited armament—Cade's Springfield and the three Colt .45s they'd salvaged from Hollister's men. To that small arsenal he was able to add a pair of cheap, single-barreled shotguns, a muzzle-loading percussion rifle, and an old Hall breech-loading carbine with seven linen cartridges of questionable quality.

Lucia fared somewhat better than the men. Being related to a few of the town's residents, she was able to procure a percussion revolver and a stubby, double-barreled rifle, both in .36 caliber.

In addition to the firearms, Cade purchased two machetes and a hand axe.

"It ain't much, is it?" Elkins observed afterward, as the men gathered around a small fire outside the corral while Lucia went off to visit with her Aunt Anna.

"It's some better than what we had before," Cade replied.

"I was hoping for more cartridge guns, meself," Riley said. He'd been assigned one of the single-barreled shotguns, and was eyeing it dubiously in the flickering light of their small fire.

"A couple of Winchesters would have upped our odds," Morgan agreed.

"I imagine they've got a few hid out somewhere, but they wouldn't trade their best for what little we had to offer," Cade said.

"T'ain't hardly fair, ye ask me," Riley said, and Poe's head snapped up.

"You want fair, go back to Texas," he said. "You know the way." Glancing around at the others, he added, "That goes for the rest of you, too."

"Here, now," Riley protested, more startled by the venom in Poe's voice than the actual words.

"He wasn't talking about going back," Morgan said. "None of us were, and I'd be tempted to fight any son of a bitch who says I was."

"No one's fighting anyone until we catch up with Hollister," Cade cut in. He was squatting next to the fire, tending an iron kettle of coffee Hector had furnished them for the evening. He looked at Poe. "Pull your horns in, Corporal. No one has to be here. They all volunteered."

"Aw, hell, I'm just blowing wind," Poe said in lieu of an outright apology. "Think I'll take a walk," he added, then pushed to his feet and headed back into the ruined town.

He looked frazzled, Cade thought, and wondered what it had been like up in those hills yesterday, trying to put the sneak on Little Fish, knowing he was doing the same.

No one spoke after he was gone, and Cade was content to let the quietness of the evening settle around them. When the coffee was ready, he announced it to the men, then filled their cups as they filed past. While they drank in reflective silence, he added pieces of venison to the frijoles and warmed them over the coals. It was a skimpy meal and the coffee was as weak as it was bitter, but he considered it a welcome reprieve to the monotony of jerky, hardtack, and tepid water that had been their fare the past couple of days.

Normally the men would have roundly complained about such a poor meal, but tonight, each of them lost in their own thoughts after Poe's outburst, they let it slide. Darkness seemed to drop over the village without warning, twilight blending into full dark while Cade tended to his chores. Lucia returned as he finished cleaning the kettles and hung them on a post for Hector to find the next day. She was munching on a tortilla wrapped around a stewed apple from who-knew-where. Poe showed up a few minutes after she did, but Cade didn't ask if he'd eaten. Frank was a soldier. He knew better than to take off with a meal on the fire. If he missed out, it was his own damn fault.

They settled back in silence and Cade let the fire die to coals. Elkins and Riley dozed. Morgan sat with his back to a gatepost and stared moodily across the street at an empty house not much bigger than a lean-to. Frank paced nervously. Cade had known the man for several years—he'd been the one who recommended Poe for an extra stripe and his promotion to corporal—but had never seen him this edgy.

They rested until the moon crept up over the Sandbars, then quietly readied their stock. Elkins drew the short straw and would have to make do with a blanket instead of a saddle. Cade took one of the Indian ponies, a wall-eyed dun mare that watched his every move with suspicion. He gave Morgan a gray of equal size to his dun, and just as flighty. The third horse went to Poe, an older sorrel that acted docile enough. Elkins and Riley accepted the mules with low mutterings and dark scowls, but didn't otherwise protest the divvy.

Cade led the dun out of the corral, then pulled her to one side to allow the others to pass. Lucia was last in line, leading Roman by the reins. She eyed him suspiciously when he fell in at her side.

"I wish you'd stay here and wait for us."

"Hattie didn't want to come when I accepted your soldiers' offer to ride the train from El Paso to Fort Stockton, but I talked her into it. It's my fault she's along, and my fault she was taken."

"It's not your fault. Her safety was my responsibility."

"You are wasting your time, Andrew. Unless you intend to go

back on your earlier promise."

"No, I won't go back on my word. But no matter how tough you think you are, you being along is going to put a kink in our tails."

"It won't be me who puts a kink in your tails, or anywhere else." She came to a halt, and Cade stopped with her. "I'm going, Andrew. With you or alone, but I'm going. You can't change that."

After a pause, he nodded acceptance. "All right, but when we catch up with Hollister, you'll have to obey orders just like any other trooper under my command. Is that understood?"

She smiled and turned to gather her reins above Roman's neck. "It is understood," she told him, looking back over her shoulder. "It remains to be seen if it will be obeyed." Then she hooked her toe in the stirrup and pulled herself into the McClellan's cradle.

Cade walked away, leading the dun into the street before climbing into the saddle. The horse snorted and took a couple of small crowhops, but he pulled her head up and brought her back to where the others waited quietly. As the men gathered around him he gave the order to move out—southwest, along the road to Villa Lobos.

CHAPTER NINETEEN

They pushed on into the night, trace chains jingling as Ed Dodson kept the bone-weary mules at a steady trot. Although Ray had ordered Fanny to bring up the rear on Jethro's Acorn, he was pretty sure some of the army horses she was supposed to be watching had dropped out in the dark. It irritated him—not the loss of the horses, since he would have cut them loose as soon as they crossed the Rio Grande if it had been up to him—but the fact that he'd told her to keep them bunched, and all she'd done was complain about being left alone in the dark. Ray knew she was angling to come with him when he left, but she was going to be damned disappointed about that. When he needed a whore, he'd go find one, not pack one along like a damn bag of flour.

It was a couple of hours after sunset when Ed brought the ambulance to a halt in the middle of the road. Ray had been riding point, but when he heard Dodson holler "whoa," he swung his horse around and rode back to find out what the problem was.

"It's too dark," Ed replied to Ray's query. He and Henry McDaniels had climbed down and were examining the off-front wheel in the light of the bull's-eye lantern, its narrow beam focused on one of the spokes.

"That road's plain to see, and we need to keep moving," Ray charged.

"The hell that road's plain to see," Ed sputtered, his head

221

jerking up from where he'd been running a finger along the spoke. "I ain't even sure it's a road no more."

"I can see it just fine. What's the matter, you going blind?"

"We can see the trail," Henry confirmed. "But we didn't see that rock in the middle of it. Ed ran over it."

"Cracked a spoke," Ed added.

"It's been rough on the wounded, too," said a woman's voice from the shadows of the Rucker's interior.

"You mind your own business, Wilkes, and let us mind ours," Ray snapped.

"We're not going to lose that much time if we wait for moonrise," Henry said, staring east toward the hint of cream domed above the horizon. "Not like we would if we busted a wheel."

Ray was silent a moment, his thoughts spinning. He was aware of Fanny having ridden up on Acorn, and of Hattie half-standing in the ambulance's front entrance. They were all watching him, waiting for his decision, and it suddenly occurred to him that it wasn't his to make. With a gruff bark of laughter, he slipped his nickeled Colt from its holster.

"Boys," he announced with sudden authority. "It's time we parted ways. If you two want to stay here and wet-nurse a couple of jugheads that ain't likely to live 'til morning, that's your license, but I'm claimin' my share of the Largo money and cuttin' my pin tonight."

"Ben says we'll split the money in Villa Lobos," Ed protested.

"Ben ain't here, and I'm leavin'. But not without my cut." He swung his revolver toward Hattie. "Get those bags out here, girl."

"I don't have them," she said.

"Goddamnit, I ain't gonna tell you twice. Get those bags out here where I can see 'em."

He thought he could hear laughter in her voice when she

said, "Lucia took them."

"What!" Ray and Henry exclaimed in nearly the same breath, and Ed said, "No!"

"Last night, when she snuck away," Hattie confirmed. "She took the money with her."

"And you didn't say anything?"

"Why should I?"

"You bitch," Ray growled above the cool sound of the Colt's hammer being ratcheted to full cock.

"Don't pull that trigger," Henry said sharply. "You do and you're liable to call every damned redskin in the area down on top of us."

Ray hesitated, recalling the gunfire they'd heard earlier. "I ought to," he grated, but he knew McDaniels was right. Lowering the hammer to half-cock, he said, "Ed, bring that lantern over here and check the toolbox."

Dodson came over and rummaged quickly through the vehicle's side box, then climbed inside to continue his search. Ray watched with a smoldering anger as the lantern's thin beam of light stabbed across the canvas sidewalls while Ed prodded under the bunks, then tore the blankets off the wounded. When he finally poked his head out the front of the ambulance, he looked like a kid who'd just discovered coal in his Christmas stocking.

"It's gone, all of it," he nearly bleated.

"Son of a bitch," Henry breathed, turning hot eyes on Hattie. "This is your fault, girl."

"No, it ain't, it's Ben's fault," Ray said, returning the Colt to his holster. "He's the one brought these whores along, and chained us to an ambulance that ain't done nothin' but hold us back. We could've been in Villa Lobos by now, instead of out here in the dark dodging Apaches."

"So what do you plan to do about it?" Henry countered.

"I'll tell you what I'm gonna do about it. I'm going to track down that Mexican bitch and get my money back, and if I find out Hollister had a hand in it, I'm gonna drill a .45-caliber slug through that bastard's heart."

"Ben wouldn't desert his brother," Hattie said.

"Girl, Ben Hollister ain't no better than the rest of us. If he got a chance to skate off with all that money, he'd take it and never look back." Ray heeled his mount over to where Fanny had been silently observing the conversation. "What about you?" he demanded. "Did you know your friend—"

"I didn't, Ray, I swear it. I knew she took off, but I didn't know she stole your money."

"I reckon you're as big a liar as any other whore," he replied coldly. "Get down."

"Ray, please, don't leave me here."

"Get off that horse, or I'm gonna knock you off with the barrel of my Colt."

A sound somewhere between a gasp and a sob escaped her throat, but she clambered down. "Are you coming back?" she asked him.

"Sure I am, Red. Just as soon as I get that money, I'll come right back and share it with everyone." He leaned from the saddle to take the sorrel's reins. "You wait for me, and see what happens."

"You bastard," she whispered.

"To the core," he agreed, and heeled his horse into the middle of the road, leading Acorn with him as he started back toward San Ignacio.

Luis dismounted some distance away and walked over to where José was talking with Antonio Carrillo. Breaking off in mid-sentence, José waited for the scout to reach his side. In a quiet voice, he asked, "You have found them?"

"Yes, they've stopped, and now one man is going back. I sent two of my men after him."

José grunted his approval. "And of the others?"

"Two old men, one of them wounded, and two women dressed as men in *Yanqui* uniforms."

José scowled at that. "Women? You are sure?"

"I have not been away from Villa Lobos that long."

José smiled. Like himself, Luis Huerta was faithful to his wife. It was another reason to consider bringing him deeper into the fold of his trusted companions—a tiny faction consisting only of Antonio, Pedro Suarez, and Javier Diaz. At one time, Juan Carlos Cordova and Francisco Castile had occupied an honored place among these few, but Francisco was no longer with them after the Apache attack below the Sierra del Capulíns.

And Juan Carlos?

José let that problem slide from his thoughts. Right now he needed to deal with these *Tejano* invaders his scouts had discovered traveling the road to Villa Lobos. What had brought them here? First the old lawman and his deputies, and now these men and women in a wagon bearing the markings of the *Norteamericano* military.

José felt certain the Federales would be interested in the *Yanqui* army's presence in Mexico. Perhaps enough to furnish a reward for anyone bringing that information to their attention. But he also suspected drawing the government's attention to this isolated part of Chihuahua might prove detrimental to his own plans. Mexico's scoundrel of a president, Manuel González Flores, would not appreciate the competition from José and his marauders. No, this was a matter better dealt with locally, by his own men, his proud Hunters of the Dunes.

"Your orders, *Capitán*," Luis inquired gently.

José eyed the younger man quietly for a moment, then said, "Tell me your suggestions."

Michael Zimmer

Luis's startled reaction amused him.

"I . . . I am honored," Luis said, bowing slightly. And then, after only a moment's reflection, he went on. "My suggestion is that we wait along the road for the men in the wagon to come to us."

"And of the man who is attempting to escape?"

"My scouts will bring him back for your consideration if possible. Or kill him if that is what he prefers."

"Very good," José approved crisply. He motioned for Juan Carlos to join them.

For a moment the lieutenant stared back warily. When he did come forward, his steps seemed hesitant, his eyes darting. José considered that telling, and his distrust of the man grew even larger.

"Sí, mi capitán?" Juan Carlos said.

"How many of your command are able to ride?"

"They all are, but three still suffer from the wounds they received in the Apache attack."

"Select all who can ride and fight, and have them report to Luis Huerta. Make sure they understand that they are to obey him as they would me."

"All of them? My entire command?"

"Your entire command . . . what remains of it," José acknowledged.

"Am I to take over Francisco's command, then?"

"No, you are to remain close, as I may have need of a messenger."

Juan Carlos's head came up. Even in the thin starshine, José could see the sharp flare of the man's nostrils, the sudden, hardened thrust of his jaw. Keeping his right hand shielded from the lieutenant's view, José wrapped his fingers around the grips of his revolver. He wondered if he had misjudged the man's limits. Then Juan Carlos nodded, and José knew he

226

hadn't. But he also understood that he would have to watch his back closely from this moment onward. Juan Carlos obviously recognized his captain's motives, as well as the steady undermining of his authority. He would not take such degradation lightly, not for long.

Returning to his men, Juan Carlos bluntly repeated José's instructions to consider themselves under Huerta's leadership. The Hunters glanced uncertainly at one another. Several looked in José's direction. Then they quietly broke apart and went to find their horses.

"Antonio," José said softly.

"*Sí?*" Antonio Carrillo replied. He had eased back several paces as José and Luis shaped their plans. Now he stepped quickly forward.

"Bring me my horse. I want to follow along and see how Luis handles these *Norteamericanos.*"

"The buckskin?"

"*Sí.*"

José had ridden the old lawman's roan through what remained of the day, but he wanted an animal he could trust tonight, with the desert's floor distorted by shadow.

They rode out single-file through the scrub toward the narrow trace of road connecting Villa Lobos with several tiny villages along the Rio Grande. José had yet to see the wagon Luis had spoken of, nor was he sure where the *Americanos* had stopped, but he trusted the scout's judgment, as well as his sense of direction. By the time the moon was halfway past its burrow in the Sandbars, Luis had his men spread across the road with their weapons drawn, horses held on tight rein. Others were placed in the scrub flanking the road. After motioning for the rest of his command to wait behind with Juan Carlos, José jogged his horse up next to Luis.

"You are sure of this plan?" he asked.

"I am sure," Luis replied without glancing around.

"*Bueno*," José said, smiling. He liked the scout's self-assurance.

Behind them, one of the men assigned to Luis began to roll a cigarillo. The rustling of the trimmed corn husk was slight, but Luis's head immediately snapped around.

"Ernesto!"

The man looked up, meeting Luis's condemning gaze with bewilderment. Then, realizing what he had done, he spilled the tobacco back into its sack and returned that and the husk to the side pocket of a short wool jacket.

Of this, too, José approved.

It wasn't long before the faint rattle of chains drifted up the road toward them. Drawing one of his revolvers, José guided his mount off the road so that the men would have no doubts about who was in charge. The moon was barely free of the distant mountain range when the wagon began to take shape in its dingy light. It was trailed by several horses, following without leads. As the vehicle's contours became clear, José realized it was an army ambulance, and he wondered about the cargo it might contain.

Luis's men remained unnoticed until the ambulance was within thirty meters of their position. Then a surprised shout came from the vehicle, and the mules were pulled to an abrupt stop. The men Luis had sent down the trail stepped quickly out of the brush along the road. They shouted for the driver to raise his hands, but instead he reached for his revolver. One of Luis's men shot him from the wagon's seat, his strangled cry nearly smothered by a woman's scream. The second man, his right arm in a sling, immediately held up his good hand and called out in perfect Spanish, "Don't shoot, friends. I will not fight you."

Luis heeled his mount forward. José followed a few paces behind.

"If you are carrying a weapon, throw it to the ground," Luis instructed.

"I have a revolver, but I'll have to reach across my body to get it out of my holster. Don't shoot."

The rest of Luis's men quickly swarmed the vehicle. One of the scouts stepped from his saddle into the ambulance's open rear entrance. A woman's loud protest was silenced by the sharp smack of a hand on flesh, and a couple of minutes later two figures—women, José saw after a second glance, both of them attired in *Yanqui* uniforms—tumbled out the back. One of them, red-haired and of slender build, sprawled face-first onto the hard, rocky trace and cried out in pain. The other reached to help her up, but one of Juan Carlos's *soldados* kicked her away. The scout's head popped out the front of the ambulance.

"There are two others in here," he informed Luis. "Both appear badly injured and unconscious."

José rode forward. As captain, it was time he assumed command. Motioning to the old man still seated on the wagon—shaggy gray beard and bloody sling—he said, "You speak my language, *Abuelo*?"

"Yes, sir," the old man replied.

"What is your name?"

"Henry McDaniels."

"Where did you learn the Mexican tongue, Henry McDaniels?"

"Different places."

"You are from Mexico?"

"No, this is the first time I've been here."

"Ah, then it is your bad luck, eh?"

"I hope not," Henry McDaniels replied. "It looks to me like you could use a man who can speak both our languages."

His pronouncement brought a laugh from José. "You think fast, my friend. I admire that, although I do not always trust it. Maybe your suggestion should be considered, but first I have other matters to attend to." He motioned to the women. "Who do these belong to?"

"They don't belong to anyone."

Cocking an eyebrow, José said, "They are *mujeres soldados*?"

"No, sir, they aren't soldiers, they're hostages. That one with the auburn hair is also taking care of our wounded."

José thought about that for a minute, then shook his head. "There is much here that I do not understand, *Abuelo*. Maybe I should keep you alive, at least until I discover all of your motives."

"That sounds like a good idea to me," Henry McDaniels replied, and José smiled thinly. He motioned the women forward. "What are their names?"

"That auburn-haired woman is Hattie Wilkes. The other calls herself Fanny O'Shea."

José leaned forward in his saddle to study the redheaded woman. "I think, my friend, that you have lied to me. This one with the hair like copper has the looks of a *putana*."

"I suppose she was, before she became a hostage," the *Americano* agreed.

"Tell me, are there others?" He watched the old man, waiting for his reaction as much as his response.

"There were three others, but they headed back toward the states," Henry McDaniels replied without hesitation, and José nodded, satisfied that he was telling the truth.

"Why are you bringing these wounded men into Mexico?"

"We robbed a town in Texas, and came down here to spend our money."

"Money? Gold?"

"It was mostly paper, but a third woman took off with it.

That's why the other two men aren't here. They went after the woman."

José glanced at Luis. "What do you think? Does he tell the truth?"

"Perhaps. Let's see what the other one says when my men bring him back."

José nodded to the women. "Take these two to the side, but don't let the men have them yet. You, old man, climb down here where I can see you better."

"What of the two men still in the wagon?" Luis asked.

"Pull them out here," José replied. "I want a better look at them."

Luis passed along these instructions, then dismounted to help remove the injured men from the ambulance. José rode around back to watch. There was no gentleness among the Hunters as they dragged a youth out of the wagon and let him flop to the ground. The dark-haired woman shouted a protest and tried to come forward, but one of the guards forced her back. José grunted; her reaction seemed to lend credence to the old man's claim that she was the nurse.

The second man came out like he was drunk, his face shining with a fevered sweat, his limbs like reeds in the river. He looked around and said something that sounded like *"Acorn,"* before a *soldado* swung his foot under the man's legs and spilled him to the ground. The scout who had first entered the ambulance rummaged around inside for several minutes, then appeared at the rear entrance with a couple of cartridge belts and a carbine clutched in one hand. "There are guns," he announced happily. "Rifles and revolvers, and ammunition for both."

"There are even more in here," another exclaimed, pulling holstered revolvers from the ambulance's side box. "Pistols and carbines."

"Is there any gold or silver?" Luis asked.

"There is none here," the man at the side box replied.

"Nor any that I could find," said the second. "Although if I had a torch, I could search more thoroughly."

"Here is a lantern," a *soldado* said, coming around back with a tin bull's-eye he'd pulled from the driver's box.

It took only seconds to light the candle and pass it up to the scout. Growing weary of the exchange, José reined away. Luis came with him.

"What do you wish done with our new prisoners, *mi capitán*?"

After a moment's reflection, José said, "Kill the wounded, then put the old man and the women on the mules."

"And the wagon?"

"Leave it. Perhaps I will send someone back for it later, but tonight I am more concerned with all these *Norteamericanos* wandering around in our country."

"Do you believe they are truly robbers?"

"It's possible, but that doesn't explain the ambulance, the women, or how they allowed money taken at gunpoint to be lost." He shook his head. "There is too much to be explained yet to kill these prisoners." He looked at Luis. "You are in charge of them, my friend. See that no harm comes to them."

Nodding solemnly, Luis said, "You can trust me, *Capitán*."

José's eyes narrowed as Luis strode away. It seemed an odd choice of words, and for the first time since they'd left *Rocas Quebradas,* he wondered if he hadn't been too hasty in putting his trust in the young scout.

CHAPTER TWENTY

They rode through the night, stopping only briefly when the moon went down, then starting again at first light. The sun wasn't quite all the way up when they found Owen Plunkett and his deputies at the base of a swirling kettle of vultures. Cade ordered his men to fan out through the desert to either side of the road, but he didn't expect them to find anyone. Whatever had happened here had occurred hours before. When he got closer—dismounted now, his dun spooking at the smell coming off the corpses—he estimated at least twelve hours, probably more.

The troopers trickled back one at a time to report no sign of anyone nearby, although Morgan had discovered a deep arroyo where a number of men had apparently spent some time waiting.

"How many?" Cade asked.

"A dozen, more or less."

"Apaches?" Riley asked.

"I don't think so," Morgan replied. "Some of the horses were shod, and there were cigarette butts nearby."

"What kind?" Cade asked.

"Corn husks, but cut straight. Mexicans, I'd guess."

"What do you want to do with them?" Elkins asked, motioning toward the dead.

"We'll bury them here as best we can."

Scowling, Poe said, "That'd work if we had more time, but

we're already pushing our luck being down here."

"We're not leaving these men here for the buzzards," Cade replied firmly.

"We don't even have a shovel," Poe argued.

"We've got two machetes and a hand axe. That's more than we had for Schultz and Hendricks." Cade felt a moment's empathy for the corporal, and annoyance at his obstinance. "We'll catch them, Frank. Don't worry about that."

Poe's lips parted as if to dispute the matter, then snapped closed.

Signaling to Elkins and Riley, Cade told them to start chopping a grave out of the hard ground.

Even with an early morning breeze and switching off every ten minutes or so, they were all sweating heavily by the time they had a hole deep enough to bury the four lawmen. Cade, who had been standing off to one side with Lucia, supervised the arrangement of the bodies. Then Poe and Morgan shoveled the dirt back in on top of them. It was a poor excuse for a grave, but better than letting them feed the scavengers. After speaking a few words over the mound, Cade ordered his men back into their saddles. Two hours later, he spotted the ambulance parked in the middle of the road half a mile ahead, and his gut tightened with dread.

"It's them," Poe said tersely, reaching for his revolver.

"Hold up," Cade told him, then raised a hand to bring the squad to a halt.

"I don't see anyone," Morgan said.

"I do," Poe replied. "Horses, too."

"Yeah, I see the horses."

"Off to the right there," Cade said. "Close to the ambulance."

"Damned if it don't look like the bogger's digging a grave, too," Riley said.

"All right, let's go in slow," Cade ordered. "Spread out as

soon as we get within rifle range and keep your eyes peeled for an ambush." He turned to Lucia. "You stay here until I wave you forward, understand?"

She shot him a dark look but didn't argue, and Cade gave the command to move out. They advanced slowly, fanning wide to come in on the ambulance from three sides. But there was only one man there when they arrived, so intent upon his chiseling into the hard ground with a short-handled pick he didn't notice their approach.

Cade recognized him from a couple of hundred yards away, but didn't call out. Morgan, on Cade's right, said softly, "Hell, he doesn't even know we're here."

"He doesn't act like it," Cade agreed. They'd stopped about twenty yards out, the country to either side of the narrow road featureless save for the same desert scrub they'd been trudging through the last three days. "Stay here," he told Morgan, and nudged his dun forward.

Ben Hollister was working steadily on a kind of cavity Cade recognized all too well. He recognized the pick, too, part of the equipment they'd brought with them from Alto Station, stored in the ambulance's toolbox. Hollister didn't seem to notice Cade even when he dismounted and hitched his mare to the Rucker's rear wheel. What looked like a pair of bodies were laid out under the canvas that had once covered the ambulance's overhead ribs. Cade drew his revolver and moved closer. "Ben Hollister!"

Hollister hesitated, then straightened and looked around. He seemed puzzled at first. Then recognition dawned. "Is that you, Sergeant?"

"It's me."

"All this way, huh?" His gaze dropped to the revolver clenched firmly in Cade's hand. "You won't need that. My fight isn't with you anymore."

"Drop your pistol, Hollister."

"I can't do that. I'm going to need it later."

"Put it on the ground, right now."

Ben paused as if in thought, then shook his head. "No," he said, and went back to chipping away at the sunbaked earth.

Cade glanced around uncertainly. "What's going on here?"

"I'm burying these men," Ben replied calmly, tipping his head toward the bodies under the tarp.

"Who are they?"

"Jethro Hill and Ed Dodson."

"Who killed them?"

"Bandits."

"Bandits," Cade repeated. "Did you see them?"

"Not here, but I saw them yesterday when they killed that Rio Largo lawman and his deputies."

There was another plot of freshly turned earth several feet from the grave Hollister was currently digging. "Who's in there?"

Ben paused without raising his head. "That's Bobby," he said huskily.

After a second's hesitation, Cade holstered his revolver and walked over to the smaller grave. There was no wood nearby for a marker, but Ben had placed a stone at its head, then scratched a message into it with something sharp. Cade moved closer to read what it said.

Robert Earl Hollister

B. 1868

D. 1884

Brother Son Friend

Cade did the math in his head, then looked at Ben. "He was young."

"Too damn young for this kind of life," Hollister agreed, and started digging again.

After motioning the others forward, Cade eased the pick from Ben's grip. "It looks like you could use some help."

"No, I'm fine," Ben replied, but the paleness of his skin and the trembling in his arms told Cade otherwise.

"Are you hurt?"

"No." Then he took a couple of staggering steps backward, and might have fallen had Cade not grabbed him around the waist and helped him into the Rucker's shade. He slipped the Smith and Wesson from Hollister's holster without the outlaw's notice and tucked it under his belt.

"Rest here a minute," Cade told him. "We'll finish this."

Ben nodded and tipped his head back against the wheel. He closed his eyes, and didn't open them even when Cade's men and Lucia rode up several minutes later.

Poe moved closer, and Cade readied himself in case he tried anything, but the corporal seemed more curious than contentious. He looked at Cade with a question in his eyes.

"He said it was bandits," Cade explained.

Morgan had already walked over to examine the canvas-covered bodies. "Two of them," he announced. "That kid who rode the sorrel and the old man who drove the ambulance."

"Hill and Dodson," Cade said, then motioned to the grave already filled in. "That's Hollister's brother over there."

Lucia gave a small gasp and looked at Hollister, and Cade saw sympathy in her eyes.

"You men finish digging this grave," Cade ordered, handing the pick to Riley. "Miss Mendoza, would you take a look at Hollister? He's acting . . . out of sorts."

Nodding, she dismounted and loosened her canteen before walking over to where Hollister sat next to the ambulance. Cade and Poe began exploring the wagon. They found the water kegs inside, still mostly full, but little else. The guns and cartridge belts were gone. So were most of the items that might have held any value to the marauders. Only the harness and some of the odds and ends from the toolbox—a tin bucket of axle grease, a jack and hub wrench, and some dirty rags—remained.

"I wonder why they didn't take the ambulance," Poe murmured.

"Maybe where they're heading it's too rough for a wagon."

"Andrew," Lucia said quietly.

He walked over to where she was kneeling at Hollister's side. Ben's eyes were closed and his breathing seemed rapid and faintly uneven, like he was struggling with something in his sleep. Lucia had removed his hat. Now she gently brushed the hair atop his head to the side. Cade swore softly at the raw flesh.

"There's not a lot of blood, but this whole area." She waved a hand slowly over the wound, like a magician getting ready to pull something exotic out of a hat. "It feels . . . indented."

"Fractured?"

"I'd say so, but I'm afraid to press on it too much." She shook her head and motioned toward the graves. "I don't see how he's done what he has."

"Is he unconscious?"

"Probably. I've tried talking to him but he doesn't answer, and he hasn't drunk anything, either."

Cade gritted his teeth and looked at Poe. Here was another responsibility they didn't need, but they couldn't just ride away and leave him out here to die.

"Let me take the men and we'll go ahead," Poe said.

"No," Cade returned flatly, then made a cutting motion with his hand when Poe opened his mouth. His voice held an edge when he added, "Let it go, Frank."

"Then, damnit, shoot him and let's bury him with his friends."

"What the hell's gotten into you lately?"

"I was there when Schultz died, and when Talbot was knifed, that's what's gotten into me. I owe those sons of bitches, Andy, and it's a debt I intend to pay."

"I owe them, too," Lucia said. "But if we leave this man or kill him to ease our troubles, then we are no better than those we are chasing."

"There's no need to shoot me," Ben Hollister said wearily, lifting his head and wiping his lips with the back of his hand. "I'm going with you, Cade."

"I don't think you're fit to go anywhere, Hollister."

"What you think doesn't interest me." Ben moved a hand to his holster, then raised it to stare at his empty palm. Noticing the Smith and Wesson tucked in Cade's belt, he said, "Damn you, Sergeant."

"You don't need it, Hollister."

"I will soon enough. They killed Bobby and they killed my men, and they stole the women."

Poe cursed like he was spitting rotten meat from his mouth, and Lucia guffawed.

"You are no better than they are," she said. "You kidnapped us with your word that we would be freed when you reached Mexico, but when that time came, you refused."

"That's enough," Cade said. He was studying the outlaw doubtfully. "Do you think you could stay in the saddle if we took you with us?"

"You can tie me there or I can tie myself."

"Or you could head on back to Texas and get your head looked at."

"No, I'm going after the men who took Hattie and . . . the other one." He frowned. "What was her name?"

"Fanny," Lucia said.

"Yeah, her." He looked at Cade. "That's why I'll need my

pistol, Sergeant."

"I think I'll keep it awhile," Cade replied. "Your rifle, too. Morgan, slip that lever gun out of Hollister's scabbard and hang onto it. We're going after Misses Wilkes and O'Shea, and if Hollister can keep up, it'll make our job easier." He glanced at Elkins and Riley, standing hip-deep in the hard soil. "You men about ready?"

"For what we're planting, it's deep enough," Elkins replied.

"Then let's get it done," Cade said.

With the dawn, José led his men south, even farther from the road. He was a firm believer in never taking the same route twice to a familiar location. It wasn't always possible to avoid a well-laid trap. The *Indios* south of the Sierra del Capulíns had driven that point home. But if a man was sly like the fox, if he watched the horizons like a pronghorn and the arroyos like a hawk, then his odds were improved. That was something he believed his Hunters took notice of, and appreciated.

The spoils brought home from their wide-ranging patrols also helped. José had worried that this latest expedition had undermined his standing among the men, who had only a limited patience for ineptitude. But the old lawman and his posse, then the outlaws with all the extra arms, ammunition, horses, and women, had tipped the scales back in his favor.

José had put his *Cazadores de los Médanos* into motion at first light. Now, as the sun slipped its shackles from the horizon and the cooling breeze tapered off, he signaled a stop. He motioned Luis and Juan Carlos forward, then surveyed the rolling plain. Antelope moved in the distance, wandering away from the column as if sensing danger. Had so much food not been uncovered in the ambulance, José might have sent a couple of men out to bring in some fresh meat, but they had enough hardtack, beans, and dried beef for a quick breakfast. Barring the unforeseen, he hoped to make Villa Lobos by late afternoon.

It would be good to be home again. Still, as he caught sight of the prisoners being ordered down from their mounts, he realized he wasn't as eager for a reunion with his family as he had been in preceding days.

"*Mi capitán,*" Luis interrupted.

José turned. "Have the prisoners caused any trouble?"

"No, they have been like sheep. The old man especially has been eager to please."

José smiled. "He senses his own mortality, that one, as well he should. What of the women?"

"Obedient."

"And the auburn-haired woman?"

"She is the most resistant, but she understands that her choices are limited."

"Obey or suffer the consequences," Juan Carlos added with a low, crude laugh.

Ignoring the lieutenant's remark, José continued to address Luis. "Does she seem frightened?"

"No more than is to be expected."

José nodded. The auburn-haired woman intrigued him. She was a fighter, that one, and in daylight he saw that she was beautiful as well.

To Juan Carlos, he said, "I am putting the old man and the women in your charge, *Teniente.* You will see that no harm comes to them, and that the men stay away. Is that understood?"

Frowning, Juan Carlos replied, "I understand your words, but not your reasons. The women we capture have always belonged to the men."

"The women we've captured in the past were Indians. These women are different."

"They are *Norteamericanos,*" Juan Carlos replied without bothering to hide his confusion. "But they are still women."

"The one with the red hair will bring a good price in Chi-huahua City."

"And the other, whose hair is not as red?"

After a pause, José made his decision. "That one I will keep as my own."

Juan Carlos's eyes widened in surprise. Even Luis reacted with a faint arching of his brows. José was notorious, even respected, for remaining faithful to his wife. He never raped or sought release in a brothel. The Church forbade that, and José was true to its teachings—as far as fidelity was concerned.

"What of Consuelo?" Juan Carlos asked. "What of your children?"

"You would do well to mind to the matters of your own family, *mi teniente*," José replied rigidly. "And you, Luis? Do you also have an opinion?"

"If I do, it is that a good soldier does not question his *capitán's* orders."

José clamped a hand to the younger man's shoulder. "This," he said to Juan Carlos, "is an example of a loyal soldier. You could learn from him, my friend."

Juan Carlos's lips drew tight and bloodless. "As you wish, *mi capitán*," he replied.

"Exactly," José agreed in a vaguely menacing tone. "Tell me, Juan Carlos, do you understand my orders?"

"Yes, I am to watch over the prisoners, and the women in particular, to see that no harm comes to them."

"To fail in those orders could mean the firing squad. You understand that, as well?"

"Yes, I understand," Juan Carlos replied, and left to carry out his duties.

José turned to Luis, intending to issue further orders, but broke off when he noticed the scout's intense concentration on the trail behind them. Following the young man's line of sight, he spotted a swirl of dust rising above a nondescript shape he knew to be a horse and rider.

"Do you recognize them, Luis?"

"It is either Raúl or Arturo, but not both." The tautness of Luis's words betrayed his concern.

"You sent them both to bring back the escaping *Yanqui*, but now only one returns?"

"No, there is more than one."

José looked again, his eyes straining to make out what Luis saw clearly. Yes, there were two—no, three horses—and a man clinging weakly to the saddle of the second mount. "Do you recognize him yet?"

"Yes, I think so. It is Raúl, and he has a prisoner."

"You are sure it isn't Arturo he brings us?"

"I am sure," Luis replied grimly.

They spoke no more as they awaited Raúl's arrival. When he was closer, José saw that the scout had been injured. His shirt under his left arm was damp with blood, as was a bandana tied around his throat. He slowed from a canter to a trot, then a walk. The sorrel hair covering his mount's neck and shoulders was dark with perspiration. The man on the second horse—a *Yanqui*, slim, balding, his face pale and dripping sweat—was tied to the horn. His left leg hung limp, the foot dangling outside the stirrup. The third horse belonged to Arturo; his revolver, rifle, and machete were fastened to the saddle, but the scout was nowhere to be seen.

"I was afraid I might not find you," Raúl said to Luis, tossing him the reins to the second horse.

"How badly are you hurt?"

"Twice this bastard's bullets stung me, but I am alive." His lips turned down in a scowl. "Arturo is not."

The wounded *Yanqui* raised his head and looked around. Even through the pain evident on his face, José could feel the man's malevolence. It radiated off of him like the odor of rotting meat. Turning to where Juan Carlos stood with the prisoners, José shouted, "Send the old man over here."

Juan Carlos spoke briefly, and Henry McDaniels rose and sauntered over as if taking an evening stroll. But José noticed his gaze was keenly focused on the tableau before him, his expression as vigilant as a rabbit venturing into an open field.

Reaching up with his good hand, Raúl loosened the knot holding his prisoner to the saddle and gave him a hard yank. The man cried out as he was spilled from the back of his horse, making a pitiful shrieking sound as he writhed slowly on the ground. Stopping at José's side, McDaniels studied the wounded man dispassionately.

"You know him, old one?"

"I know him," McDaniels replied in Spanish.

"What is his name?"

"Ray Beeler." He looked at the horse. "That one's name is Acorn."

"That one is a horse, and has no name," José replied irritably.

Raúl had been glaring balefully at the elderly man. Now he took a threatening step forward. "Your friend killed my friend, *viejo.*"

"He isn't my friend," McDaniels replied, then raised his eyes to the bleeding scout. "And you are lucky he did not kill you."

José studied McDaniels for a moment, then said, "He is that good?"

"He is a killer," the old man confirmed. "I'm surprised your man caught him. I wouldn't have expected it."

"Is that true, Raúl?"

The scout hesitated, then shrugged. "It was a long shot, and a lucky one," he acknowledged. "My first two bullets missed, but the third found its mark." He walked over to put a boot on Beeler's chest to stop him from rolling back and forth, then pointed to his hip. "The joint is shattered. When he was struck, his horse jumped sideways, but he wasn't able to hold on. He crawled into some brush, and was mostly unconscious when I found him."

"Why did you bring him back?" Luis asked.

"Because you told me to, and because he killed Arturo. I thought perhaps you would want vengeance for his death."

Luis looked at José. "He is your prisoner, *mi capitán.* What do you wish done with him?"

"My wish is for you to remove this offal from my presence, as he has no use to any of us. But first." He looked down at the condemned man, unable to prevent the sneer he felt creeping over his face. "Get him on his feet," he ordered, and Luis motioned for two of the men from Juan Carlos's former command to lift the groaning *Yanqui* from the ground.

"You, old man," José snapped to McDaniels. "You will make sure this filth of a hog understands what I say."

McDaniels nodded quick assent and came over to stand at José's side as the *soldados* dragged Beeler in front of them, one on each side to hold him up.

"Ask him if the death of a true soldier of Mexico was worth his own death."

McDaniels seemed momentarily perplexed by the question, but then shrugged and repeated it in English. Beeler stared back as if equally puzzled, and his eyes moved slowly over José's face. Then his lips peeled back in a ghoulish grin and he spoke in a voice ragged with pain. McDaniels listened, swallowed audibly, and looked at José.

"He says if he could, he would piss on the corpse of your dead mother."

José's lips parted in astonishment. It wasn't the answer he'd expected, but it was one he admired, as he had the old lawman he had killed yesterday. "I think you are right, old man. This is *mal hombre,* a very bad man."

"He has killed a lot of people in Texas," McDaniels confided.

"Well, even the worst of us have good qualities, but killing Texans, though worthy of praise, will not save his soul today. Not after the death of a trusted scout. Raúl, did this pig have a knife on him?"

"*Sí, mi capitán,* in his boot." Raúl walked to the *Yanqui's* horse and slid a long, slender dirk from inside the roll of blankets behind his saddle. Its blade was like a razor, its handle made of some exotic wood José was unfamiliar with; the bolster looked like polished steel. Taking the knife, José stepped in front of the man called Beeler and said, "You are to be killed, but first I will give you something to remember me by."

He waited for McDaniels to translate, then a beat more for Beeler's reply. Smiling, the wounded man spat instead, a glob of bloody mucus hawked up from deep in his throat. The spittle struck José's shirt close to his neck, and José's eyes widened in shock and rage. With a cry, he jabbed the slim dirk upward through the bottom of Beeler's jaw, through his tongue and into the sinus cavity behind his nose.

The gringo's reaction was instantaneous. His entire body convulsed—knees bending upward until his feet cleared the ground, his arms turning as rigid as a bent rifle barrel. He didn't scream, though. His nose ran blood and snot and his eyes streamed tears, but the sounds that strained the tendons in his throat remained unuttered.

Leaving the dirk embedded in the man's face, José took his own knife and cut a piece of fabric from Beeler's shirt. He used the material to wipe the spittle from his chest. Then he pried open Beeler's lips and wadded the piece of shirt inside, pushing it against the dirk's bloody blade.

"Now," he said, breathing harshly. "Take this dog away and do as you wish with it."

Turning his back on the prisoner, José stalked over to where Juan Carlos waited next to the women. Grabbing the auburn-haired woman by the wrist, he yanked her to her feet and told her to come with him. She didn't understand. Not the words. But she knew what he wanted. They all did.

CHAPTER TWENTY-ONE

Poe, Elkins, and Morgan wanted to follow the bandits' trail straight into the desert, but Cade refused. Surprisingly, Hollister sided with him.

"They'll be watching for you," Ben said. "Their kind always does."

"Their kind, or your kind?" Poe challenged.

"Anyone who's smart and wants to live. If you try slipping up behind them, they'll spring a trap you'll never escape."

"That wouldn't be too damn easy," Poe shot back.

"It wasn't hard in the Sandbars. How many men did Little Fish kill, and how long did it—"

Ben stopped talking when Poe started toward him. Morgan grabbed Poe's arm, and Cade stepped between him and Hollister. "Get ahold of yourself, Corporal. You're a soldier, not a brawler."

"I'm going to kill that son of a bitch, Andy, I swear I'm going to kill him."

"You're going to obey orders or get your ass back to the States. Is that understood?"

Poe sucked in a shaky breath, then relaxed his stance. "Let me go," he said to Morgan.

Morgan looked at Cade, and released his grip. Poe stood steady, but his eyes bled hatred. "Those were my friends your half-breed killed, Hollister. When hell's froze over and we're all locked in ice, I'm still going to remember that."

Ben nodded acceptance. "I wouldn't expect anything less, but first we need to rescue those women. There's a town southwest of here called Villa Lobos. I'd lay odds that's where they're headed."

"Then why'd they leave the road?" Elkins asked.

"A road doesn't necessarily follow the straightest path," Ben replied.

"He is right," Lucia said. "When my father traveled to San Fidel, what is called Villa Lobos today, he would use the road only when he carried the wool in his cart. If he didn't have anything to sell, he would take burros across country. He said it cut nearly two days off his journey."

Cade stared speculatively at the bandits' trail, lost in the creosote less than twenty yards off the road.

"I think it's a good bet they're heading for Villa Lobos," he said. "I also think Hollister's right about it being too risky to try to follow them. We'll stay with the road, for a while, at least." He looked at Lucia. "Any idea how far it is to this village?"

"No, I've never been there. I only know what my father told me. A quiet village except on the night before Mass, when the young men gathered in the cantinas to drink and brag. It is supposed to be several times larger than San Ignacio. There was a trader there that my father dealt with. He took our wool in exchange for what we needed, then sent the fleece and whatever other crops he'd acquired on to Chihuahua City. If these men, these bandits, are not at Villa Lobos, then that is where they will go. But Chihuahua is much farther, many days travel from here."

"Well, let's go see where the road takes us," Cade said. He walked over to loosen the reins to Little Fish's coal black gelding. "Elkins, you can have my dun, unless you'd rather ride that mule with a blanket for a saddle."

"I believe I'll switch, Sergeant," Elkins replied. He pulled the blanket and bridle off the mule and set it free, then approached the dun. Putting a hand on the Springfield carbine Cade had left tied loosely to the saddle horn, he said, "You want this, Sergeant?"

"Keep it." Cade took off his cartridge belt of .45-70 rounds and handed it to Elkins. "This, too. I'll use Fish's Spencer. It might be older than the Springfield, but we know it's accurate."

Cade led out on the black gelding, ordering Lucia to stay in back and the men to spread out in between so they wouldn't make too tight of a target. The mule Elkins had turned loose followed along as if on an invisible lead, as Cade had hoped it would.

They rode until noon, alternating between a jog and a walk, before stopping to rest the horses. Cade kept an eye on Hollister, leaning against his grulla and hanging onto the saddle horn. Hollister was staring at the hardpan in front of his boots, but Cade didn't think he was seeing it.

Lucia led her mule forward. "I've been watching him," she said, meaning Hollister. "I don't think he will last much longer."

Cade shrugged. There was nothing he could do about Hollister now. The man would live or die, and the rest of them would continue on regardless.

Stepping away from his horse, Cade cocked his head to the south. "Does anyone else hear that?"

"Hell, I smell it," Elkins said, wrinkling his nose.

"So do I," said Morgan.

Cade did, too. The musky wet-wool odor of goats or sheep. A few minutes later, hearing a distant bleating, he decided it was sheep.

"They be comin' this way, from the sound of 'em," Riley said.

The men had all moved up close to where Cade and Lucia were standing next to their mounts, but it was another ten minutes before the first of the mob appeared over the crest of a low hill west of the road. Cade could hear the faint tinkling of the leader's bell, and spotted her a few seconds later, a woolly ewe larger than the rest, like she'd grown into her position as queen over the years.

Cade had heard it said that a smart shepherd never got rid of his leader. They became like old friends, partners who knew their roles and performed them like professionals. The dogs had a part in it, too. He saw one of them now, a black and white collie trotting over the hill alongside its flock, head lowered like he was thinking of taking a bite out of any sheep that considered straying. The posture must have worked, because the herd looked tight and under control as it flowed past less than a hundred yards to their right.

When the shepherd finally hove into view, he was everything Cade would have expected. Slim and gray, dressed in worn clothing and a straw sombrero fraying at the edges of its wide brim. A sun-faded serape draped over one shoulder offered the only color—thin lines of red, blue, and gold across a brown background. The revolver strapped around the old man's waist seemed an oddity, yet Cade knew it shouldn't. It was a foolish man who didn't carry some kind of weapon out here.

Motioning Lucia to her mule, Cade said, "Let's go talk to him. The rest of you stay here and keep your eyes open."

The shepherd had already noticed them. Now he stopped and pulled his serape back so that he could more easily get at his revolver. Cade kept both hands out in the open where the shepherd could see them, and when they were within range, Lucia shouted something in Spanish that caused the herdsman to relax. Not enough for him to flip the wool back over his gun, but he didn't seem as anxious when Cade and Lucia rode up.

Lucia spoke first and the shepherd replied, and soon they were engaged in a rapid conversation in Spanish that Cade could only guess at. Then Lucia gasped and dropped from her saddle. She had tears in her eyes as she embraced the elderly man, and he was grinning and nodding and babbling in return. At one point he held his hand out with his palm flat, as if indicating the height of someone no more than nine or ten years old, and Lucia laughed and turned to Cade.

"This is my father's brother, Gustavo."

"Buenos días," Cade said, expending a fair portion of his Spanish in that simple greeting.

"Good day to you, I think," Gustavo replied.

"You speak English?"

"Sí, un poco."

"Not well," Lucia cautioned.

"A little," Gustavo emphasized, holding a thumb and forefinger up for Cade's inspection, barely half an inch separating the two appendages. "Very a little, you know?"

"Yes, I know."

"Tío Gustavo used to run sheep for a man in El Paso," Lucia explained. "He learned some English there." She turned back to the older man and they spoke rapidly in Spanish for several minutes before Cade finally interrupted them.

"What's he saying?"

The two spoke a moment more, then Lucia came back to stand next to Cade's black, looking up at him in his saddle. "What he says is not good."

"Tell it anyway."

She did, explaining how a bandit named José Yanez had come to San Fidel with only half a dozen followers, and how from there he'd recruited an army of nearly fifty.

"Yanez calls them his *Cazadores de los Médanos,*" she said. "It means Hunters of the Dunes, in honor of the sand dunes that lie north of the village. When he first arrived, Yanez promised the people of San Fidel that with his help and a small tax he would protect them from the Apaches, and for a while, he did.

But as his army grew more powerful, the promises he'd made seemed less important to him."

It was a story Cade had heard before, although not one he'd ever come face to face with. "Now the protector is worse than the enemies he once protected them from?"

"So it seems. Yanez's men have taken over the town, and no one there is safe. My uncle says that for a time, families would send their daughters away before they became of age, for fear they would be claimed as wives for the soldiers. Then Yanez learned of their actions and called it treachery. He executed a father who was caught trying to smuggle his thirteen-year-old daughter to the Guadalupe Mission in Juarez. After that, very few families have tried to send their children away.

"Now Yanez and his men use San Fidel as a base from which they raid north and east, stealing cattle and horses from ranches in the *Estados Unidos* that they sell to merchants in Chihuahua City. They take scalps from Indians that they sell to the Mexican government, and prisoners they pass on to the big rancheros close to the mountains in the west, where the graze is good for their stock and there is plenty of water all year."

"Slaves?"

"Yes, slaves. But there is something else. I told him why we were here, and he told me of some *Norteamericanos* who had a copper mine near the dunes, before Yanez and his men arrived. The *Yanquis* left in a hurry because of the bandits, and had to leave some of their supplies behind."

"Guns?"

"Maybe better, maybe not. Dynamite."

"Dynamite," Cade repeated softly. "Yeah, that might be better, if it's still there and still good."

"No one speaks of the mine for fear Yanez will learn of it and force the people to reopen it."

"Does your uncle know where this mine is?"

"Yes." She pointed west. "A day's ride in that direction, in a canyon north of *Los Médanos.*"

"*Los Médanos?*"

"The dunes south of the springs at Samalayuca."

"These the same dunes Yanez named his army after?"

She nodded.

"Can your uncle guide us there?"

She spoke briefly to Gustavo, who immediately shook his head no.

"He will not leave his flock," she told Cade. "It is his life."

Cade chewed thoughtfully on his lower lip, staring in the direction Lucia had pointed as he considered their options. Perhaps two days lost for explosives of unknown quality—they could be worthless if too old, or if they'd gotten wet—versus the old man's estimate of fifty bandits waiting for them in Villa Lobos.

"Damn," he breathed, easing back in his seat. "All right, ask your uncle if he can at least give us directions to that mine."

"I already did. He said we will see the trail the *Yanquis* used to haul their copper north to El Paso." After a pause, she added, "Are we going after the dynamite, Andrew?"

"I think we have to."

"Did you also think about what might become of Hattie and Fanny if we take too long finding it?"

"Yeah," Cade replied grimly. "I thought about that, too."

José's scowl deepened as he and his men wound their way through Villa Lobos. He had sent Antonio ahead to alert the citizens to their arrival. Having done so, he had expected large crowds along the street as he led his embattled troops into town. So where were they? Where were the alcalde and the town's leading businessmen?

And the priest? Where was he to offer his blessings at their successful return?

José's angry gaze raked the street, lined with milk-colored adobe buildings and dusty cottonwoods. Nearly three hundred citizens lived here, yet not even a child stood alongside the village's winding thoroughfare to welcome them home.

As they rode into the central plaza, the only sounds to greet his ears were the clopping of their horses' hooves, the rattle of bits and spurs, and the creak of saddle leather as the column came to a ragged halt. But at least here, at last, there was someone to greet them. Pierna Mala—Bad-Leg—stood in front of what used to be a trading post before José and his men confiscated the building for their own use. Bad-Leg wore a large grin and a dirty canvas jacket that had once belonged to a German officer of indeterminate rank, supposedly sent to Chihuahua as a military observer. Bad-Leg had once confided to José that he hadn't questioned the foreigner's business in Mexico before killing him; it had been enough, he claimed, that the blond-haired stranger had been traveling with Federales.

"It was his sole crime," Pierna Mala confessed, "but it was all the evidence a true son of Mexico needed."

That had been many years ago, José knew, before he lost his leg to the *Guardabosque Tejano*—the Texas Rangers. And before he arrived in Villa Lobos to take up the cause of freedom. Or free living, as Bad-Leg called it.

"No rules, eh, *mi capitán*?"

At first, José had refused to consider allowing him into their ranks. He was a cripple on crutches, and possibly a buffoon to hear him talk. But time and familiarity had softened José's opinion. Bad-Leg was as shrewd as he was reckless, and commanded more respect on his one leg than men like Juan Carlos ever would on two. Perhaps he could not ride, but he could command a garrison, watching José's back from home even as he sent men out into the surrounding countryside to recruit more Hunters.

Pierna Mala stood at attention as José approached, his palm raised to his forehead in a crooked salute. *"Mi capitán,"* he called, his voice ringing across the plaza.

Smiling, José gave the order for his men to dismount and disband.

"Go to your homes," he told them. "Take care of your wives and sweethearts. Then return here at dusk and we will celebrate our return with a fiesta."

The men cheered and the tension of the past week—ever since locating Geronimo's camp in the Sierra del Capulíns—evaporated like drops of dew in the morning sun. It was good to be home again, José thought. Then his gaze fell on Juan Carlos and their prisoners, and his smile dimmed. He motioned the lieutenant forward.

"Take the captives to the priest's house and see that they are fed and made comfortable," he commanded.

"All of them?"

José's gaze lingered on the auburn-haired woman, her face bruised, eyes lowered.

"Yes. Tell the priest I will be by later with an urgent matter for him to attend to."

"Sí, mi capitán," Juan Carlos replied, returning to the captives and motioning them toward the church that occupied the opposite side of the plaza like a small castle.

"A celebration?" Bad-Leg asked as the Hunters dispersed. "Even after . . ." His words trailed off potently.

"The Apache ambush?"

"I thought maybe, when Antonio told me of the men who were lost, that you might postpone the fiesta."

"No, with so many soldiers killed, it is more important than ever to show the men that life goes on."

Bad-Leg's hesitation almost caused José to question his decision. Then he dismissed the idea as absurd. Death was a steady companion, the opportunity to dance and drink and fornicate as rare as rain in this parched country. They would celebrate tonight, sleep off their debauchery tomorrow, then have the priest hear their confessions so that they could continue their lives with unblemished souls.

But first, José had his own business to conduct with the priest.

"Is Father Alfredo in his rectory?"

"No, he has gone into the country to visit those too old or infirm to attend Mass in town."

José frowned. It was annoying that the priest wasn't available when he was needed. José considered his presence among the men as important as a medical practitioner's—if they'd had a doctor—but the padre never saw it in the same light.

"They are all the Church's children, near and far," he'd insist whenever José brought up the need for him to remain close to town. And José could never summon enough courage to countermand the opinion of a man of the cloth. José Yanez feared neither man nor beast, but the thought of displeasing either the Savior or the Holy Virgin could turn his spine to liquid.

Rubbing his heavily stubbled jaw thoughtfully, José turned his back to the imposing structure. Then he smiled. "So be it, eh?"

Laughing, Bad-Leg bobbed his head. "So be it. Shall I order a beef slaughtered?"

"Order five of them slaughtered," José said. "I want everyone here tonight to share in the joy of my news."

"Your news?"

"I am to be married, my friend."

"Married?" Bad-Leg's eyes widened almost comically.

"To my new wife."

"Ah, the gringa? But . . . what of Consuelo?"

"Don't worry about her, Pierna Mala. I will talk to Father Alfredo as soon as he returns. My marriage to Consuelo will be annulled, and then I will wed my new love."

"But that . . ." Then he smiled. "As you wish, *mi capitán!* Five fat steers, and plenty of vino and mescal."

"And fireworks? Are there any left from the night we celebrated Christ's birth?"

"Some, I think. If there are any here, I will find them."

"Good. And now, I go to tell my wife the bad news. Perhaps, if you see her at the dance tonight, you might offer her some comfort."

"If not me, then I will find someone who will," Bad-Leg promised.

José Yanez paced anxiously across the small placita of his home, just off of Villa Lobos's central plaza. The house had once belonged to a wealthy merchant who dealt in wool and hides from the surrounding ranges. At one time, the products of the vast herds of sheep and goats that ranged these desolate hills surrounding San Fidel had been the community's chief source of income. But in recent years the herdsmen had been avoiding San Fidel. They referred to it now as Villa Lobos and took their flocks elsewhere to trade.

At first José had resented the implication of the title—that he and his men were somehow more predator than protector—but in time he had come to not only accept the term, but embrace it. He considered the villagers' refusal to recognize his role as their defender as license to dissolve his original contract with the town. It also freed him of any obligation to remain close—other than for a small home guard to protect the interest of his soldiers—allowing him and his Hunters to roam farther afield in search of plunder.

The villagers' decision, while not openly acknowledged, was

widely understood. They rejected the presence of José's *Caza-dores de los Médanos*, yet lacked the courage—or at least the arms—to do anything about it. The consequences had worked out much better for José and his men than it had for the people of San Fidel.

There were annoyances, though. José faced one now, with dusk settling over the town and the padre not yet returned. Already, Bad-Leg and his men had spread the word that there would be a celebration tonight, honoring not only the Hunters' return, but also the wedding of their *capitán* to a gringa. And the men had made it clear the townspeople were expected to attend, wearing their best clothes and bearing large smiles and good wishes for the happy couple, as well as a small gift as a token of their respect.

José knew any gifts would be trifling. His men had already ransacked the village of anything of value. It was the gesture that counted. That and the power of his authority to demand such a tribute.

Now he worried that the priest would not return in time. He had sent men into the country to search for him, but so far the padre's whereabouts remained unknown. If he was not located soon, the fiesta would have to be called off, the wedding postponed until Father Alfredo could vacate José's marriage to Consuelo, clearing the way for a new wife.

A delay would not have been so distressing if José didn't fear he'd already offended the Church. In a moment of weakness following his confrontation with the *Tejano* killer called Ray Beeler, he had sinned terribly by consummating his marriage too soon. He fretted also that the gringa's fierce resistance may have made matters worse, at least in the eyes of God.

His faith harbored some confusing beliefs toward matrimony. As a matter of course, José had always felt safe in copulating only with his wives, and he had taken pains over the years not to change them too often. It was just that there had been so many Hunters killed this time. Not only the scout, Arturo, but those murdered in the Apache ambush as well. So, with the *Tejano's* sputum still damp on his shirt, José had sought to alleviate the darkness by taking the *Norteamericano* woman before their vows.

After much prayer and reflection, José had convinced himself that what he had done would not be considered a sin if he could end his marriage to Consuelo, then marry the gringa—he would need to find out her name prior to the ceremony—before nightfall, for it was not only proper, but expected, that a man make love to his new bride on the day of their wedding.

So where was that damned priest?

The gate to the courtyard squeaked as it was pushed inward. José spun, his hand darting instinctively to the revolver on his hip, but it was only Bad-Leg, come to report on the fiesta's preparations, and on the padre's whereabouts. José scowled as he read the answer to the latter question on his subordinate's face. He knew the rest would not matter if the priest could not be located in time.

"Your wishes, *mi capitán?*"

"You don't even bother to present me your news?"

"You already know my news," Bad-Leg replied. "Without a smile on my face, you can be assured the priest has not been found. It is the celebration I inquire of. The beef already roasts over coals, and the tables have been arranged in the plaza. I have also assembled a band of trumpets and guitars."

"Have the people begun to gather?"

"Not yet. I sent word they will be summoned by the ringing of the church bells."

José nodded approval. "Sometimes I wish you were not a cripple, Pierna Mala. You would make a fine field officer."

"Ah, it is true that I often wish the same thing, but the Savior, in His wisdom, had other plans."

"And did the Savior have any revelations regarding the location of Father Alfredo?"

Bad-Leg smiled wistfully. "If He does, He has not yet shared them with me."

José exhaled loudly and glanced to the door of his house. No sound emanated from the dwelling where he had informed Consuelo that afternoon that she had until nightfall to gather her things—and he included their two young daughters among her possessions—and leave. He had told her they were to be divorced that evening, and that she would be free to find a new husband tomorrow. Consuelo had taken the news in the same stoic manner she had accepted his proposal at her first husband's funeral.

"Mi capitán," Bad-Leg cautiously intruded.

After a moment's pause, José said, "Let us wait awhile longer and see if the priest returns. If he has not arrived by midnight, we will call off the celebration."

"As you wish," Bad-Leg replied, bowing slightly as he retreated toward the heavy gate leading to the plaza.

José waited with a patient smile until the man had left the placita, drawing the gate closed behind him. Then he resumed his pacing, his expression growing steadily darker.

CHAPTER TWENTY-TWO

Riding through the night like they did, it was luck and little else that brought them to the copper mine Gustavo Mendoza had told them of. If not for the slim cart track leading into the canyon and the old shepherd's assurance that a mine existed there, Cade doubted he would have bothered to explore the narrow crevice.

Through disuse, the road had grown over almost entirely in bear grass, with towering prickly pear, yucca, and tarbush growing along its periphery. Mexican poppies, like yellow paint splashed from a bucket, covered the hills to either side of the canyon's entrance. To the southeast, *Los Médanos*—The Dunes—stood between them and Villa Lobos like lines of infantry, ridge after ridge of pure, pale sand. Cade knew he'd have to decide soon whether to cut straight across those barren spines, or circle them to the north, adding perhaps another day to their already delayed pursuit of the bandits.

The canyon was narrow enough that they had to navigate it single file. Cade sent Poe in first, at a thirty-yard advance, and had Morgan bring up the rear. Lucia rode toward the middle of the column where she could keep an eye on Hollister; the outlaw leader hadn't given them any trouble since they picked him up the day before, but he was prone to falling asleep in the saddle or briefly blacking out.

The canyon's walls turned sheer almost as soon as they entered, its floor graveled and rocky. Traces of dried mud indicated running water at some point earlier that year, but it was dry now. Yet there was a hint of moisture on the air that flowed past them on a downdraft, pleasantly cool after their long sojourn across the desert.

They were a hundred yards in before the canyon widened, its sides becoming less perpendicular, the floor giving over to a type of lush grass with which Cade was unfamiliar. The horses and mules recognized it as desirable and immediately began stretching their necks for bites that they chewed as they walked, the excess sticking out past their bits like frayed cigars. Under different circumstances Cade would have ordered his men to keep their mounts' heads up, their attention focused on the route before them, but they'd been so long without decent graze that he kept his mouth shut and let the stock grab what they could.

They found the mine without difficulty, sunk into the canyon's south wall fifty feet above the floor. Tailings fanned out beneath it like a woman's fancy wedding train, with steps carved into the earth at its side. A stone hut near the center of the canyon was surrounded by grass even more lush than what they'd passed so far. Cade pulled his horse to a stop some distance away. Poe had already dismounted to inspect the hut. He emerged from it now and walked over to where the rest of the squad waited.

"Nothing in there," Poe reported. "There's a shallow well in back, but it's dry."

"Any sign of the men who used to mine here?"

"Not even a track in the hut. I'd say this place has been deserted for some time."

Cade glanced over his shoulder and his gaze settled on Hollister, sitting his grulla with his reins slack, eyes closed.

"Maybe we ought to leave him here," Poe suggested quietly. "There's good grass for his horse and shelter from the sun, and there's water somewhere, I'd bet my last nickel on that. We just haven't found it yet. We could pick him up on the way back." He looked at Cade. "Or leave him here."

"Your obsession with Hollister is getting tiresome, Frank," Cade replied in equally low tones. "You need to put it aside until we're back in the States." Then he raised his voice for the others. "Dismount and unsaddle the horses. One of you get a fire started and heat up some venison and beans. Morgan, help Lucia get Hollister off his horse. Frank, you come with me."

Cade dismounted and handed the black's reins to Elkins. Then he and Poe climbed the rust-hued talus to the mine's entrance. He'd been inside a few shafts over the years. Never all the way into their bowels, but far enough past the entrance to expect a wooden frame to reinforce the roof and timbered bracing every ten feet or so. He saw none of that here, and his scalp crawled when he envisioned the tons of rock and dirt that hung unsupported above his head.

About ten feet into the adit, Poe spotted a lantern sitting on an empty crate on the floor. He picked it up by its harp and gave it an experimental shake, his brows arching in surprise at the sound of splashing from the reservoir, the pungent odor of kerosene. He looked at Cade. "Have you got a match?"

Cade handed him a packet and Poe tore off one of the little wooden slivers and struck it alight. He waited until the sparks and sputtering tapered off, then raised the glass and touched the flaming head to the wick. When the light caught, Poe tossed the match and lowered the globe.

"That's better," Poe said, brushing the worst of the dust off the glass before adjusting the wick for maximum illumination.

Shoulder to shoulder, the two men ventured deeper into the shaft. About sixty feet in they came to a stack of supplies covered with a tarp. Poe stood back as Cade slid the paulin away. Underneath, they found numerous implements for digging, a twenty-gallon keg filled with iron spikes, several crates of candles, canned foods such as tomatoes, peaches, and sardines, some blankets, and a pair of packsaddles. And to one side, almost as an afterthought, half a crate of dynamite.

Poe whistled when he lifted the lid. "Looks like that old shepherd knew what he was talking about."

Reaching over Poe's shoulder, Cade ran a finger along one of the sticks of dynamite, then gently rubbed his fingers together. The feeling was damp and slightly oily, the smell reminiscent of rotting eggs.

"This ain't good, Frank."

"What do you mean?"

Cade held up his fingers, the tips covered with a faint sheen. "It's sweating."

Poe muttered a curse and quickly backed away, taking the lantern with him. "That throws a kink in the cow's tail," he said.

Cade followed him, and they backed off another dozen paces. Not far enough if the deteriorating dynamite blew—Cade doubted if any place in the entire canyon would be safe if that happened—but at least far enough back that an errant ember wasn't likely to escape the lantern's ventilated chimney and land inside the crate.

"What now?" Poe asked.

After a moment's thought, Cade replied, "Let's get out of here."

Hollister was awake by the time Cade and Poe returned to the stone hut. Sitting with his back to the wall, arms crossed over his chest, he watched their approach with expressionless eyes.

Riley had kindled a fire and put some meat and frijoles on to heat, and he and Lucia were monitoring it. It would be the first warm meal they'd had since leaving San Ignacio, and the eagerness in Riley's eyes as he watched over the steaming beans attested to his hunger. Cade figured they were all feeling it; parched corn and jerky kept a man moving, but did little to satisfy his cravings.

Elkins was squatted nearby, smoking a cigarette and keeping an eye on the grazing stock, but Morgan was nowhere to be seen. Sensing the question in Cade's roving gaze, Elkins said, "Morgan went back to keep watch from the canyon's mouth. I planned to relieve him after I ate."

Cade nodded, pleased with their initiative. Lowering himself next to Lucia, he said, "Your uncle was right. We found half a dozen sticks of dynamite in a crate about sixty feet inside the mine."

She smiled. "Then the trip was worth it?"

"I'm not sure," he said, then told them what he and Poe had discovered.

Riley's expression was worried when he said, "I worked a spell in a lead mine in Missouri, Sergeant. I never handled dynamite meself, but knew a few who did. They'd get white as me mother's fresh-washed sheets when anyone mentioned sweat and dynamite in the same breath."

"It's dangerous," Cade allowed.

"Why?" Lucia asked.

"It means it's deteriorating," Ben supplied quietly. He was speaking to Lucia, but looking at Cade. "It means a man'd be a damned fool to mess with it."

"That's about the size of it," Cade admitted. "It seems we've wasted more time than we had to spare coming out here."

"No . . ." Lucia breathed.

"Unless you can find someone damn fool enough to carry it," Ben added.

Cade hesitated. "What are you saying, Hollister?"

"We're going to need the edge that dynamite will give us, Cade."

"Not if we blow ourselves up before we get there."

"Then whoever carries the dynamite will need to stay far enough away from the others that he'd be the only one who died if it went off." He chuckled. "Him and his horse, of course."

"I'd not ask anyone to volunteer for that kind of duty," Cade said.

"I won't be volunteering, Sergeant. But I will be carrying it."

Poe snorted. "Hell, you'll fall asleep before we're halfway there and leave nothing but a crater in the ground where you fell out of your saddle."

"Then there will be nothing lost, and you won't have to waste any more time glaring in my direction, Corporal."

"Oh, I don't mind glaring," Poe said. "Thinking about you and me settling accounts when this is over is what keeps me going."

"That's enough, Poe," Cade said. He looked at Hollister. "You figure you can pull this off?"

"There'll be nothing lost in my trying, and quite a bit gained if I can do it."

"I won't argue that," Cade replied. "All right, let's eat first, then give the horses a couple of hours to graze and rest. After that I'll pull out with my men, and you can follow along half an hour later."

Hollister's smile was slim to the point of skeletal, vaguely haunting in light of his goal. "If you hear a bang, Sergeant, don't bother coming back to see what happened."

"I wasn't planning to," Cade replied stonily.

By midafternoon, José's rage was nearing its peak. Already, the last of the riders Bad-Leg had sent out the day before to locate the absent padre had returned with no news of the man's whereabouts. Luis had sent out a few scouts as well, but José's hopes of them finding the priest were shrinking steadily. Meanwhile, yesterday had passed, and so had his chance to wed the gringa—her name was Hattie, according to the bearded outlaw called McDaniels.

There was little doubt in José's mind now that he had sinned badly in the eyes of the Church. Had raped, when the charge would not have been brought up at all if the priest had been in his rectory where he belonged.

José fumed and paced, and from time to time he would drink deeply from a reed-wrapped bottle of wine looted from the sacristy behind the church. Consuelo had left last night, following his instructions and taking only her clothes, a few personal items, and the children, the oldest toddling at her side, clinging to her skirt, the other suckling at Consuelo's breast even as she exited the placita.

José felt only a momentary regret at the loss of his family. It was not the first he had left behind, and he suspected it wouldn't be the last. But a moment of remorse was all he could afford with the absent priest claiming his attention; the need to wed the gringa before another day passed and the immorality of his actions sank him deeper into despair.

The heavy wooden gate leading to the central plaza had been left open upon Consuelo's departure. It remained open now, as the sun crossed a pale sky devoid of clouds and the heat within the hacienda's enclosure grew even more oppressive. Sweat—from drink as well as the sun's rays—streamed from José's face and darkened the fabric of his shirt, and his belly churned from too much wine and not enough food. His vision swam briefly when he spotted a slim figure gliding through the gate. At first José didn't recognize the man; he even thought it might be the wayward priest, returning to seek pardon for his absence. Then he realized it was Bad-Leg, nearly as swift on his crutches as most men were without them.

Bad-Leg stopped uncertainly, his gaze dropping to the bottle of wine in José's right hand, and the other bottles, empty, sitting on the wooden table behind him.

"What news have you brought me, Pierna Mala?"

"None that is good, I am afraid. The priest is still missing. I have sent more men out to scour the countryside. I am sure he will soon be found and returned to Villa Lobos."

"This is all you have to report?" José slammed the bottle down on the outdoor table where he had hoped to feast in celebration of his nuptials.

"There is a question the men wish me to ask. It concerns the beeves that were roasted last night. They fear the meat will go bad if it is not soon eaten, and the Hunters are hungry. There has been little for them other than corn and frijoles."

"No one cares about the Hunters' bellies," José murmured darkly, before turning away.

"It is wasteful to let it rot."

"Then don't. Drag it into the desert and let the wolves and coyotes feast."

"And the men, *mi capitán*? Your loyal Hunters of the Dunes?"

José put both hands flat on the table. His head felt full, and his mind seemed to swirl in alcoholic eddies. "Tell me, my friend, am I in the saddle of a bucking *caballo*?"

Bad-Leg chuckled knowingly. "I think what bucks is too much wine. It fuddles the brain, no?"

José opened his eyes to stare at the empty bottles staggered across the table. "I wish I had not drunk so much," he confessed.

"*El resaca* is like the bite of the scorpion on a man's ass," Bad-Leg agreed. "Not so bad now, but worse tonight and tomorrow."

José turned carefully to wave the man away. "Celebrate, Pierna Mala. Break out the wine and mescal for the men, order the villagers into the plaza and serve the meat and chili, the tamales and frijoles. The pastries, too, with lots of sugar. Make it all available to my brave Hunters. When the sun sets tonight, no man, woman, or child should be hungry . . . or sober. That is my decree!"

"The band?"

"Yes, of course, the band. Let there be dancing along with the feasting, and after the sun sets, light the fireworks. You found some, no?"

"Yes, a few rockets and some pinwheels."

"*Bueno!*" José cried, then belched loudly and swayed back until his hips hit the edge of the table. Laughing, he said, "I only wish I could be there, *mi amigo.*"

"You will be," Bad-Leg predicted. "Sleep now, and when you awaken, the priest will have returned and you can marry your pretty gringa and be happy again, eh?"

"Yes," José muttered, slewing his eyes toward the yawning door to the hacienda. "Sleep, then tonight . . ." He stopped, scowling. "Where is my bride, Pierna Mala? I haven't seen her."

"She and the others are still under the watchful eye of Juan Carlos Cordova, in the church rectory."

"Cordova!" José spat, then wiped away what clung to his chin with the back of his hand. "That swine is not fit to watch goats. Bring them here." He looked at Bad-Leg, squinting until he was able to see him clearly. "They will be under your charge now, my one-legged friend. Is that understood?"

"*Sí*, of course."

José nodded, then returned his attention to the dark entrance of the hacienda. There was a low cowhide *sofá* inside, and blankets he could roll out on the floor if he wanted. Or a bed in one of the back rooms if that was his choice. And it would be cool and quiet inside, so that he could sleep off the effects of the wine in peace. Pushing away from the table, he made his way carefully toward the hacienda's door.

"Go," he instructed without looking around. "Start the fiesta. I need only a few minutes to . . ." His voice trailed off as he reached the door. He frowned, trying to remember what it was he needed. Then he saw the bottle of wine in his right hand and laughed. That was it, he decided. He needed more wine, and lifting the bottle to his lips, he drank deeply as he lurched inside.

They'd found a spring inside the canyon. With that much grass and as green and lush as it was, Cade had known there had to be water somewhere. In addition to full canteens, they had also raided some of the supplies the American miners had left behind, taking along tins of food and extra blankets, carried on the mules using the packsaddles he and Poe had found inside the mine shaft. They were better outfitted now than they had been since their first night on the trail, and with packs instead of a cumbersome ambulance, they could make better time, too. And at that moment, time was something they desperately needed.

Exiting the canyon's mouth, Poe twisted in his saddle to catch Cade's eye. "Which way?"

He pointed southeast, toward the pale rise of dunes. "That way."

"Straight across?"

"As close to true southeast as we can make it. We'll pick up the Villa Lobos road on the other side, then find out if that's where they were heading."

The sound of a horse's iron shoe clipping a stone somewhere back in the narrow canyon caught Cade's ear. He glanced over his shoulder, but Hollister was still out of sight. Wanting to keep it that way, he said, "Let's move out."

Although the chore had rattled his nerves, Cade had gone back into the mine to help Ben stow the dynamite in his saddlebags, three on each side. They'd wrapped the sticks individually in strips of wool cut from a blanket, then sprinkled water over the coarse fabric to keep the dynamite cool. Cade didn't know if the moisture would help prevent the explosives from detonating prematurely, or if it might ruin the already compromised munitions. Had it been only him and his men he would have left the dynamite behind, judging it too risky. But Hollister had been adamant, and Cade had elected not to argue. He'd already decided that if they managed to get back to the States, he wouldn't try to bring Hollister with them. Poe might object, but that was a bridge they could cross later. Unless the dynamite blew too soon and settled the matter for them.

They reached the northern rim of *Los Médanos* within an hour. After that, travel proved difficult, and in places, even dangerous. The dunes were a land like no other Cade had ever passed through. Steep tan mountains of sand rippled by the constantly buffeting winds, fine-grained and dragging at their every step. In most places the horses sank into it past their fetlocks, and the heat seemed to sear into their flesh like a farrier's fire, as blistering from below as above. The taller ridges rose sixty feet or more, and Cade wondered if this was what it was like to be in a ship crossing a vast body of water, cresting one powerful wave only to plunge into the trough behind it, before rising again toward a cloudless sky.

At one point they came to an undulating heath, and in its middle they discovered the remains of a trio of small wagons, ringed by the bleached skeletons of oxen. There was no sign of human remains near the wagons; they found those a few hundred yards past the last sun- and wind-scoured vehicle, three men half-buried in the shifting sands, their skulls showing the deep gouges of scalp knives.

"Apaches?" Riley asked, dabbing at his cracked lower lip with the back of his hand.

"Not likely," Cade said. "Apaches don't normally take scalps."

"Scalp hunters," Morgan speculated, and Lucia concurred.

"These men here." She motioned toward the corpses. "They were probably Mexicans, or half-breeds, but their scalps would sell as well as any Apache's."

Cade ordered a short break and water for their horses. No one suggested burying the dead. It was too hot, and the moving dunes would soon reopen the graves. Given time, Cade figured the sand would cover them again, at least for a while.

They pushed on into the seemingly endless drifts, and in late afternoon came to familiar terrain. The land here was more gently rolling than it had been in the lower regions along the Rio Grande, and had a larger variety of flora. Cade called another halt, and they unsaddled the stock and hobbled them before turning them loose to forage on the spotty grass.

The deep sands had taken a toll on all of them, as had the long days of travel with scant sleep, poor food, and seldom enough water to satisfy the deep thirst of slow dehydration. They couldn't stop now, though. According to what Lucia recalled from her father's stories as a child, and what her Uncle Gustavo had told them yesterday, Villa Lobos wasn't far ahead.

"Before nightfall," Lucia predicted, and Cade hoped she was right.

Moving out, he sent Poe and Morgan ahead to scout, while he, Elkins, Riley, and Lucia followed with the pack mules. Cade hadn't seen any sign of Hollister since leaving the canyon near the Samalayuca springs, but no one had reported hearing a distant explosion, either, so he figured the outlaw was probably still following them.

Despite his sense of urgency, Cade kept the small squad to a walk after leaving the dunes. By sunset they'd reached the San Ignacio road, running more directly south here than it had before; it was as if whoever had laid out the route wanted to steer clear of the dangers lurking within *Los Médanos*. There was no sign of the bandits' passage in the dust, but Cade hadn't expected any. Yanez and his men had left the road yesterday, after plundering the ambulance. Their trail would be farther out in the desert—if they'd come this way at all.

As they turned onto the road, Cade glanced back the way they'd come, but there was still no sign of Hollister. The outlaw's absence was starting to nag at him. He kept remembering the dullness of the man's expression, the slackness of his facial muscles, and the way he'd doze off in his saddle—nothing at all like the stern-faced outlaw who had raided their camp in Texas. Cade wondered if it was Bobby Hollister's death that had taken so much starch out of Ben's spine, or if it was the blow Little Fish had given to his head.

Thoughts of Hollister continued to occupy Cade's thoughts as the sun gradually sank below the horizon. Dusk was closing in around them like a hot, dry fog when he brought his gelding to a sudden stop, throwing a hand up to halt the others. A group of horsemen had appeared on the road before them. Cade considered ordering his own men to scatter into the desert, but something about the approaching figures stopped him. He counted three horses, and when they drew closer, he spied a fourth figure riding a burro.

Easing his dun up alongside Cade's black, Elkins said, "That's Poe out front, isn't it?"

"Looks like him," Cade agreed. Poe in front, then Morgan leading a horse with a prisoner bound to the saddle. And behind them, a rotund figure in a brown robe and a low-crowned, flat-brimmed hat, pushed back on his head to reveal a florid, clean-shaven face.

"And damn if it doesn't look like they found a padre," Elkins added in surprise.

CHAPTER TWENTY-THREE

He awoke to the murmur of voices whispering in his ear, and his hand dropped instinctively to his revolver, his body jackknifing into a sitting position even as the gun's muzzle came level with his shoulder.

He stared into a land as blank as a piece of canvas, pale tans and soft browns, all of it without feature—at least at first. Then, with his heart pounding and sweat coursing down his face in rivulets, he blinked to clear the haze from his mind and took a second look around. He saw dilapidated wagons in the moonlight, the ivory glow of bones nearly entombed by sand, and wondered where he was . . . who he was.

A horse standing hipshot not far away looked more like a ghost than a living, breathing creature. If not for the saddle cinched to its back he might have believed it was dead, too—a memory of some past tragedy not yet ready to leave the scene of its slaughter.

It was the saddle that caught his eye, that brought his scattered thoughts back in bits and spurts. He recognized the rig, recalled buying it from a shop . . . somewhere. Lowering the revolver, he stared at its polished steel and walnut grips, and recognized that, too. A Smith and Wesson American model, .44 caliber. Glancing at the ghost-gray horse—a grulla—he knew there would be a rifle in a scabbard on the far side that fired the same cartridge.

He became aware of a burning on his face, a tightness to the flesh between his eyes and the scruff of his whiskers. He touched the cheek and flinched and knew it was burned, perhaps even blistered. Looking at his legs, he saw the sand piled against them and understood that he had been there awhile. Hours, if not days.

Slowly, he climbed to his feet, then stood a moment until he was sure of his balance before returning the revolver to its holster. The confusion persisted. He knew the horse was his, and that the Smith and Wesson shot a .44, but he didn't know where he was or how he'd gotten there. When he took a couple of steps forward, his head began suddenly to ache. Within seconds the pain was worse than what he felt from his ulcered cheeks and lips.

Reaching up to explore his scalp, he discovered his hat glued to his hair with some kind of sticky residue. He peeled it off gingerly, saw blood at the crown, and wondered if he'd been shot. Then his eyes crinkled at the memory of a swinging rifle butt slamming down on top of his skull. The man behind it was called Fish, but there were others lurking out there, as well. He smiled remembering someone named Mose and how they'd been good friends. Mose was gone now. So were others, including some he was supposed to take care of. A brother, but there had been women, too, one of them with auburn hair and soft brown eyes flecked with gold. A gentle soul—Hattie, she was called—and with that, it all came back in a rush, like a thousand chutes opening at once.

His own name bobbed within the flotsam, but it was Hattie Wilkes, she of goodness and a promise for his own future that he clung to until his mind quit spinning and he was able to walk to where the grulla patiently waited.

Ben took the horse's reins, even though the animal showed no disposition to wander off. Remembering the dynamite in the saddlebags, he opened the near-side flap. The wool wrappings had dried out during the day. He freed one of his two canteens from the saddle and gently poured water over the blanket scraps. He did the same on the other side, then took off his hat and filled it with what remained from the canteen. The grulla drank greedily, and Ben felt anger that the horse had been forced to suffer because of his own failings.

The grulla drained the hat and snuffled for more, but Ben knew he'd need to ration their water until he located another source. He did press the damp felt to his cheeks, the moisture momentarily easing the effects of the sunburn, although the sting came back as piercing as ever when he returned the hat to his head.

He tipped the canteen to drain what few drops remained past his own lips, then checked the cinch and mounted. After waiting a moment for the dizziness to pass, he lifted the grulla's reins and croaked out a rusty, "Hup," that set the horse into motion.

The tracks made by Cade and his men were easy to follow in the moonlight, and the grulla fell into the trail without hesitation. It was a good thing, Ben decided. He could already sense the darkness returning, the throbbing from the top of his skull becoming more demanding as his mount lurched through the deep sands.

Cade ordered his men to dismount while Poe and Morgan escorted their prisoners to them. The man Morgan had tied to his saddle looked surly, half-starved, and dirty, his shirt stained with old blood.

The padre was younger, and clearly the softer of the two. His belly pushed out against the coarsely woven robe that covered his frame from shoulders to ankles, and his sandaled toes looked like fat little grubs. Although he was smiling, the expression looked strained and uncertain. It was the priest who spoke first, going on for several minutes before Cade motioned Lucia forward to translate.

"He says his name is Father Alfredo Hernández, of the Church of the Virgin Mary of San Fidel. He says—"

The padre started talking over her explanation, until Cade interrupted him with a sharp command.

"Tell him to shut up," he said to Lucia.

She spoke briefly, and the priest nodded and clamped his lips closed with exaggerated firmness.

"Frank, what have you got here?"

"Damned if I know," Poe admitted. "Neither of these men seem to speak American, and I don't savvy Mexican. That skinny fellow tried to throw down on us when we showed up, but me and Morgan already had our revolvers drawn. Considering the way he acted, I decided we'd better put a rope on him. The padre didn't seem like the running kind, especially on a burro, so we just motioned for him to come along. He's tried talking to us a few times, but I didn't recognize more than a word or two, and nothing I could string together to make sense of."

"I'll bet that burro could tell us a few things, if it could talk," Morgan said. "I'd hate to put that fat priest on a stout mule, let alone a short-legged jackass."

"I was thinking the same thing," Cade said. He turned to Lucia. "Tell the padre to get down, before he breaks that burro's back."

"I would imagine that burro has been carrying the priest for many years," she replied, her displeasure at their remarks evident in her tone.

"That may be, but I want him on the ground now. Then let's hear what he has to say."

Lucia spoke and the priest nodded and dismounted, then immediately began speaking. Cade let him drone on for several minutes before he held up a hand to stop him.

"What's he saying?" he asked Lucia.

"He says a lot of things, including who his bishop is and where he was born. It's what he says about San Fidel that is important."

"Then that's what I want to hear."

"He confirms what we already know about José Yanez. He says he has not been to town since the bandits returned from a raid to the northern part of the state, but that he has learned much from this man, who Yanez had sent out to find him and bring him back. He says Yanez's men were ambushed by Apaches, and that many of his men were killed. He also says Yanez returned to San Fidel with three prisoners, one man and two women, and that one of the women has red hair."

"Fanny O'Shea," Morgan added needlessly.

"Fanny and Hattie, and the man is probably Henry McDaniels," Lucia agreed. "Father Alfredo says Yanez wishes to marry the auburn-haired woman, and that is why the priest was sent for. He is to dissolve Yanez's marriage to the wife he has now, so that Yanez can marry Hattie."

"Can he do that?" Cade asked dubiously. "Dissolve a marriage, I mean?"

Lucia repeated the question in Spanish, and the priest vehemently shook his head. After a brief outburst, he quit talking and looked to Lucia to translate. Smiling wryly, she said, "No."

"How many men does Yanez have under his command?" Lucia asked, and the priest replied.

"He isn't sure, but probably between thirty and forty."

Cade looked at the second man. "Who's he?"

"One of Yanez's men, called Raúl. He is considered a scout with the rank of corporal, although I don't think the people of San Fidel would consider it a legitimate position."

"Ask him how many men Yanez has."

Lucia asked and Raúl laughed, then spat toward Cade's feet. Lucia shrugged. "He says ten thousand, maybe more."

"Okay, then ask the padre if he knows if the women have been harmed."

"I already did. He says he doesn't think so. He says the prisoners are being held in the church rectory, and that the men were instructed not to molest them, under threat of execution. Yanez wants to marry Hattie, then sell Fanny to a brothel in Chihuahua City. He thinks her red hair makes her valuable."

"Yanez sounds like a real nice guy," Poe said sarcastically.

"He sounds like what he is," Lucia replied matter-of-factly. "A murderer, a thief, and a kidnapper. Those dead Mexicans we saw with the wagons in *Los Médanos*, I'd expect something like that to be Yanez's work, as well."

"Did the padre say how far away we are from Villa Lobos?"

"Following the road, another three hours. We could be there by midnight."

"Ask him where the church is in town, and where Yanez's men stay, if there's any one location. Get whatever information you think we can use."

Lucia turned back to the priest, and Cade motioned Poe aside. "What do you think?"

"We can't take Yanez's army in a straight-on fight. There're too many of them."

"Our only choice seems to be slipping in quietly and sneaking the women out, then making a run for the Rio Grande."

"That's a tall order," Poe said quietly.

"It is, for a fact."

"What if Hollister shows up with the dynamite?"

After a pause, Cade said, "I don't think Hollister is going to show up. I think he either passed out and lost his horse, or

280

maybe the dynamite went off and we just didn't hear the explosion."

"Well, it's no loss as far as Hollister is concerned, but I hate to lose that dynamite."

"That stuff was so unstable, I'm not sure I would've trusted it anyway."

"What do we do with these two?" Poe asked, indicating the priest and the bandit.

"We'll hog-tie Raúl and leave him here, but take his horse and guns with us. As far as the priest." Cade eyed the chubby padre silently, then shook his head and swore softly. "Hell, I don't know what to do with him. If we leave him, there's a good chance he'll untie Raúl and let him go, but he's too fat and slow to take with us."

"We could tie him up and leave both of them here in the middle of the road. Somebody'll find them."

"Yeah, that might work, although he'll surely holler about it."

"Let him holler," Poe said. "There won't be anyone out here to hear him."

Lucia spent another ten minutes interrogating the priest, then came over to join Cade and Poe. "Yanez's men, those who aren't married to local women, share a garrison on the main plaza across from the church." She crouched and begin tracing lines in the dirt of the road, too faint to read in the available light, but the directions of her hand gave Cade perspective.

"Here is the plaza, and here is the church," she continued. "The rectory where Hattie and Fanny are being kept is here." She poked at a spot beside the church. "Over here, in this corner across the way, is a building that used to be a warehouse. It is where the buyers stored the fleece and hides the shepherds brought in for trade. It is the garrison now, and here, to its side, is the trader's hacienda, with a small placita and a strong gate to prevent intruders from coming inside. This is where José Yanez lives with his wife, unless he's already killed her or told her to leave."

Cade looked up. "Is Yanez so cold-blooded he'd kill his wife to marry another woman?"

"Father Alfredo says that he is, but that he suspects Yanez will force her out, instead. The bandit chief considers himself a good Catholic, and would try to avoid murder. At least right in San Fidel, where the people of the village would know what he did and judge him for it."

"What kind of good Catholic kills the way this Yanez does?" Poe asked.

"Father Alfredo says only José Yanez considers himself a good Catholic. The padre says he is evil, and suspects he has made a pact with the devil."

"Could be," Cade agreed, standing. "But it doesn't change our job. Riley, Morgan, take care of those two. Elkins, grab that bandit's rifle and revolver, and any other weapon he might have on his saddle."

"Wait," Lucia said, stepping in front of Cade. "What are you going to do to the priest?"

"We're going to tie him up and leave him here."

"You can't do that. Father Alfredo isn't like the rest of us. Tomorrow, when the sun rises, if he is still here, unprotected . . ."

"If you want to stay with him, you can, then turn him loose in the morning. But right now my priority is getting Hattie and Fanny out of Villa Lobos alive, then getting the three of you back to El Paso."

Even in moonlight, there was no mistaking the fire in Lucia's eyes. "This is a man of the cloth, Andrew. You can't treat him like some wretched bandit."

"I can't take the chance he wouldn't free Raúl as soon as we're out of sight."

She took a deep breath, then let it out slowly. "I am going with you, but let me talk to Father Alfredo first, so that he knows you mean him no harm."

"Tell him if we can, we'll come back this way and cut him loose."

"He will be hurting, with his hands tied all night."

"I expect he will, but it can't be helped."

She didn't reply, and Cade watched her stalk to where the priest stood next to his burro, dwarfing the small equine. She spoke briefly, and he immediately started hammering back in Spanish, shaking his head emphatically and saying "No" several times in succession.

Leaving them to their argument, Cade went over to watch Riley and Morgan haul Raúl off his horse and begin binding him hand and foot with a length of reata cut from his own gear. Lucia joined him as the troopers finished restraining the bandit.

"He is afraid," she explained simply. "Of being left out here to die, or wolves, and rattlesnakes and scorpions."

"It can't be helped."

"What if he promised not to release Raúl until morning?"

Cade shook his head. "The fact is, I wouldn't trust him to keep his word."

"He is a priest."

"He's also a man. If Raúl threatened to cut his throat if he didn't turn him loose, I suspect he'd do it."

Her smile was like ice clinging to her lips. "Tell me, Andrew, how will you justify these actions to God?"

"Morgan, tie up the priest. Don't hurt him, but make sure it's tight enough he can't work himself loose." He glanced at Lucia. "It'll be better this way. If he was free and refused to untie Raúl, then Raúl or someone else would eventually kill for it."

"I hope you are right," she replied coldly. "And I hope our

283

Father in Heaven sees it that way, as well." Then she stalked to where she'd left her mule, her spine as rigid as a steel bar.

"You know, I still can't figure out whether she likes you or hates you," Poe said softly.

Behind them, Alfredo was protesting loudly as Morgan and Riley closed in on either side of him with ropes.

"I wouldn't want to place a bet on it either way," Cade replied. But absently, his attention already focused in the opposite direction, toward the bandits' stronghold at Villa Lobos.

The priest had been wrong when he estimated the town of San Fidel lay three hours away. They made it in less than two, guided the last few miles by the red and white bursts of fireworks arching over the central plaza. Cade led his squad off the road and called a halt while still a quarter of a mile away.

"Looks like they're having a celebration," Poe observed.

"A weddin', maybe," Riley speculated, and Lucia hissed something heated but unintelligible under her breath.

Another rocket climbed above the church steeple to explode with a hollow bang and a blossoming of light, but Cade was struck by the silence that followed. The few firework displays he'd seen in the past had always been accompanied by shouts and cheering from the spectators. Whatever was going on in Villa Lobos, it didn't appear that the townspeople were sharing in the joy.

"Frank, you and Morgan slip into town—"

"No," Lucia interrupted, heeling Roman forward. "A couple of *Yanquis* creeping through town like thieves, how long do you think it would take for word to reach Yanez?"

"You have another idea?"

"I'll go. It is the only plan that would work if you hope to learn anything without raising suspicion."

Cade hesitated, even though he knew she was right. Lucia

was Mexican. She understood the culture and spoke the language, and Villa Lobos was large enough that she could slip in and mingle without attracting too much attention to herself. If anyone asked where she was from, she could tell them she was visiting relatives, or that she had come in from one of the smaller settlements nearby—a shepherd's daughter, or a vaquero's wife.

"She makes sense," Poe said quietly.

"Yeah, I know."

Smiling, Lucia said, "Is it as distasteful to acknowledge as it appears from your expression, Andrew?"

"We're cavalry, Miss Mendoza. Sending a woman into a dangerous situation to scout the enemy grates on a soldier's pride."

"Do you have a better idea?" she asked.

"Unfortunately, I don't." He eyed the revolver strapped around her waist, the rifle carried in a sling wrapped around her saddle horn. "Maybe you'd best leave those behind. They'll only draw attention to the fact that you're an outsider."

After a moment's consideration, she nodded agreement. She loosened the rifle first and handed it to Riley, then unbuckled the gun belt and did the same. She kept the revolver, though, tucking it behind the belt under her *rebozo.*

"I don't want you to use that if you don't have to," Cade said as the revolver disappeared from sight.

"I am not a fool, Sergeant."

"I didn't say you were. Have you got extra ammunition, in case you do need it?"

"A few rounds . . . enough, I think."

"We'll be waiting out of sight, but I'll have a man close to the road to watch for you. Get back here as soon as you can."

"I will." She stopped and looked at him, and he felt something alien lurch in his chest.

"Be careful, Miss Mendoza."

Her smile was warmer than he'd seen it in a while. "You be careful, too, Andrew. I don't want to have to rescue you and your men, as well as Hattie and Fanny."

"We'll manage," he replied with a solemn grin. Then she tapped her heels against Roman's sides and made her way back to the road, and Cade's smile disappeared.

CHAPTER TWENTY-FOUR

There was a larger crowd roaming the side streets than Lucia had anticipated. She would have expected most of the villagers to be either home in bed or in the central plaza viewing the fireworks. Not out here lurking in the shadows.

Reining into an alley fifty or so yards shy of the festivities, she dismounted and felt her way along the dark passage until her hand came to a *carreta*, parked close to the flat wall of a nondescript adobe building. The cart's wheels were nearly as tall as she was, carved from slabs of cottonwood stumps, but the racks were made of widely spaced limbs, and she hitched Roman to one of them and told him to behave himself. Pulling the *rebozo* protectively over her head and making sure the revolver was still secured behind her belt, she returned to the main road.

Yanez's men did not know her, so she wasn't worried about being recognized, but she was also young and attractive, and that did concern her in a village dominated by outlaws.

Fate lent a hand. She was still well clear of the pulsating light from the central bonfire, as well as the lanterns and torches set up around the perimeter of the plaza, when she spied a woman slipping away from the revelry. She was dressed in attire similar to her own—a simple skirt and blouse, a dark *rebozo* drawn over her head. For those still in the plaza, their vision muted by firelight, Lucia thought the fleeing woman would be difficult to see, and that would work to her own advantage as well. Hurrying across the street, Lucia was within a dozen feet of the woman before she was noticed.

The woman stopped with a gasp and made as if to flee back toward the plaza.

"Don't run," Lucia pleaded. "I mean you no harm."

"Who are you?"

"My name is Lucia Mendoza de San Ignacio."

After a pause, the woman repeated, "San Ignacio?"

"*Sí.*"

"You are the woman of Yanez or one of his men?"

"No!" Lucia made no effort to hide the loathing she felt at the suggestion. "I am a woman, not a pig."

The woman's voice softened, and the tension—the sense that she was on the verge of flight—left the silhouette that was all Lucia could make out. "Nor am I, but it is difficult to avoid them, especially when they are drinking. My name is Estela de la Cruz, of San Fidel. You should not have come here, Lucia Mendoza, of San Ignacio. This is a dangerous place for women. For anyone who is not a soldier of José Yanez."

"I am aware of the danger, but I came for a reason and cannot leave yet." She nodded toward the plaza. "What are they celebrating?" she asked, then held her breath waiting for the answer.

But Estela's reply was pragmatic rather than informative. "We can't stay here," she said. "We are too close to the plaza. Come with me."

"Where?"

"Never mind, just come."

She brushed past Lucia, who hesitated only seconds before following the other woman away from the gala. They hurried down the main road, hugging the deeper shadows close to the buildings until they came to a door that opened directly onto the street. Estela threw a single, furtive glance over her shoulder, then knocked softly. The door was opened almost immediately, and they both slipped inside. The door closed behind them, leaving them in near total darkness until a small but heavy curtain was pulled back from a cupboard. A candle in a small pewter holder burned within, and a brown hand reached up to lift it from the tiny alcove and carried it, guttering, to a table in the middle of the room. Left alone, the candle's flame grew and its light pushed back at the darkness until Lucia could make out several figures standing back in the shadows. She sensed they were all women.

"It is all right," Estela assured the others. "She is from San Ignacio."

"How do we know she isn't lying?" said a voice from the gloom.

"Because I believe her."

Several women edged into the light. Offering Lucia a slim, apologetic smile, Estela said, "We all have reason to distrust Yanez and his men."

"That butcher murdered our husbands," another stated, her face lined with grief, eyes bright with hatred. She looked to be in her late thirties, but already worn down by life and tragedy.

"Our husbands and our fathers," Estela reminded the older woman, and placed an arm affectionately around the shoulders of a girl no more than fourteen. "This is Carmen. Her father was also killed by Yanez's men when two of them came for her. By his death, he allowed his daughter to escape, but life has not been easy. She spends her days here, in hiding."

"Life has not been easy for any of us since Yanez and his men took control of our town," another pointed out.

"True," Estela replied. "But I think it is harder for the very young."

"It is hard for all of us," the woman with hate-filled eyes reiterated. Then she turned her gaze on Lucia. "Why are you here?" she demanded.

289

"This," Estela told Lucia calmly, "is Serena, but as you can tell, her life is no longer serene."

"That is understandable, considering her loss," Lucia replied, and Serena's expression relaxed ever so slightly.

"You still haven't told us why you are here," Serena said.

Lucia paused to consider her reply. Perhaps a lie would have been wiser, considering her occupation, as well as Hattie's and Fanny's, but lies were so complicated, so easy to lose control of.

"I came because my friends were taken by Yanez's men. I intend to free them and take them away."

It wasn't the whole cloth, but it wasn't a lie, either.

"The gringas?" Serena asked with a suspicious lift to her brows.

"Yes."

"You said you are from San Ignacio," Estela reminded her. "I was not aware of any *Norteamericanos* living near there."

"My parents were Edwardo and Rosa Mendoza. They were killed in the Apache raid on San Ignacio . . . how many years ago? Ten?"

"Ten," agreed Serena. "I remember hearing about it when my youngest was still crawling on the floor. They say many men were killed."

"Many women were killed as well. And many children and younger women were taken captive."

"And you?" the older woman asked shrewdly.

"As you wish to believe," Lucia replied. "I was later sold to a rancher, a *Yanqui* named Hardy, from Sonora."

Serena nodded smugly and looked at Estela.

"I was not raped by the Apaches, if that is also what you wish to believe, and we were legally married when the rancher took me into his home."

"What does it matter?" Estela said, then surprised Lucia by speaking English. "Don't let her shame you."

"Where did you learn—"

"To speak the language of the *Yanquis*? From the miners above *Los Médanos*, near the springs at Samalayuca. Do you know of them?"

"Yes, we stopped there on our way to San Fidel."

Switching back to Spanish, Estela said, "Perhaps it would be best if you told us everything."

"I think maybe you are right," Lucia replied, also in Spanish—and then she did.

Cade heard Roman's slow clopping before he spied the weary jack coming down the road. When he was sure—by her silhouette against the moonlit sky—that it was Lucia, he softly called her name. His gut tightened unfamiliarly as she reined up beside him.

"You were gone a long time."

"Was I? It didn't seem like it."

"Did you find Hattie and Fanny?"

"I didn't see them, but I found the building where they are being kept, and a back way into it. It is as Father Alfredo said, they are being held in the rectory until the padre can annul the marriage between Yanez and the woman he is still married to." She looked past him. "Where are the others?"

"Waiting in an arroyo east of here. They're not far."

"Good, because if we want to rescue Hattie and Fanny, we should do so now, while Yanez's men are drunk."

"Can you lead us in?"

"Yes, but there is another in town who knows the way better than I do. She has promised to take us there." At Cade's hesitation, Lucia went on. "Do not worry, Andrew, she will not betray us. She is one of the survivors of Yanez's occupation of San Fidel. She and others despise his men."

Cade consented with a shrug. He didn't like it, but he knew

they didn't have much choice. If they were to be betrayed by this woman Lucia had put her faith in, then it had likely already happened; the trap ready to be sprung. And if she truly wanted to help, then it would make their job easier. But Lucia was right. Whatever they did, they needed to do it quickly, before dawn.

"Wait here," he told her, and hurried away.

The men weren't far, and as on edge as they were, it took only seconds for them to ready their mounts. In the black's saddle, Cade led them to where Lucia waited in the middle of the road. Eager to return to Villa Lobos, she pulled her mule around as soon as she saw them approaching through the scrub. Cade jogged his horse up beside Roman, each of them occupying their own wheel rut. Poe and Morgan were immediately behind them, then Elkins and Riley bringing up the rear with the extra mules on lead ropes.

When within a couple of hundred yards of town, Lucia motioned to the right, and Cade let her have the lead. They followed a shallow dip in the land toward an alley on the north side of the village. As they drew near, a figure stepped out of a lean-to shed and spoke Lucia's name.

Halting, Lucia said, "These are the men I told you about. Sergeant Cade, this is Estela de la Cruz. She is the one who showed me the rectory where Hattie and Fanny are being held."

Cade said, *"Hola, señora,"* but Estela didn't reply. She moved to one side where she could see the others, then glanced questioningly at Lucia.

"There are not many," she said in English.

"I told you there were not many."

"I was expecting more."

"This is all we have," Lucia replied, "and it will have to do. We—I—won't leave San Fidel without my friends."

Estela pointed to the lean-to. "Leave your animals there. We will go the rest of the way on foot."

Cade relayed the command, then added, "Riley, stay here with the horses and don't let anyone come near them, man or woman."

"Aye, Sergeant," Riley replied, accepting the black's reins and leading both animals into the lean-to.

Estela waited until their mounts were secured, then motioned for them to follow her. Cade went first, carrying Little Fish's Spencer with a full magazine and a round chambered. His Colt rode butt-forward on his right hip, the cavalry holster's flap unbuttoned to allow quicker access; like the Spencer, it also carried a live round under a hammer set at half-cock.

Although dark in the alley, it wasn't so bad that Cade couldn't follow de la Cruz as she led them in a roundabout way toward the central plaza. The sounds of carousing were winding down, and he hadn't seen a rocket's burst in a couple of hours. Lucia remarked on the lack of music.

"The musicians went home when Yanez's men became too drunk to notice they'd left," Estela explained, her voice floating softly back to them. "The bandits will sleep away most of the morning, but the rest of us must be up early to do as much work as possible before it becomes too hot."

"Where does the whiskey come from?" Cade asked, and Estela threw a puzzled look over her shoulder.

"The beer and mescal," Lucia corrected.

"Ah, *sí*, the beer. San Fidel makes its own. There is a brewery on the edge of town, and a spring with good water that supplies the village. More springs to the south allow us to grow our corn and wheat. The rest is traded for from Chihuahua City." Her voice took on a wistful quality. "At one time, San Fidel was known for its wool. Before Yanez came, we wove blankets and lighter clothing that our village traded in Chihuahua City, Ciudad Juárez, even El Paso del Norte, to the *Americanos*." Then her words turned bitter. "When the bandits came, our way of life was lost."

"Why?" Lucia asked.

"Because Yanez does not want knowledge of what happens here to become widely known. He can't stop the rumors, but he tries to slow them down, and to paint them as false when outsiders come to San Fidel." Her voice hardened even more. "Those who would be missed if they did not return to where they came from are allowed to leave, but those he thinks would not be missed . . . they often don't leave at all."

It took them twenty minutes to reach a spot just off the plaza, where hoarse shouting, drunken curses, and wild boasts echoed between the buildings. Cade didn't understand the words, but the tone was familiar, no different from what he'd heard a thousand times before in the states and territories, saloons and cantinas. Standing at a corner of the building they were huddled behind, Estela motioned Cade forward. She stood back when he got there, and he peeked around it into the plaza at the far end of a short alley. Other than the shouting and loud boasts, there wasn't much activity. He spotted several men lounging on a low wall enclosing what he assumed was a well or shallow pool. They were laughing and talking loudly, but many others were already asleep or passed out under the surrounding porticos.

Pointing across the plaza to a high wall with a wooden gate in its middle, Estela whispered, "That is Villa Lobos, the hacienda where Yanez lives."

"I thought the town was Villa Lobos?"

"No, not to the people of San Fidel. Only the villa of Yanez and the garrison beside it deserve that name."

Cade studied the large building next to Yanez's hacienda, its front wall scarred with bullet holes, the pale adobe around them blotched dark. "What are those stains?" he asked, even though he thought he already knew.

"Blood," Estela confirmed. "That is where they execute the men and women who refuse to obey Yanez's commands."

Cade glanced overhead, where the church's steeple rose monolithically toward the stars, then to the building they were standing behind. "Is this the rectory?"

"Yes." She stepped back and pointed to a solid wooden door in the rear wall. Then she pulled an iron key from the bodice of her blouse and handed it to Cade, the metal warm from her breasts. "That is the key to the rectory. Entry to the church is through a door in the side wall. The key was given to us long ago by Father Alfredo, so that the women of the village could come in and clean both buildings when it was needed."

"Does Yanez know you have this?"

She shrugged. "Possibly, but he wouldn't care. Until his return yesterday, he never used the rectory. At one time he would have considered keeping prisoners inside its walls sacrilegious. Now he no longer cares."

"Has he gotten worse?" Lucia asked.

"Steadily worse," Estela replied. "But lately . . ." She let her voice fade.

To Cade, Lucia said, "I have seen this in men before."

"So have I," he replied.

"If he is not stopped, the bloodshed will only worsen."

"According to your padre, Yanez has between forty and fifty men under his command. I've got five."

"He no longer has that many," Estela said. "His army was attacked by Apaches when they were returning from the north. With the men he left here, under the command of a one-legged lieutenant named Pierna Mala, he has maybe thirty left." She shrugged acknowledgment. "Still, it is less than forty or fifty."

"Not enough less," Cade replied.

Leaving the women at the corner, he rejoined his men. Looking at Poe but speaking to them all, he said, "Did you hear all of that?"

"We heard it," Poe said.

"All right, so we know what we're up against. Frank, stay out here with Lucia and Estela. Morgan, Elkins, and I will slip inside and see if we can find Hattie and Fanny."

"What do you want me to do if one of Yanez's men shows up?"

"Overpower him if you can. Otherwise, try to hide. And if you're seen, give 'em hell. We'll hear you and know we're out of time. But I'd rather go in quiet and leave the same way." He turned to Estela, who, along with Lucia, had followed him back to his men. "How many guards does Yanez have watching the prisoners?"

"Two, under the command of Juan Carlos Cordova. When Serena took them their food earlier today, she said both men were in chairs near the front door, and that they looked half asleep. If they managed to get some wine or beer, then perhaps they are fully asleep."

"We can't count on that," Cade said. He paused a moment to consider leaving their long guns behind, then decided to take them along. There was no guarantee they'd be able to retreat through the rear door to the alley. If they had to make a run for it in a different direction, he wanted the Spencer with him.

Inserting the key into the lock on the rear door, Cade felt the tumbler turn inside, the bolt sliding back with a faint thump. He removed the key and handed it to Estela. With a final glance at those crowded behind him, he said, "Let's get this done and go home."

Juan Carlos Cordova stood at the edge of the portico in front of the Church of the Virgin Mary of San Fidel, one of the few sober ones left of Yanez's Hunters. Even the merciless *capitán* had surrendered to the comforting embrace of vino, imported from Mexico's southern regions to supplement the harsher liquors brewed locally.

Juan Carlos found the *capitán's* acquiescence to alcohol ironic—he, who held himself in such high regard above all others, as drunk now as any common bandit—though hardly amusing. And when he awoke in the morning and realized yet another day had passed since his violation of the gringa, Yanez's rage would soar even higher, as if on the same wing as the vultures that had followed them south from the slaughtered Mimbreños. By tomorrow, if the padre had not returned, Juan Carlos would not want to lay odds on the holy man's survival.

It had not always been that way. It was true José had been unpredictable from the beginning, quick to anger and often brutish. But he had also been logical, willing to listen to the advice of his lieutenants or the wisdom of the elders.

Not that long ago, if anyone had suggested they try to trade with the Apaches—their lifelong enemies, the people they hunted like animals to sell their pelts for money—José would have banished him from their ranks. He would say, as he often had over the many years Juan Carlos had ridden with him, that there was no room in his command for the ideas of fools.

Personally, Juan Carlos considered them lucky—and maybe it was a fool's luck, at that—to have ridden away from Geronimo's camp with their heads still attached to their shoulders. He suspected it was only the audaciousness of their proposal to the war leader that he hadn't ordered them killed.

It had been there, while he waited for José's return from Geronimo's camp, that Juan Carlos began to understand the growing depths of José's eccentricity. It had been there, as well, that he began to plan his desertion. He might have already been gone had not Luis talked him into staying. And that, Juan Carlos realized, he also found ironic, and amusing—that José would abandon him, his old lieutenant from their earliest days riding the bandit's trail, to embrace the man who actually sought to betray him.

Juan Carlos had listened, as foolish men often do, but he held no illusions regarding the outcome. Even if Luis Huerta's planned coup proved successful—an unlikely proposition, Juan Carlos believed—there would be no place in the former scout's militia for an aging lieutenant once loyal to the man he had displaced.

So why was he still here? Why didn't he seek flight now, while the Hunters wallowed in debauchery? With his rank, there was nothing to stop him from commandeering a horse and as many supplies as he'd need to take him far from José's reach.

Standing within the rectory's portico, Juan Carlos stared broodingly across the plaza at the garrison. Earlier, he had stood directly in front of it, staring at the bullet holes that pocked the thick adobe walls, the brown stains of the blood from . . . who could even recall how many men and women had been executed there?

Juan Carlos closed his eyes, flinching as the thunder of the firing squad's carbines echoed in memory. Yes, he had once been a loyal follower of José Yanez. But now, finally—and hopefully not too late—he recognized the futility of his own aspirations, the fallacy of placing those dreams in the hands of a lunatic. He needed to go—tonight, before José awoke from his drunken stupor.

Before his own body was placed before the garrison's wall to face a madman's wrath in the muzzles of the firing squad's guns.

Juan Carlos straightened with purpose. And then he froze. A noise had come from within the rectory. A sound that should not have been made in a nearly empty building. He stared reluctantly at the heavy front door. The only men still on their feet were those gathered around the fountain, and he feared if he ordered them to accompany him, they would not even be able to negotiate the thirty or so yards to the rectory's front door.

The smart thing to do, he decided, would be to ignore whoever was inside. Abdicate whatever responsibility he still had and flee Villa Lobos before the sun made its appearance. But in the end, he sadly realized that a soldier's duty could not be ignored. Not even in the midst of desertion.

Drawing his revolver, Juan Carlos stepped toward the front door, unlocked now that the prisoners had been removed to José's personal quarters across the plaza.

There was a loud creak as the narrow door swung inward on forged hinges. Cade cringed, waited a moment for some kind of challenge, and when none was forthcoming, he stepped inside.

A candle in a sconce at the end of a short hall guttered in the draft created by the opened door. Cade pried it free of its tallowed base and raised it above his head, where the light wouldn't strike his eyes. Morgan and Elkins moved up beside him, as keenly alert as foxes. Estela had mentioned two guards somewhere near the front of the house, but that had been earlier in the evening. There was no telling where they were now.

The three men eased silently down the flagstone hall to the entrance of the sacristy, the small room separating the church from the padre's living quarters; it was where the priest donned his vestments prior to Mass, the altar boys their cassocks and cottas, and where the Eucharist and sacramental wine were kept in an ornate cabinet. They paused there only a moment before making their way deeper into the rectory, where Estela claimed they would find Hattie and Fanny.

Coming to an arched entry into the main house, they stopped once more. With the candle held aloft, Cade peered into the padre's spacious living quarters. This was the parlor, richly furnished with upholstered chairs and ottomans, a bookcase lined with leather bound tomes, and elaborately woven rugs on a polished oak floor. Sideboards of mahogany and mountain pine were set against the walls, along with paintings of men and women working in fields, of flocks of sheep and bounding deer, and religious images. To their right was the rectory's front door, opening onto the plaza. But it was the muffled sound coming from one of two closed doors on their left that caught Cade's attention.

"What the hell was that?" Elkins whispered tautly.

Moving the candle in that direction, Cade said, "Let's go find out."

They approached the farthest door cautiously. Morgan flanked it on one side, Elkins the other. Cade stood back, partially shielded by a bookcase, and held the candle at arm's length in case whoever was inside decided to start shooting. But when Morgan turned the knob and shoved the door open, there was no gunfire.

After a beat, Cade leaned forward to peer inside. Sleeping quarters, he saw, with candles burning from brackets on the walls, a heavy wardrobe and chest of drawers, and a canopied bed with a thick mattress.

And in the middle of the bed, a knot of human flesh.

The three men stepped quickly into the room, the muzzle of Cade's Spencer sweeping the shadows, but there was no one else there.

"Who is it?" Elkins asked.

It took a moment to piece it together—the arms bound behind his back, ankles drawn back as well and tied to his wrists. The face was a mess of blood and matted hair; the colorful handwoven blanket under him was crusted with it. From where one eye had been there now oozed a creamy pus, and his right arm was sodden with blood. That was the key to the man's

300

identity, the torn flesh where an army mule called Lester had bit into the muscle.

"It's McDaniels," Cade said, and Elkins swore quietly.

"I wonder what he did to make them so mad."

Cade shook his head and set the candle down on a small bedside table. He knew it could have been anything, or nothing at all. After witnessing the carnage left behind at the ambulance, he wouldn't have been surprised by any explanation.

"Let's cut him loose," he said, drawing his knife.

Elkins moved around to the other side of the bed; Morgan kept watch at the door.

"Be easy with him," Cade cautioned. "Move him too fast and he's liable to cry out."

"I don't think so," Elkins replied, tipping McDaniels' head to one side to reveal a blood-soaked gag shoved into the man's mouth.

Cade nodded. "All right, but let's cut him loose first. We can take the gag out later."

It took only seconds to slice through the hemp keeping McDaniels hog-tied. They helped the man straighten his protesting limbs to the bed, then gently rolled him onto his back. When Cade eased the gag from his mouth, he saw that someone had taken a blunt instrument to his face, knocking out most of the teeth on his left side.

"Jesus," Elkins hissed.

In the shape the old outlaw was in, Cade didn't know why they'd even bothered to hog-tie him. McDaniels moaned softly as the blood started to flow back into his hands and feet, and Cade leaned close to speak into his ear.

"McDaniels, listen to me. Where are the women? Where's Hattie and Fanny?"

McDainels groaned softly and turned his head to study Cade's face in the glow of candlelight. "Thargeant?"

"That's right. Sergeant Cade. We've come to rescue Hattie and Fanny. Do you know where they are?"

McDaniels turned his gaze back to the canopy's underbelly, and for a second, Cade was afraid he wouldn't answer. Then he began talking, a mumbling discourse pushed stubbornly past a broken jaw and wrecked mouth. Cade caught most of what he said. One of the men, an officer, had come to get the women that afternoon. He'd taken them to Yanez's quarters across the plaza. He didn't know what happened to them after that. Others came in afterward led by a man named Luis Huerta, who wanted more information about the money they had robbed from Rio Largo. McDaniels told them what he knew, but Huerta wasn't satisfied. That was when they started beating him. After a while he told them Hollister had hid the money in a town called San Ignacio, and that only the two of them knew its location, but he didn't think Huerta believed him.

"Tha keep me 'live," McDaniels stammered through swollen lips. "Mebbe tha look."

He stopped talking then, but Cade understood what he'd tried to explain. Beaten nearly to death, McDaniels had babbled whatever ruse his reeling mind could come up with to get them to stop. Cade knew the reprieve would be temporary. Huerta would send men to San Ignacio, and no doubt their efforts there would be no more productive than Huerta's had been here. Cade didn't know what had become of the money taken in the Rio Largo raid, nor was he overly concerned about it, but he knew Hollister wouldn't have hidden it in San Ignacio, where the chances that one of the townspeople would discover it would be too great.

"What do we do now?" Elkins asked.

Cade considered the question with a hard sinking in his gut. He'd caught only a glimpse of the hacienda's high front wall and solid wooden gate, but he knew it wouldn't be broached easily. Or quietly.

"We'll ask Estela if there's another way into Yanez's quarters," he said. "Elkins, stay with McDaniels. One of us will be back in a few minutes."

He nodded, and Cade and Morgan returned to the alley behind the rectory. Cade told Poe and the woman what they'd learned, and Estela shook her head.

"There is no rear entrance to either the garrison or the hacienda."

"How do we get in?"

"If the gate is locked from inside, you will need a cannon."

"Hollister," Lucia said hopefully, her gaze darting to Cade.

He shook his head. "We don't know where he is, or if he's even alive." He spoke to Estela again. "Are there any big guns in town, cannons or howitzers, something like that?"

With her lips turned down resentfully, she said, "Yes, there is a cannon. A small one. It is locked inside the garrison with Yanez's men."

"Then we'll need a diversion of some kind," Cade said. "Something that'll draw Yanez out of his lair."

"I can do that," Lucia said.

"No, not that kind of a diversion."

"Why not?"

"It's too dangerous."

"I'll go," Estela volunteered. "They know me." Her voice soured. "They have been after me for a long time. Tonight, I will let them think I have changed my mind."

"No, I can't let you do that," Cade said.

She fixed him with a hard glare. "You cannot stop me, soldier." Then she dodged to the side, out of his reach, and started swiftly down the alley toward the plaza.

Cade swore, but couldn't step out from behind the rectory without risk of being seen by the men standing around the low wall of the central fountain. He cursed again when Lucia slipped past him.

"Get back here!"

"I'll go partway with her," Lucia replied.

"Damnit!" He shook his head in helplessness. "Then stay out of the plaza, out of the light," he ordered as loud as he dared with Yanez's men so close. Even drunk, he knew they would be dangerous.

Backing away from the corner, he told Poe to stay put and keep an eye on the women. "If they need help, get out there as fast as you can. We'll be right behind you."

Poe nodded and stepped up to the corner, edging an eye past it to follow the women's progress. Cade turned to Morgan.

"Let's get inside. We'll have a better field of fire from the front of the rectory than we would from here."

They reentered the rectory, moving swiftly down the short hall past the sacristy to the parlor. Cade halted when he saw Elkins helping McDaniels into one of the upholstered chairs.

"What's going on here?"

"He wanted to get out of bed," Elkins explained, bent at an awkward angle as he paused with McDaniels only halfway into his seat.

The wounded man cried out at the unexpected stop. Sliding free of Elkins's grip, he flung an arm out to catch himself, but the only thing handy was a lamp with a deep blue glass shade. The back of McDaniels's hand struck the lamp and sent it crashing to the floor. Shattered glass and jagged pottery shards flew in every direction. The men froze. Even McDaniels sensed the gravity of his clumsiness, perched on the edge of the seat with his bloody gums and broken teeth exposed to the candlelight.

For a long moment, no one moved, and Cade began to think maybe they'd escaped detection. Then the front door swung inward and a stocky man with a drawn revolver filled the entry. Behind him, flickering light from the plaza revealed the men standing idly around the fountain.

The man spoke loudly in Spanish, his tone demanding as he sought a cause for the noise McDaniels had made. When he spied Cade, his eyes widened in surprise. He raised his revolver, but Cade was quicker and slammed a thick chunk of lead deep into the man's chest. The bandit gurgled some kind of protest as the revolver spilled from his fingers. He staggered outside, clutching at the front of his shirt, then collapsed beneath the portico.

Cade swore and ran across the parlor to slam the door closed as the men at the fountain came uncertainly to attention. A couple of them were already drawing their weapons, and Cade felt a bullet's impact through the wood as he latched the door. Then he remembered Estela and Lucia, and the muscles across his chest tightened until it felt like he couldn't breathe. Throwing a desperate glance over his shoulder, he snapped, "Get over here!" and Morgan and Elkins moved quickly to comply.

"Cover me," he shouted, and flung the door open before they'd even reached his side.

"Sergeant!" Morgan yelled, but Cade was already on the move.

He ran to one of the broad adobe columns supporting the portico's outer rim and put his back to it. Half a dozen or more bullets smacked into the outside of the pillar, chewing out fist-sized chunks of adobe that flew off, trailing little clouds of grit like the tails of comets. Morgan also slipped outside, darting to the second flanking column and throwing himself to his stomach behind it. Elkins remained at the door, crouched where he could take advantage of its thick oak planks.

Peering past the edge of the pillar, Cade spotted Lucia hunkered down close to the outside wall of Yanez's hacienda,

305

fully exposed but so far unnoticed by the intoxicated *soldados* firing at the rectory. Estela had ventured even closer to the big gate in the front wall. A water keg offered her partial conceal-ment, but Cade knew neither of them would remain hidden for long.

The men who had been lounging near the fountain had already scattered across the opposite side of the plaza, seeking shelter wherever they could find it. Others stumbled from the garrison half-dressed, eyes darting wildly as they fought the alcohol's solid grip on their senses. Cade counted seven men returning fire so far, but knew those numbers would swell rapidly as the bandits from the garrison gathered their wits and weapons.

"Morgan," he called, then signaled his intentions.

"Don't do it, Sergeant, you won't make it."

"Gotta try," he returned, then pushed away from the column and sprinted toward the fountain's low wall.

He'd hoped to use the stone mure as a shield before making a final sprint to where Lucia and Estela were trapped in front of Yanez's hacienda, but Morgan was right. Cade had barely covered ten feet when the first bullet struck him a solid blow to his left leg, halfway between his knee and hip. He cried out and staggered to the side, the move saving him from taking a second round to the gut; instead the slug burned across his side just below his ribs like a white-hot iron. Tripping over his own feet, Cade went down hard on his hands and knees, the Spencer fly-ing from his grasp. Two more bullets struck close enough to kick dust into his face. He spat and swore and started to crawl after the Spencer, but the shooting suddenly intensified and he had to scramble back behind the portico's bullet-chewed column on his hands and one good knee.

"Sergeant?" Elkins called.

"I'm all right," Cade gasped, pulling a faded red bandana

from around his neck and tying it as best he could above the wound in his leg. The bullet had punched a hole through the fleshy part of his outer thigh, but missed both bone and artery.

"Sergeant," Morgan said, and when Cade looked up, Morgan pointed across the plaza with his chin.

Bending at the waist, Cade peeked around the edge of his pillar. A short, slim man wearing boots and blue trousers but no shirt or hat had appeared at the hacienda's gate. He was carrying a revolver in one hand, a holster and cartridge belt in the other, and he immediately started bellowing questions and commands.

Yanez, Cade thought; it had to be.

"Can you get a shot at him?" he asked Morgan, palming his Colt and squirming around for a better view.

"No," Morgan replied, then swayed back when a bullet gouged into the column close to his nose.

Stretched out on his stomach, Cade leveled his Colt on the Mexican captain, but his vision suddenly seemed to tilt and blur, and his shot went so wide he doubted if Yanez was even aware he'd been fired upon. Then the bandit spotted Lucia crouched against the hacienda's front wall. He yelled at her, Spanish words Cade couldn't make out and wouldn't have understood if he had. Yanez took a step toward her and raised his revolver, and Cade cried out and tried to bring his own weapon to bear, but the sights kept jumping around and he couldn't get them to steady on his target.

Yanez was going to kill her. There was no doubt in Cade's mind of that. But as the bandit chief leveled his revolver, he abruptly stiffened, arching his back and raising the muzzle until it pointed well above Lucia's head. Cade spotted movement behind him. Then a woman stepped clear, lifting the revolver from Yanez's hand like a mother taking a doll from a child. Yanez dropped to his knees, and Hattie pressed the revolver to the back of his skull and pulled the trigger. There was no hesitation on her part, and no questioning the result. Yanez was flung forward like a rag, arms flopping limply as he struck the ground. After that, he didn't move. Estela and Lucia stood and Fanny dashed out the open gate; then the four of them were racing toward another alley, in the plaza's corner.

"Sergeant," Morgan called, and pointed to where men were spilling from the garrison's front door like wasps from a battered nest. "We've got to get out of here," he shouted in a strained voice.

Cade struggled to his feet, leaned briefly against the pillar to gather his strength, then pushed away to lurch awkwardly toward the rectory door. Morgan opened up with Ben Hollister's Winchester, laying down a steady fire, while Elkins ducked outside and wrapped his free arm around Cade's waist to help him inside. Morgan quickly followed, and Elkins slammed the door shut.

"Hell's breaking loose out there," Morgan said tautly, feeding fresh rounds through the Winchester's port.

Cade nodded and leaned against Elkins to take some of the weight off his left leg. He looked at McDaniels, who stared back with resigned stoicism.

"I goin' nowhere, Thargeant, but I thure like a chance to kill couple tha boys."

"You're too beat up to fight, McDaniels."

"Too beat up tha run, but put a pistahl in my good hand." He held up his left arm. "I give 'em hell 'til tha thylinder run dry."

"Sergeant, we've got to move," Morgan said, still in that high, tight voice that had come inside with him.

Cade glanced at the door, spotted the revolver the first bandit had dropped, and told Elkins to get it. He looked at McDaniels. "Good luck."

"My luck'th done run out, Thargeant, but I'll do wha I can to help you and your boys get tham women outta here. You got 'em, don't you?"

"They should be waiting for us out back," Cade confirmed.

"Then you'd better get movin'," McDaniels said, and turned his remaining eye to the front door, where shouts and angry cries from the plaza were growing in volume.

"Let's go," Cade said, and this time he shunned Elkins's assistance and hobbled out on his own.

They found three of the women standing close to Poe, who was peering down the alley next to the rectory.

"Where's Estela?" Cade demanded.

"She went the other way," Lucia replied. "She has friends on that side of town who will hide her."

Cade studied the other two women in the dim light reflected off the adobe walls. Fanny appeared weary but untouched, but Hattie had obviously been roughed up. Her lower lip was swollen and there was a bruise along her jaw, but she seemed steady enough otherwise.

Poe sent a round down the alley, then ducked back as return fire whistled past his ear.

"How many?" Cade asked.

The corporal glanced over his shoulder, frowned briefly at the wet shine of Cade's leg, and said, "Can't tell for sure. They keep looking this way, but seem shy about introducing themselves."

"Can you keep them busy for a few minutes?"

"Oh, yeah, for a few and then some, if you need it." His gaze returned to Cade's blood-soaked trouser leg. "Can you make it?"

"I'll make it," Cade vowed. "Give us five minutes if you can, then get back to where we left the horses. We'll be waiting for you there."

Michael Zimmer

Poe nodded and returned to his job, while Cade led the others back the way they'd come. After a few yards Lucia came up beside him and slipped her shoulder under his arm. He started to protest, then looked into her eyes and found himself smiling instead.

Glaring, she said, "You're lucky they didn't blow your fool head off out there, Andrew."

"You're welcome," he replied, and decided that was enough for now.

CHAPTER TWENTY-FIVE

He sat up at the sound of galloping horses and crabbed partway around to face the east. Although the sun wasn't up yet, it wasn't far away, either, and the land he stared across was bathed in the soft, pearl light of its coming.

The horses appeared from the south, bunched tight and moving fast. He smiled when he spotted Hattie Wilkes. For a few seconds he debated calling out to her, but caught himself in time. Even as muddled as his thinking had become, he'd accepted that any chance the two of them might have had together was far in the past. He was glad she was safe, though, and hoped she stayed that way. He hoped she lived a full life somewhere above the Rio Grande.

He wasn't counting on as much for himself. He'd embraced his own fate last night, hopelessly lost in the vast, dark desert, surrounded by scrub and sand, his head throbbing diabolically as fresh blood trickled from inside his right ear. With death seemingly beating the brush for him in every direction, he'd pulled his saddle and bridle from the grulla and turned him loose. Then, leaving his rig behind, he'd taken only his saddlebags and a canteen and began walking. He hadn't the faintest idea where he was when he finally plopped down and pulled the dynamite and fuses from his saddlebags, but some inner compass must have been at work, because there was Cade and his men and all three women, mounted and riding hard to the north as if they had hounds trailing them.

Or something worse.

He watched them out of sight, then struggled to his feet and waited for his balance to return—something that was taking longer every time he stopped and sat down for a spell—before beginning his final hike to the road.

He had come to some conclusions last night. For one, he knew the grulla would be okay on its own, and that was important. And he felt he'd done as well by his brother as was possible, considering his own poor choices in life. He might have wished for better, but didn't have a solid enough past of his own to provide it, and he supposed that was all right, too.

Something else he had was confidence that Cade would get the women safely back across the Rio Grande to El Paso, and the thought pleased him. He was glad it did. It made what he had to do—what he had to *try* to do—almost vital. And maybe it could wipe the slate of his own forsaken history clean. Or at least tidy it up a bit. Because what he'd come to understand last night in his hazy wanderings was that if you wanted to kill a snake, you didn't chop off its tail. You removed its head.

Halting in the middle of the narrow trace that passed for a road, he stared south toward a town whose name he'd forgotten—names were the hardest to recall, he was finding, and his own seemed to elude him more than most—and set the saddlebags down beside his boots. The sun was nearly up now. A few more minutes and he'd be able to feel its warming rays. He looked forward to that. Last night had been miserably cold without a blanket to drape over his shoulders or a coat to pull on.

He took a stubby Durango cigar from his pocket and put it in his mouth. The dust from Cade and his bunch was already settled, but he could see another cloud taking shape to the south, low on the horizon, like a smeared fingerprint on the sky. He tried to focus on what he needed to do, playing it out in the winding tunnels of his mind.

The dust was climbing higher as the first rays of the sun touched his face. He could see the horsemen now, quirting their mounts fiercely, filling the narrow road. He wondered how many there were, but didn't want to try to count them, didn't want to risk losing his train of thought this close to the end.

They spotted him from some distance away and halted their horses. He could see them looking right and left, leery of an ambush. He didn't recognize their leader, but couldn't recall if he should have. Then, at a command from a younger man on a steeldust gray, the mounted column moved forward.

He puffed furiously on the cigar to keep its tip burning. Reaching down carefully, he removed his gun belt and held it out to his side in full view of the bandits. He let it drop to the ground, then waited as the horsemen closed in around him, a tight circle bristling with gun barrels, all of them pointed at him. The man on the steeldust barked out some kind of command in Spanish that Ben didn't understand. Nor did it matter. Nothing mattered now except cutting off the serpent's head.

"My name," he began, the stubby Durango bobbing at the corner of his mouth. He stopped and his brows furrowed. Then he went on. "Well, I don't guess my name is important, but I came south with that sergeant you're chasing. Do you know him?"

The man on the steeldust glanced around at the others, as if seeking someone who might know what this strange gringo with the blood running out of both ears was chattering about. At his side, a man said, "*No entiendo,* Luis."

"Luis," he said, and then his own name came to him and he raised his hand and poked his chest with his thumb. "I am Hollister, Ben Hollister."

"Hol . . . Hollister?"

"*Sí,* yes, and you are my enemy. Do you know that word?"

313

The bandit leader's expression began to darken with impatience, and Ben knew he was running out of time. He reached up slowly and took the cigar from his mouth, then gently blew away the ash. Lowering the cigar to where an inch of fuse protruded from the front of his shirt, he said, "*Adios, you sons of bitches,*" and touched the fuse with the cigar's glowing tip.

Luis scowled, and Hollister laughed. "Don't know what it is? Well, you soon—"

CHAPTER TWENTY-SIX

El Paso, Texas–August

"Looks like rain," the ticket agent observed. He was a slight man, bald as an eight ball on top but with a wiry fringe of gray around the edges. His eyes looked pale and watery behind thick glasses, his fingers slim and deft.

"It does," Andrew Cade agreed without looking up.

"They're late this year, the rains."

Cade didn't reply. He shoved his money through the slot under the dusty glass of the pass-through, then waited while the agent did a quick recount.

"Nothing you can do about it, though," the ticket agent continued absently, a tongue-dampened thumb moving swiftly over the bills. "Weather's gonna do what she wants, but at least it ain't as hot as it was last week."

Cade kept his mouth shut, wishing the old codger would stop talking and focus on the job at hand.

Finishing his count, the agent placed the cash in a drawer, then drew a couple of forms from a wooden box at his side and scratched out dates and destinations. He placed them in a half envelope with the Southern Pacific Railroad logo on the front and slid them back through the slot into Cade's waiting hand—tickets for two, California bound.

"Enjoy your trip."

"Enjoy the rain," Cade returned, glancing skyward as he stepped out of the line of customers and headed for the far end of the platform where there weren't as many people. The old man was right. It was overcast and noticeably cooler than last week, but he didn't think it was going to rain. Not today. It felt too dry for that.

He was still worming through the crowd when he heard a voice hailing him. Stopping, he turned and smiled when he spotted a lean figure in army blue making his way toward him.

"Andrew Cade!"

"Hello, Captain," Cade replied, reaching out to shake Miller's hand. "I didn't expect to see you here."

"We're back in El Paso for a few days, before moving on to Arizona."

"What happened to duty at Fort Stockton?"

Miller grimaced. "The army changed its mind. Geronimo finally came back across the line, and we're to report to Fort Bowie to await further orders."

"Is the whole troop with you?"

"They are, except for Colonel Hawthorne. He went on to D.C., presumably to request additional troops to pursue the Apaches."

Cade doubted the captain's explanation, but he'd been in the military long enough to know that any good officer never spoke disparagingly of another to an enlisted man. Still, he figured Lawrence Hawthorne would remain back East as long as he could manage the ruse, turning the responsibilities of his command over to junior officers—men like Ward Miller. Whether Hawthorne saw it that way or not, Cade knew the overbearing lieutenant colonel was doing the troop a favor. Miller was a capable leader who cared about his men, and for a minute, Cade almost wished he was returning to Arizona with him.

As if sensing his thoughts, Miller said softly, so that they wouldn't be overheard, "I heard there was some debate on whether or not to hold you for a court-martial."

"There were those who wanted to," Cade acknowledged. "Then word came down from Washington that I was to be given a medal instead. I was told Colonel Hawthorne was one of the officers pushing for a court-martial. I sort of wondered if you were one of those who opposed it."

"I definitely opposed it," Miller said, "but my opinion was never sought. I did write a letter to the War Department with my assessment of your devotion to duty and qualifications for command, but I don't know if it did any good." He smiled. "I'm glad they made the decision they did, though. It would have been a travesty to charge you with . . . whatever they were considering."

"Treason was one."

"Treason!" Miller scoffed. "That sounds like Hawthorne's doing." His eyes dropped to Cade's clothes—a dark suit in a herringbone pattern, shoes on his feet, a bowler on his head. "Have you made a decision about what you're going to do with the rest of your life?"

"Not entirely." He held up his tickets. "These are for San Diego. After that, I guess I'll see what I can find in the way of a job."

"If you ever want to come back to the army, drop me a line," Miller said earnestly. "I'll do everything in my power to make it happen."

"I won't, but I appreciate the offer." He held out his hand. "I need to see to my bags, but thank you for stopping by, Captain. I appreciate it more than you might realize."

"You're welcome, Serge . . . Mr. Cade. Or is it Andrew?"

"It's Andy to you, and good luck in Arizona."

He smiled, watching Miller walk away. Even in his deep blue uniform, the captain was soon swallowed by the milling crowd on the station's platform—people inbound and leaving, family and friends to greet or see them off. Cade hadn't expected to see Miller, and he'd already voiced his goodbyes to Poe, Morgan, Elkins, and Riley—shipped east the week before to rejoin the troop at Fort Stockton. Now they were probably on their way west again, through El Paso to Fort Bowie. Cade had heard about the renewed Indian trouble in southern Arizona. The papers claimed Geronimo was behind the outrages, but Cade knew it could have been him, or some other Apache upstart. Either way, it was no longer his responsibility.

Turning his back on the swarm of men and women fronting the ticket window, Cade found a semi-isolated spot at the far end of the depot platform where he could fill his pipe and smoke it in peace. Staring at the low, gray clouds rolling in from Mexico, his thoughts returned, as they often did, to those desperate days following their flight from Villa Lobos.

Although she didn't confess to it until they reached the spot on their way back, it turned out that Lucia had stolen the outlaws' money when she fled the ambulance southwest of San Ignacio. She'd stowed the bags of cash under a creosote bush less than a hundred yards from where the wagon was parked. A simple search probably would have turned it up, but Hollister's men apparently hadn't considered looking close by.

When Lucia pointed out where she'd stashed the money, Corporal Poe had ordered it retrieved and brought back with them to Camp Rice. From there, it had been returned to Rio Largo.

It was at Camp Rice, on the Texas side of the Rio Grande, that they'd reported to the commanding officer and related their experiences in Mexico. Four of them had been immediately confined to barracks, while Cade was taken to the infirmary in a delirium of fever. The wound in his thigh had worsened after twenty-four hours in the saddle, and he'd lost a lot of blood. The camp surgeon had worried infection might set in, but by the time they were ordered to Fort Bliss, under armed escort,

318

Cade was back on his feet, albeit with crutches.

They'd camped that first night after leaving Camp Rice near the crossing south of San Ignacio they'd used going into Mexico. Lucia slipped off after dark to visit the town and say goodbye to the people who lived there.

"I may never see *Tía* Anna again," she'd told Cade before leaving, and from the deep sorrow in her voice, he'd understood it wasn't just an aunt she was saying goodbye to, but a part of her life that she'd probably never revisit.

At dawn, she still hadn't returned, and the sergeant in charge of delivering them to Fort Bliss was nearing a state of apoplexy by the time Cade suggested she'd crossed the river into Mexico. Keeping his expression neutral, he'd added, "You were ordered to see that all of the women were transported safely to El Paso, Sergeant. What are you going to do about this?"

"Don't try to rile me, Cade," the sergeant had nearly sputtered in response. He was glaring across the river, balled fists planted firmly atop his hips.

"There's a crossing right there," Cade said, tipping his head toward the low bank where the tracks of the Rucker's passage a couple of weeks earlier were still visible in the moist soil close to the stream.

Although the commander at Camp Rice had refused to go into Mexico to retrieve the ambulance, Cade had paid a couple of Mexican laborers two dollars apiece to cross the river and bring it back. The commander hadn't been happy with Cade's accomplishment, but he was pleased to have the ambulance. It allowed him to keep his own vehicles on-site, and use the Rucker to transport the women.

After several minutes of furious contemplation, the sergeant informed Cade that this situation was different from the one Cade had faced after the women were kidnapped.

"If she went of her own accord, then my responsibility is fulfilled."

"You figure your commander will see it that way?" Cade asked.

"Andy, if he don't, then he can damn well go into Mexico himself and bring her back."

But by the time they'd packed up to pull out, Lucia had returned. She'd had a good visit with her aunt, and learned even more about what had happened in Villa Lobos in the days following their escape from the town.

"Their leaders were killed. Yanez we know about, but a lieutenant named Cordova also died, and Hollister killed the man who attempted to take charge of the Hunters, a scout named Luis Huerta. Hollister killed many more, as well."

Cade was aware of Hattie's heightened interest when Ben Hollister's name was mentioned, and noted the shock on her face when she learned the outlaw had lost his life in stopping Huerta and his men. The quick tears she blinked back when Lucia related how he'd died revealed a depth of feeling Cade hadn't realized existed between the two.

"He was a hero in the end," Lucia said, then shook her head as if unable to balance her own conflicting views of the man.

"He didn't kill all of them, did he?"

"No, but with Yanez's men so disorganized, the people were able to break into the garrison and arm themselves." Her expression was sober when she looked at Cade. "*Tia* says maybe five or six bandits escaped, but no more than that, and maybe none at all. Villa Lobos is dead, Andrew, and San Fidel has returned."

"Then some good came out of all the bloodshed," Cade said softly. He wasn't thinking of the bandits, or even Hollister's men, but of Schultz, Hendricks, and Talbot, as well as the Rio Largo lawman and his deputies.

"It would not have happened if not for you, if you had not

come after us."

"It seems to me you did your part, too."

"I did what I could, but I could not have done it alone." She flashed him a hard look. "Don't argue with me, Sergeant. I am not in the mood for arguing."

Laughing, Cade said, "You be sure and let me know when you are in the mood for it, and we'll pick up where we left off." Then he wheeled his horse—the coal black gelding that had once belonged to Little Fish—and rode ahead to join his men.

They were taken to Fort Bliss, where the three troopers were put in the stockade and Corporal Poe was confined to barracks. Cade had been released on his own recognizance, but with orders not to leave the post under any circumstance. With growing impatience, they waited for the braids in Washington to decide how to handle the patrol's quiet invasion of Mexico. In the end—lacking any outrage from Mexico City or President Manuel González Flores's representatives in Washington—the Army had done what Cade considered wisest. They elected to ignore it.

Morgan, Elkins, and Riley were released, and with back pay, had gone into El Paso to celebrate. Frank Poe went with them, and Cade thought he looked mighty proud of the new stripe added to his shirt—a sergeant now, already assigned to take Cade's place under Miller.

The women had scattered upon their return. Fanny O'Shea had immediately gone back to the Cosmopolitan Saloon, where she found herself a minor celebrity among the other whores. Hattie Wilkes had purchased a train ticket to Tennessee, leaving behind the mystery of what had originally brought her West, or what she hoped to return to. And Lucia . . .

The conductor's voice rang above the teeming crowd. "All aboard! Nine a.m. to Tucson, Yuma, San Diego, and points in between. Let's get onboard, folks. This is the final call."

Fingering his tickets, Cade forged his way into the crowd. He was limping slightly—the wound still bothered him occasionally—but it was nothing a few months in the California sun wouldn't cure. He found Lucia waiting near the rear steps to the middle passenger car.

"I was beginning to think you'd changed your mind," she said as he came close.

"No, not in the least."

"You look sad, Andrew."

"I guess I am, a little. The army's all I've known these last twenty-odd years."

"Are you sure you want to do this?"

He looked into her eyes and smiled. "Yeah, I'm sure, Mrs. Cade." Then he took her arm and escorted her to the car, following her up the steps and inside.

ABOUT THE AUTHOR

Michael Zimmer is the author of eighteen novels. His work has been praised by *Library Journal, Booklist, Publishers Weekly, Historical Novel Society,* and others. *City of Rocks* (Five Star, 2012) was chosen by *Booklist* as a top ten Western novel for 2012. *The Poacher's Daughter* (Five Star, 2014) received a starred *Booklist* review, and was awarded the National Cowboy & Western Heritage Museum's prestigious Western Heritage Wrangler Award for Outstanding Western Novel (2015). He is a two-time finalist for the Spur Award from the Western Writers of America, and author of the American Legends Collection series. Zimmer resides in Utah with his wife, Vanessa, and their two dogs. Visit his website at www.michael-zimmer.com.

The employees of Five Star Publishing hope you have enjoyed this book.

Our Five Star novels explore little-known chapters from America's history, stories told from unique perspectives that will entertain a broad range of readers.

Other Five Star books are available at your local library, bookstore, all major book distributors, and directly from Five Star/Gale.

Connect with Five Star Publishing

Visit us on Facebook:
  https://www.facebook.com/FiveStarCengage

Email:
  FiveStar@cengage.com

For information about titles and placing orders:
  (800) 223-1244
  gale.orders@cengage.com

To share your comments, write to us:
  Five Star Publishing
  Attn: Publisher
  10 Water St., Suite 310
  Waterville, ME 04901